Ned Mutton and the Fiendish Fish Finger Conspiracy

By Adam Mansell

Copyright © 2018 Adam Mansell

ISBN: 978-0-244-07582-8

All rights reserved, including the right to reproduce this book, or portions thereof in any form. No part of this text may be reproduced, transmitted, downloaded, decompiled, reverse engineered, or stored, in any form or introduced into any information storage and retrieval system, in any form or by any means, whether electronic or mechanical without the express written permission of the author.

This is a work of fiction. Names and characters are the product of the author's imagination and any resemblance to actual persons, living or dead, is entirely coincidental.

PublishNation
www.publishnation.co.uk

Prologue

With trembling hands, the man in the tweed suit opened his binocular case. Although it was January and snow was forecast, it was what he saw that made his hands shake and not the chill wind. His face flushed and his heartbeat quickened as he adjusted the focus and the blurred object came into view. It was perched on a winter bare ash tree growing inside a fenced-off old building complex. This winter visitor was rare in the twitter world of bird-watchers, very rare indeed. He recalled reading that its multicoloured plumage had not been seen on these shores for at least forty years. And now here it was, flicking its head from side to side and chirping sweetly on this freezing day. He looked around the complex with his binoculars and saw at one point in the tall security fence there was a ragged hole where the wire seemed to be have been pushed outwards. He scanned the fence in more detail and suddenly huge black letters came into view. Putting down the binoculars, he saw more clearly what they read: **Private property. Keep out or you will be severely punished. By order of VA Estates and Securities.** He had always been a law-abiding man and never broke any laws or even bent them a little, but the bird of exquisite rarity that sat on a branch within the forbidden fence was too much for him to ignore. Think of the envy it would cause within the bird-watching world if he was the first person in the country to report it and even produce a photo of this little avian. He would be the envy of his 'tweeite' club, the toast of the Royal Society of Bird Protection; he would have articles written about him and maybe get on TV with the bloke who has the afternoon show that all the old ladies like to watch. Thinking of old ladies made his mind up. His mother would possibly think he was, at long last, good for something. His forty-eight years of living in the shadow of his forever disapproving mother might change if he only took a risk.

Quietly, he replaced the binoculars in the case and walked towards the fence, always keeping the little birdie in sight. As he stepped through the hole in the fence, his trouser leg caught on the wire and the rattling sound startled the bird. It flew off the branch and he froze, praying it would not go far, praying it would settle again within sight of him. His prayer was not answered in the manner he sought, but better. The bird fluttered down onto the fence just directly above his head. He let out a slow breath and fondled for his digital camera. He licked his lips and perspired under his tweeds but the little bird took no notice of him. Slowly, he switched the camera on and moved it to his eye. Leaning past the fence, he looked up at the rear of the bird. It made a small movement and greyish-white droppings splattered down his forehead and dripped onto his nose, but he did not flinch. Instead, with the coolness of a professional wildlife photographer, he lightly touched the button. As he did, the bird turned its head to look directly down into the lens. It was a perfect shot.

He went to snap a second photo but suddenly there was the sound of metal banging loudly against something and the startled bird flew off in the direction of the buildings. The man went back through the gap in the fence. Elation of the picture he had taken receded as the thought of arrest entered his head. He waited but saw no one coming to intercept him or any sign of security men doing their rounds. In the meantime, the little bird had settled on the skeletal, rusty frame of the building and was tempting him again with its delightful song. As courage flowed through his veins, his daring returned. After all, who would be out on a freezing day like today, and why protect such a set of old, dilapidated buildings? So he started climbing through the hole again. Then he stopped. His mother's word came back to him, all those years ago. Instead of cosy stories to tell him at night, she would tell him terrible tales of ghosts and rotten monsters. He recalled the tale of a large white ogre that haunted a disused temperature-controlled food storage unit or, to the uneducated locals, the 'chiller factory'. The creature used to prey on innocent people who came too near to the factory or who stuck their noses into its business. With a gulp of horror, he realised this was the fabled 'chiller factory' and the creature's lair. He readied himself to turn around, but then the bird's song started again and the beautiful tune seemed to dispel his mother's dreadful nightmare story.

So he went through into the factory complex. He cursed as he saw the bird fly off into the buildings, and so, with a final nervous glance back, he followed it. Past an old fallen chimney he went and into the heart of the broken buildings. Then he saw the 'chiller factory' and it chilled him. It was old, and if a building could look wicked then this one did. Rusted corrugated sheets hung on the walls like dragon scales. There were no windows and broken drain pipes pitched down at odd angles to form what looked to him like a monster's frowning brow. Dark patches of mould and moss underneath this looked like large, sinister eyes staring down. At the bottom was a large metal door that had been smeared in white paint. It looked like the mouth to another world. The metal door creaked on its hinges and sounded like it was crying out in an awful, tortured voice.

The man's nerves failed him and he went to run back, but then he saw the bird fly down in front of the door. It hopped over to where there seemed to be something on the ground. Uttering a little song, the bird looked around, then started to peck at the earth. It did not see the paving slab that was thrown from the dark entrance, but the man did. He uttered a scream and then, realising where he was, quickly tried to cover his mouth. A larger white-mitten hand beat him to his mouth and another dragged him upright, then pulled him towards the door. His eyes bulged in terror as he saw what had hold of him. The stories were true. It was not human; it was horrible. He struggled and struggled against the inhuman grip. With a last effort of supreme willpower he tried to get free, but the hands that held him were far too strong. He saw the paving slab on top of where the bird had been. What remained were a few bright feathers that flew away in the wind. Then he was pushed through the doorway and landed with a splash on a wet concrete floor. Free from the grip of his captor, the man screamed aloud, but the steel door was slammed shut, cutting off his howl of terror.

Something cold and hard hit him around the head and a dreadful, icy tone cut across the darkened room. "You will get the same as the birdie if you don't shut up that row!"

He passed out and the creature that had dragged him into the building now leaned down and took hold of his tweed trouser legs. "Take this walking patchwork quilt to the gallery of fools to join the others," the icy voice ordered. Then it broke into a wicked laugh that echoed in the darkness.

Chapter 1

The boy stared at the spider. The spider, with its many eyes, stared back. From the glass that imprisoned it, the spider saw the distorted face of the boy. His nose was large and engorged with spots ripe for popping. His eyes were splayed over the side of the face like a goldfish and below this, a miserable downturned mouth contemplated the arachnid. A mass of curly brown hair grew on top of the head and sat there like an unkempt hedge. The convex view of the face did not change when the boy moved from behind the glass. As he walked towards his secret box, the overcast day revealed the boy's true features. He was indeed hideous, and it was not the glass that distorted his features but a cruel twist of family genes that made him so fish-monkey-ugly in appearance.

As he opened his secret box, the boy looked at the contents inside. He contemplated which tool to use to pull the legs off his prisoner. Should he use pliers or his mother's tweezers he had stolen that morning? Or maybe he should carve them off with his father's new nasal hair trimmers? He was interrupted from these torturous dreams by a wicked shout from below: "Ned Mutton. Get down here now and put your toys away; it's starting to snow."

Ned ignored the order and, scratching his chin, deciding at last on the nasal trimmer to de-limb the creature. There was stamping from the stairs and he quickly hid his box under the bed. Outside his bedroom door, a hoarse voice railed, "Toys, now!"

He opened the door and, without any acknowledgement to his mother, stomped downstairs. In a surprisingly short time the snow had started to settle outside and covered his toys that were in the backyard. Ned put his boots on without tying the laces and walked into the snow. His footsteps marred the unblemished snow. He reached his bike and kicked it into the garden shed. Then he kicked his go-cart inside. Then he kicked his trampoline upside down and before it landed he booted it against the wall and in doing so smashed his father's prize clematis. Although it was not in flower, the frame severed the stem so it would not be flowering at all. Ned pulled the trampoline away from the plant and tore the bare tendrils from the wall. He yanked it and yanked it until there was no clematis left on the wall. It lay mangled and entwined with the trampoline. He couldn't be bothered to free it, and anyway it was dead and he had grown bored with the toy, so he threw it—clematis and all—over the yard wall into the alley behind the house. There was a loud curse from behind the wall but Ned ignored it and, walking to the shed door, he gave the remaining toys one last kick. The toys lay there, dripping inside the shed, and a huge puddle was spreading in the doorway. Then he walked back to the kitchen door, kicked his boots back outside into the snow, and stomped back upstairs. As he entered the room, his mother was opening the palm of her hand over the windowsill and letting the spider go. Before he could object, she slapped him across the head with her free hand. "Don't be cruel to animals."

He looked at her with disdain. "It's not an animal, it's an insect. Or, to be precise, it's an arachnid."

His mother slapped him again. "Don't be cheeky, Ned. I don't care what it is, just don't be cruel to it."

"If you don't care what it is, then what do you care what happens to it?" Ned asked before ducking, as another slap was heading his way.

"One day, Ned Mutton, you will regret being a bully and being cruel to things. All bullies get what's coming to them. You mark my words, young man."

He guffawed as she left the room. Then he reached under his bed again and found a library book on insects. It was dog-eared and tatty and overdue by a year, but its contents held Ned in awe. Here he had learned the word arachnid, though it had taken him half a day to master its pronunciation. And inside there were more wonders—illustrations of dismembered insects, insects skewered by pins, legs of insects, heads of insects, pincers, wings, and other dissected delights for the discerning young entomologist serial killer. He had studied this book but had not had the opportunity to copy these cruel amputations. He had nearly succeeded in his first operation today but his mother had let the patient out of the window. The book was not his. He had been lent it by an even crueller and more demented little swine who lived in a very large house on the periphery of Ned's estate. Ned had met, or rather fell over, him on his way back from school one day. The boy, for that is what he was, had got a large earthworm and was attempting to force-feed it to a little girl, who was lying on the path with her mouth clamped shut and shaking her head in a vain attempt to thwart the force-feeding. Ned tripped over the head and over the boy and as he cried out, the boy, quick as lightning, pushed the worm into Ned's mouth. He tried to spit it out but the boy jumped on Ned and pushed his jaws together, forcing Ned to chew. The girl took the golden opportunity and ran. Ned, meanwhile, tasted the slightly warm and rubbery earthworm. He was not pleased, but the boy was. He had started to laugh and as he did, he relaxed his grip. So Ned, like the girl, took the golden opportunity. He did not run but kicked the boy in his scrotum. The boy's laugh turned to a scream. Tears ran down his face as he crumpled on the pavement and began to groan, one hand massaging his now swelling goolies. Ned started to laugh but then his stomach suddenly reacted to the earthworm hors d'oeuvre. He convulsed and then he vomited. It splattered over the agonised boy.

 There, on the pavement, was one boy who lay panting with sick down his front. The other was rolling forward and backward in an effort to make the pain go away before he could wipe vomit from his own face. Ned looked at the boy and laughed again. The boy looked like he was about to burst into tears, but he succeeded in wiping the sick from his face and then he flicked it at Ned. A piece of worm hit Ned in the eye, but he didn't stop laughing. He laughed even louder and now the boy started to laugh. People were walking past and looking at the two boys with disapproval.

 The sick-covered boy groaned between giggles as he attempted to rise. Ned stood up quicker and held out his hand to help. With one hand on his goolies, the boy held out his other hand. Ned recoiled at the sick on it. The boy spoke between groans and giggles. "It's only your vomit, you imbecile. Now help me up." He had a high-pitched voice and Ned did not know if this was natural or that his kick in the boy's testicles had caused the falsetto squeal. A very upper-class accent, not the usual encountered on the streets of this area of town, accompanied the shrill voice. Before Ned could reply, the boy had grabbed his hand and was upright. He started to shake Ned's hand. "Boy, you are an ugly bugger. Father would have drowned you at birth if you were his. By the way, Fabian Vaughan-Abbott's the name, and torture's the game." Ned let the boy shake his hand. He couldn't believe a person could be so rude when introducing themselves. His own parents had taught him to be polite when meeting someone for the first time. Still, he decided he liked the boy, even though he had tried to force-feed him a worm, and so introduced himself. "My name's Ned. Ned Mutton."

Fabian Vaughan-Abbott guffawed. "Mutton! Mutton? Now, that's not a common name. It's an odd name, no doubt about it, but it's not a common name, and I don't want to associate with people who have common names. I'm going home for tea and buttered crumpets. Would you care to join me?"

Ned's stomach felt slightly hollow after he had emptied it on the boy and the pavement. It was groaning at the mention of a buttered crumpet. "Are they hot or cold? Only if they're cold, I won't, if you don't mind."

"Cold crumpets?" Fabian shouted. "I wouldn't let Crichton serve me them. I'd have him flogged if he did, and Father would endorse the beating as well."

Ned did not follow. "Who's Crichton?"

Fabian crossed his arms and sighed. "Crichton, my obtuse new friend, is our manservant. He was Father's batman in the army and now he's mine. Did your father serve his country?"

"He works for the council, if that's what you mean?" Ned replied enthusiastically.

"Hardly, I would say. What capacity does he work for the council?" Fabian Vaughan-Abbott looked slightly disgusted. "Is he a waste minimisation officer, per chance?"

"A what?"

The boy sighed again. "A bin man, you thick plank."

Ned's face grew red. Even though he railed against his parents most of the time, he was very protective of what people thought his mother and father did for a living.

"No, he isn't a bloody bin man! He's a dispatch manager."

"Oh, he's an internal postman, then?"

Ned went redder, then swallowed hard and answered, "Yes."

Fabian snapped his finger and, with a shrill voice, acclaimed a victory. "Yes! I knew it. Am I right, or am I right all the time? It's all in the breeding and education, you know. But saying that, you wouldn't know, would you? Because I bet you go to that school for thickies down the road."

"You mean Westfield Boys School?"

"Unfortunately, yes, I do," replied Fabian.

There was an uncomfortable silence. Then Ned made a suggestion.

"Hot crumpets?"

"Top hole, my thick chum."

With that, Fabian walked off, and Ned took that as a cue to follow. Fabian set a quick pace and marched off across the road and through a tree-covered area and onto the race course. He climbed over the white-painted fencing and Ned crawled under.

"How far is your house?" enquired Ned.

Fabian didn't stop walking or look at Ned he just pointed to a very large mansion set up on the brow of a hill. "The Manor House, that's what it was called when Father purchased it last year. But we changed the name to 'Stalingrad Towers'. Well, Father did."

"The House of Frankenstein, you mean?" Ned was referring to what the locals called the old mansion before it was refurbished. For years an old couple had lived there, and they had only ventured out very rarely. Some rumours flew about that only at Halloween they came out from behind the high walls. And they dressed, as Ned had been told, or rumour told, in long, faded, flowing robes of black silk, just like Dracula and his bride. Even worse was the rumour that they had a son who only walked the streets and parks on freezing winter nights. He was huge with pale white skin and a pronounced limp. People in the town had disappeared on such nights and in the morning the huge imprints of feet were left in the snow. One large-size foot and one maimed, crippled foot being dragged behind.

Fabian stopped and turned. "I beg your pardon?"

A tinge of nervousness awoke in Ned, and it wasn't the dark legends of the house. He wanted some hot crumpets and if the truth be known, he could do with a new friend. But the boy's attitude was starting to set Ned on edge. Looking at the house and how the boy talked, and worse, how they employed a servant, Ned knew his family and his background could never equal Fabian Vaughan-Abbott's breeding and social standing. It was going to be difficult, but he was willing to deny his background and start telling some lies. Besides, he wanted to see inside Stalingrad Towers. He wanted to impress the other kids at his school. He had always wanted a ponce as a friend, and all that came with it: the toys, the food, the parties, all the rich trimmings from the table of self-indulgence. But right now, he wanted hot buttered crumpets.

"Er...that's what the locals call it, at least the stupid ones. I think it looks great."

Ned racked his brain to think about a programme his father had insisted on watching last week. It was an unbelievably dull one-hour special about country houses. He had groaned most of the way through it but now he looked at the mansion, his new friend, and a golden opportunity awoke within. He tried to remember what the presenter had said. It was time for Ned Mutton to impress.

"Yes...I think it looks magnificent. Er...possibly of the...er...shallot period?"

Fabian Vaughan-Abbott looked mystified. Ned took this as a sign that his historic building assumption was correct.

"You think our mansion looks like a member of the allium family?"

This time it was Ned that looked mystified. "Allium?"

"It's an onion, you cretin!"

"Er...no...shallot?" Ned countered desperately, trying not to lose face.

Fabian tutted loudly and raised his eyes to the sky. "You mean baroque, you stupid oaf!"

"I'm not stupid!"

"I think you'll find you are."

"No, I'm not!" Ned was getting angry now. He hated being called stupid, even though he knew deep, deep down inside that he was a little thick.

Fabian smiled sadistically. "So you're not thick, are you?"

Ned gulped. He knew that a question to gauge just how stupid was going to be asked. He needed to impress. Just how much was going to depend on the answer he gave.

"I'm no good at history, or sport, come to that," Ned said, trying to influence the subject matter.

"I know that already!" Fabian added. "Culture and the arts aren't your forte either. So let's try geography."

Gulp. Outside his town, Ned didn't know the slightest thing about geography.

"Alright, Mr Thicky, what is the capital of South Korea?"

Ned screwed up his face in concentration. Again, he racked what passed as his brain. He concentrated so hard that his face started to turn blue.

"Come on!" cruel Fabian demanded.

It wasn't on the tip of his tongue, or anywhere near it. But he had heard of somewhere recently on the news. A name came to him. So he blurted it out.

"Iran!"

Fabian Vaughan-Abbott's explosive grunt of laughter actually took leaves off a nearby tree. "Oh my, I've struck gold this time! I have the thickest friend in the whole universe."

The word 'friend' outweighed the hurt of being titled 'thicky of the world'. Ned looked sheepish. He stared at the fallen leaves and managed an attempt at saving face in front of this upper-class tormenter. "If you're so clever then you tell me where Iran is, then?"

Fabian gave Ned a supercilious smile. "Why, it's in America, of course." And with that, he started off again in the direction of Stalingrad Towers.

Ned was impressed with his newfound friend's geographic skills and ran after him. "You know a lot of stuff. I'd like a friend who was clever. Where do you go to school?"

"I go to St Geoffrey's. It's a boarding school in the countryside, and after that I've got a place at Cambridge. Father has assured me of that."

Fabian stopped and, facing Ned, put his hands on his shoulders. He looked up at the house and drummed his fingers near Ned's ears. He seemed to be making a big decision. He turned and looked quizzically into Ned's goldfish-like eyes. Fabian Vaughan-Abbott clicked his tongue, then took a deep breath. "Now, look, I must admit I have an ulterior motive here, old boy. I'm only home for the summer break and I would like to lease you as a friend for that period. Father and Mother will be in awe that I've made an acquaintance with a local thicky—er, I mean boy—so quickly," Fabian apologised hurriedly. "And there will be something in it for you, plus there could also be a bonus in any denomination you choose." Ned's eyes widened in anticipation of money, or that's what he thought Fabian meant. He was using a lot of big words and Ned wanted to stop him and ask him to explain some of them. But Fabian continued regardless. "Now, look, there is a class divide. That we know. I'm from the landed gentry and you're a working-class lout." Fabian held up a hand as if stopping a reaction from Ned. "No, no, don't thank me for telling the truth. Father says it's my best trait, and he has a gift of seeing the best in people. Also, Father is disgustingly rich and this morning, at early luncheon, we discussed a business proposition. Not only will you pass as my friend, but you can help us in our endeavours to further the Vaughan-Abbott Empire. How does that sound, eh? I bet you'd like that. You don't get many opportunities where you're from to help one of the oldest and wealthiest families in the county. It's all for the good of the country, you know. Did I mention I've met Her Majesty?" he added. "No? Well I have."

He turned to Ned's side and with one arm on his back, led him towards Stalingrad Towers. "Now, when we go in the house, where Father and I will agree your salary for the summer term and the potential bonus, I shall address you by your surname and you shall refer to me as Mr Fabian. Please don't look at Father directly. Lower your head in his presence, and you must only address his feet. Okay?"

No, it wasn't okay. But then Ned thought of the measly amount of pocket money his mother and father gave him and how much he could fill his pockets if he allowed himself to be used as a personal servant. Or what he could buy at the shops. How he could be better than all the other kids on the estate because of the money he had. It didn't sound that bad after all, and it was only for the summer.

So 'Mr Fabian' it would be. Never was a soul bought so easily, and the actual wages had not even been discussed. Ned was truly thick and becoming increasingly immoral.

Chapter 2

They started up the rise and joined a road bordered with flowers and saplings. The sun shone as if in hope and Ned's nerves tingled as the automatic gate creaked open and they walked into the courtyard of Stalingrad Towers.

It had been a dark and gothic looking place but the dressed sandstone, fine stone lintels, and carved mythical creatures had now been replaced by blue and brown stone cladding. The ancient stone framed windows had been replaced by UPVC plastic ones. Above the entrance foyer there had been a great coat of arms. Now it was replaced by a huge satellite dish. Even to Ned's plebeian mind, it looked nothing in comparison to its former gothic wonder.

"Don't you think it's brilliant? Mother chose the exterior. She can't stand the cold, and this place was draftier than Inuit's crack. Ah, here she is." And walking down the steps came a vision of rejuvenated plastic beauty. Fabian stole a quick glance at Ned and tapped his nose. "She's not my real mother, you know."

Ned didn't hear. If he did, he wouldn't have cared. She was beautiful. Her skin was orange, her hair rigid with spray. Her eyelashes would put a cow to shame and come to that, thought Ned, so would her udders. Her surgically enhanced bosoms stuck out in front of her like the twin guns on a battleship. The nails on her fingers were like great pink eagle talons. She wiggled down the steps and planted a quick kiss on Fabian's forehead, then held out her hands to Ned and smiled.

"Fabian, you never told me that you had such a good-looking young friend," she squeaked. Ned was dumbstruck with puppy love. His stomach started to ache with it. A dark thought of his mother in tracksuit top and bottoms entered his mind. He shook his head to dispel the horrible thought. This was the mother that he wanted; glamorous, beautiful, charming, and with a nice carroty orange hue. He felt like he would refuse the money he was to be offered for friendship and service if only he could fall into her arms and be caressed by those talon-like fingers. Then he started to dribble.

"Mother, this is Mutton. He is my friend for the summer and he's going to help down at the lake and over at the chiller factory," Fabian announced.

"Oooh. That's very good of you, Mutton. By the way, my name's Simone," she squeaked again. Then she smiled impishly and giggled. "That's not your first name, is it?"

Ned was hypnotised. He just stared, and a large globule of dribble hung from his chin.

"No, Mother, it's not his Christian name, but we, as in Father and I, will refer to him by his surname, which is Mutton, and you should also."

Before any further questions could unfold, a door opened at the side of the steps and a man appeared carrying a dustpan and brush. He was immaculately tailored in a black suit and over this he wore a pinny. His hair was greased back to his skull and he had a pencil moustache. Cold blue eyes darted suspiciously around and then landed on Ned. A look of disgust registered on his face as he extended his arm with the dustpan in it and caught the dribble hanging off Ned's chin.

"Ah, Crichton," Fabian announced happily. "Where's Father?"

"He is in the study, young sir," Crichton said with exaggerated pomposity. He withdrew the dustpan and produced a starched hanky which he dabbed delicately on dumbstruck Ned's chin.

Fabian looked at Ned, then to Crichton. "Relieve him of his stupor."

Crichton folded the handkerchief expertly with one hand, then with the other hit Ned around the head with the dustpan. It had the desired effect.

"Ooouuuch!" Ned shook his head and seemed amiss as to where he was. He saw Fabian, then a man brandishing a dustpan, then the vision of beauty again. The image of the latter calmed him down.

"Now, now, decorum please," uttered Crichton.

Fabian grabbed Ned and led him off up the steps. He looked back to where Fabian's mother was. She waved and giggled. Ned smiled inanely and waved back without looking where he was going. He tripped up and fell over and his face landed on a pair of immense shoes.

"Now, that is what I call service! Know your station in life, boy," a voice roared.

Ned's eyes were momentarily blinded by highly polished boots. They were like a tan brown mirror and they seemed to go on forever, rather like the deck of an aircraft carrier. He raised his head and a globule of dribble from his mouth landed on the perfect shoes. Before he could clean it off, an equally huge hand grabbed Ned's hair and started to polish the spittle into the shoes. The heat generated by the follicle buffing made Ned cry out.

Fabian started laughing, his stepmother started screaming, and the polisher's voice rose to a crescendo of what seemed like ecstasy. The sound was like a baritone gorilla having trouble breathing.

Fabian shouted above the obscene noise, "Father, this is Mutton."

The hand pulled poor Ned's head away from the shoes as Fabian's father inspected the polishing. There seemed to be a discussion between the family. Fabian was saying that the shoes still needed a further buffing and his stepmother was pleading to use the services of Crichton to finish off the shoes. Fabian's father was scrutinising the gleam of leather. In all this, Ned tried to gasp for breath, and just as he thought his heartbeat had settled to normal, his head was suddenly thrust down again and the buffing resumed.

"Damn it all! There's nothing wrong with my spit or Crichton's spit, but this boy must be malnourished. I can't get a blasted sheen as I normally do." He pulled Ned's head up to his face. Ned's eyes were still rolling from the movement, but he registered what he thought was a large beetroot with bulging eyes, a handlebar moustache, and very, very fake black hair.

The vegetable head narrowed its eyes and studied Ned, and then it looked down at its shoes. "It's no good, Crichton, you'll have to give them the beeswax treatment tonight. I want them to shine like Orion by 05:30 hours tomorrow." With that, he dropped Ned onto the steps and walked off into the house.

Fabian had stopped laughing and came over. He slapped Ned on the back. "You're a damn good sport, old boy." And then he ran after his father. Simone wiggled over and started to cradle Ned in her arms. He instantly forgot about the humiliating hair buffing and his overall degradation at the expense of the male side of the Vaughan-Abbotts.

"Are you alright, young Mut...?" she stopped and showed what Ned thought was some kind of compassion by asking his real or first name.

"It's N-N-N-Ned," he stammered, lost again in her synthetic beauty.

Something grabbed him, and as Ned closed his eyes, he imagined it was his heart flying away to a brighter world with Simone, but it was Fabian yanking him off to the house for an interview with his father.

"Stepmother, leave Mutton alone! Father and I have business to discuss."

Fabian pulled Ned into the entrance foyer. It was ghastly and seemed like Simone had had a free hand at interior design as well. They stood on a highly polished marble floor. A lilac chaise longue sat near a gold decorated glass table. On this was a gilded framed picture of Fabian as a baby. To Ned, he looked like a smaller version of his father—all purple with jet black hair and frog-like eyes. A silver and glass chandelier hung from the ceiling and a shag pile carpet ran up the spiral staircase.

Fabian heaved on Ned again. "Come on. I'll show you my room on the way to Father's study."

Like Simone, Ned thought the house—or mansion—was beautiful. He thought of his house, which didn't even have a hallway. You just opened the front door and walked into the lounge. This was a wellspring of opulence and he was lapping it up.

On the first floor landing there was green and mauve flock wallpaper and oil paintings of Fabian, Fabian's father, Simone, and an old man.

"Stalingrad Towers has five floors, three reception rooms, an internal croquet lawn, swimming pool, and tee-off balcony," Fabian, sounding like a tour guide, boasted.

"Wow! Look at these!" Ned ran over to a glass display cabinet. Inside it was full of collectable die-cast cars, lorries, buses, and other toy vehicles. They were in pristine condition and looked as though they had never been played with. Indeed, on the bottom shelf were all the original boxes stacked carefully on top of one another. Excitedly, Ned pulled at the brass handle. An alarm went off.

"You idiot! These aren't my toys, they're Father's. I've never been allowed to play with them. He'd tan my skin if I did," Fabian looked up the corridor in panic. "Oh, what have you done? He's going to kill me."

"They're just toys," Ned said reassuringly.

Fabian's face was starting to tick. He looked terrified. Then he turned to Ned and croaked, "Not to Father, they're not."

He pulled Ned and started to run.

"Fabian Vaughan-Abbott!" His father's voice boomed from behind a door along the corridor.

Fabian let go of Ned and fell to his knees. "Oh heavens, I'm for it now." His fingers were at his mouth and he started to make strange babbling noises.

Ned bent down and looked into Fabian's face. "Look, I'll take the blame. It's not your fault. I'll tell your father it was me."

Fabian stopped the noises. Momentarily, he looked mystified, as if he could not comprehend what Ned was offering. Then he smiled. "Yes...yes...you take the blame. After all, it was you!" He said the last word with added accusation, which Ned did not like.

A door opened and the voice boomed, "You have exactly five seconds to get in here, or I will get the Baron out!"

Fabian squealed. Ned started to worry as well now. "What's the Baron?" he asked.

Fabian gulped. "It's Great-Grandpapa's reinforced iron slipper."

"What's your great-great-grandfather's footwear got to do with you? Is he still alive?"

Fabian just shook his head in dismay, but then went into a detailed history of the Baron.

"Father beats my arse with it and it stings like hell. He considers it good discipline for a growing young boy. He says that his father beat him with it and his father beat him with it and so on. It's been in the family for years. Grandpapa had an accident with one of the stud bulls and he got his foot crushed. The only thing he could wear was a reinforced slipper. And he insisted he remain in charge of the farm, so he had the Baron made by Great-Grandmamma and the local blacksmith. 'Comfort with protection' was how he described it." He looked at Ned. "There you have it, the history of—" Fabian stopped suddenly. He realised that he had talked too long.

"Five seconds is up! Here comes the Baron!" Out of a door came his father, clutching an enormous tartan wool and iron-shod slipper. He smacked it wickedly in the palm of his hand.

Ned yelped, knowing that Fabian would volunteer him for a good thrashing. They both backed up the hall. And, as if Fabian could read Ned's mind, he stammered to his oncoming father, "It wasn't me, Father. I swear it wasn't me."

His father smacked the slipper harder in his palm.

Fabian collapsed on his knees and put his hands together in prayer. "Please, Father. Please hear me. I didn't do it!" Fabian moved one arm and pointed down the hall. "It was—"

"Me, dear," Simone interjected. "I brought you up a drink and knocked the silly thing as I passed."

Fabian and Ned stared at her open-mouthed. She winked back at them.

Mr Vaughan-Abbott looked like he was about to explode. He studied his wife whilst panting rapidly in annoyance. Then he quickly turned away and strode back into his room. From there he started to shout, "Damn it, woman. You're not supposed to be on this floor. This is my space, not yours. Don't touch a bloody thing here and give the drink to the boy to bring to me."

Simone gave the drink to Fabian and smiled, then walked off down the corridor.

"And get that loafer Crichton to bring me refreshments in the future!" Fabian's father hollered.

Ned looked at Fabian. He just held the drink in a shaking hand and tried to steady it with the other. Ned indicated that they should do something. Fabian shook his head to indicate they should not. He then inclined his head towards the direction of his father's room and seemed to be waiting for something.

The silence was broken by an order. "Well, come on, boy. Bring my drink."

Fabian nodded in satisfaction, then seemed to glide towards the door. Ned stood where he was. He was not sure whether he wanted a further acquaintance with this terrible man. But then he saw that Fabian was indicating with determined jerks of his head that Ned should follow him. He took a deep breath, then followed. At the door, Fabian took a handkerchief from his pocket and wiped the glass. He counted silently to ten, then knocked on the door.

"Come."

Ned followed Fabian into the room.

If the cabinet in the hall was full of wonder to Ned, then the inside of this room was incredible. Ned lost his fear and stared in wonder at the ceiling. It was full of plastic aeroplane kits, all made up, painted, and hung on sewing threads. They were arranged so that it looked like a huge air battle was taking place, and some even had grey painted cotton wool streaming from their engines, as if on fire.

Ned looked around, and by the bay window there was another battle going on, this time with plastic tanks, armoured cars, artillery, and infantry. The battle ground was made out of papier mâché and painted green and brown, interspersed with sponge hedges.

The planes hanging from the ceiling were out of reach but Ned automatically went to touch one of the tank models. As he did, another alarm went off and a glass partition slammed down in front of his face, nearly taking his nose off.

"Look but don't touch." Fabian's father's voice cut through the noise of the alarm. He sat in a leather chair with his back towards Ned, who had not noticed him when he entered the amazing room. Mr Vaughan-Abbott picked up a remote control and pointed it over his head towards the battle scene. With the press of a button, the noise of the alarm ceased.

Ned turned around as the leather chair creaked on its axis to face him. Ned quickly looked away, not wanting to face the spiteful beetroot. He saw on the walls lots of paintings of soldiers from ancient history to present day. There were Romans, Saxons, Vikings, Norman knights, and down through the ages to fusiliers, artillery men, armoured corps, parachutists, and many more. And there were photos too. All of them were showing what Ned thought to be a smaller, younger beetroot in uniform. One was smiling, shaking hands with some royal dignitary. Another showed the beetroot holding a flag Ned couldn't recognise. Another was a beetroot in pants standing on a burnt-out tank.

"Do you like the ops room?" the beetroot spoke.

Ned looked away from the photos and came face to face with the talking beetroot.

"The what?" Ned nervously said.

"The ops room, boy, the operations room!" he bellowed. "The operations room is where I execute plans that will expand the Vaughan-Abbott empire." He slapped the leather chair's arm, then held out his hand for the drink. "My empire!" he added with another slap.

Ned could see the Baron sitting on Mr Vaughan-Abbott's lap. It looked like a pet cat curled up on its master's lap. He took his eyes off it in case it saw him and decided to pounce.

Fabian dutifully handed the drink to his father, who snatched it away and took a long gulp. He wiped his mouth with the back of his hand, then leaned forwards and beckoned to his son. "Who's this young whipper-snapper?"

Fabian bowed to his father, then, trying not to stammer, and, like Ned, to notice the Baron, he started to explain. "Father, this is my new friend for the summer. I've decided to lease him for that period. His name is Mutton."

"It's Ned," Ned butted in.

Father and son ignored him. Fabian continued, "If you please, kind sir, we need to discuss his wages and duties, if you know what I mean?" He stole a glance at his father, winked quickly, and tapped his nose again. He had done that when he introduced his mother and Ned didn't know what it meant. Maybe he had a nervous tic, or maybe it was being in the presence of his father that made Fabian nervous, Ned thought.

He looked directly at Fabian's father, who looked back at his son. A depraved smile grew on his face and then he winked and tapped his nose too. Ned now knew it must be a family affliction. After all, his family had a multitude of disorders. He got a clearer picture now of the beetroot-coloured person. The face was large, jowled like a bulldog, and purple. He had an engorged reddish nose at whose bottom sat a curled handlebar moustache that was waxed to perfection. Ned thought that another cat-like thing, not unlike the Baron, was asleep on the top of Mr Vaughan-Abbott's head. But under closer scrutiny, Ned realised it was a shiny black toupee. He tried to suppress a giggle and two big bulbous eyes whirled in their sockets, then fixed on Ned.

A terrible shout cut the titter off. "What are you looking at, boy?"

"I...I...your syrup," Ned blurted out. "I mean, your hair."

"You don't look at my hair, you common little twerp! You look at my feet when you address me, my feet!" And Fabian's father stuck his brogued feet in Ned's face. "That's what you do in my presence, you address the feet!"

Fabian pushed Ned forwards into his father's feet. For the second time today, he had a mouth full of shoe.

"Now, Mutton, you are to be hired as my son's friend this holiday. Is that correct!" Mr Vaughan-Abbott stated rather than asked. With a foot in his mouth, Ned muffled a yes.

"What was that?"

Ned nodded this time, causing Fabian's father's legs to shake in the chair.

"I take that as affirmative," and he pulled his shoes from Ned's mouth. With the support gone, Ned fell over and landed at the feet again.

"Damn me. This boy's keen to serve. Never known such a keen groveler," Fabian's father leaned over. "Well, get up, boy. You've proved your point, and we can't discuss wages and a performance bonus with you staring at the floor."

Fabian pulled Ned, who stood waiting on unsteady feet for the next verbal assault, up by the scruff of his neck. But it did not come. Instead, Mr Vaughan-Abbott beckoned his son and Ned forward. "Sit!" It was an order, and both boys, seeing there were no other chairs in the room, sat on the floor. Each had a polished brogue pointing at them.

Mr Vaughan-Abbott reached into his pocket and pulled out a gold-plated money clip that strained to clasp the largest wad of notes that Ned had ever seen. The hand shook the wad in front of Ned's eyes. The eyes followed the flapping money as if hypnotised. "Now listen, boy. This will be yours, all yours, if you agree to be my son's friend, personal vassal, and so on…"

He was still nodding in action to the movement of the money. It stopped and hit him around the head. "Well?"

Ned's eyes rolled but he managed to say yes.

"Good! Now with this lucrative responsibility there are a few other conditions I want you to accept."

Ned raised his eyebrows in question.

Mr Vaughan-Abbott continued. "You must stop your friendship and acquaintanceship with any other former friends," he enforced the last word. "And if you see them in public you will ignore them, alright?"

Ned didn't have too many friends anyway. There were a few, but as Ned's parents had moved recently they were now outside the area where Ned's old school was and therefore so were a lot of his old friends. He had not been happy and for the first six months at secondary school had virtually kept himself to himself, making very few friends and, if he did, they would be classed more as acquaintances. He had railed against his parents and said he hated them. He had locked himself away in his room for ages and had only recently started to go out again. There were some people at his new school that had befriended him. One was a slightly scruffy boy with large bi-focal glasses and an immense head that sat on his shoulders like a huge inverted triangle. His name was Gideon Pale or, to others, as he was a swot and exceedingly clever at science, he was known as 'Professor Pyramid' or 'The Bouncing Brain' as he 'bounced' when he was kicked across the sports field by the school bullies. Ned had started to hang around with a tiny boy called Darryl Percival but, on account of his minute height, he was renamed 'Percy the Pygmy'. He was barely four feet tall but he thought he was a right hit with the girls. This advantage was countered by a fat pie eater called Twenty Tonne Trevor. He was always—without fail—next to Percy. This boy could not, or would not, go anywhere without Percy the Pygmy. Anywhere Percy went, Twenty Tonne would go or would appear in an instant. It was as if he was attached to Percy by an invisible cord. The Triple T—as Twenty Tonne Trevor's name was shortened to by the thick boys in school, because they could not remember long words—was as wide as Ned was tall. Everything that Percy said, Triple T agreed with. Every joke that Percy said—even though they were terrible—Triple T would collapse into laughter. So if you wanted Percy the Pygmy as a friend, it came with a condition; that condition was Triple T. Lastly, there was a girl. A portly blonde girl called Lola, or as everyone called her 'Lola the Loon'. Ned had met her on the first day after school and she had walked home with him. He now avoided her like the plague. He thought she was nice at first. But then she kept asking him questions about his family, his house, his relations, what he ate, what side of the bed he slept on, when he went to the toilet, and lots of other personal things that you don't ask people when you first meet them. Then Ned started to worry. And when he said he didn't know her well enough to tell her such things, she started to scream and shout out that she would cut her own head off because he was being unreasonable. Then Ned had also decided: evade at all costs. And when she actually produced a pair of scissors she carried in her bag, he knew that the fledgling friendship was doomed to die, and moreover, he wished he had walked home without her because now she knew where he lived. She apologised the next day and said the scissors were there in case she was abducted by aliens and she would cut her own head off before they kidnapped her. Ned lived in hope. So, all in all, he was not potentially missing any deep and meaningful relationship by giving up the friends he already had.

"Okay," he said with a smile.

Mr Vaughan-Abbott inhaled deeply through flared nostrils. His eyes seemed to penetrate Ned and screw him to the spot. There was an uneasy silence. Ned's eyes roved about and landed on Fabian, who shrugged his shoulders and forced a smile. Their uncomfortable silence continued; then Mr Vaughan-Abbott burst forth again, shouting orders this time. "You will also be at our beck and call day and night and your parents—you do have parents, don't you?—aren't relevant to you anymore. Furthermore you are never to discuss anything that involves me or my empire with them. Is that clear?"

Such a statement would shock any other young person, but not our Ned. He thought of his father in his nylon suit going to work on the bus. He had apparently been in the same department at the local authority since he left school and had worked his way up. His father seemed very content and happy, but to Ned, now surrounded by such lush, tacky, and kitschy extravagance, he couldn't fathom the menial existence that he felt his father had scraped out. And having witnessed Simone standing before him like a modern-day Cleopatra, the very thought of his mother was making him nauseous. Oh, how he felt like falling to his knees and begging the Vaughan-Abbotts to adopt him. Like abandoning his so-called friends, abandoning his parents would not be a bad thing really. He felt that he needed to strike out on his own and make his millions. After all, opportunities like these didn't knock twice, and he had a good head on his shoulders—even though Fabian said he was a thicky—his father had said. Like a young fledgling about to leave the nest, Ned Mutton was flexing his wings and looking forward to money and rewards offered at the Vaughan-Abbotts' generous bird table.

"Crystal clear," Ned announced.

So there it was indeed, Ned had sold his soul to the highest bidder. He had sold his friends off, his mother and father off, and he didn't seem to care one little bit. He was not becoming the soaring bird of opportunity he thought he was, but he really was developing into a disgustingly foul little brat.

Mr Vaughan-Abbott smiled at Ned as if knowing his inner thoughts. Ned didn't care; he had wanted to shout out 'Father' in fond affection, but then Mr Vaughan-Abbott threw something at Ned. He tried to catch it but dropped it instead.

"Idiot!" hoarsed the horrible foster parent. "That's a top of the range mobile phone. Now pick it up!"

Eagerly, Ned did. He had never, ever had a mobile phone. Not in all his young years. He was so excited that he dropped it again. Both father and son groaned.

"Now, boy, that's programmed to receive only. So you can't make calls to former friends or family members. Certain things will need to be done and they may not be too pleasant, but you look to me like you have very little intellect or scruples, so here's to a financially rewarding summer." He tossed the wad of money to Ned, who caught it eagerly. Then Mr Vaughan-Abbott clapped his hands together and said, "We will call you when we need you. Okay?"

Ned cradled the money and phone lovingly. He looked at Fabian's father and mouthed a thank you.

Mr Vaughan-Abbott rose from the chair and went to leave the room. "You will await our call. And you may call me Beetie from now on. It's what the regiment used to call me." He turned around and his large eyes fixed on Ned. "You are in my new regiment. I am commander, with Fabian here as captain and you will be a plebeian: that is to say private, or in the ranks. Now, both of you, bugger off!"

Fabian smiled a horrible sickly beam as his father left the room. Ned, who knew a bit about army stuff, saluted.

Fabian let out a deep breath, then very excitedly spoke to Ned. "I can't believe it! I just can't! You've only just been introduced to Father and he's given you a wad of cash and mobile phone." He then nudged Ned playfully. Ned frowned and pushed him backwards. "Hold off, old man. I wasn't being giddy, I just can't believe he is going to let you call him Beetie. I can't even call him that." Fabian smiled horribly again and then shook his head in mock surprise. "Beetie. Beetie, eh? Crichton, who saved Father's life more than once, isn't even allowed to call him that. You must have impressed him, my thick chum."

Pride awoke in Ned. He had never impressed anyone, not even his parents, or so he believed. But now, within the space of an hour, he had been given a wad of money, a mobile phone, and the honour to call an ex-warrior by his nickname of Beetie. He looked through the window and into the outside world and he could see this world bending to his will to bring him fortune and respect from others who had always thought he was an ugly failure. Yes, he had impressed. He had impressed a very powerful businessman and he felt good about it. He still harboured thoughts about adoption from Mr Vaughan-Abbott and beautiful Simone, but then he realised that Fabian would be his stepbrother and it dampened the dream somewhat. Still, his pride was there in him now, and with this newfound elation he turned on his would-be sibling. "Yes, I did impress, and I did because I'm not thick!"

To Ned's surprise, Fabian didn't contradict him and put him on the spot with an intensely hard geographical teaser, he just nodded. "I know you're not thick, my new friend, and furthermore, Father obviously doesn't think you're obtuse either or he wouldn't have enlisted you."

Ned's pride just made him smile and nod silently in agreement. Mostly because he didn't know what obtuse meant.

Fabian nudged Ned in the ribs again. "Come on then, let's bugger off. I'll see you to the gate."

As they left the room, Fabian turned to close the door and gripped the door handle hard in an attempt to stop himself laughing out loud.

Chapter 3

So with a new friend, new phone, wad of dosh, and new dizzy heights to climb to, Ned left Fabian at the gates of Stalingrad Towers and started a long walk home. Immediately depressed at leaving his new would-be family and friend, and not looking forward at all to reaching his squalid house, he couldn't wait for the call from dear Beetie.

As Ned neared his house, he started to kick at things in the street, taking his frustration out on flowers, fences, bushes, and poor old Mrs Marshall's terrier. He was daydreaming about a particularly brave deed he would perform for Beetie when he spied the little dog out of the corner of his eye but he did not see Mrs Marshall holding the lead. His foot, by this point, was in automatic kick mode and before he could stop himself, his foot went for it. The dog jumped aside but still got a swift boot on the arse that made it yelp out loud. It was very lucky for Ned that Mrs Marshall was on the way to have her monthly ear draining session at the medical centre, and more fortunate that she suffered from severe myopia. She could not see a thing clearly unless it was right under her nose and Ned was not right under her nose. She in fact thought Ned was a tree. "Don't walk into trees, Minty," she said in a very orderly voice. Then it softened. "You could hurt yourself. You do your business up the tree like a good boy. Go on." Minty obeyed his short-sighted mistress and began to relieve himself over Ned's leg and ankle. Ned immediately stopped daydreaming and gave little Minty a side sweep that would put a football striker to shame. The dog was swept back and gave a strangled yelp as the lead in Mrs Marshall's hand went tight. She took that as a sign that Minty had done its business and hauled on the lead hard. The dog shot forwards but managed to strain against its lead to turn and growl at Ned. He laughed and scampered after the dog, which, tail between legs, ran in between Mrs Marshall's legs. It was a mistake. This was the one thing she could not stand her dog doing. It was dangerous, she had told Minty so often, as she could easily stamp on him or trip over him. So she, usually so kind to her little pooch and other miniature dogs, gave him a kick, which in truth, and much to Ned's delight, was a lot harder than he had done. Poor Minty howled yet again and got out of the danger area quick. Ned slapped his soiled leg and laughed out loud, which Mrs Marshall did not hear.

He reached his house shortly after and, with a resigned sigh, unlocked the front door. A voice called out instantly, "Ned, is that you?"

"No," he answered, and walked up the stairs to his room and slammed the door. He hid the wad of cash in an empty model aeroplane box, then stuffed it under his bed. He kept the phone in his pocket. It was good to feel it close, and anyway, Beetie might call day or night. Ned heard footsteps on the stairs and knew his mother was coming to see him.

He judged when she was just about to turn the handle of the door, then shouted, "Knock, please."

Mrs Edwards opened the door and walked in the room. "What did you just say?"

Ned was lying on his bed. He rolled over and faced the wall. "I said knock."

Mrs Edwards looked furious. "I will not! This is mine and your father's house. You live here because we pay the mortgage and keep you. So your father or I will not knock before we enter your room. And you look at me when I speak to you, young man!"

Ned still stared at the wall. He slowly rolled over and faced his mother. She was resplendent in tracksuit top and bottoms. She also wore furry slippers and had a matching hair bobble that tied her brown hair back. Ned thought of Simone and how beautiful she was in comparison to the revolting image he now looked at.

"Anyway, Ned, I'm not here to bother or embarrass you." Ned muttered something that sounded like 'Like a lot, you're not'. He then stared at the aircraft kit hanging from his ceiling.

"What was that?" his mother snapped.

"Nothing."

"Good, because I've got a hundred and one things to do before your father gets home and I'm in the middle of cleaning the house and I've got to go and fetch Mrs Marshall's prescription when she gets back from having her ears done. Oh yes, I've got to go to the post office and I've promised to help paint the neighbours' house. That reminds me..." Ned shut his eyes as his mother reeled off a list of to do's. His mind wandered after Simone. He was snapped out of the sweet image by a slap from his mother. "You're not listening to me, are you?"

"Ouch." Ned sat up and pretended to rub the injury. His mother was still talking. "So, with all this to do, I want you to walk Mrs Marshall's dog, Minty."

"But I've just kicked it." He corrected himself. "I mean, seen it going for a walk with that old cabbage boiler."

He ducked another slap. "Don't you call Mrs Marshall a cabbage boiler. She's a very kind old lady and she's offered to pay you for walking Minty. Oh yes, and your friends called around too. Maybe you could walk the dog with them?"

Ned looked dumbstruck. "Are you mad, woman? Do you think I want to walk that little rat dog in public with some friends?" He turned away from her, then turned back. "Anyway, who were they?"

Mrs Edwards looked dumbstruck now. "I don't know, they never said. Or if they did, I didn't hear them." She looked past Ned and stared at the wall. "Maybe I need some of Mrs Marshall's ear wax remover. Your father says I've got selective hearing anyway." She went off again into her own narrative of lists of woes and unending tasks. Ned drummed his fingers on his knee, then jerked her tracksuit to get her attention.

"So, who was it?"

She looked startled, then stared around his room as if she was unsure of where she was.

"Who were they?" he said again, and when she still didn't answer, Ned spoke slowly, exaggerating the pronouncement of every word. "W-H-O C-A-L-L-E-D A-R-O-U-N-D T-O-D-A-Y- T-O S-E-E M-E?"

Mrs Edwards looked annoyed now. "Oh...I don't know. One was very small and the other was very fat."

Ned smiled sarcastically at his mother. "Thank you. It was Percy the Pygmy and the Triple T. Now you can leave the room and get on with whatever you've got to do."

To his surprise, but still looking annoyed, Mrs Edwards turned around and left the room. For an instant, Ned could not believe it, so he quickly slammed the door before his mother could remember anything else that would involve him helping neighbours, or household chores, or the dreaded homework he was supposed to do by yesterday.

The summer was rolling along and Ned had not heard from Fabian or anyone at Stalingrad Towers. He had to wait a further four agonising days for the call, which, to Ned's delight, came directly from Beetie.

He was eating dinner at the table with his parents and was just biting into a piping hot minced beef crispy pancake. His father had opted to cook tea and had misread the cooking instructions. He microwaved the pancakes for ten minutes instead of two. They looked normal to the dining eye but inside the golden breadcrumbed shell was liquid mince that was the temperature of the earth's core. Ned had been playing outside with his catapult and had worked up quite an appetite after shooting last year's Christmas nuts at various living things. If there was one meal that Ned loved, it was crispy pancakes, chips, and mushy peas. He stabbed one of the pancakes with his fork and greedily rammed it into his salivating mouth. As he bit down, the crust broke and released a cauldron of super-heated mince onto his palate. He could hear the lining of his tongue and the skin on the roof of his mouth sizzle. Ned screamed and spat the mince and blistered skin tissue out. It spattered the face of his father, who received scorch marks across his face. Even the tablecloth seemed to blister under the intense heat. Ned grabbed the vase on the table, nuzzled the lilies out of the way with his gherkin nose, and drank deeply from the grey water. He was panting like a dog when he finally drained the vase, and then he ran over to the sink and sucked greedily at the cold tap for the next minute. His mother was administering first aid to her husband's scorched face when Ned stopped slurping. He held the sink for support and breathed deeply. Then he turned on his father. Ned's tongue was as red as Beetie's face and was starting to swell like a balloon. "You stupid idiot! Call yourself a father. Yooooo mooo iike a bwooody..." His verbal attack could not continue because Ned's tongue had now expanded so much that it filled the whole of his mouth. Instead, he jumped up and down and mumbled threats at his father and shook his fists at his mother. Then, from his pocket, his mobile phone rang.

Beetie thought there was a cow on the other end of the phone when it was finally answered. All he could hear was mooing noises. He looked at the phone in disgust and hit it on the top of his bureau, then shouted at it. "If that's Mutton, then moo once for yes."

There was silence, and then a single moo.

Satisfied, Beetie carried on. "Right, you've taken the money and the phone, now it's time for payback. Be at Stalingrad Towers in five minutes." With that, he hung up.

In the dining room, Ned shook a final fist at his parents, then ran out of the house towards Beetie and, moreover, towards his beloved Simone. He ran, panting heavily and sounding like a vacuum cleaner blocked by a pair of underpants, and as he did he thought of his first mission for Beetie. He could perform heroic deeds and afterwards have his deformed tongue massaged back to normality by Simone.

*

Panting, he arrived outside Stalingrad Towers. His tongue's swelling had subsided slightly and Ned could move it about inside of his mouth. He practiced a few words outside the gates, trying not to sound bovine, and was so engrossed in attempting to speak properly that he did not notice the fence that had been erected around Stalingrad Towers. It was high and hung with wire, and Ned walked into it. There was a flash, a loud bang, and sparks as Ned was thrown back by a high voltage charge from the newly installed electric security fence. He got up unsteadily and patted out his singed clothes. His hair was standing on end and his ears were ringing. On the periphery of his hearing, he could hear what he thought was a bull roaring. He shook his head and looked around to see Beetie on his knees laughing like a maniac. Ned tried to look as normal as he could and, with a great effort, walked towards Beetie with his head held up high. The laughing subsided and Beetie struggled to stand up.

"Alright, Crichton, you can turn the power off now. Test successful, I think."

Crichton pulled a large switch down. It banged and sparks shot out, so he let go quickly and retreated. Beetie was still struggling and his manservant went to help.

"I don't need help, you idiot!" Beetie roared. "Go and open the gate for the boy." And Crichton did his master's bidding.

To Ned, it was like the gates of heaven opening. He did not even consider that the full voltage of electricity could have killed him. Ned was going to the place he loved: Stalingrad Towers.

On seeing Beetie having trouble standing, Ned rushed forwards to help, but his offer of assistance was brushed off.

"Ah, the guinea pig has arrived. What do you think of my new security system, boy? Keeps the filth out of Stalingrad Towers, don't you know." He eventually succeeded in rising and started to massage his knee. "Got one in the kneecap back in the jungle; never healed, still open to the elements. Gives me some gyp in the cold weather. Still, king and country and all that." He slapped Ned on the back. "Come on. Fabian's waiting inside. You've got work to do."

Singed and lightly toasted, Ned walked in awed silence behind Beetie. Crichton appeared from behind the opened front door and bowed them in, though he looked distastefully at the presence of Ned entering the house.

"Fabian Vaughan-Abbott, down here at once!" Beetie roared.

Fabian appeared very quickly on the landing. He was red-faced and Ned thought he might have had a beating with the Baron. The thought did not distress him; in fact, the thought of adoption by his beloved Beetie and Simone occupied his mind. His dreams were wandering into a kind of sibling rivalry with only one outcome. Fabian's high-pitched voice brought Ned out of his revelry. He was studying some papers and did not notice that there was a guest.

"So sorry, Father. I've been looking at the quantities involved in the new housing development and I think it would be beneficial if we brought in some rather disreputable surveyors." Fabian stopped when he noticed Ned. He looked at his father. "Is he in?"

"Yes, of course he is! He's taken the money and phone and will take a great deal more, I would surmise. Wouldn't you, Mutton?"

"Err, esh, hir, I ud," Ned answered, trying to sound un-swelled and normal.

"What?" Beetie and Fabian asked in unison. Eager for more rewards and getting to understand his place and just how the Vaughan-Abbott household operated, Ned just nodded in reply. It seemed to satisfy both father and son.

"To the study then," Beetie commanded. "Run ahead, Fabian, and get the prisoner."

Ned wondered what sort of thing he was getting as he watched Fabian turn on his heels and disappear back up the landing. Beetie launched off up the stairs. Ned followed and noticed curiously that his limp had disappeared. As he climbed the stairs, Beetie shouted out orders to invisible people. "Crichton, G and T in my study now! Something edible as well; a cucumber sandwich with horseradish sauce and jelly, and better get soft drinks for the children. And keep that awful woman that purports to be my wife out of my vicinity for the next hour."

They reached the study. Beetie pushed the door open and sat straight on his leather chair. A mahogany desk had been placed in front of the chair and Ned stood in front of it. Fabian shuffled up close to his father and then placed on the table a jar. Something was swimming in it.

Before Ned could notice what it was, there was a knock at the door. Beetie shouted, "Enter!" and from behind the door, Simone appeared. Ned's heart bounced a foot in the air, his legs went into a jelly-like state, and a hot flush came over him. Simone eyed him quickly as she entered the room. Beetie was going and getting a hot flush as well, but it was not a blushing puppy love but the start of a brooding eruption of intense rage. He gripped the arms of his chair and you could hear the leather squealing as it was constricted. A button popped off and landed with a plop in the jar. "Get out of this study, woman!"

Simone ignored Beetie's eruption of rage and wiggled over to place a very large glass of gin and tonic and a cucumber, jelly, and horseradish sandwich on the table. There was the sound of shaking crockery as Crichton entered carrying a silver tray with a jug of orange juice and two glasses on it. All the time he was tugging at a pretend forelock and making quick bowing movements towards Beetie. Ned noticed that Fabian had retreated towards the curtains and was half hidden by the time Beetie pulled his wig off and threw it at Crichton. "You bloody Quisling! You're supposed to lay down your life before me, and here you are sucking up to a wretched girlie. Now get out, you blaggard, before I set the Baron on you!"

Crichton set down the quivering tray and withdrew from the study faster than lightning. Simone did not. She waited patiently for Beetie's anger to abate. He was still gripping the chair arms but then released one and downed the gin and tonic in one. There was a hissing sound like red hot metal being quenched in water. Beetie's eyes set on Simone as he ground his teeth loudly. The sound made the hairs on Ned's neck stand up. All the while, Simone leant against the wall and polished her long fingernails with a pink nail file. This went on for minutes, the grinding and filing getting louder as if competing against each other. It seemed to reverberate around the room until Ned could not stand it any longer. He was about to scream when Beetie slammed his palm down on the desk. The jar nearly tipped over but Ned caught it.

"No, you can't go shopping!"

"Why?" Simone asked coolly.

"Because I said so, damn it!" Beetie retorted. "And it would be my money you would be spending."

"I need to go out and get some things for me," Simone said. "Some personal things—"

"Send that lily-livered servant of mine!" Beetie interrupted.

"He can't get what I want, and anyway, I need a new hairdo and because of your temper and shouting no mobile salon will come within a mile of this place."

Beetie stuttered, "This place…this place…this place has a name. A very expensive name, I'll have you know!"

"Do you want me to look perfect or do you not?" Simone asked.

He was silent for a while and looked around the room awkwardly. "Can't you get Crichton to cut it? He always does mine, and the boy's too."

This time it was Simone who exploded. "No, I can't! How dare you think I'd look good with a short back and sides?" She advanced on Beetie and pointed at his uncovered scalp. "Anyway, baldy, you wear a bloody syrup!"

Ned guffawed as Beetie touched where his wig would have been. He ignored the rude outburst from Ned and leaned back to delve in his pocket. Simone picked up the wig and threw it back at Beetie. He caught it, placed it delicately on his head, and patted it reassuringly.

"How much?" he asked with a sigh.

"Two hundred and fifty pounds," Simone said casually.

Beetie pulled out his wallet, then stopped. "HOW MUCH?!"

"Two hundred and fifty pounds, to look beautiful?" Simone said with a purr.

Beetie raised his eyebrows quickly and breathed excitedly. Ned breathed excitedly too. She had put on the voice of a vamp and boy, did it work. Beetie handed over the money. She reached for it but Beetie snatched it back. "Crichton will drive you, wait for you, and bring you back."

Simone reached for the money and uttered in that seductive voice again, "But of course he will, my dear Beetie, of course he will." He handed over the money and as Simone turned and walked out of the room, Ned saw a look of anger and frustration on her face, but from where Beetie and Fabian were they could not.

"And get that idiot to refill me immediately!" Beetie shouted. Ned thought he could hear a sob outside the door, but the sound was cut off by Beetie slamming his fist on the table again. Ned turned to look and saw Fabian reappearing from the curtains. Beetie was holding up the jar and studying it.

"Right, Mutton, what's this in the jar?"

Ned leaned forward and recognised what was floating in water.

"It'th a oot."

"What?"

Ned breathed heavily and concentrated. His tongue was slowly becoming less swollen, so he tried again. "An n-o-o-o-w-t!"

Beetie and Fabian looked puzzled and shook their heads. "What in heaven's name is an oooot?" Beetie asked.

Ned took a deep slurp of orange juice. It stung slightly as he swished it around his mouth. He could feel strips of skin hanging down from the roof of his mouth and recalled the detailed drawing of a whale's mouth with its baleen plates that it used as filters to syphoned krill from the sea. He thought this was how a whale feels as he siphoned the sweet juice over his blistered mouth. The freshness made him feel better and so, like a tourist trying to grasp some new language for the first time, he licked his lips and spoke slowly.

"That is a newt."

"Correct," Fabian said.

"But what kind of oot, err, newt, is it?" Beetie asked. Ned didn't know. He thought a newt was a newt. Thankfully, before he was further pressured for an answer, Beetie explained, "It's a very expensive newt, that's what it is! Because this ugly little lizard thing is costing me an awful lot of money."

"Oh," was all Ned could find to say.

Beetie started to go red again and Fabian sought the curtains again.

"Oh! Oh! Is that all you can say? When this…thing is holding up my housing development at Fulwood!"

Ned knew of the Fulwood Housing Development. It was always on the cover of the local paper. There had been major opposition by the local people to the proposed development. They said it was an area of natural beauty, a place where they could go and relax, and moreover, a place where rare wildlife was found. His father had been involved in looking at the planning application for the local council. Ned remembered him being dead set against it, but he had to be impartial because of his job. That didn't stop him donning a disguise and dragging Ned down to the site to protest. Actually, Ned had to admit it was one of the rare times that he had enjoyed being with his dad. They had booed and hissed at the digger drivers and had formed a human chain across the proposed new road. The police came and broke it up and the diggers continued to dig, but now it seemed there was a new obstruction in the way: a newt.

Beetie was looking at Ned. The rage was slowly brewing. Ned remembered where he was and, with a rare insight that Beetie and

Fabian could not have guessed, Ned took the lead and, now able to speak coherently, he surmised, "So, this little newt is an endangered species that has been found down at Fulwood?"

Beetie looked astonished. He then turned to look at his son, who looked equally astonished.

Beetie shook himself from his astonishment. He held up the jar and studied the creature. "The great crested newt. The bloody expensive newt, more likely." With a thump, he placed the jar back on the table. Beetie clicked his fingers and Fabian brought two small fishing nets out from behind the curtains. "You two will take these and collect each and every one of those little blighters. You will then get rid of them in whatever way you deem fit. Make them die or do what you want with them. Flush them down the bog for all I care. Just get rid of them and free Fulwood housing estate of them!"

*

So Ned and Fabian went off to the Fulwood site to collect great crested newts. They walked along the security fence and tried to find a hole to crawl through. There was none, so they looked for places where the fence was loose and the ground was soft. Ned eventually found one near to an oak tree. He was about to pull the wire up when he saw a man in a hard hat and high visibility yellow vest coming out from behind the tree. He was struggling to pull up his trousers and complaining about a new takeaway restaurant that had opened recently. Ned and Fabian waited for the man to wander off. The moaning receded so Ned took the nets and buckets and threw them over the fence. Then he got down and started to crawl under the wire. Fabian looked around nervously, then followed. Fabian tried to hurry through the gap and started to push Ned, who was only halfway through when they heard the man's voice again. "Alright, alright, I'll get yer paper. Sorry I forgot it. The sports section's missing though." Ned looked in the direction of the voice and then to Fabian. He looked to Ned like he was about to wet his pants, and as the man drew nearer, he did. Fabian panicked and tried to scramble past Ned but he got caught up in the wire. He grabbed at Ned and shrieked, "Don't leave me! Don't leave me for that bully!"

"Oi! What are you two doing? This is private property, so you get out of there and clear off sharpish!" the man yelled at them.

Ned tried to pull away and managed to wiggle out of Fabian's embrace but as the man closed on them, Fabian grabbed Ned's foot. He started to kick Fabian so as to get away from this approaching gorilla. Ned may have wanted money and all the trappings of the high life, but he didn't want a criminal record for breaking and entering.

The man was nearly on them. Ned readied his boot for a final kick to Fabian's head so that the little coward would release him. Fabian was shaking uncontrollably but would not relinquish his grip. It put Ned off his aim and he kicked the fence post instead. Then, miraculously, the hold eased and, as if giving into fate, Fabian turned to his would-be executioner. The effect was instantaneous. He let go of Ned and started to shout abusively at the man, "You brute, you swine, you cruel old bugger! Frightening innocent children like that; you should be ashamed of yourself! Get over here and get me out of this wire!"

Released from Fabian's hold, Ned scrabbled through and looked back at the scene. He could not understand the change from lily-livered coward to rampant lion-like warrior. Then he noticed the print on the man's vest. In bold black lettering it read '**VA Estates and Securities**'. The man was on Beetie's payroll, ergo he would do whatever Beetie, or in this case Fabian, would ask.

The man looked confused. Then he pulled up his sleeves and cracked his knuckles as he finally closed on Fabian.

The lily-livered role overcame Fabian again. He gave a high-pitched yelp and managed to free himself from the wire. A hammer-like fist smashed into the wet mud where Fabian had been. The fence now separated them. The man grabbed the wire and shook it like a maniac. Fabian ran behind Ned, then squealed like a sow. "I'll have you flogged for that, you plank! Do you know my father is your employer? He pays your wages that you buy beer and chips to fill your fat belly with!"

The guard didn't register that he was an employee of Mr Vaughan-Abbott and shook the fence even harder. One of the wooden poles was coming out of the ground and both Fabian and Ned retreated. As the pole tore free, it seemed that the guard suddenly saw the error of his ways. He looked left and right, let go of the fence, and ran behind the tree.

Fabian regained his arrogance and started to goad the guard. "You dim-witted oaf, come out from behind there and get back to guarding my father's property. Honestly, talk about thick. He's nearly as stupid as you, Mutton."

Ned didn't take kindly to being called stupid. He aimed a punch at Fabian.

Fabian sidestepped and held up his hand. "Now, now, Mutton, there's no need for that. I'm just putting people in their place. Anyway, I've had training in the martial arts, you know, so you'd be picking a fight with a champion. Also, do you want to be sacked by Father?"

Ned lowered his fist. He was still angry at Fabian and could not believe what a cowering jelly he had been a minute ago.

"Okay, piddle pants, if you're so clever, why didn't we go and just enter this site through the gate?" Fabian gave Ned a very patronising look, but before he could say anything, Ned continued, "And why doesn't your dad use that idiot who's hiding behind the tree to get the newts?"

Fabian raised his arms to the sky. "Heaven save me! Am I surrounded by cretins?"

From behind the tree, the guard's face appeared. Fabian saw him, "Ah, there you are, you doltish idiot." He beckoned him with his finger. "Come here and explain to this boy why you can't rid this area of those little newts."

The guard crawled over and mumbled to Fabian, "Ah, forgive me, young master. I had no idea who you were. I don't want to lose me job or have no beer and chips. Please don't tell his lordship Mr Vaughan-Abbott about this."

Fabian waved him away from his feet. "Alright, alright. Now tell Mutton here about the newts."

The guard looked from side to side, let out a cry, then started back towards the tree.

Fabian tutted loudly. The guard scurried off to safety behind the oak. "Go on and do as I said. Get back to the gate to guard my family's investment," Fabian shouted.

With a deep sigh, Fabian turned to Ned. "Right, listen. The guards here have to be seen to be protecting the place. There are protesters outside the gate most days and if they see one of the guards disappear for long then they will get suspicious. And if those newts suddenly start to disappear as well then Father will have a big problem. If no one sees anyone dodgy going through the front gate and the guards are seen as doing their duty then no one will suspect a thing. In the meantime, we—innocent children on, say, a nature watch—are seen." He stopped and pulled two creased stickers out of his pocket. "Here, stick this on." Ned looked at the sticker. It said, 'Save the Great Crested Newt'. He obligingly stuck it on his shirt. Fabian continued, "And if we're also seen to be supportive of the do-goody newt lovers then, hey presto, no one will suspect a thing when the newts suddenly vanish!"

Ned stared ahead without saying anything. Fabian took it as stupidity. "Do you want me to explain it again, more slowly this time?"

"No. I understand alright." Ned thought for a millionth of a second what his parents might think. He remembered again when he and his dad protested against the development and suddenly thought that his dad may be now, at this very moment, protesting for the great crested newt. He shook the thought away. They walked on through long grass and over marshy ground. The last of the year's butterflies flew lazily on the warm air. Fabian tried to clap his hands together and squash them. After a while, the ground rose slightly and they could see willow trees on the crest of a small hill. Both boys pushed through the overhanging boughs and there, hidden in the centre of the trees, was a beautiful pond. The water was still in the summer haze with only the occasional ripple of fish breaking the surface.

"Right, this is where the newts are. Let's get them," Fabian said.

"What are we supposed to do with them when we've got them?"

"I don't know what you're going to do with yours but I've got big plans for mine. I might put one in the microwave and see what happens. That would be good, wouldn't it?"

Ned ignored Fabian and took off his shoes and socks. He was rolling up his trousers when he noticed that Fabian was lying against a tree not getting ready for the task ahead.

"Oi, come on. We're going to have to get in the pond and get them," Ned explained.

"Oh no, not me, old man, I'm too well bred to get wet. You'll have to do it."

"You can get stuffed, old man. We get in there together."

"You do it for me. Remember whose son I am?"

"Beetie would want you to do it too," Ned said half sarcastically.

Fabian was on him in a shot. In a show of unconcealed anger, he pushed Ned backwards. "Don't you ever call my father Beetie in front of me! Do you understand? He's my father, not yours!"

Ned was surprised by the sheer rage that Fabian directed at him. Fabian had laughed when Ned had addressed his father as Beetie. He had encouraged him, and now he was like this. Still, although he knew that Fabian was not a particularly nice person who was spoilt, rude, toffee-nosed, and a bully, Ned had said he would be his friend for the summer. And anyway, he thought, think of the benefits: the money, working for Beetie, and being close to Simone.

But then Fabian realised that he had stepped too far and this outburst could make things difficult for him and his father. He looked down at his feet, then to Ned, and held out his hand. "Look...sorry, old man. I overreacted a bit. No one has ever had the privilege of calling Father Beetie, least of all a commoner...er, I mean a fellow young boy. It's a lot to take in, you know. Shake?"

Ned shook and then took both fishing nets and a bucket.

"You're a good man, Mutton. Just for that, you can keep my share of the newts."

Ned nodded, then waded off in the shallows. Fabian sat on a tree stump and brought out from his pocket a pipe. He packed it with tobacco, lit it, and started to puff away. The smell of the pipe smoke mixed with the smell of fallen leaves and drifted over the pond. After a short while, Ned caught a newt, and as he emptied it into his bucket he saw Fabian blowing smoke rings over the still water.

Chapter 4

This was the first of many tasks that Beetie set Ned. Fabian helped, or rather accompanied him, on these 'missions'—as Beetie called the tasks—and as Ned did more of these, he came to think Fabian was there only to oversee the deeds and check that Ned was doing them properly. He always kept a discreet distance from Ned, who also suspected that at any sign of trouble or intervention from the forces of law and order, Fabian would not be seen for dust.

They, or rather Ned, moved some boundaries at a factory development and the foundations were dug before anyone from the local authority could stop them. There were protests but the planning department deemed it too much trouble to go through the courts and the site was expanded and passed. On another development, there was an ancient monument that had stood for hundreds of years. It bore the legend of a battle fought nearly a thousand years ago but it was in the way of Beetie's new fast food takeaway drive-through and it had to go. Ned waited until there was some Royal Gala in town when loads of fireworks would be set off at night. The countless loud bangs, crackles, and explosions hid the sound of the sledge hammer blows that Ned inflicted on the ancient monument as he took it apart. Again, the authority thought it too troublesome to replace, and anyway, they were offered a year's discount from the takeaway, so that helped settle matters.

Ned was operating solo by this time, as Fabian was doing other things at home that Beetie would not tell him about. But because of this, he was becoming a budding young vandal with expanding criminal tendencies. He didn't care if he broke the law. It was small reptiles, places on a map, old pieces of stone that no one cared for, buildings out of use for so long that they should be demolished, things he thought no one should really care about. As long as he was not caught, he was happy. The money was not exactly rolling in though. After his initial payment from Beetie he still had seen any further cash. Beetie had promised him wads of cash and heaped back-handed praise on him, but he still had not opened his wallet. Ned's parents didn't seem to suspect anything. He did most of his 'missions' at the weekend, bar the ancient monument; that was in the week and he said that he was going to bed early, then climbed out of the window and ran to the stone smashing session.

The weekend before Fabian left for St Geoffrey's School he had a leaving do and Ned was invited. He went because he thought he would see Simone and he thought he would ask Beetie for some money. But when he got there he felt so out of place that he tried to leave at the earliest possible moment. A few of Fabian's school friends had come along and they did not think highly of Ned. Fabian was sticking with them. Ned caught pieces of conversation about class, breeding, and council houses but he was clever enough to ignore them. Maybe due to his criminal activities he was becoming more astute and devious, because before he would have been unaware that he was being the target of insults and jokes. And if he had, he would have lost his temper and shouted back at them, maybe even picked a fight, but now he thought he was being collected in his thoughts. He thought he was being wise and calculating, as a criminal mastermind should be.

Simone was nowhere to be seen and so he left the ballroom and tried to spy Beetie. He walked up the stairs quietly. The sound of the party receded as he reached the landing. He passed the oil painting of the Vaughan-Abbotts and stopped to listen. There was a sound of shooting and banging, the rat-tat-tat of machine gun bullets and earth-shaking explosions. Ned crept forwards. The battle sounds were coming from the room. He reached the door and started to turn the handle when a voice spoke behind him.

"The master is expecting you." It was Crichton, and Ned nearly wet himself in fright. A guilty thought came to him that he certainly was not the criminal mastermind that he thought he was, but like all guilt-driven notions, he shook it away before turning, in surprise to himself and the manservant, on Crichton. "You idiot! What are you doing creeping around here like Frankenstein? You nearly had a pair of trousers and pants to clean." And to both of their surprise, Ned carried on the verbal attack. "What the hell does Beetie want? And what's that noise? And what's the idea of jumping out on people?

I'll...I'll...I'll do something nasty to you next time if you do that again."

Even in the darkened landing, Ned could see Crichton bowing his head and reaching for his forelock. "I beg your pardon for startling you, young master Mutton, but sir suggests you join him in there." He pointed a shaking hand at the door.

Ned calmed down and felt slightly embarrassed by his outburst, but then his pride started to overtake the former feeling. This man, albeit a manservant, called him young master. Crichton, who only recently had hit around the head and looked down his nose at Ned, had called him master. This was definitely progress in the scheme of becoming a criminal mastermind. Ned pushed out his chest and reached for the door handle. He turned to Crichton. "One more thing, Crichton. Call me sir from now on, not young master." Crichton reached for his forelock and disappeared backwards into the shadows.

Down the landing, Crichton flicked his hair backwards and strode with his nose high in the air. He looked back at Ned and grunted through the raised proboscis. "Disgusting little plebeian," he muttered under his breath.

When Ned knocked on the door, the sound of explosions stopped. There was a groan and sounds of heavy footsteps. Then the door opened. Beetie looked more beetroot-like than usual. He was also huffing and puffing and between these he ordered, "Come in, lad."

Ned saw that the model airplanes, tanks, and soldiers were covering the floor. He had to tread carefully to avoid breaking them. Beetie just piled through them, breaking a regiment, three battle tanks, and two aeroplanes on the way to his desk. Ned stopped to pick one of the broken models up but Beetie suddenly opened up with a pretend machine gun, shouting, "Rat-tat-tat-tat-tat-tat." Ned looked mystified for an instant, then he grabbed his chest and fell backwards, uttering a cry. Another regiment and tank were crushed and Beetie rushed over to stand above Ned, who in horror thought he had overstepped the mark by crushing the models and tried to get up, but Beetie was on him first. "Damn good show, boy. But never leave a comrade behind." Then he offered his hand out. Ned was astounded. This was Beetie, who craved and loved his models. Not even his own son was allowed to play with them, let alone break them. Ned let himself be pulled up. Beetie patted his shoulders and tottered over to his desk. There was an empty bottle of whiskey on there, and various crushed beer cans under it.

Ned decided to speak first as it seemed Beetie was in a good mood. He opened his mouth but Beetie got in there faster. "Now, boy, you've done well. You've done very well for old Beetie and your reward is coming. You have had an initial down payment which I hope you have not squandered on unworthy causes. That boy of mine doesn't show as much promise as you and he's going back to boarding school next week. Your summer lease period is up but I want you to stay on with me as you're a grand little vandal. Anyway, it's time to up the ante, so to speak, you know, solo missions." Ned was about to correct Beetie on the fact that he had been a solo operative for the last few missions when Beetie loudly started to reminisce. "Done plenty myself in the past. Operating behind the lines and all that, can't say any more." He tapped his nose. "Official Secrets Act, you know. Though there was the South Atlantic and the Congo. Of course, there was also China and that little incident down in Colombia." He chuckled and had a wistful look on his claret coloured face. Then, as quickly as it had come, he snapped out of it. "Anyway, if you prove yourself as a solo operative by wrecking this piece of old rubbish then Christmas will come early this year for you!" Beetie crunched a few soldiers as he moved to an easel. It was covered by a black cloth, and Beetie pulled it away in dramatic fashion. Ned stared at an aerial photo of a truly dilapidated old industrial building. It looked as though it was near to falling down. In fact, it looked as though it had been bombed and this was a post-mission aerial reconnaissance photo that squadrons used to judge whether it deserved another high explosive pounding. Corrugated roof sheets lay in piles on the ground. Pipes and conduits criss-crossed each other in bent and buckled paths. There was a half-collapsed chimney and a mess of scrap metal everywhere.

"What a dump," Ned said.

Beetie turned and eyed him intently. "You may think that, my boy. But let me tell you that this 'dump' is the most expensive piece of land or real estate in the county. Beyond that crappy façade is a view to die for: Rolling hills, parkland, and a river running beside it. People will kill for that or they will pay big money for it. This 'dump' is a former chiller factory or cold store where they used to keep things frozen, food stuffs and all that. It went out of business thirty odd years ago. I bought it for a song ten years ago but some do-gooders in the bloody council have put a preservation order on it. Can you believe it? A run down old crap-hole like that, and they say it deserves recognition for its industrial heritage to this area!" Beetie kicked the easel and it tremored. He watched it quiver and then, with a look of hatred, kicked it again. The easel flew against the wall and collapsed but the photo detached itself and gently floated down to rest at Ned's feet. He looked at it. Then he looked at Beetie, who raised his eyebrows, then frowned at the photo. Ned lifted his boot and stamped on it.

"That's my boy. Destroy it. Bring down that dump by any means available—so long as you're not seen. And it needs to be done by Christmas, so get it done and you can have a nice bonus for the holiday."

Ned was floating on a cloud of self-importance and pride from the words Beetie had said. He trusted him over his own son, who was downstairs being childish with his friends, whilst Ned was doing adult business things upstairs. He was appreciated by this great man, this developer, this self-made entrepreneur and war hero. He truly was, even though he had not been paid for ages. Ned was giddy with dreams of becoming Beetie's trusted number two. He would become his enforcer, just like in the films. He might even try to grow a moustache. That would make him look the part. He pulled out his phone from his pocket and fiddled with the settings.

"Erm...Beetie, may I make a short film of you with this phone you gave me? I've been looking at it and it has a video player on it and...well...you know, you're the kind of father and employer that I've always wanted...if you see what I mean?"

Beetie looked puzzled but then succumbed to Ned's dreadful crawling. "Yes, I suppose so. You're a good lad even though you're as common as muck, so yes, I'll do it." He went to the desk and in a drawer found another bottle which he opened and drank deeply from. Beetie straightened himself up and adjusted his wig expertly and without aid, for there was no mirror in the room. He cleared his throat. Ned pointed the mobile phone at Beetie and pressed record.

"Well, now then...mmmmh..." He was not used to being filmed, and the situation clearly put him off his guard. On top of that, he could not think of what to say until his eyes fell on the photo of the chiller factory. "Ah, yes...here's my retirement nest egg. That former factory will bring me rewards beyond anyone's dreams. I will do anything to achieve that. I mean anything." He screwed a bloodshot eye towards the camera. "I tell you, I'd kill for that site. Anyone who dares to come up against me then they're dead meat. I own that building and all that is in it. I have done since I purchased it all those years ago. There. How was that? Okay, because that's all you're getting!" Beetie grabbed the phone from Ned and pressed stop. He studied it, looked at Ned dubiously, and then went to put the phone in his pocket. Beetie's eyes zeroed in on Ned. He guffawed loudly and threw the phone back. "That's something to show your grandchildren, boy," he chuckled again, and slurped down another long swig from the bottle. Then Beetie belched loudly, hiccupped, and bent down to pick up the photo of the chiller factory. He staggered to the window, fumbled with the lock, and threw the photo out into the night air. "Be gone, foul thing," he muttered, then slumped back down in his chair.

Ned left, still feeling elated, and he had not even set eyes on Simone. He was swimming in the sea of devotion and the captain of that water was Beetie. Ned went to say farewell to Fabian but when he approached him, Fabian turned away and spoke to his fellows from St Geoffrey's School. Ned chuckled in spite of the deliberate insult, but he did not care. After all, Beetie favoured him above his son, and being Beetie's man, who could stand against him now?

As Ned walked out of Stalingrad Towers, the electric fence opened automatically and he made his way down the road. Still within sight of the lights, he felt a gentle brush on his shoulder as the photograph of the chiller factory drifted past to settle on the ground in front of his feet.

*

Over the next few months, Ned was busy at school and the detestable homework. He tried to stay away from home in the day at weekends. His parents would try desperately to encourage him at home with planned trips to the seaside or promises of days out to interesting places but Ned did not want any of it. He was growing frustrated with a lack of action. Apparently, Beetie's plans were on hold due to some bribe not working. So Ned had to wait for the planned demolition of the chiller factory to begin. He was getting used to breaking things, smashing things, and general destruction, and Ned was now starting to get withdrawal symptoms due to his inactivity. He needed to annihilate something: mineral, vegetable, and—even in his darkest thoughts—animal. Winter came quickly with the arrival of cold weather. The model aeroplane kits that he and his father had built were the first to suffer. They hung from his ceiling on cotton, chasing each other in mock dogfights. He had taken an added interest in these after seeing Beetie's collection at Stalingrad Towers. The kits were from his father's collection—a collection that had been built up over many years and had been stored away "for a rainy day". To his credit, Ned's dad had been positively overjoyed that his son was taking an interest in something that they both could do. They had started with some old inexpensive models and together had built and painted sixteen World War II aircraft. Ned had eyed some very expensive ones after that. His dad said that they were very special and were also very rare. Ned suspected that his dad had bought them without consulting his mother and when he mentioned this, his dad went a reddish hue and changed the subject rather too quickly. So Ned knew it was true, and so made a deal to build a big Messerschmitt fighter all by himself and paint it whatever colour he wanted if he forgot about the expensive stash of model kits in the attic. He painted it in lurid colours, which his dad said were not accurate to that type of aircraft, to which Ned told him to "get a life" and then delicately brushed hundreds of kill marks on the fuselage and tail of the kit. Ned was fascinated with these; he had seen these in his dad's books on the fighter planes of the Second World War. Pilots stood by their aircraft and pointed at crosses, stars, or roundels—depending on which side they were on—to signify how good they were and how many enemy aircraft they had shot down. Some had a few, others had hundreds. He looked now at the model with all its kill marks. Then he went down to the shed. From here, he brought out some turps, some cotton wool, and a box of matches. Ned then pulled the models down from the ceiling and stuffed them with cotton-wool-soaked turps. He then set fire to them and threw them out of his bedroom window. They flew down to smash in burning lumps of stinking black plastic. Fifteen blackened lumps of plastic were stuck to the drive and Ned suddenly thought of his father's love for these former plastic kits. But fortune favours the demented mind sometimes and, fortuitously for Ned, his parents were out and the deformed remains were covered up within the hour. The first snow had started to fall. It caught the local authority by surprise and by the time the gritting lorries were loaded and ready to roll, the roads, paths, towns and villages, and the countryside were covered in a thick white carpet.

From his bedroom window, Ned looked down at the now-white street. He could see children playing joyfully in the snow. They threw snowballs at each other, pushed sledges down the paths, and built snowmen. Laughter and happy thoughts filled the street apart from in Ned's bedroom. He scowled at the high-spirited children and brooded in his self-imposed prison. He needed action and he needed it now. Then, as if in answer to some deranged prayer, Beetie called. "It's on," were the blunt words from his employer. "Get down there and obliterate!" The phone then went dead. Ned squealed with delight. This was it. After all the waiting, his demolition dreams were on again. He felt like an athlete getting ready for the big marathon; trained and ready to run, at the peak of fitness, and probably the best in his league. Except his was not the arena of sporting achievement but the arena of mass destruction. In his bedroom he looked again at the last remaining fighter plane, the big one with all its kill marks. Then he looked at the children building snowmen. Dark thoughts filled his mind as he grabbed a pen and ran downstairs. Ned darted into the kitchen and wolfed down the remains of a cold takeaway from the night before. He wiped the grease from his mouth with his sleeve, belched loudly, and went to the hallway. On the doormat was a letter. He stuffed it in his pocket and ran out of the door for a date with destruction.

In number two's front garden, Jennifer and Jackie Jones were admiring the snowman they had just made. It was small and rotund with three coal buttons, a red scarf, and a broad-rimmed Stetson hat. The young girls giggled joyfully as they placed a parsnip that would be its nose below the two coal eyes. Their joy turned to horror as a boot broke the head apart. The coal eyes fell out and the parsnip nose nearly speared Jennifer in the ear. Ned had launched himself with such force at the snowman that he knocked the two girls back in the snow and carried on over the small privet hedge. Without a second thought, he was off down the street to the next snowy white victim. At number nine there was another snowman. The family stood inside their lounge, warming themselves by the fire and looking at it. A boy ran into their vision and stamped the snowman into pieces. The parents ran out after the little hooligan but he was gone, on to find another kill. For that was what Ned was doing. He was being a fighter pilot, flying into the snowmen and shooting them down in a storm of smashed and broken snow. By the time he had reached the end of the estate where he lived, Ned had achieved acedom three times over. By the laws of aerial combat, if you shot down six enemy aircraft then you qualified as an ace. Ned was a triple ace, as he had demolished eighteen snowmen on the estate. Children were left crying. Mothers were left apoplectic with rage. Fathers sought vengeance.

Ned halted, panting but elated, at a winter-bare oak tree. He leaned back against the cold bark and pulled out the pen and letter from his pocket. On one side of the letter were his name and address. It was unopened, so he opened it. It was his report from the school. He groaned and screwed it up, then threw it over somebody's garden fence. The envelope was the important thing here. Then Ned heard the sound of a vehicle turning the corner into the estate. He recognised the drab grey van of the local grocer called 'Grumpy' Giles. All the kids loathed him as he was the most miserable person in the town and it was obvious he could not stand kids. Parents used to call into the grocer's shop and take their children in with them. As he served the parents with fruit or vegetables or both he would eye the children threateningly and growl under his breath at them. He was old and bitter. Rumour had it that he lived in a caravan and years ago some kids from another estate set fire to it. So Grumpy hated children. He also did home deliveries and Ned remembered hearing his mum on the phone placing an order with Grumpy. Obviously this was the order coming around the corner. Ned forgot the envelope for a second and put it away and then he rolled a snowball super-fast. Grumpy came into range and, to Ned's delight, he had his window open. The grocer drove up the incline to the estate, unaware that he was being targeted. Suddenly, an extra-large snowball exploded on the side of his head. Grumpy momentarily lost control of the van and headed for a cherry tree opposite Ned. He swung the wheel away from it and then, correcting the steering, managed to miss the tree at the last moment. Ned watched the moaning old grocer weave up the road unsteadily. A fist appeared from the open window of the van and shook feebly at Ned. He howled in laughter and then rubbed on his cold hands. The snow had chilled them as he had brought no gloves.

When the warmth and circulation had returned to his fingers, Ned brought out the envelope and neatly tore it in two. One side had his name and address on. The other was clear, so he scrawled eighteen silhouettes of snowmen on it with a cross going through each of them. As an afterthought, he added the silhouette of a van as well. This was his score. His kill marks, to proclaim what an ace he was. Ned smiled happily. He put the score board in his pocket and was going to throw away the piece with his details on when he heard a low growling. Initially, he thought it was Grumpy returning, but from the corner of his eye he saw a mass of angry men walking towards him. He realised quickly that these were the parents out for his blood and, like a fighter ace outnumbered and low on ammunition, he decided to flee. The crowd saw him and roared as they broke into a run after him. Ned shot across the road and, luckily for him, the snow had slowed the traffic to a crawl. He darted across the front of cars and over a fence that led to a park. In the distance he could see Stalingrad Towers, but with that mob on his back Ned knew he would never make it to the safety of Beetie's retreat. He scanned the other end of the park and saw the old chiller factory. With a quick glance back, he saw the mob at the road and he decided to head towards the factory. From the photos that Beetie had shown him, Ned thought that he could lose this maddened mob in the maze of broken buildings, if only he could reach it.

He ran into the trees and cursed loudly as he noticed his footprints in the snow. Even if he outran these vengeful parents they could still follow his tracks. Putting on a burst of speed, Ned hoped that, being younger, he would be fitter than his pursuers. He bolted from the trees and into open country. There was another howl of maddened excitement as Ned was spotted and the chase was on.

He was absolutely without cover and the snow was getting deeper as he ran into the middle of the park. From the trees the parents erupted. Ned turned his head as he ran and saw that they carried makeshift weapons. He saw garden hoes, shovels, large sticks, branches, and one ruthless individual carrying a double-headed axe. Ned's legs nearly buckled at the sight of this, but he kept running forwards. He was quicker, but the mob split into three groups when they reached the open park. Two headed to the left and right of Ned to outflank him while the third continued from behind. It was as if they were herding him towards the chiller factory. Ned didn't worry; he wanted to get there and lose himself in the maze of old buildings. But the muscles in his legs were beginning to burn, a stitch was growing in his side, and he was getting breathless. The deep snow was slowing him and making him tired, but it was falling much heavier now. He fell over and got a face full of ice cold snow. Behind, the parents saw their victim collapse and they scented blood. It was advantageous for Ned that he fell because the cold shock gave him a renewed energy and he leapt forwards as the mob hit the deeper snow. They slowed as Ned accelerated. Through the white flakes he saw the rusted fence ahead. Instead of looking like a prison's enclosure, Ned viewed it as sanctuary from above. Snow had drifted up against it, making a deep trap, but Ned could just make out an old wooden plank leaning up against one of the concrete posts. It too was covered with snow and maybe it was rotten. He did not know whether it would hold his weight but he did not have time to check, for the crowd following directly behind had waded through the deep drifts and were gaining on him again. They thought that their quarry might escape in the blizzard of snow and they wanted Ned's blood. To Ned's left and right the parents were approaching as well. The drifts of snow were not as deep as behind him so the two groups were converging on him quicker. He yelped and ran up the wobbly wooden board. It shook and quivered. It cracked and groaned and, as Ned reached the top, it snapped. But he launched himself like an Olympic diver over the fence and it seemed like he was actually flying through the air. The joy was brief as gravity caught up with him and with the grace of a sack of potatoes he fell into a snow-covered pile of rotting donkey dung. The thick outer shell of this putrid heap was hard enough to walk on but it collapsed under the impact of a human missile. Ned screamed and then disappeared into the depths of the decaying manure mound.

*

Three hours passed before, gasping for breath and spitting out old rancid bits of dung and hay, Ned's head appeared. It was like a newborn chick emerging from an egg. He had been knocked out by the impact and woke in pitch darkness. Terrified, Ned cried out, but, in doing so, got a mouth full of manure. Full of panic and disorientated, he scrabbled and fought against the gooey mess and burrowed in the direction he thought was upwards. Scraping away like a deranged mole, eventually, through muck-covered eyes, he could make out daylight. Grabbing and scooping pieces of dank smelly dung, he crawled towards the light coming out where he had so violently entered. Ned shook his head and small clods of manure fell off. He wiped his eyes, then cleared out his ears, and was just going to pull himself free when he heard voices. He shrank back into the mound as he remembered the maddened mob. Then he craned his neck and listened. Keeping his head still, he moved his eyes to look where the voices were coming from. As he was covered in dung, Ned's head showed out against the snow-covered mound. Only the whites of his eyes camouflaged well with the snow which was still falling heavily and was quickly starting to cover his head.

"Come on, let's go home. I'm starving, wet, and cold," one of the voices said.

"No. We've got to wait until that little bugger's found," another voice answered.

Ned's eyes locked on two men not three feet away from him. He tried to shrink further into the manure.

"It stinks round here. I'm going home, and you would if you've got any sense. The boy's long gone anyway. Come on, let's get some grub."

"It's alright for you," the other man complained. "You haven't got two daughters to console after seeing their snowman's head kicked off."

His companion took out his wallet and offered the other some money. "Look, take this and buy them something nice. Say it's from Uncle Ernie. Get them a plastic snowman that won't melt or lose its head."

The man looked at the factory, then to his friend. He seemed to be deciding whether to retreat to warmth and food or to stay hunting for the wayward snowman serial killer. His eyes took in the money and then he turned and they fell directly on Ned, who froze. He saw the man snatch the money and walk towards him.

This was it.

Ned had been found and was about to be captured and executed by the intense look of hatred on this man's face. He closed his eyes and waited for rough hands to grab hold of his head and start pulling. He tried to burrow backwards into the manure and succeeded a bit in wiggling into the smelly depths. It was warm inside and he curled up into a ball so as to make extraction as difficult as possible, then waited for hands.

Nothing happened.

He thought they had gone for some tools, maybe a spade or a pick to dig him out. In times of crisis, Ned liked to suck his thumb. It was a habit he had never broken since he was a baby. He stuck it in his mouth and then spat out a lump of dung. Then he heard something. It was like a muffled cry. It certainly was not the sound of tools digging away to get at him. Ned cocked his head to try to hear better from his donkey poo prison and he thought he could hear a struggle going on outside. Then a voice screamed but was cut off in mid-howl.

Ned was mystified but then he heard the sound of something sniffing at the entrance to his hide. He shrank back again.

From the compact cack, Ned could hear it. Sniff. Sniff. Then there was a pause, then a sniff again. One of Ned's eyes saw what looked like a carrot poking into the hole. He didn't move. What was it? He was terrified. The old stories of the haunted chiller factory suddenly came to him in the dark. He remembered one Halloween his grandfather had told him the tales of giant ghost-like monsters that lived there and on dark nights carried people off to their terrible fate. In the confines of the mound he could not see what was looking for or smelling him and guessed it was one of the monsters. He bit down on his thumb to stop himself from screaming. From above there was one long sniff and then an exhalation of breath and strangely, Ned got a whiff of vanilla ice cream. Then there was silence.

Ned didn't move a muscle for ten minutes. Eventually his legs and arms were screaming from the cramps, so he moved very carefully. He stayed in the new position for another ten minutes before shifting again and so on until very tentatively he put his head through the hole. There was no sign of the two men and there were no tracks. The snow was still falling but it had eased a little. Ned stayed in the hole for another fifteen minutes. He scanned every area and looked in the shadows of the buildings in case anything was waiting.

Very nervously, he lifted himself out of the manure. He scanned the area again. There was no movement. Maybe in his exhausted, dung-covered state he had imagined it. At the base of the mound he found a nice thick and straight branch. He shook off the snow and tested the weight. It felt good to have a weapon of some sort and it renewed his confidence. He decided to not head back to home just yet. Beetie had ordered Ned to start demolition of the chiller factory today, but he needed a bath, he needed a change of clothes, and he needed a weapon far more destructive than a branch. Ned also needed to avoid the estate where he lived until it was dark and he could slip back to his house without being seen by vengeful parents. So he decided to do a reconnaissance of the chiller factory. Anyway, he thought, Beetie would be proud of him doing a 'recon'. That's what good soldiers did, and he wanted to be the best for Beetie.

The snow hid the true dilapidation of the buildings. As Ned walked around the decaying complex, he saw that the photos did not do it justice. It was a dump only fit for demolition. The buildings were rusting or rotting or in a state of partial collapse. Ned passed a huge wall of corrugated roofing sheet. It seemed that someone had half-heartedly attempted to strip part of the building of its roof. The pile now had its own roof of thick snow and as Ned passed it, he saw the skeleton frame of one of the buildings that it had been stripped from. There was a collapsed chimney ahead of him with a sign on the base that was half covered with snow. He brushed it off to reveal writing telling people to beware of dangerous buildings. To wreck all these remaining buildings was going to be a big job. A very, very big job. He thought that maybe he had bitten off more than he could chew, so to speak, but then a light ignited in his mind.

Arson.

He would have to wait until the buildings had dried out a bit, but then he could set fire to them all. Yes, that was good. He would set fire to them and burn whatever monsters or fiends lived in the buildings. That would take away that feeling of terror he had suffered cowering in the poo mound. He'd have the beast running scared. Oh yes, he would.

And, walking around the corner, he nearly bumped into it.

Chapter 5

Ned screamed in shock and he dropped his weapon. He ran to hide behind the fallen chimney, then stopped and looked again. Ned looked over the bricks cautiously. The creature stared back at him and Ned furrowed his brow and then started to laugh.

"You old nag, you scared the piddle out of me." He moulded a snowball and threw it at the creature.

An old black and white donkey heehawed in protest and backed away from the assault. Ned leaned against the bricks and chuckled. The donkey must have chased the two men that were about to get him. It must have been sniffing the pile of manure that he was hiding in, and the carrot he saw must have been what the animal was sniffing for. Also, it explained the vast pile of cack. Though where the vanilla breath came from, Ned could not explain. Maybe the mule liked ice cream and it had originally been made at the factory and there was a tub or two left here. It was a stupid thought, but Ned was good at stupid thoughts. He felt like he had solved one of life's great mysteries and, with great bravado, he picked up the branch and swung it across his shoulders like a machine gun-toting mercenary. The donkey avoided him as he passed it. Ned was about to pelt it with another snowball when he noticed something more worthy of assault. It was the reason he had been hunted and ended up covered in donkey poo and smelling disgusting. It was the object of his hatred. The thing in front of him had to die.

Ned threw the snowball aside. This thing deserved a severe beating with his branch. Black expressionless eyes stared back at him.

It was a snowman. Not just any old snowman; this one was quite magnificent. It was not roughly moulded by gloved hands, or lopsided. It was made of pure white snow and was nearly seven feet tall. The black eyes were made of coal and the nose was a carrot. It had a tartan scarf on and a velvet bonnet and under its arm was a stick.

Ned swung the branch menacingly as he approached the snowman. He looked at it and saw that it was different to the others he had so recently obliterated. This one looked strangely alive.

Still, to Ned it was the target of all his recent shame and anger. He quickened his pace as he closed on it. The branch was taken in two hands now, and he swung it over his shoulders for maximum smash.

"I'll take your head off, you great lump!" he shouted as the branch sailed over his shoulder to decapitate the snowman. But instead of the sound of wood smashing against snow, there was a sharp crack of wood hitting wood. The snowman's stick had come up to meet Ned's branch head on. And holding onto the stick was a very angry snowman. Ned stood with his mouth agape as the snowman deftly turned his stick and cracked Ned hard across the knuckles.

"Ouch!" Ned cried out and dropped the branch and before he could do anything else, the snowman grabbed him.

"Come here, you horrible little swine."

Ned could not believe his eyes or ears. The snowman had spoken. It had also hit him and his hand was starting to swell. His mind could not take this in, but his body could. He tried to run. But the snowman pulled him closer and then got him in a headlock.

"Phooh, you stink! We have ways of dealing with you horrible little fleshy things." And it started to drag Ned towards one of the buildings.

"Help! Help! Help me!" Ned cried out. He heard his own voice reverberate across the old buildings. The only reply he got was a smack across the back of the head by this irate snowman. "Shut up, you little swine."

From his locked head, Ned's eyes registered where he was being dragged to. Terror filled him as he saw the old battered door and more terror overflowed in him as he thought about what it was that lay behind the door.

Ned tried one more cry for help, though this one was to his great mentor. "B-e-e-e-e-e-tie pl-e-e-e-a-se—"

But this plea was cut off as the snowman's huge arm muscles constricted his throat. Ned struggled and kicked the snowman but he was far too strong for a young boy. The door was getting nearer. Ned tried to plead but he was held fast and could not get a word out of his throat. He kicked and kicked and, in doing so, managed to crawl up the snowman's back and at the end of it he was still in the snowman's hold but completely inverted and staring straight at the chiller door. Though it was upside down, it still held utter horror for him and he struggled even more violently against his tormenter. Ned's donkey manure-covered head proved more slippery than his captor could manage and, with a pop, he shot out of the headlock and backwards. Flying through the air, Ned landed in a roll and before he stopped he was on his feet and running for the fence. Shoes slipping and sliding through the snow, Ned gathered speed and shot past the broken chimney. But snowmen are made of the same icy substance that Ned was trying to outdistance his hunter on. As the fence came into view, Ned urged his legs faster. Behind, the snowman was rapidly gaining, and when it saw the fence it launched itself in a rugby tackle at Ned's feet. Both snowman and boy crashed in a pile of snow, only to stop inches from the wire boundary.

Ned cried out in anger and frustration and the snowman grabbed his feet and started back to the chiller factory door. Face down and head in the snow, Ned's nostrils and mouth started to fill up as a small mountain of snow built up around his head. He coughed and shook the white suffocating flakes away. He could not see the door but knew it was approaching rapidly. Once more he cried out, but the sound just echoed off the old buildings once again. The snowman was out of breath and stopped. He went to readjust his hold on Ned, who felt the grasp loosen and tried to make a bolt for it.

A thick, heavy snow foot stamped down on Ned's back. The snowman had had enough. "Oh no you don't!" He put more pressure on Ned's back and then bent down to mutter in his ear, "You're coming to meet the master, you foul thing. He knows what to do with the likes of you, oh yes he does." Then the snowman laughed a horrible high-pitched giggle. The snow around Ned's trousers turned a yellow hue and he was dragged off again. Not a minute passed and they were outside the door. It was battered and dented and someone had made a very, very bad job of repainting it. The finish was as if a huge gloved hand had just smeared paint on in an ever-widening circle. The fresh marks in the snow where the door had been opened recently revealed a mess of paint on the concrete.

Again, Ned was stamped on and the snowman banged loudly on the door. "Open up. It is me, Heinrich."

There was a muffled sound of voices and then a short, sharp giggle. "Open it yourself," a sniggering voice retorted.

Heinrich snowman's hand went for the handle but he quickly pulled it back and looked most annoyed. "You know I can't!" he shouted at the door.

There was more sniggering from inside. "What, a big snowman like you can't open a door? Why is that, Heinrich?"

Heinrich's body slammed the door and then shouted, "Because I have no fingers; none of us have got any fingers. Now, open the damn door!" Ned had turned his head and was listening intently to the strange exchange of words. The door remained silent. Nothing moved and the door did not open.

Heinrich had a mystified expression on his round white face. And although snowmen do not possess eyebrows, Ned could tell Heinrich's brow was furrowed in thought. He stayed like this for a while and Ned tested the weight of Heinrich's foot on his back. It was still too heavy to break out from. The snowman cupped his chin in one hand and tapped his cheek as he thought.

"Excuse me?" Ned interrupted. "Could you let me go, please?" Startled, Heinrich actually did let go of Ned and, with a look of triumph, he hammered on the door again.

"I've got a fleshy swine with me!" he shouted out.

The response from behind the door was instantaneous. "You're a liar!"

"It's true," Heinrich pleaded.

"Prove it."

"What?"

"Prove it, you fat fool!" voices behind the door demanded.

"How?" Heinrich said. The mystified look had started to grow on his face again.

"Heinrich, you're as thick as the snow that fell this morning. If you've got a fleshy one then squeeze it hard so that we can hear it!"

"Oh, right you are." He pulled Ned up and hit him across the head.

"Oooooouch!"

Frantic voices chattered from inside the building. A bolt was drawn back and the door swung inwards. Heinrich pushed Ned in.

It was dark inside. A small naked light bulb seemed to hang from nowhere in the blackness. Ned tried to adjust his vision. Outside it had been glaring white everywhere but inside here the darkness made him feel sick. Squinting his eyes, Ned could slowly make out six white, black-eyed faces staring at him. They murmured together, then crept towards him. He backed up and stood on Heinrich's feet, who let out a cry of pain, and the shadowy faces retreated again. Heinrich pushed Ned into the group and in the darkened area they started to prod him with their mitten hands. They uttered words like 'eeeyuck' and 'horrible'.

Ned's mind still could not believe this was real. He started to shake and brought his thumb from his pocket.

"This little swine was going to take my head off with a branch," Heinrich explained to his revolted kin.

They started to laugh at that.

"It wouldn't make much difference if you didn't have a head, Heinrich," one of the snowmen said. The others all agreed and the laughter got louder.

Then, from out of the shadows, a voice shrieked, "Silence!"

The snowmen stopped giggling and shot to attention. From somewhere in the darkness there was the sound of a maimed leg pulled along the floor and then a lower, deeper sound of a stick hitting the floor. Scrape, donk, scrape, donk, scrape, donk, it went. Ned's eyes had got used to the bad light and he looked at the fear etched on the snowmen's faces. He felt it too, and even though his mind was telling him "This cannot be real", he started to turn his head in the direction of the sound. The snowmen were holding each other's hands. Ned took hold of Heinrich's and he didn't protest. The sound grew louder and Ned could feel Heinrich begin to shake. Ned was terrified yet mesmerized as, through the darkness, a huge, menacing snowman appeared. Ned, who had little respect for authority, realised this could only be the chief snowman.

Dragging its left leg and rearing up to full height, the snowman stood in the half-light. It leaned on a gnarled walking stick and stared at the other snowmen. They looked straight ahead, not daring to meet the cold eyes. They were as black as the room's darkened corners and the only life in them was the faint glow of red that burned with a sinister intensity. Its carrot nose was bent and slightly withered and the mouth had a snarling look of perpetual wickedness.

Heinrich shook off Ned's hand and bounded forward to salute. "Lord Marshall Melton, sir, I caught this vile creature outside our fortress. The swine was throwing snowballs at your beloved steed. Also, he was going to take my head off with a tree branch." The last sentence was said in a very accusing tone.

The coal eyes of Marshall Melton narrowed and he brought his stick up level with Ned's face.

"You vile, fleshy fiend, how dare you assault my stallion? You will pay for your crimes. That I guarantee!" The voice was high-pitched and full of fury. The other snowmen nodded eagerly in agreement. Ned was going to pay for assaulting their master's war horse and for trying to decapitate a snowman. Melton poked Ned in his chest and leant down. "But we will not make you pay with your life today."

The snowmen started to tut and moan. Melton rounded on them and nearly fell off balance in the process. Heinrich went to his aid but was shouted away. "Get off me! And the rest of you, be quiet!"

He pointed his stick at them and they all dropped their eyes from his gaze. Melton gave a short evil laugh, then spoke. "Do not be disappointed, my minions. This despicable little twerp will indeed pay for trying to behead that idiot." Melton swiped the stick at Heinrich, who backed away before it hit him. "But he will perform a service to us first; something that I have been planning for a long time." The other snowmen now all seemed to have a look of bemused happiness on their faces. Melton looked at them, then tutted loudly. He brought his stick up again and pointed at them, then slowly, and with deliberate aloofness, he let it rest in front of Heinrich's nose. "You lot can join the ranks of that idiot. You really are not expected to understand how a complex and devious mind works, so don't try to. You just do as Uncle Melton says. Okay?" He produced a horribly patronizing smile that hung on his white face for what seemed like a lifetime. Ned did not understand a thing. His eyes darted to the door. It was bolted and Heinrich was in the way. The silence continued, only broken by the sound of dripping water. Ned started to creep towards the door. He looked at Heinrich, but he was staring ahead. It seemed that he was in some kind of trance. Ned edged around him. Then the silence was shattered by Melton's scream. "Get that slug and empty his pockets!" Snowmen jumped in the air and ran into each other in confusion. Melton was barged into and took to hitting them with his stick in retaliation. They ran about the room howling and ended up bowling each other over like nine pins. Only Heinrich remained upright, and he grabbed Ned. Melton limped over to him and patted the snowman on the head. "There's a good boy. Well done." He then turned to the pile of snowmen and selected one. "You there, empty his pockets."

The snowman extracted himself from the pile and walked towards Ned. As he did, he turned to Melton, then started to say something but decided to stop. He stood in front of Ned and hesitated. Ned saw the look of nervous confusion on his face. His eyes were darting everywhere and Ned swore he could see beads of sweat appear on his forehead. He looked quite kindly in a strange way, but the look of dread fear grew over the benevolent façade. This simple task was taking too long for Melton.

"What on earth are you doing? Empty his pockets!"

The snowman gulped and, with shaking hands, turned back to his master. He held out his hands as in explanation.

"WHAT?" Melton was apoplectic.

A tiny voice came out of the snowman. "Errr, I…I…can't empty his pockets, sir, master…errr, your lordship."

"WHY?" Melton screamed back.

"I got no fingers, sir," was the brief explanation.

"IDIOT!" Melton shrieked. The sound shook the room until it faded to silence. Melton closed his eyes and breathed deeply and slowly. Eventually he calmed himself down. He started to drum his stick in the palm of his left hand, then spoke smoothly to Ned. "You, boy, will empty your pockets and give the contents to the cretin in front of you. Is that clear?"

Outnumbered, imprisoned, and dreadfully confused, Ned nodded and handed over what was in his pockets. But he managed to slide his mobile phone into his pants through a hole in his pocket. It was very uncomfortable, but he dare not let it fall into enemy hands.

Melton's horrible smile returned. "Thank you for that. You!" He eyed the snowman who had the contents of Ned's pockets. Ned thought he was going to order the snowman to search Ned but instead he barked an order. "Take the little slug's items to my office now." Off he went, and Melton looked at Heinrich. "Bring that foul child downstairs to our..." He paused and cocked his head to one side. "...To our gallery." And he tucked his stick under his arm in military fashion and limped out of the room.

Heinrich pushed Ned forwards. His legs were like jelly but he managed stay upright and walk in the direction that Melton was taking.

"Enjoy what's in our gallery," the other snowmen sniggered.

"W-w-what's the gallery?" Ned asked.

Melton had reached the top of a rusty spiral staircase. "You will see soon enough how we deal with vile, interfering, fleshy swine like you." Water was dripping down into the darkness below and Melton took hold of the handrail and started to walk down the stairs. They creaked and groaned in protest and as Ned was pushed onto the stairs, he felt the old corroded steps give slightly as he walked down.

Heinrich managed to trip over something and he fell into the topmost railings. The whole thing shook wildly. Ned grabbed at something. It felt cold and clammy.

"Get off my nose, you foul little beast!" Melton brought up his stick and tried to hit Ned but he struck Heinrich in-between the legs instead. The snowman cried out and, doubled over in agony, went straight over the side of the stairs. Ned heard his cry continue until it was cut off sharply as Heinrich hit the floor below with a wet thud.

Melton retrieved his stick. "What a dolt. Do you know first aid, boy? I think that cretin may need some medical attention. Come on." He limped downstairs and Ned, for some strange reason, followed. Maybe it was a kind of cruel fascination in him that he had to see what one of these snowmen looked like splattered.

They arrived at the bottom of the stairs to splash in cold water. A dirty fluorescent light hung off the ceiling and emitted a flickering blue glow on the wet floor. Melton looked around and eventually found the prone body of Heinrich. He limped over and the strobe light gave his action a slow-motion effect, like someone's relative dancing very badly at a family party. Ned leant on the bottom rail and saw Melton's jittery movements take him towards Heinrich. When he reached the unconscious heap, the chief snowman leant on his stick and bent down. Ned could see Melton talking into Heinrich's ear—wherever it was—but he got no response, so with his good leg, Melton kicked him.

"Get up!"

There was still no response. So Melton kicked him again. It had no effect. Heinrich was out for the count.

Melton prodded Heinrich a few times but got no result, so gave up.

"Oh, come on, boy. We'll have to leave this lump of a snowman. I suppose as usual I'll have to do everything around here myself." He beckoned Ned with his hand. "And don't think of trying to escape this place because it's a maze and I've got an army of loyal snowmen guarding every exit."

Ned did not doubt that, but he still eyed the top of the stairs in hope, but saw the other snowmen staring down at him. They had heard the commotion and, risking Melton's rage at leaving their post, had come over to see what was going on.

"Come on," Melton called like a master to his pet. Ned sighed and stepped down into the shallow water. He splashed near to Heinrich and, seeing Melton not looking, he stepped on the snowman's carrot nose. There was a moan and then Heinrich shook his head and suddenly got up, dripping cold water. He was very unsteady on his feet and, rubbing his nose, tried a few tentative steps. He staggered and grabbed Ned for support. The weight of him was incredible. Ned could feel the great strength in the snowman's grip and cried out.

Melton turned around. "Ah, the idiot returns." He hit the floor with his stick, soaking Heinrich, who waddled unsteadily towards his master. They waited for Ned, who splashed up and followed them into a tunnel lit as badly as the previous room, though in this one the light was not flickering on and off but reflected off the water-covered floor. In fact, the whole of the lower level of the chiller factory was under near ankle-deep water. Ned's trainers were soaked through but the water did not seem to bother the snowmen.

There certainly was a light at the end of the tunnel but not one with a sign of hope for Ned. This grim light showed another short corridor, whose end was a huge steel door. Like the exterior of the building it was rusty and aged, and at its side, a dull red light glowed above a recessed button.

Melton smiled callously and put his stick down. Ned was looking at the door. Fear was growing in him at what could lay behind it.

"Now, vile fiend, behold the snowman's gallery!" Melton pressed the button.

Nothing happened.

He pressed the button again.

Nothing.

Melton punched it.

Still nothing.

He punched it again and winced in pain. "Oooouch! Damn, damn, damn these hands."

He hit it again with his other hand and then quickly whipped it behind his back and massaged the throbbing hand out of view from Ned and Heinrich. There was a pause while he tried to suppress the pain and regain a little dignity. His eyes fell on Heinrich. "You there, idiot, open the door."

Heinrich waded through the shallows to the side of the door. Melton and Ned looked questioningly at each other as Heinrich bent down and picked up Melton's stick. He walked to the door and jabbed the end of it into the recessed hole. The red light turned to green and, with a groan of protestation, the door opened inwards.

A look of fury appeared on Melton's face. Then, it quickly vanished as he remembered that he was not supposed to show that he could be upstaged by a lesser snowman. He leaned on the door frame and started to nod. "Ah yes...the err...the stick. I wondered when you were going to use the stick. It's obvious, really. I just wanted to see if my intellect and guile had rubbed off on you, Heinrich."

Heinrich did not reply. He offered the stick back to Melton and pushed Ned through the door. Melton swiped the stick at Heinrich as he passed but he ducked quickly and then Melton tried to kick him but in doing so nearly lost his footing and had to grab the door frame for support. He saw Ned nearing the first in a line of glass-fronted tanks. "Now...whoops." He slipped down again but managed to pull himself up and hold an arm out in a theatrical pose. "Now...you...you...now behold...the...the gallery of fools."

Ned had stopped in front of the nearest tank and was staring in horror at what was inside.

"Yes," Melton said. "Meddling fools like yourself who stick their noses into the business of snowmen."

Through mildew-covered glass, a face stared back at Ned. It was frozen in ice and had the same look of terror that Ned had on his face. It was not unlike a mirror image, except this was a man, or a postman to be exact, dressed in his uniform and still clutching an electricity bill. Mesmerized by the contents of the tank, Ned noticed there were others lined down the room. He moved down the line. In the next tank was a bird-watcher dressed in tweeds and frozen in an attitude of stark terror. Opposite there were two roofing contractors wearing overalls, high visibility vests, and hard hats. Ned's head turned from left to right as he walked along. Various poor unfortunates were frozen in different poses; one even had a complete family picnic outing in it. The father was iced up eating a cucumber sandwich, the children iced up playing with a ball.

Ned turned away and shook his head in disbelief. "I've read about these in the papers. That family, the twitcher, and the roofers, they said they must have been abducted by aliens." He seemed to recall something else. "Come to think of it, there were reports of large white aliens seen in the area."

"You now see the fate that awaits those who meddle in snowmen matters," Melton said. "Fools, all of them. There are twenty tanks down here. Eighteen tanks are occupied by your frozen foul fleshies." And then he added with glee, "Just two more need to be filled to make a full house."

Ned's befuddled mind caught up with him. "Hang on. That must have been you lot!" He shook his head again. "No, no, snowmen can't walk or talk or attack people. It's impossible. It can't be!" He continued to try and rationalize with himself. "Snowmen can't do that. They melt. They get smashed up by children. This can't be. It just can't be. I must be dreaming. It's all the hard toil that I've been doing for Beetie. Somebody pinch me, please."

Melton smiled at this. He nodded to Heinrich. "Do as he asks."

Heinrich shifted uncomfortably and moved back out of range from the stick's radius of attack.

"Do it!" Melton erupted.

Heinrich held up his hands and mouthed, "No hands."

"Then hit him!" Melton screamed.

The backhander Heinrich gave Ned snapped him out of his daze. "Oooouuuch."

Ned reacted by kicking Heinrich in the shin. Heinrich then shouted out in pain and went for Ned, but the snowman that had earlier emptied Ned's pockets came running through the door and ploughed into him. Heinrich rocketed backwards and bounded off the thick plates of glass as the other one fell to his knees in a splash, then lay flat out in front of Melton.

"Forgive me for interrupting you, my lord," the snowman spluttered, with his face in the water. Heinrich raised himself up and hobbled over to Melton, who totally ignored the injured snowman. He looked down at his feet.

"Well. What is it? Didn't I order you to take the contents of his pockets to my office? Why have you disobeyed me?"

Chapter 6

The snowman lowered his face further in the water and spluttered something that neither Melton, Heinrich, or Ned could understand.
"Lift your head out of the water, you simpleton," Melton ordered.
The dripping head was lifted clear and the snowman coughed and fought to regain his breath. In the palm of an outstretched hand, he offered Melton a soggy piece of paper. "It...it...it...it is just this, dear master."
Melton took the sodden paper and looked at it in a mixture of disgust and mystery. He scrutinized it for a long time. Then his brow creased and his face went from white to pink and then to a violent scarlet colour. Sizzling came from behind his eyes and he exploded in rage. "You...you horror, you killer, you foul devastator of delightful snowmen!" He could not find enough words to express his anger and rage, so he started hitting the floor with his stick and splashing water everywhere. Heinrich backed away but had no idea why his master was so hopping mad. He was very dense and did not think that he had done anything in the last minute to upset his master so. But Ned knew why Melton was so enraged. The piece of paper was Ned's score board. It had all his kill marks on; black outlines of snowmen with crosses scribbled through them. They marked all the snowmen he had smashed up.
"Eighteen snowmen, eh, boy? Eighteen beloved snowmen, all dead." The black eyes glowed red. "Oh, you're going to pay for this," Melton advanced on Ned.
He backed away from the raving snowman and trod on the prone one. A leg jerked upwards and kicked Ned forwards into Melton's path, who had his stick ready to strike. Steam issued from Melton's ears and the stick started to descend.
"My lord, excuse me, my lord," the snowman lying in the water spoke. "Marshall Melton, sir?"
"WHAT?" Melton turned from Ned. He could hardly control his rage.

"Look, sir. We found this as well." The soaking snowman offered another piece of paper.

Melton was halfway through a step when he stopped and bent down to read the piece of paper that was still in the snowman's shaking hand. His head went up and down as he tried to focus on the soggy print. He grabbed at the shaking hand. "Hold still, damn it." The red eyes eased back to a natural black colour. He blinked a few times and the steam lessened from his ears. The look of intense anger slowly gave way to a smirk, and then Melton spoke suddenly. "Ned Mutton."

"Yes," Ned replied without thinking and quickly slapped his hand over his mouth. He had not expected Melton to know his name. How could he? Ned gulped as he realised what he had admitted; now they knew his name.

Melton snickered. "An added bonus, I think." Then he looked around as if searching for something. His eyes found the snowman still lying prostrate in the shallow water.

"What are you doing lying on the floor? Get up, you nincompoop!"

With a splash, the snowman obeyed. Melton bent his head and whispered something in his ear. There was a mystified look from the snowman so Melton smacked him around the head, then whispered again. This time, the snowman nodded his head in understanding and then ran off.

Melton rubbed his hands together and chuckled evilly. He turned to Ned. "Now, follow me to the nerve centre of my great empire."

The rusting green slime and mildew-encrusted room seemed hardly like part of a great empire, but Ned stumbled forwards as Heinrich pushed him from behind yet again. Ned's temper started to break through and he turned back to Heinrich. "If you do that once more, I'll get Beetie to kick your arse really hard."

Heinrich stuck his tongue out to Ned.

"What is a Beetie?" Melton's voice echoed back through the room.

Ned was still very scared but the pride of working and knowing a war hero beat the fear of these snowmen down momentarily. He stood where he was and, trying to stop his knees from wobbling, confronted Melton. "He's a war hero who'll come to rescue me and make you snowmen into a pile of slush!"

Melton looked slightly perplexed but then shrugged it off as if it was nothing. "Oh well, if you say so, you little twerp." And he limped to the end of the room.

Ned could not think of a decent enough retort so he quickly moved forward before Heinrich pushed him again. At the end of the room they went through an open door and there was a lift. Melton reached out to the button to engage the lifts descent but then thought the better of it and started to walk towards another eroded spiral staircase. Ned didn't like the look of the staircase at all so he pressed the lift button. To his surprise, a clattering and whirling sound started above and grew louder as the lift started to descend. Melton considered the ascent by rickety old steel, then turned and stood next to Ned and waited for the lift. They both looked around the room's dark interior awkwardly. Ned drummed his fingers on his thighs while Melton whistled an inane tune. Behind them, Heinrich twitched nervously.

A ding announced the arrival of the lift. Heinrich barged through and pulled the old cantilever steel door open. Melton shoved Ned aside and walked into the lift. Heinrich followed and Ned suddenly yanked the door shut with a crash and ran for the stairs.

He did not look back but could hear Melton cursing the lift door and then Heinrich. Ned just ran up the old stairs, heedless of their unsafe appearance and groaning sound. He caught sight of Melton's walking stick trying to lever the door open. To Ned's fortune, it had jammed when he had slammed it.

At the top of the stairs there was very little light and Ned stopped briefly to decide which direction to take. He could make out what looked like an old foreman's office and then, to the opposite, he saw a corridor. Above, roof lights partly covered in ivy showed what Ned hoped was a way out of this terrible place. Melton had warned him of the presence of snowmen guarding every exit but none pounced on him. He started for the corridor just as he heard the sound of splintering wood from below. Any minute now, Melton would be free from the lift. Ned could hear the deranged old snowman screaming for his snowy minions to come and get him.

And out of the office came the snowman that had been ordered to search Ned. He stood there and stared at Ned, who momentarily froze. He would be on him in an instant and, judging by the strength of Heinrich, Ned knew he would not be able to escape easily. The snowman took a step forward. Ned backed off and then, to his utter astonishment, the snowman nodded curtly and then ran in the opposite direction.

"Wait!" Ned cried out. But the snowman disappeared into the darkness. Ned did not follow. It might be some trap arranged by the unhinged minds of snowmen. But then, why did it not grab him and hand him over to Melton, Ned thought.

There was no time to ponder it anymore as the staircase started to shake, announcing that Melton and Heinrich had escaped from the lift and were now in hot pursuit. Ned took off down the corridor. He did not know where he was going but anywhere was better than next to Melton. The corridor gave way to an open balcony. Below, Ned could see a large shop floor area filled with chairs and tables. Standing around these were a lot of snowmen. They shouted out when they saw Ned and, throwing chairs everywhere, started after him. Ned shot across the balcony and straight through an open door into rooms filled with decrepit-looking machines. The stitch was coming back now and he ran behind one of the machines to pause and get his breath back. Behind, the voices grew. Above them all, Ned could make out Melton's enraged cry. He poked his head around the machine and, to his horror, saw snowmen coming down the direction he was about to take. To the back of him, Melton's voice was getting louder. It seemed as though Ned was about to be trapped in the room. The old pieces of machinery were dented, rusty and leaking oil, but they offered some form of cover. He darted between another two and tried to make a winding route to find another exit but saw glimpses of white coming through the door. Ned flattened himself against the oily metal panel of one machine. He turned his head quickly and swore as his nose banged against a steel ladder. Ned suppressed a cry of pain, rubbed his nose, and eyed the ladder. It led up to the top of the machine and above that he saw metal ceiling tiles. Some were damaged and hung down lazily; others were intact and looked solid, so Ned crept up the ladder. He crawled along the top of the machine trying to keep low and out of sight. It was slick with old oil but it helped Ned slide along without a sound. The ceiling tiles were not far above his head and one of the hanging ones offered what looked like an escape from the room. There looked as though there was enough room to manoeuvre himself between the tiles and the grey concrete ceiling and hopefully out of the snowman-infested room. As it was, it seemed the only option. He needed to lift himself up and see if the suspended ceiling would take his weight but then close by he heard Melton's voice, so Ned slithered along the oily machine top and risked a look over the edge. He could just make out the back of Melton's head. The wicked old brute was out of breath and wheezing.

"Right…who…..saw…the….foul…little…beast…come….in this…room?"

"I think I, err…I mean, I think someone saw him come in here, my lord," a nervous voice said.

"Well, did you or didn't you?" Melton's terrible voice harangued the snowman.

"I, err…it was him that thought he saw the fleshy swine," the accused snowman announced, accusing another of his kin.

"No I didn't, you bloody liar!" the second accused snowman shouted. An argument broke out and then fists started to fly. A major punch up started between the snowmen. Ned felt the machine shake with impact as snowmen bounced off it or were thrown into it. As it shook, Ned saw an old oil can vibrate its way across his vision. He reached out and grabbed it. Even in this near-fatal situation with snowmen below fighting and Melton so near, Ned's sense of mischievousness could not be resisted or suppressed. He pumped the plunger with his thumb and felt the satisfying pressure of oil squirt out the end of the nozzle. It shot over the edge of the machine.

"What the…urgh. What's this mess?" Melton's voice sounded disgusted. "Stop fighting, you plebeians. You've broken the machines and I am covered in sticky black oil."

Ned bit his teeth, trying not to giggle. He risked leaning over a little more to see Melton's head splattered with oil and saw Heinrich wiping Melton's head with his hands. All he was doing was turning his master's head an oily black colour. In return, Melton smacked Heinrich. He wiped oil from his eyes and turned on the snowmen.

"Which one of you saw that brat come in here?"

The scrap stopped in mid-brawl. Fists were poised over heads. Feet were ready to kick. It seemed everyone was balanced precariously in mid-swing, ready for the starter's orders again. One snowman's head was nodding back and forward where he had been punched repeatedly, his opponent holding a mitten hand full of chest, with his other hand readying for further strikes with a crunched up mittened fist. The punch-drunk snowman's eyes rolled around in their sockets and, with his head rocking like a heavy metal fan, he lifted his hand and pointed towards the top of a machine. Like an inebriated cow, the snowman shouted, "'Eeesh 'ere."

Ned saw all the snowmen snap their heads in his direction. In his eagerness to see his tormentor covered in oil, he had reached out too far and been spotted. Quick as a snake, he pushed backwards across the top of the machine and the oily surface propelled him rearward with the speed of a rocket. He cleared the tops of three more machines before crashing through an office window and falling backwards into a torn and scabby leather chair.

Melton's voice broke through Ned's concussion. "There he goes. Get him!"

Ned spun around in the chair and the oil coating on him threw him off at the same speed he had just been lifted off the machines. He rocketed into the snowmen that were coming for him. They tried to grab him. They tried to tackle him down. They tried to jump on him. But Ned's slippery clothes were making it impossible for them to pin him down. He rolled and slid across the floor and the pursuing snowmen tried to turn and follow but they careered into each other on the slick oil trail that Ned left.

Leaving them in a pile, Ned slid along the floor and bounced off the machine he had just vacated. He fell on his front but continued to slide, and his eyes caught sight of Melton leaning on his stick and raising his one good leg, ready to stamp on Ned as he passed under him. Ned hit the oil slick he had squirted from the can and his speed increased. Melton misjudged his timing and still had his leg raised as Ned shot between. The maimed leg started to fall, but Ned—

practiced in goolie kicking—brought his leg up backwards and landed a kick right in-between Melton's legs. The old snowman screamed in such a high-pitched voice that the sound shattered the dials on the machines.

Sliding at a rapid speed now, Ned hit the balcony and careered over the edge. There was a dull flopping sound as he miraculously landed on a strategically placed games cushion. The impact blew the thing apart but cushioned Ned's fall. Feathers and dust flew everywhere and these stuck to Ned's oil-covered body making him look, from a distance, like a strange white feathered bird.

Overhead, the snowmen and Melton's recovery was slow. The heaped snowmen managed to extract themselves from their own pile and came immediately to the aid of Melton, who lay against a machine and whimpered as Heinrich wiped the tears from his eyes. As the snowmen came towards their master, they stood on the broken dial glass that covered the floor and started to scream and cry and jump about in agony.

Ned stole a quick glance up at the mayhem and ran off. Some of the snowmen saw him but were in too much pain to pursue. He scarpered through the room and off into the darkened corridor ahead. Again, he had no idea where he was going but he wanted to be away from the concentration of snowmen and hoped they were all in the room he had just left. The noise of snowmen receded the further he went, which was good, but the light was getting worse and Ned feared that he was heading deeper into the factory and not towards the exit, wherever that lay.

There was a column of light shining down at an angle ahead and Ned slowed as he approached it. It cast a dirty grey glow on the floor in front of him. He stepped forwards carefully and as he passed into the light a door to his right started to shake violently. Ned nearly jumped out of his skin. He shot a glance at the door and saw eyes staring at him through rusted bars. They were bloodshot and wide with madness. Ned tried to tear his gaze away but he couldn't. The eyes seemed to penetrate him and look into his soul. He was about to plead with this new terror to stop staring at him and explain that he was only an innocent young boy lost in a world of horror when a hand from the cell door opposite grabbed him. He screamed and nearly wet his pants for the umpteenth time.

"Don't touch it! Look at it. It's some kind of monstrous chicken freak that the snowmen have created," the red-eyed man shouted.

"Sssssh, you idiot, you'll bring down the bloody snowmen on us!" the man who had hold of Ned said.

"But it's a mutation!" the other insisted.

"No it's not, you dummy. It's a boy under all that dust and feathers," his friend tried to reassure him.

A face came close to the bars and Ned thought he recognised it from somewhere. He was still scared and pulled back against the hand that had hold of his collar. The grip intensified but the voice was pleading as it spoke this time. "Please! Help us."

Ned was still confused. He calmed down slightly and started to brush off the dust and feathers, then asked, "Who are you?"

"We're the two blokes who chased you into the factory grounds," the other person said from behind the first door. "It's your fault we're in here. Those snowmen are horrible bullies. I haven't felt like this since I was at school. They kept prodding and pinching us. And that leader is a right horror." He started to sob.

"He's been like that since we were captured this afternoon, been sobbing all the time. That's why his eyes are all bloodshot," the other prisoner explained. So he wasn't mad, Ned thought, he was just terrified.

A strange sense of comfort came over Ned. Though he was being chased by deranged snowmen and had little time for reassurance, he didn't feel alone anymore. These imprisoned men were captives like himself and once freed could even up the odds a little. He did not know how many snowmen there were hiding and living in the chiller factory. Above the shop floor and looking down on them all he had guessed there were roughly about twenty but there were bound to be more lurking in the dark recesses of the building. You could count on Melton posting sentries outside as well. Still, three against a load was better than one against a load.

Ned looked at the steel doors. A huge metal catch that was opened by a central wheel held the doors firmly shut. He gripped the wheel and started to turn it anti-clockwise, then stopped.

76

"Hurry up, boy! There's no time to lose," the man inside pleaded.

"If I let you out, you'll forget the incident this morning, won't you?" Ned asked.

Both men responded quickly, "Yes, yes. Of course we will! Now hurry up before that big lame snowman comes."

Ned turned the wheel again and before the catch had lifted fully, the man inside kicked his door open. He looked up and down the corridor, then pushed Ned aside and started to turn the wheel again to open the door with his friend in. Ned cocked his ear down the corridor. He could hear something. It was a sound like thin metal being flexed mixed with a squealing sound. Ned looked left and right then but could not get a bearing on where the sound was coming from. The man had undone the wheel and was pulling on the door to release his friend when Ned sensed the sound was coming from above. He knew what it was before he started to look up. Next to the roof light was a vertical duct and sliding down this headfirst was a snowman.

Ned backed off as the snowman fell out of the duct and landed on the floor between the men and Ned. It rolled over in a ball and quickly stood up, ready to grab Ned.

"Move!" one of the men shouted, and Ned jumped aside. The man raised his leg and kicked the snowman into the cell. It hit the wall with a splat, turned, and walked unsteadily towards the door. As the snowman's head came level with the doorframe, Ned slammed the door shut with all his might. The bars on the door actually gouged into the snowy flesh. The snowman's face was indented and it looked like a griddle pan. Its eyes looked like burnt tomatoes and the nose an orange-brown sausage sizzling on this weird cooking implement. Insensible with concussion, it smiled inanely and its teeth started to fall out. Then it collapsed against the wall.

"I think you killed it," the newly released man commented as he came over to stare down at the heap.

"Good. The swine deserved it!" his friend commented angrily. He looked at Ned with a mixture of fear and respect. "You sure make short work of snowmen, boy. You're a right killer, you are."

Ned looked down at the snowman. He leant down to listen for a heartbeat but the men pulled him back. "Come on! We've got to get out of here now!"

And so Ned ran off again with the men. They ran through the lower levels for what seemed like ages. They went left and right at junctions. They tried to find stairs that led upwards and kept their ears open for sounds of pursuit but thankfully they heard nothing apart from their own steps echoing around the dark depths of the factory.

All were getting desperate now, and as they approached another junction, Ned saw a faint glimmer of red light. They had been past this intersection before but no one had noticed the dull colour in the distance. Ned skidded to a halt and headed down towards it. The men followed behind him.

The passage he was running along was unfamiliar but as he went farther the light grew brighter and he knew he had seen it before. Not far from this was a stairway that they could climb and beyond that was a door to the outside world.

Ned stopped at the red light. He was panting and drawing deep breaths as the others came up to him.

"What's this place?" one asked.

Ned looked at them both and pointed to the door next to the light. "Behind that door is a gallery of terrors. The snowmen have frozen their victims in glass cubicles."

The two men grabbed each other and shook with fear.

"Why on earth have you led us here?" the snowman kicker asked. The other man continued to shake.

Ned faced them and thought of how Beetie would behave in this near-death situation. They were all on edge; their nerves were shredded. These men had endured untold horrors and the slightest thing could push them over the edge. Team leadership and a strong hand was the recipe needed and Ned Mutton was the chef to deliver this stalwart dish.

"Because I was brought here earlier and just down there is a staircase that will lead us to the ground floor and our freedom."

The two men stopped shaking and looked at Ned with newfound respect and admiration. They smiled and patted each other's backs in reassurance.

"You lead us out of here. Our nerves are shot and you're—"

The chiller room door opened inwards. From inside, Melton's voice boomed out and finished the sentence: "A foul little turd who is going to pay!"

The snowmen jumped out of the door and grabbed the two men. The men fought as they were pulled backwards into the room. One screamed as he disappeared into the white scrum but the other kicked at the snowmen and had hold of the doorframe. He was managing to aim some excellent boots at his attackers. Coal eyes were popping out of sockets and carrot noses were snapping under the man's steel toe-capped assault. Melton kept out of range from the blows but was haranguing his bruised and battered servants. "Get the little turd! I want him now!"

Ned had not run. He watched the other man being pulled to his doom and their eyes met.

"Go, boy! Run and get the law!" he cried out, as at last the snowmen grabbed his legs and heaved him in.

"Go, now. Go. Go and tell my kids I love them…eee-aaaaaagh!" And he too was pulled inside the room.

Chapter 7

Ned went. He ran towards the staircase. He did not have time to scream or cry out for the two men. Earlier they had been enemies, but then they all had been drawn together in a fight for survival. Now escape was everything. They had sacrificed themselves for his chance to flee this foul place. He would get out of here and come back for vengeance. No going to the police; this called for justice with no rules and Ned knew where to go. He would go to Stalingrad Towers and get Beetie.

The stairs were in sight. Ned did not let up the pace he was running at. He leapt up the stairs two at a time with the intention of ramming any snowman waiting for him over the edge of the rails.

Near the top, Ned saw white feet. He drew his head down and powered into them like a bull. There was an unbalanced cry of terror and then there were no feet on the stairs. The cry reached a crescendo as the snowman's full bodyweight fell on the already rusted stair supports and the spiral staircase came crashing down on top of it.

Ned hooted with delight then turned ready to face more evil snowmen. The room ahead was in darkness; no dull light shone. They could be hiding anywhere, but Ned strode ahead, ready to meet any snowy sentry head on. Into the entrance room he walked, expecting an attack. He screwed up his fists and breathed deeply. Silence met him. Utter silence, except for the occasional drip of water on the concrete floor. Ned could see a thin line of light breaking through the darkness and as he moved towards it, he saw it was sunlight breaking through the gap in the top of the steel entrance door. There was freedom. After all the horror he had been through, there was his escape. Ned forced himself to look behind just in case one of the men had managed to make it. But he knew it was hopeless. They were gone and he would be too if he did not hurry up. Hopefully all those wicked snowmen were trapped below and could not get up here.

Ned made for the door. He glimpsed old electrical wire looped on the floor ahead but the thought of freedom made him ignore it. The bolt for the door was tantalizingly close. Ned reached for it and as his hands closed around it and pulled it back there was a snap and the sound like a fisherman's reel rotating lightning fast. Ned was jerked backwards as the electrical wire noosed around his ankle and pulled him upwards to hang upside down from the ceiling.

Suddenly the light was switched on and Ned could see snowmen walking forwards and clapping their hands in congratulations.

"Bravo. Bravo. Bravo indeed, my brainless minions! You have proven that you can learn the rudiments of physics." Hanging upside down, Ned knew the voice even before he saw an inverted Melton limping towards him.

Ned turned his mouth down in loathing, but upside down it looked like a smile. Melton returned the smile and reached out to Ned, then spun him around. The room turned faster and faster as Melton spun Ned more eagerly. All the snowmen were following the turns of Ned like kittens watching a toy mouse turning on a string. They were laughing and giggling, and then Ned was sick. The cold takeaway that was part-digested had endured enough, and the inverted spinning that Melton was making it undergo blew the safety valve. A Catherine wheel of spew spattered the snowmen. Melton received a half-digested sweet and sour chicken ball in his eye. Then a staccato of warm fried rice hit the snowmen. Some tried to cover themselves from greasy carbohydrate attack, others tried to grab him and stop him rotating. Melton shouted, hands grabbed, pandemonium ensued, and then Ned's phone rang.

The tone made the snowmen jump backwards. Ned was momentarily confused. Then it suddenly came to him what the noise was. He struggled to reach the phone which was lodged awkwardly in his pocket. He wriggled and wriggled and then his hand reached the phone and Ned pulled at it. His fingers were inadvertently pressing buttons and he hoped he didn't cut off the caller because he knew who it was. He knew this was his salvation on the other end of the line; he knew it was Beetie calling and if he could speak to him then Beetie would come right down and rescue him. At last the phone came out of his pocket but it slipped out of his hand. As it sailed through the air, he could hear Beetie's aggressive voice amplified and reverberating around the small room. Ned's fingers had accidentally hit the speaker button in his struggle to retrieve the phone from his pocket and he could see the phone on the floor and hear his saviour shouting aloud, "Where the blazes are you, boy? Answer the bloody phone now or I'll come down there and tan your hide with the Baron."

It was the sweetest sound that had passed Ned's ears for days. Hanging upside down and captured so close to the door to freedom, he could now taste the renewed tang of liberty in the scolding words from Beetie.

The snowmen gradually moved towards the phone. They approached it with a mixture of suspicion and trepidation, but Melton did not. The old swine pushed through them and tried to grab the phone. It kept slipping out of his mitten hands and was heading towards the stairwell when he put a foot on it and leaned down so his head was just above it. Beetie was rising to a fervour of rage. "Damn you! You little squirt, answer the phone now!"

Melton looked puzzled. Then Ned shouted out, "Beetie. Beetie. Beetie! Help me! It's Ned and I've been kidnapped!"

The phone bellowed, "WHAT?"

Melton looked at Ned, then back at the phone. Ned knew he would not have much time.

"I'm here at the chiller factory and I've been kidnapped. Please come and rescue me. I need immediate extraction!" Ned added, remembering that was a military term, and should do the trick.

The phone went silent.

Melton intervened. He cleared his throat. "Mmmm...to whom am I speaking?"

"Be-e-e-e-tie he-e-e-e-e-lp!" Ned shouted again.

Still, the phone was silent. Melton kicked one of the snowmen and nodded towards Ned. The snowman tentatively moved forwards, then looked back at Melton and put his hand to his mouth and nodded at Ned. Melton smiled haughtily and nodded. The snowman moved forwards and muffled Ned with its mitten hand.

Melton returned his attention to the phone and spoke again. "Well, hello there. Is that Beetie the war hero?" He sniggered. "Do you know a squalid little beast called Ned Mutton, perchance?"

The phone replied. "Errrrrr...I don't know who...or what you are talking about. I...err...certainly don't know or have ever known a person called Ned Motton."

Ned's eyes bulged in horror at what he suddenly realised was Beetie denying all knowledge of him or the operation to wreck the factory. Melton saw Ned's fear and sniggered again. "It's Mutton, not Motton," he corrected Beetie. "And he's here right now. Do you want to talk to him, Beetie?"

"I don't know a Motton or Mutton." Beetie's voice balked. "...Err...and my name's not Beetie. In fact, this is a recorded message. The time will be exactly...err...ten past...goodbye." And the phone went dead.

Melton turned to Ned. He had a triumphant smirk on his face. "A friend, was it? Or rather this Beetie was a former friend who has now denied all knowledge of your existence and left you in the lurch." He pulled at the cable and it released Ned, who landed in a heap on the floor. Melton leaned over him. "You're on your own, boy, and I've got a job for you to do." He strode over to the centre of the snowmen. "Heinrich, take this beastly little fiend to my office. The rest of you, go back to work. Come on now, all of you, back to your toil." He clapped his hands together and seemed to chivvy them along like a farmer with his chickens.

Ned was marched into a dilapidated office. He let Heinrich shove him forward because he felt the world around him had collapsed. What Melton said was true; he was alone and Beetie was not coming. He had heard Beetie deny that he knew Ned. His own hero, his valiant mentor, his guru, had renounced him. All the dreams of domination with Beetie at his side were now scattered to the dark corners of this dingy office. Ned was stuck here at the mercy of these snowmen and their deranged leader. No one knew he was here except Beetie, and he had abandoned Ned to what seemed a snowy fate.

He looked around the office to try and change his depressed state of mind but the interior of the room made it worse. It was horribly shabby and run down. The wallpaper was mouldy and peeling off the wall. In some places it had abandoned its grip on the plaster and lay like a shed skin on the floor. One section of wallpaper was still in its original condition and Ned could see that it had been hidden behind a radiator that had been removed. There was some form of graffiti that had been scrawled across the pristine wallpaper but it looked illegible. In one corner of the room was a plant pot with a dead Christmas tree sitting askew in it. An office table sat in the centre and was covered in white spatters of what Ned thought was paint, and beside this was a pile of half-broken chairs. Ned crossed to look at the graffiti; he bent down and could barely make out what was written so he stepped back and squinted at it from different angles. He started to read it out slowly. "M-e-l-t-o-n is a d-i—"

Suddenly, the door burst open. "What was that?"

Ned jumped back. He turned and saw Melton leaning on his walking stick.

"I was just reading this bit of graffiti," Ned explained.

Melton furrowed his brow and looked where Ned was now pointing.

"Ah, yes. One of the many loyal slogans my snowmen daub around this fortress."

Ned suppressed a giggle. "Oh, really, is that right?"

Melton's eyes narrowed menacingly and he leaned down until he was level with Ned's face. "Yes, really. That is right. Now, you repulsive child, take a chair and sit down at the table and I will explain to you what you are going to do for the greater good of snow-mankind." Ned shook a chair free and placed it in front of the desk. As he sat on it, the wood creaked and groaned, so he put some of his weight onto his legs in case it did collapse.

Melton paced in front of the desk. "You must be the most appalling, vile, and loathsome little fleshy swine I have ever laid my coal eyes on. You firstly destroy my own kind and then have the utter scorn to celebrate it by keeping this!" He slammed the scoreboard on the table and Ned jumped out of the chair. He landed back on it quickly and it splintered, cracked, and then collapsed, leaving Ned on the floor.

"Ha! That's where you belong, you swine, right at our feet!" Melton howled. "I would have no compunction to make you into slush, but that would be far too good for the likes of you and it would be far too merciful for the likes of me. Now, pick another chair and sit down."

Ned shook the remaining chairs apart. Out of five, only one had four legs, so he opted for that one and sat even more carefully again in front of the desk. The wood protested at his weight but thankfully it stayed together.

Melton lifted his walking stick and hit the desk with it. "Heinrich, down!" The snowman got down on his hands and knees behind Melton. Heinrich braced himself and Melton sat down across his back, then lifted himself slightly and gave Heinrich a back kick. The snowman-chair shuffled closer to the desk. Melton put his hands out to the desk and, seemingly not satisfied, kicked again. Heinrich shuffled closer and, when Melton judged the distance correct, he slapped Heinrich across the head with the stick and the shuffling stopped. Heinrich the snowman-chair did not seem at all put out by this. It was as if it was part of every snowman's duty towards their callous master.

Melton settled down in his 'chair', then opened a drawer in the desk and started to rummage through it. There was much cursing from Melton and prodding with both arms but eventually, and using both hands like oven gloves, he managed to extract a rather limp frozen food magazine. He placed it on the table and, with more difficulty due to his large mitten hands, started to flick through it. Ned looked on in puzzlement until a shout announced that Melton had found the desired page. He turned it around to face Ned.

Ned's eyes bore down on a section of frozen fish dishes. His puzzlement deepened.

Then Melton's hand jabbed down at the bottom of the page. Ned's bulbous eyes followed the hand and came to focus on a photo of a packet of fish fingers.

"There!" Melton shouted.

Ned looked from fish finger packet to Melton and back again. He repeated this action until Melton skewered the page with his stick. "There, you idiot! Just there!"

Ned pushed out his bottom lip and shook his head in defeat. He had absolutely no idea what Melton was shouting about.

Melton dropped the stick, rubbed his face wearily with his hands, and sighed. "You are looking at fishy fingers."

"Yes, I know. They're actually called fish fingers, not fishy fingers."

Melton took up his walking stick and held it level with Ned's eyes. "I think we'll call them fishy fingers, won't we?"

Wondering how many snowmen had been beaten to slush with the stick, Ned could only agree. "Okay, okay, we'll call them fishy fingers."

"Good!" Melton smiled and put down the stick. He leaned back in the snowman-chair, but it had no back and he over-balanced. His arms started to flail in the air until, from below, Heinrich shifted his weight and Melton crashed forward into the table.

Ned started to giggle but Melton grabbed the stick and aimed a swipe at him. He ducked back just in time, but his chair started to creak and groan, so he held up his hands in surrender. Melton sat heavily on Heinrich and he groaned like Ned's chair, but they both ignored it.

"Now, you little piece of excreta, let me explain to you the facts about our great and noble race. We righteous snowmen have been around for centuries. Once children loved us and revered our beautiful race. They would play with us and laugh with us and weep their sweet little eyes red when the sun came out and melted us. But now you mock us and deride us. You call us idiots and simpletons."

Ned thought that it was Melton that called the snowmen idiots and simpletons, but he decided not to mention it, and Melton had not finished with his speech. "Yes, you scoffed at the idea we could walk and talk, but for some deranged reason you dolts thought we could fly." He started to laugh and then shook his head in displeasure. "Oafs and dotards all of you..." He put a hand into the draw and rummaged again. To Ned's surprise, Melton produced a pipe and put it in his mouth. "We hid ourselves from your vile race and the world for a long time...long enough to learn and devise a plan. A plan so devious, so monstrously clever, that your race could never dream of it and would quake in their soggy socks if they ever found out about it." Ned leaned forwards to try and understand what Melton was saying because the pipe was distorting his voice. To Ned's relief, he took the pipe out and held it like a wooden prop, trying to reinforce his speech. It fell out of his hand and clattered under the desk. A white hand came out from under the desk and held the pipe in its open hand. Melton snatched it out of Heinrich's proffered palm without comment. He studied it briefly, then threw it across the room where it landed with a crack and broke in two. "And it was I, Melton Mowbray the Third, that perfected that plan; a plan that will rid us of fear and allow us to take our rightful place in the world!"

Ned nodded in polite bafflement because he had no idea what Melton was on about or what it had to do with fish fingers.

Melton then rose and kicked Heinrich aside. He started to pace behind the desk. "I…or we snowmen, have one major disadvantage—apart from the sun, that is—these!" He held up his hands, then continued. "Snowmen are created without digits, or fingers, to you. We proud people cannot open doors easily, press buttons, eat crisps, hold a cup of tea with aplomb, use cutlery with etiquette, pinch people, pick our noses, tie shoelaces, or operate complex machinery, et cetera, et cetera, et cetera, so you!" Melton pointed the best he could at Ned. "Will bring us fishy fingers from the frozen food shop so we can have our own FINGERS!" The last word was shouted and it echoed around the office.

Poor Ned just sat there with his mouth open. He did not know what to say. This mad snowman was demanding that he go out and get some fish fingers so that the snowmen could use them as fingers. He sat in the rickety old chair with his mouth agape until dribble started to run down his chin and the gentle tickling snapped him out of his reverie.

He wiped away the spittle and flicked it on the table. Melton looked disapprovingly at it and covered it over with the magazine.

A befuddled Ned looked up at the snowman. "You want me to go and get some fish…err…fishy fingers for you?"

"Yes, and when we fit them we will be complete and the world will be our oyster and you will be the micro-organisms that we feed on."

Needless to say, Ned did not know what a micro-organism was, but he did not say so.

Melton continued as if making a great oration. "Yes, my vile fleshy swine. We will fit our new digits and be the apex of the planet's creatures, and then we will take our revenge out on you human insects. You who mocked us and sought to destroy us, you who have kicked my brethren apart and despoiled our race, you will personally be responsible for this. For you will be the key to unlock our bonds and open the door for glorious snowmen to conquer the world!" He stamped to attention and raised his head high whilst his right arm shot out in salute.

"You mad old bugger. It'll never happen."

Melton's eyes sizzled and he slammed both hands on the table. "Oh, won't it? Well, we shall see, won't we? Heinrich, I think it's time this little beast visited the gallery of fools again. Bring him now!"

So the prodding and pushing began again and Ned was led out of the office by Heinrich. Melton told Heinrich to meet him outside the gallery of fools in ten minutes. Heinrich nodded and bowed, then grabbed Ned by the scruff of his neck and pulled him back inside the office. He shut the door and looked around nervously, then rubbed his hands together and started to pace the room. Back and forth he went, counting loudly very slowly to three, then starting again. This went on and on until Ned could not take it anymore.

"Please! Can't you count above three? Your pacing is driving me mental. If you want to know how long ten minutes is, it's about five minutes away."

Heinrich shook his head.

Ned smacked his own head with the palm of this hand. "Look, I'll tell you when five minutes is up, alright? How far is the gallery anyway?"

Heinrich screwed his face up in thought. "About a fifteen-minute walk."

"You dimwit, you just said you can't...well, never mind...we'd better go." Then Ned stopped. "Anyway, why does Melton want us to meet there anyway?"

Heinrich just shrugged.

If freedom could be gained for a packet of fish fingers then Ned was willing to do as he was asked. But there was a nagging suspicion growing in his head as to why they were to meet where the frozen people were interned.

It took nearly half an hour for Heinrich to locate the gallery due somewhat to the spiral stairs having collapsed. But they arrived out of breath and sweating— well, at least Ned was sweating.

Melton was not happy. He was dressed in an old dinner jacket decorated with food stains. On his head sat a tatty old top hat and skewered into his right eyelid was a gold monocle. He leaned on his walking stick. "Where the hell have you two blundering idiots been?"

Heinrich fell onto his knees and started to kiss Melton's hand. Ned stared on as a look of pleasure grew on Melton's face. Heinrich's kissing started to move up Melton's arm and he suddenly quivered like a jelly and let out a high-pitched giggle. Ned was astonished, but then Melton withdrew his arm and returned a hard smack around the back of Heinrich's head. The chief snowman composed himself and rubbed his hands together. "You, Heinrich, like this fleshy swine, are on very thin ice. One more lapse in your duty as my personnel valet will result in you being slushed. Do you hear me? You follow me like a dog! Like an obedient dog! Now get up and stop this snivelling behaviour."

Hienrich took the hand and started to smother it with kisses again and Melton allowed this sycophantic behaviour to continue for a while until he pulled his hand away and the snowman fell to the ground at his feet. Melton patted his head. "Good boy, good boy. Now fetch the Frozen Death Squad."

Heinrich actually ran off on all fours and whilst he was gone, Melton turned to Ned. "Now, I've got twenty-three snowmen here and according to the fishy finger boxes they contain twelve in each box, so I require…" He held out his hands to count but then realised he had no fingers and quickly put them behind his back. "Errr…you go to school surely and do sums. So…now I'm checking, of course, because I know already how many I need. So how many boxes do I require?"

Ned thought briefly, then said, "Three million!"

Melton nodded. "Yes, that's the correct...eh...what...*that* many? Well, it's a good job I'm going to get you some help then, isn't it?"

Before Ned could protest, Heinrich came back with two large snowmen wrapped in heavy overcoats that came down to their feet. One had a bowler hat on, the other was bare-headed. They both had brightly coloured scarves on and wore large lensed sunglasses that nearly covered their faces. Heinrich curtsied in front of Melton. The two snowmen pushed him aside and snapped to attention.

Melton tucked his walking stick under his armpit, then took out his monocle and scrutinized them closely. He frowned at the hatless one. "Where is your hat?

"Sir, begging your pardon, but I couldn't find one, sir!" he shouted back.

Melton sighed. "You're no good to me if you can't blend in with the fleshies." He took off his top hat and handed it to the snowman. "Here, take this." The snowman went to take it, but Melton pulled his hand back. "But make sure you look after it."

"Sir, yes, sir." The snowman took the hat and placed it on his head. It slid over his sunglasses and completely covered his face.

Melton breathed a sigh of woe. "Never mind, never mind. You'll have to hold it up."

There was a muffled "Sir, yes, sir," from under the hat.

Melton slapped his good leg with his stick and looked around to find Ned. "Let me introduce you to these very special warriors. They are the elite of our fighting force. They are trained in the art of Arctic warfare and fighting behind enemy lines; by that, I mean your lines. They know no pain and will fight to the last snowball and they will never, ever surrender." Ned saw the two snowmen looking questioningly at each other at this, but Melton did not see and carried on. "And their motto is 'No victory, no surrender'. They are the Frozen Death Squad and they will accompany you on your mission."

Ned looked at them. They looked big and mean, but they did not look particularly elite.

"Whoa! Now hang on, I was only joking about having to get three million boxes. If you've got twenty-three snowmen then you are going for four fingers and a thumb on each hand, yes?"

Melton had not a clue of how many fish fingers he needed but he did not want to admit this. "Errr...yes, four thumbs and a finger...that's right."

"Well, in that case, you'll need..." Ned started to count. He went through his fingers, did it again and again and again, and so on, until: "You're going to need ten fish fingers per snowman, so that's two hundred and thirty, then divide that by twelve, that's...well, that's..." He picked up a large wooden splinter from the floor. "I need something to write on."

"Heinrich, bend over!" Melton ordered.

A huge white posterior presented itself to Ned and he started to calculate and divide by scrawling very hard into Heinrich's backside. Ned jabbed the numbers into the white bottom and Heinrich started to yelp and whine.

"I can't concentrate with him whimpering like that," Ned said irritably.

Melton hit the floor with his stick. "Heinrich, you will suffer in silence or face the consequences!"

The whimpering became quieter and Ned continued. He had worked out the answer but kept jabbing the stick into the snowman butt in revenge. Then, with one final hard jab, he announced, "Twenty boxes or there about, is what you're going to need." And with that, Heinrich ran off screaming.

"Excellent," Melton clapped his hands together.

"And I won't need your elite soldiers either, so they can stay here," Ned added.

"Oh, I wouldn't dream of sending you off on a mission on your own. And I wouldn't dream of sending you off without a little incentive either." Melton smiled wickedly. "You see, what's to stop you buggering off and never coming back. That's why my fighting elite are joining you, and..." A deep laugh started in Melton's belly. "Well, why don't you go and look in freezer tank number twenty? I think you'll find something interesting in there."

Ned was puzzled by this, but Melton pushed him into the gallery. Even though he knew what was in the tanks, Ned still did not want to look in them, but he had to. The postman, the roofing contractors, the twitcher, the family were all there. He walked up to tank number nineteen and saw the two men he had set free earlier. One was frozen with his head in his hands, the other was frozen whilst in the throes of a rebellious two-fingered salute. Ned looked to the floor in sorrow, then looked into tank number twenty. His mother and father were staring back at him. Ned slammed his palms against the glass and screamed, "Mum! Dad! What are you doing here!?" They were tied back to back on a stool and were shivering all over. Ned's dad looked at him and smiled weakly. His mum looked incredibly angry.

Melton walked in and spoke. "They are not frozen yet, unlike your friend in the next cell, but they will be if you don't get me the fishy fingers in twenty-four hours."

Ned looked into the cell again. His mum struggled against the ropes and looked fiercely at Melton. From behind the thick glass, Ned could hear a muffled tirade of abuse directed towards the snowman. For months now, Ned had thought his parents more and more embarrassing and annoying. At times he had wanted to disown them; indeed, his fantasies about being adopted by Beetie had taken over his home life. But now, after all he had been through, after Beetie's rejection, and looking now in the cell at his helpless mum and dad, his anger at them collapsed. He pushed against the mildewed glass as if trying to get in and be closer to them. Ned's nose touched the glass and a tear broke over the rim of his eyelid. It fell onto the glass and trickled a watery path down until it slowly froze. He turned on Melton. "You're a rotten old swine, Melton. It isn't fair grabbing innocent people and freezing them." He slammed his fist against the glass. "How the hell did you get them here anyway?"

Melton started to chuckle. "Well, it's all down to you, really."

"What do you mean?" Ned shouted.

"You had your name and address on the piece of paper in your pocket, remember? So, in effect, you have sealed your parents' fate. All we had to do was send the boys around and grab them. And now they are going to be exhibit number twenty in the gallery of fools unless you get the fishy fingers."

Ned's temper exploded. He knew it was his fault and he hated himself for it. If he had not taken the school report and not kept a score board this would not have happened. Then again, if he had not met Fabian and Beetie this also would not have happened. In truth, it all came back to Ned. In his anger, he kicked Melton in the shin. The old swine howled and the other snowmen went to his aid but he put out a hand to stop them and with his other he felt for a switch on the side of the cell. Melton pushed it down and the cell with Ned's mum and dad started to fill with a cold mist.

"No!" Ned screamed. Melton did not listen. He kept his hand on the switch.

"Please! Stop it!" Ned cried out. Melton looked down at him with a sneer, then flicked the switch up.

"You dare kick me, you little bugger. Anymore funny business again and Mummy and Daddy are frozen fish."

The mist started to clear and Ned saw his parents. They were covered in a thin skin of ice and were shaking a lot more, but thankfully they were alive.

"Right, then," Melton said. "Let us pick up your escorts and you can proceed with your mission."

Before Ned could think, he arrived at the entrance door he had recently so nearly escaped from—though this time he was squashed between the two Frozen Death Squad snowmen. Melton ordered the door to be opened. A dull and overcast late afternoon light seeped into the room. Ned was pushed out and as his escorts followed him, he heard Melton's voice in the background. "Go, my super troopers. Go and seek our destiny. Go and bring the fishy fingers." Then the door slammed shut.

Chapter 8

Outside, the two snowmen walked at Ned's side, each with one hand on his shoulders. He tried to shrug them off. Ned's anger was still boiling and it was with himself for what he had done. Now he had to fetch twenty boxes of fish fingers and return to the chiller factory so his parents would be set free. He also had these two with him and even if he did escape them, what could he do? He could not go to the police. Would anyone believe that snowmen lived and breathed, and even if they did, by the time they got back here then you could guarantee that Melton would have frozen them. The thought of Beetie brought a nasty taste back in his mouth. That wig-wearing lout would not help at all. Ned felt a horrible resentment towards him. Beetie had sent him on this mission and had abandoned him. Dark thoughts of revenge filled his mind as he looked over towards Stalingrad Towers.

"Oi! Come on, we've got to get Melton his fishy fingers," the snowman with the bowler hat said.

Ned turned on him. "Alright, alright, I know!"

The bowler-hatted one pulled at Ned's shoulder. "You heard what Melton…errr…I mean Lord Melton Mowbray the Third, said."

"Any funny business and your mummy and daddy get frozen," Top Hat cut in.

"I wanted to say that," the Bowler retorted.

"You can't remember your own name, let alone what old peg leg said," Top Hat commented as he took Melton's hat and crushed it together in his hands, then returned it to his head. "That's better, it fits now. Got a big head, has old Melton."

Bowler Hat stopped and flapped his hands in panic. "Don't do that to his hat. And don't call him peg leg. Not here, he'll hear us; you know what that old tyrant's like. He can hear loads around here and he'll have us court-martialed and slushed."

"Get away with you, you old flake," Top Hat said scornfully. "I'm not afraid of that gammy-legged old bugger." All the same, he snuck a quick glance towards the factory just in case.

Bowler started to roll up the sleeves of his coat. "Don't you go calling me a flake. I'll poke your coals out if you do it again."

Top Hat stopped. "Flake!" he shouted.

Bowler advanced on him and put up his mitten hands. "Come on, then. Come on," he roared.

Top Hat waved him away with a large hand. "Shut up, you big fat flake. You can't poke me eyes out because you ain't got any fingers. So stick that up your carrot!"

Ned watched the confrontation with a bemused look. Top Hat had started to take off his coat and as he did, Bowler launched a flying kick at him. Top Hat had managed to get one sleeve off and swung the big coat in an arc at the flying snowman. It wrapped around his neck and the wet hem caught Bowler in the nose with a wicked sharp crack.

Top Hat slapped his thighs and started to hoot with laughter. Ned suppressed a giggle while Bowler landed with a crash in the snow and started to sob.

It was not dark just yet, and anyone seeing these two snowmen fighting could bring disaster to Ned's parents. So he walked between the two and held up his hands. "Alright, that's enough. We haven't even left the factory and you two are fighting. How can we be successful in getting the fish fingers if you do this?"

Top Hat stood and considered Ned, and Bowler stopped sobbing. They looked at each other and shrugged. "Okay, okay," they said reluctantly. Top Hat walked over and held a hand out to Bowler. As he was just about to accept Top Hat's hand, Ned said, "Right, you with the top hat, apologise to your bowler-wearing comrade."

Top Hat turned to Ned. "What?"

"I said, apologise to him," Ned repeated.

"You can stick that where the sun don't shine, you little fleshy swine," Top Hat said angrily.

Ned backed off a little. From behind, Bowler got up and brushed snow off his coat. "You heard what he said, apologise to me."

"Get stuffed!" Top Hat answered.

Ned was pushed aside as Bowler advanced on Top Hat. They started to size each other up again like very amateur boxers.

This time, Ned shouted. "You two, stop this!" He stomped between them and, like a tiny referee before a boxing match, gave them his thoughts. "Now listen. We've been sent on a mission to get fish fingers and that's what we're going to do. This is a top-secret mission and we can't have morale fall apart, can we? My mum and dad are in there." He pointed back to the chiller factory. "And I want to get them free and the only way I'm going to do that is to get twenty boxes of fish bloody fingers for your boss, so stop this nonsense and come on!" He folded his arms together and the two snowmen just stared down at him. Ned looked at them both with suppressed anger and then shouted out, not caring if anyone saw or heard, "And that's an order!"

The two snowmen looked astonished. Ned followed up quickly while they were in this state, "You, soldier, apologise to your comrade now!"

Top Hat walked forward and Ned leaned back. The snowman towered over Ned and he looked down then snapped to a rigid attention. "Sir, yes, sir!"

Top Hat did a goose step march over to Bowler. He took off his hat and cleared his throat. A high-pitched upper-class twang came out of the white mouth. "Ahem...I am sorry if I have offended you, my old chum. Please accept my deepest apologies for the uncouth and loutish manner which was directed at yourself." He held out his hand and Bowler took it and shook it.

Ned was slightly baffled by this sudden change of character but he quickly forgot it and walked over to the snowmen. He patted them on the backs. "Well done. Now, what's the plan?"

The snowmen both looked puzzled. "Plan? What plan's this?"

Ned's impatience started to rise. "The plan to get the fish fingers!"

Top Hat scratched his chin for a moment. Then he seemed to remember something. "Oh yeah, the fish fingers. You're supposed to get them."

Ned bit his lip in irritation. "I know I'm supposed to get them, but where's the money to pay for them? I haven't got any with me." He had not either. In all the confused terror and assault of the senses Ned had been through recently, he had completely forgotten to ask Melton for some cash.

Top Hat and Bowler looked at each other quickly, then back to Ned. "What's money?"

"Tell me you're not serious. Please tell me that you're having a laugh," Ned cried out.

There was a look of innocence on the snowmen's faces and, before they could say anything, Ned exploded, "You don't know what money is? You cannot be serious. I mean, you're supposed to be an elite fighting force that operates behind enemy lines. You're supposed to blend in with ourselves. You're...you're...this Frozen Death thingamy that infiltrates our world and...and...you don't know about money?"

Top Hat started to laugh and Bowler took a nervous look back to the chiller factory, then started to giggle. Top Hat beckoned Ned forwards, then leant down and whispered in Ned's ear, "We made all that stuff up."

Ned blinked. "What?"

Top Hat put his big hand on Ned's shoulder, then explained. "Yeah, we made it all up so that we can get away with light duties at the fortress—that's what Melton calls that old piece of junk." He pointed back to the chiller factory. "That maimed old git's a right slave driver; do this, do that, be my chair, kiss my hand, and so on. You have no idea what it's like living with him." Top Hat shook his head sadly. "Honestly, he's a right slave driver. Always strutting about in that smelly old jacket and that poncey eyeglass and telling everyone what to do." Bowler had come over and started to speak slowly. He kept his voice low and also kept looking back to the factory as if Melton was about to come out and get them for telling tales. "So yeah, anyway, one day old peg leg...err...I mean Melton, sees this postman nosing about outside the fortress. He gets into a right tiff and orders us to go out and get him. Well, we did, but he put up a right struggle so we had to give him the old one-two." Ned did not know what 'the old one-two' was but he did not care. The tale he was being told was more interesting and bizarre. Bowler opened his jacket and Ned saw a load of opened letters. "When we got him, he had a bag full of these. We didn't tell Melton but kept them and took them back to our den in the fortress. Well, they was ever so good, loads of letters and some books, and that's where we got all that stuff about soldiers and war and special faeces."

"Forces," Top Hat corrected his comrade in arms.

Bowler ignored him. "Yeah whatever, ever so brave they was, these special faeces, operating behind enemy lines, passing unnoticed, cutting communication lines, you know, phone lines, TV aerials, and all that, great stuff it was and it was all in these." Bowler pulled out a bundle of curled and ragged papers from his pocket and Ned recognised them as war comics. The same sort of comics he had when he was younger.

Top Hat was nodding eagerly. "Oh yeah, all that Frozen Death Squad and 'No victory, no surrender', that was all in them comics. It took us a long time to read these 'cos we're not very good; mind, we eventually fooled old gammy leg. Told him we've been selected for the school of Arctic warfare and we've got to bugger off for three months. Melton swallowed it down like a tub of Neapolitan ice cream." They both started to laugh, apparently relieved to be able to tell the truth to someone after all this time. And Ned started to laugh too. It was unbelievable. These two nincompoop snowmen had abducted a postman, read some comics, and fooled that depraved old snowman, and, moreover, were still getting away with it. He could not stop himself laughing. Maybe it was the culmination of events and the initial freedom he felt now that he was away from the confines of the factory that made him howl. But whatever it was, these two idiots were joining in as well, and all were slapping each other on the backs and hooting with delight.

Ned was still laughing when he noticed it was starting to snow again. Cold flakes drifted down on the back of his neck. It made him shiver, and then a thought came to him. "What did you come back to the factory for?"

Top Hat was coughing now from laughing too much so Bowler hit him on the back. "Oi, get off!" He looked seriously at Bowler, then to Ned. "Well, before we went Melton reckoned he had this brilliant plan, said summit about us snowmen taking our rightful place at the head of society. Dunno what he meant but it sounded good, and anyway, we started to miss the old tyrant. He plays hell with the other snowmen but if he comes on all bolshy with us we tell him we've got another mission and have to go to the Arctic." He tapped his nose. "Know what I mean, eh, but we go to our den and he don't bother us, silly old bugger."

Ned shook his head to get rid of the cold snowflakes. He also shook it in wonderment that these two buffoons could dupe their evil genius of a leader. Two thoughts came to him: if these dimwits could fool Melton then maybe, just maybe, he could. The other thought was not so pleasant. "Hang on. If you kidnapped the postman, did you get all the others in the freezer tanks?"

Bowler and Top Hat smiled proudly. "Yeah, of course we did."

Ned face turned an angry red. "Then you got the people in tank twenty today then?"

The snowmen looked as if the answer was obvious. "Well, yea-h-h-h-h-h…of course we did. We got them all."

"They're my parents!" Ned shouted. The cry echoed across the ruined factory building and was finally taken away by the wind and snow.

Top Hat walked over to Ned. He bent down so he was level with him and lifted his hands in the air. "That's our job, son. If we don't occasionally do anything for Melton, he might get suspicious." He stood upright and turned. "Talking of Melton, we'd better get a move and get them fishy fingers he wants so badly."

Bowler pushed Ned forwards. "Come on, lad, no use crying over milt spilk, or whatever it is?"

Dusk was approaching rapidly as they reached the fence. Bowler took hold of the branch of a fallen beech tree that was leaning across a broken part of the fence. In an impressive show of strength, he pulled the tree back scattering snow everywhere. The mini-storm blew away to reveal a ragged hole in the fence.

"Go." Top Hat pushed Ned past Bowler and then took up a crouching position on a slight rise just outside the fence. Ned saw him put his hands to his eyes and scan the area in front. He then waved one hand in the air and Bowler came running up behind Ned. He too crouched down and put his hands to his eyes as if he was looking through something.

"What are you doing now?" Ned asked.

Bowler looked startled and pulled Ned down in the snow. "Keep your head down. We're behind enemy lines and we're being soldiers. That's what they do. And we're checking out the ground with our binoculars."

Ned looked at their hands and saw nothing. "You haven't got any binoculars."

Top Hat motioned Ned to be quiet and then crawled over. "We know that. We're just pretending we have, and you can too, here." He pulled off his own pretend ones and handed them to Ned, who stood there with his hands by his side. "Here, take them now." Top Hat insisted. Still, Ned did not move to take them. Top Hat suddenly jumped up and bowled Ned over. "And keep your head down!"

Ned started beating at Top Hat. "Get off me, you oaf."

Top Hat pinned him down. "I'm trying to save your life out here behind enemy lines."

Ned started to shout against Top Hat but then Bowler crawled over and put a huge hand over Ned's mouth and put his free hand to his lips. "Shhhhh! Someone's coming."

He pulled off his hat and knocked Top Hat's off as well, then nodded to the left of him and shuffled around in the snow so he was facing that way. The heads of the snowmen were just visible above the rise but Top Hat spread his body over Ned's so he could not move. Instead, Ned's eyes bulged out of his head with the weight of the snowman and in trying to see what was approaching them.

Bowler let out a small scream. "Bloody hell, it's Melton! I told you to shut up and not say anything about him." He crawled backwards and tried to curl up in a ball. "Oh, we're for slushing now. That old brute's coming for us alright, and worse, he's riding on his war horse, so he means business." He started to shake and panic. Top Hat released Ned and craned his neck in the direction Bowler had indicated to. He looked for a split second. Then Ned saw his coal eyes bulge. "Bugger me, he's right. It *is* the old thug!" He grabbed Bowler and shook him. "You're in the special faeces! On a mission you don't fall to pieces." Ned thought that it rhymed well but the rap needed working on. Anyway, it was enough that the overweight snowman was off him. He suddenly gasped an unburdened lung full

101

of air, then spluttered. "Wait...let me...see." And before Top Hat could stop him, he scampered over to see.

Appearing through the snow was a donkey being led by a figure, and on the donkey was another figure wrapped in brightly coloured robes. It was like a scene from a Christmas card, and how the hell the snowmen could tell it was Melton, Ned did not have a clue until a stick came out from under the robes and hit the figure leading the donkey. "Hurry up, you cretin." Ned recognised the wicked tones of Melton, and he even recognised Heinrich's whimper as his master hit him.

What on earth was Melton doing out here, thought Ned, but he was suddenly grabbed again and pulled down. "Oh, will you get off me!" he managed to say before Top Hat beckoned him to silence. "There's someone else coming," he said in a panic. Ned let himself be pulled down but strained his ears to try to hear a new sound. It was barely audible at first, but then he could make out the crump, crump, of heavy footfalls in the snow. Top Hat, Bowler, and Ned froze where they were. They could hear Melton and Heinrich and the protesting neigh of the donkey from their left. From their right the crumps got louder. Then they seemed to merge and all of a sudden stop. There was the sound of a struggle and more hits from a stick, then it seemed Melton was standing just above their own position.

His voice cut through the snow in a pleasant tone. "Ah, Brinsley, how good to see you again."

The voice that answered was not so pleasant. "I don't usually do outdoor trips. Is the boy taken care of or, judging by the phone call, have you messed it all up?" This time Ned let out a small scream. He knew the low growl of a voice. It was Beetie. Top Hat pulled Ned down again.

"What was that?" Beetie asked.

"What was what?" Melton replied.

"I heard a scream." Beetie said.

"Probably a human being squashed by one of my warriors."

Beetie scoffed at that. "Hmmmph. Your loutish snowmen couldn't squash a snowball. Now listen, that boy knows too much about my empire building. He's served his purpose and now we need to dispose of the little tyke. Is he frozen like the rest of them?"

Melton put his arm around Beetie's shoulders and walked over to where Ned, Top Hat, and Bowler were lying. They all involuntarily shrank back against the snow. Melton reached the ridge, then turned around and spoke in Beetie's ear. "You know, Beetie—that's what the plebeian swine called you, isn't it—you should learn to trust in Melton a little more. After all, my freezer tanks are nearly full to the brim with people you wanted to get rid of. Remember the twitcher and the roofing contractors, the family who went for a picnic and postman, they were all undesirables that threatened your so-called empire, and it has been down to me to get rid of them."

Beetie turned on Melton. He was breathing heavily and was out of temper. "Now you listen to me, you...you...you hobbling old fool. I am the one who pays for the electricity that keeps your ramshackled factory at sub-zero temperature so your dunderhead snowmen can survive. I'm the one who keeps you in ice cream so your idiots can get drunk on vanilla, chocolate, Neapolitan, and the rest. And I'm the one who keeps the law off your back, so you will show me some respect." Beetie shoved Melton's hand from his shoulder and rounded on him. "And to my delight, you will tell me that that brat Ned Mutton has been frozen in a chiller tank and will not bother me ever again."

From below their feet, Ned's stomach turned over. He had been set up all along. It was no chance meeting that he and Fabian had. He had been duped, and what a fool he had been. Beetie, or rather Brinsley Vaughan-Abbott, and Melton had been in cohorts together since all this began. He had done Beetie's bidding, demolishing listed monuments and getting rid of rare species, and was now supposed to have disappeared when he went to demolish the chiller factory. Looking back, he should have known. The factory was too big for one gullible boy to tear down, but his pride and greed had got the better of him. Now it was his mum and dad that were awaiting a freezing and he was on some wild goose chase to get hold of some fish fingers. Ned lay there completely deflated. He could not think straight for a minute. Then Melton kicked some snow backwards over the cowering figures and it landed on Ned's head and he thought and thought. Melton, Melton, Melton. He was supposed to have frozen him by now, but instead he had kidnapped his parents and sent him on this 'mission'. Beetie obviously knew nothing of Melton's plans and, as if on cue, Melton started to speak again.

"The foul little swine has been taken care of, so there is no need to worry," he explained calmly, then added in a brisk tone, "but my price for getting rid of your...how shall we say...'embarrassments' has risen, my dear Brinsley. After all, my tanks are nearly all full and, contrary to you, I am grateful for what you have done for me and my minions, but time moves on and we want to as well. You see, it's all getting a bit overcrowded down there and the atmosphere of the place isn't good for my boys either, all that damp and cold, so I was thinking of getting them away from there." Melton slapped Beetie on the back and got a growl in return. He ignored it and continued. "You see, as a successful properly developer, I was thinking that you could purchase—with your vast amounts of cash at your disposal—a nice purpose-built snow village for us, somewhere in the North?"

Beetie coughed in shock, then shouted out, "YOU WANT WHAT?"

Melton sighed. "A nice little winter retreat for me. The boys want one too, but they can settle with a shed."

Beetie exploded. "You ungrateful old pig; I've kept you and your freaks alive for years. If it hadn't been for me, you would have all melted away down those cack-filled drains eons ago. You get ice cream by the gallon and the law kept away from there." He jabbed his finger back to the factory, then turned it up and held it in front of Melton. "And this is the thanks I get? Well, let me tell you something, Mr Melton Mowbray the Third, I'm going to turn around and go home to my nice warm mansion. I'm going to pour myself a stiff one, then I'm going to phone the electricity company that supplies that dump of a factory and I'm going to tell them to switch off the power!"

A look of horror appeared on Melton's face. Then it slowly turned to amusement. "Well, Beetie, old man, if you do that then I'll have to send the law the video of you boasting about how you would murder to get your hands on the factory and anyone who gets in your way is dead."

That stopped Beetie in his tracks. "Video. What video?"

Melton smiled and gave a false laugh as he started to explain. "The little horror was hanging upside down in my fortress when his phone rang. Surely you remember our conversation, you denying his existence, and our little subterfuge?"

Beetie frowned.

Melton continued. "I take it that is a yes. Well, on the phone there is a video camera and even me, with my big mitten hands, eventually managed to work out how to view it, and what a performance I saw. You are a little worse for wear on it and you slur your speech a bit, but it's all there. The confession of kidnapping and murder, or at least that is what the law will conclude if they get hold of it." He grinned genially at Beetie, who frowned even deeper as a terrible fractured memory came back. He was in his study with Ned and, having drunk too much, allowed himself to be filmed making a speech of all he was going to do and how he would do it down at the chiller factory. He gulped heavily, then growled.

"Alright, I'll look into a snow villa for you but not for those dunderheads that follow you around. They can build one for themselves. But I want that phone back in my hands and I..." he tried to calm himself down before continuing. "I want you to do one more job for me as well."

Melton took Beetie's hands in his and gently squeezed them in reassurance. "You get me the villa and the building materials for a big shed and an Austrian ski instructor thrown in and I'll do one more job for you. Now, who do you want got rid of now?"

Beetie did not even bother to hide any shock that Melton knew what he wanted. He pulled one hand from the snowman's grasp, reached into his jacket pocket, and pulled out a photograph.

Melton took it and studied it. "What a sweet little thing. What's she ever done to you?"

Beetie returned to his gruff arrogance. "Never you mind what she's done to me. The address is on the back and if you get any bother squish the parent. There's only one in the house and he's a weirdo or he's out at his work most of the time, so you shouldn't muck it up." He turned to leave, then stopped. "As for the villa and extras, I'll need a couple of days to arrange things. Leave the factory door open and I'll come down to get the phone and see that the girl and Ned Mutton are frozen in your tanks. Then, and only then, you'll get your just reward." Beetie hid a smile from Melton and walked off into the snow-filled darkness.

Melton chuckled to himself. "Fool. You'll get your reward before then." He threw the photo away, then shouted out, "Idiot, bring my steed. We're going home." Heinrich pulled the donkey over to Melton, then bent down in the snow to allow his master to mount the animal. There was the sound of curses and swearing, then the donkey heehawed loudly and the trio strode off.

Ned waited for a minute, then got up. Dusk had turned to a cold and dark winter's evening. There was no sign of anyone and the tracks both parties left were starting to get covered in fresh snow. As he looked around for Bowler and Top Hat, Ned caught sight of the partially snow-covered photo and picked it up. Ned flicked the snow from it and saw that it was of a girl. She was not particularly pretty; she had curly clumps of hair that were tied tightly to each side of her head in big red ribbons and she had large green eyes, bigger even than Ned's bulbous eyes. She stared out from the picture as if in a stupor of astonishment. The trouble was, Ned knew he had seen her before, and recently too, but he could not place where it was he had. Beetie wanted him dead because he knew too much, he had got rid of all those in the freezer tanks too, but why he wanted to get rid of this girl, he had no idea.

"Have they gone yet?" Bowler said from below. Ned looked down and saw that the snowman was still curled up in a ball and not moving. He also saw Top Hat was not moving and assumed he was frightened rigid too, until he heard snoring and realised that he had fallen asleep.

Ned picked up the photo and pocketed it. "Yeah, they've gone. You can stop cowering now and wake up your elite comrade while you're cowering down there."

Chapter 9

Bowler got up quickly, dusted the snow off himself, and put on his hat. "I...I...was listening to the ground, if you must know...to...to see if there were any other people approaching."
"Yeah, alright, if you say so," Ned said coolly.
"I was, you know. We read about them Indians that did that when they was looking for cowboys," Bowler tried to reassure him.
"Well there aren't any cowboys round here, partner. Now wake up sleeping beauty, will you?" Ned ordered, and Bowler obeyed. He took a few steps over to the slumbering Top Hat and kicked him hard in the head. Quick as lightning, Top Hat was up and planted a left hook right on Bowler's chin. The snowman went down like a sack of potatoes and did not move.
"Oh, well done, you," Ned shouted. "I'm on the greatest mission ever planned by your lord and master, I've got to get twenty boxes of fish fingers, I've got no money, and you've got no plan." His voice was rising now. "My parents are about to be frozen, as is a little girl, and you've just KO'd one of the team!"
"Well, he shouldn't have kicked me in the head," Top Hat said, picking up his hat and putting it on.
"You were asleep on duty!" Ned accused him.
Top Hat shot to attention. "Sir...I...I..." But he could not seem to explain. "I...I mean, we had a bit of a leaving party with the boys last night. We...well, I, drank too much vanilla ice cream...and...and...well, I'm suffering a bit now." He took off his hat and bowed his head in shame. "I...get a bit tetchy when I ain't had much sleep and he..." Top Hat shook the unconscious Bowler with his foot. "...he winds me up, he does."
Ned stomped down to where he was. "Look, you can't go hitting people just because they wind you up. He's your comrade in arms, for goodness' sake, and you've been tasked with a mission. And..." A thought suddenly came to him. Why did Melton throw the photo away? Did he have a photographic memory? And what did he

say…"You'll get your reward first." What did that mean? Ned looked at the chastened Top Hat. "You two get the people that Beetie…I mean, Melton, wants freezing. That's right, isn't it?" Top Hat nodded. Ned lifted the snowman's head so he could see Top Hat's face. "You two and no one else?"

Top Hat breathed deeply and wiped a tear from his eye. "Just us two and no one else."

Then while these two were with Ned, the little girl was safe. After all his recent shameful deeds and selfish actions, maybe he could redeem himself by helping this girl, but more importantly, for now, he had to rescue his mum and dad. These idiots had no plan, but he must think of one, and soon. Fish fingers first, mum and dad, then try to get rid of these two idiots and save the girl. A snowflake landed on his nose and brought him back to reality.

Top Hat was still standing in front of Ned. He wore a look of intense strain and seemed to be near to bursting into tears.

Ned was about to speak when Top Hat burst out. "Sir, I will commit hari kari if you order it. Just give me a box of matches and I'll do it!"

"What the hell's hari kari?" Ned asked.

"It's the only honourable option for me, sir. I fell asleep on duty and I should be shot. We ain't got no guns, so I'll melt myself," Top Hat explained through near welling eyes.

There was a groan from below and Bowler got up rubbing his chin. "What happened?"

"You slipped up," Ned said hurriedly. He went over and supported Bowler, then turned to Top Hat and, enforcing the words loudly, said, "DIDN'T HE? HE FELL OVER."

Top Hat looked blank, so Ned kicked him. It did the job. "Ouch…oh yes, old man…you slipped on the new snow." He helped support Bowler as well. "You must be careful in the future, my old chum." He finished the sentence with a ludicrously fake smile.

Ned leaned around Bowler's back and whispered to Top Hat. "No more talk of hari kari alright?" He nodded and took the whole weight of Bowler as Ned took the lead. "Now come on, we're behind schedule and we've got a date with some fish fingers."

Top Hat and Bowler did not move. They were whispering to each other and nodding and then looking serious and whispering and nodding again.

Ned's patience was nearing meltdown. "Come on!" he shouted.

"Yes, sir," Top Hat snapped. Ned shook his sad head and started off, but Top Hat had more to say. "Excuse me, sir, but as you've been ever so good in these times of recent battle trauma, me and my chum was wondering if you would like to take command now…well, to take a higher rank than us…so to speak."

Ned stopped and calmed himself again. He paused for a while, then said quietly, "What do you mean this time?"

"Well," Top Hat said eagerly. "We're just 'non-coms', you know, in the ranks…cannon fodder, grunts, so to speak."

"Yes, I know," Ned snapped.

Top Hat looked hurt but then continued. "Well, what rank do you want to be?"

Ned was not taken aback by the bizarre idea. The situation was surreal enough; he with two snowmen hunting for fish fingers so some maniac despot snowman leader could start world domination.

Ned just smiled briefly. "I'll be a brigadier, if it's all the same to you."

Top Hat looked delighted and a weak Bowler responded with a fragile smile. They both saluted perfectly. "YES, SIR!"

The trio walked across the empty park, Ned taking the lead while Top Hat still supported Bowler. It was bitterly cold as they strode through the fresh snow. No other person was out. It seemed all the townsfolk were shut away in their nice warm homes, and it was just as well for Ned not to be seen with these two snowmen. He waited for them and wondered whether the snowmen needed a quick course in road safety as ahead of them, a major road crossed their route. He saw street lights casting their orange glow down on the snow-covered road and, to his relief, noticed that they were virtually empty of vehicles too. An odd truck or car moved along at a snail's pace, but because of their low speed, Ned was sure that they could cross the road without being seen closely. Anyway, at a distance, Top Hat and Bowler looked like large men wrapped up in thick clothing so as to stave off the cold.

Bowler rubbed his head and pulled away from Top Hat's support. "He's alright now, sir," Top Hat said. "Just needs a bit of ice cream to get his circulation going."

Ned shot him a warning glance. "No ice cream. You fell asleep on duty, remember? And I want my parents back living and breathing, not frozen, so no ice cream."

Top Hat turned away in shame. Bowler looked at Ned. "I...I'm alright now. I don't need any ice cream, sir. Maybe a little treat will do me some good though."

"We haven't time for any treats now," Ned snapped again.

"Oh, go on, sir, just a little one," Bowler pleaded. "It doesn't have to be ice cream or a sweetie. I'll settle for a look at a talking car or train."

"A what?"

"A talking car, or a talking train. Or a talking celitopter," Bowler smiled.

Top Hat turned around. "He means a helicopter."

Ned shook his head and opened his mouth but no words formed. He noticed that they had dropped the formal words of rank and he suspected that more idiot ideas were about to be proposed.

Top Hat started to explain enthusiastically. "When we nicked the postman's bag, he had some books in there as well. They was ever so good; a little car that sang and talked, a little blue train that chuffed along and raced a helicopter. It was ace."

Ned blinked in mystified resignation.

Top Hat grinned and slapped Ned on the shoulders. "Look. There's a road ahead and if we wait near it we can wave at a car and stop and talk to it."

Ned's voice came back. "No, we can't!" And he started off towards the road. The snowmen looked disappointed, then took off after him. They caught up, turned, and pleaded as they neared the road. "Please. Please. Please. Please." They kept on. Bowler had his hands clasped together as if in prayer and Bowler was nodding keenly with an inane smile fixed on his face.

"NO!" Ned shouted.

"Oh, go on. Go on. Go on. Go on. Go on," Top Hat repeated.

They reached the road and Ned stamped the snow. "NO! NO! NO! Now come on. That is a direct order." He went to pull their coats but saw Bowler pointing down the road. "Here comes a little car now. Let's stop and talk to it."

Ned turned in fear and saw an old van approaching them. It was sliding all over the road trying to gain a grip on the snowy surface. Now it was his turn to plead. "Come on, please. We've got to cross now."

"We only want to say hello," Top Hat begged.

"Noooooo! We've got to cross this instant!" Panic rose in Ned now. "We can't afford to be seen and we don't have time to stop a car." He pulled on their coats with all his might, but it was like trying to pull a concrete post out of its foundation.

"It's stopping anyway," Bowler declared gleefully.

The van was too, and even before it slid to a halt up the curb, the driver opened his door, scattering snow violently from off the vehicle. He was so eager to get out of the car that he did not even switch off the engine. It was then that Ned recognised the grey grocer's van and, worse still, Grumpy Giles advancing towards him. The vegetable peddler had done his last delivery and was carefully negotiating the hazardous road home when he noticed Ned. The two large snowmen accompanying Ned were covered up in their hats and overcoats, and to Grumpy they were, he presumed, vengeful parents ready to give the little brat a good hiding. He slapped his cold hands together with delight and strode forwards to give punishment.

"That's it, lads. Hold the little fiend down. He ruined my new shirt this morning and now he's going to pay," Grumpy shouted.

This deranged grocer bent on retribution for a cheap shirt was the last straw for Ned. His legs would not respond to his brain's command to run. They just stood there and shook in the snow. Ned looked at the two snowmen he still had hold of, but they were just smiling at the car. Grumpy was nearly on him when the base instinct for survival took over Ned's befuddled brain. From where it came, he did not know. He did not even recognize his own voice. It was the voice of a drill sergeant howling rage at new recruits, but it was Ned's voice and the order echoed across the park. "ATTACK! ATTACK! ATTACK!" he screamed.

Comic book training took effect instantly: Top Hat and Bowler un-slung pretend rifles, fixed pretend bayonets, screamed an abominable cry as only snowmen can, and charged. Grumpy's legs worked better than Ned's and he turned and tried to run back to his van. He slipped and slid all over the curb and then fell over. He was whimpering in terror as these two immense snowmen came on, approaching fast. The imaginary rifles were leveled at his backside as he scrabbled in the snow, trying desperately to reach the sanctuary of his van. It was fortunate that Grumpy had left the door open and the engine running. He made it to the van, slammed the door shut, slammed the gear stick into first, and stamped his foot down hard on the throttle. The van did not move. Its tyres were spinning helplessly on the compacted snow. They squealed in protest and Grumpy squealed in terror as he started to jump up and down on the seat, trying desperately to help the rubber tread gain purchase. Over this noise, Grumpy's hearing discerned the louder scream of the snowmen's war cry. His brain made him look in the rear-view mirror, and what he saw made him wet his y-fronts. The bayonet charging snowmen filled the mirror and a millisecond later they struck the car. Top Hat and Bowler bounced off the van but their impetus had the desired and fortunate effect for Grumpy. The van shot forwards and managed to grip on the fresh snow.

Ned was struck dumber than Top Hat and Bowler. He stood there not moving and just watched as Grumpy started forwards in the snow. The van gained momentum and in his eagerness to get away, Grumpy still had the accelerator flat out on the floor of the van. He seemed to be transfixed with the road and escape. The van was steadily getting faster and faster. Grumpy was white-knuckled on the steering wheel and panting heavily. The windscreen was misting up but he did not care. He needed to get away from these psychopaths in white and away from that horrible little git. Revenge would have to wait.

Ned saw the van going faster and faster down the road. He saw a sharp bend ahead and expected Grumpy to start slowing down but the van kept accelerating. As it neared the bend, Ned shouted out a warning. But it was too late.

Inside the van, Grumpy suddenly realised he could not see out of the windscreen. He desperately rubbed away the condensation and then saw the bend approaching. Like the captain of a ship trying to avoid an iceberg, he spun the wheel around in his hands. The van carried on forward, not responding to its captain's evasive manoeuvres. It headed towards a large yellow box, but it was the tree behind this that made Grumpy scream. As if trying to escape the terrible scene fastly approaching, he inadvertently looked in the mirror and saw a second bayonet charge coming from behind. Grumpy soaked his pants again as he smashed the yellow box in pieces, then instantly collided with the tree and blacked out. The two snowmen followed suit a millisecond later.

Chapter 10

Ned was horrified. Alright, Grumpy Giles was an old misery guts, but Ned did not want to see him slammed into a tree and gone to greengrocer heaven on his account, and after all, he had ordered the bayonet charge. The van was crumpled against the tree. Smoke and steam poured from the screaming engine into the night. The steam billowed around the car and tree as the engine sang an agonized death chant. It was like the stage show of a cheap heavy metal band before they erupted onto stage. Only, on this forum, the star was hanging out of the van door looking like it was the final curtain instead of the opening act.

Ned ran to the van. He kept to the fresh snow on the curb and avoided slipping over. Top Hat and Bowler got up on unsteady feet. One of Bowler's coal eyes had popped out and he was pushing it back in its socket. Top Hat was examining their 'kill'. It wasn't really their kill but the tree's kill, but they decided to notch it up for themselves. The two snowmen looked at the unconscious figure sprawled over the door. Top Hat picked up a stick from the wounded tree and jabbed at Grumpy. Bowler, blinking and smacking his own head in trying to focus, stood behind and goaded him on, though they both looked ready to run in case Grumpy came around. Then Ned arrived, panting in the freezing air. Bowler came to attention while Top Hat continued to prod.

"Mission accomplished, sir. The enemy is dead," Bowler shouted out. Top Hat turned and acknowledged Ned in silence. He threw the stick away and leaned into the van. He fiddled and fiddled and then cursed and eventually took hold of the seat belt that was holding Grumpy in his seat and tore it from its mountings. Grumpy fell into the snow with a soft thud.

As is part of their nature, which Ned was not so shocked with now, Top Hat kicked Grumpy and quickly ran back to his colleague. Bowler started to giggle. Top Hat did too and swaggered forward to kick again when Ned shoved in front. "Alright, that is enough. Stop that behaviour this instant."

Top Hat stuck his lip out in protest but managed a quick kick before stomping back to a still giggling Bowler.

Ned knelt down over Grumpy. "You two are thugs. The poor old sod might be a misery guts but he doesn't deserve a kick when he's down. And I'm going to put you on a charge if you don't behave."

"But he's dead, ain't he?" Top Hat moaned.

Ned looked down at Grumpy. He certainly looked dead. He did not even seem to be breathing, so Ned felt for a pulse. There was nothing.

"You're gonna have to give him the old hit and miss," Bowler said with an exaggerated cockney accent. Ned ignored him; he was still trying find a pulse when Bowler started again.

"Yeah, if you wanna save his fork and knife, you're gonna have to give him a hit and miss."

Ned turned from the unconscious grocer. He looked at Bowler. "You! Why are you talking cockney jibber-jabber?"

Bowler smiled. "Hit and miss: kiss. Fork and knife: life. You're gonna have to give him the kiss of life."

It was probably the thought of performing the kiss of life on Grumpy that made Ned snap. He forgot his recent attempt at peace and reconciliation. "You with the top hat, hit that idiot now, and that *is* an order."

"Yes, sir!" and Top Hat did, and Bowler went down again like a sack of potatoes.

Ned saw the snowman collapse and suppressed a laugh, but it was only an instant of relief from the present life and death scene. It seemed Grumpy was not breathing, and foul as he was, he needed immediate medical attention. Ned looked at the two-day growth of stubble on Grumpy's chin. He looked at the thin, chapped lips. He looked at the white spittle that was congealed at the corners of the mouth and his stomach convulsed at the thought of offering his young lips to this horror. It looked like a severe case of athlete's foot, only this was on the mouth. Why couldn't they be full, beautiful lips? Why could not this be Simone, he thought. Then he rubbed his face, gulped, shivered, and prepared himself for the kiss of life.

"No tongues," Top Hat sniggered as Ned's lips neared the fungal encrusted maw.

"You shut your mouth you...you..." Ned could not finish. Before the thought of tongues invaded his mind, he took a deep breath and clamped his lips to Grumpy's own.

A tortured taste and image of his grandmother's old and toothless Yorkshire terrier licking him awake one morning when he was a child assaulted his senses. The taste and sensation were putrid. Ned nearly cried as he performed the life-saving action. He closed his eyes tightly to shut out the foulness of it all. He coughed life down the old greengrocer's throat. Then he felt hands on him. They were pulling him away from Grumpy and he thought it was Top Hat. He tried to shove the hands away; he was saving a life, it had to be done no matter how horrible the lips tasted. Ned concentrated on the effort but more was being applied against him, and with an immense shove, Ned was thrown back in the snow.

"Get off me!" Ned cried. "I've got to save his life. It's the least I can do!"

There was a scream and Ned heard another voice. It was muffled by a hand scraping away at its own tongue. "Eeeaaurrch!" Then it cleared. "Where the hell are the gritters? Those lazy good for nothings are safe and warm at home whilst honest decent folk are trying to do a good day's work! These roads need clearing." Grumpy was up and very irate. He looked around to get his bearings, then saw Ned. His eyes rolled in their sockets and he remembered the recent kiss. He spat and spat and he spat again.

Ned saw Grumpy. He had an enormous bruise growing on his forehead. He swayed and staggered and the rolling eyes settled on Ned. A shaking hand pointed at him. "You're a sick boy, you are, a very sick boy!" Then the ungrateful grocer noticed Top Hat, who took off his hat and sun glasses and blew him a kiss. Grumpy's eyes rolled up to the heavens again and he screamed like a baby. He hawked one last almighty spit in Ned's direction and ran off up the road, blaring out to the cold dark night that snowmen were alive and attacking good honest people.

"Flee, flee, flee for your lives!" he ranted. "They're alive! They're alive!" And he disappeared into the darkened night.

Ned turned to look at the van. It was wrecked beyond repair. The steam was at last dissipating into the chill air and the engine that had been screaming in agony was coughing and spluttering, gradually slowing in its asthmatic throes. It managed one last dying choke, then seized up with a bang.

There was silence. Top Hat looked unsure about what had happened. He picked up the stick and with evident unease stepped forward carefully and jabbed at the crumpled bonnet.

"It's dead. You're alright, you've killed it," Ned said tiredly.

A look of utter joy blossomed on Top Hat's face. He punched the air and went over to wake his fallen comrade.

Ned clapped his hands together and sarcastically congratulated the car killing snowman. "Well done, killer. You and your chum are real mean and downright nasty muthas."

Top Hat looked back in obvious elation. "Thanks, mate, but we really wanted to have a chat with this little motor. Do you think it felt any pain when it hit the tree?" He suddenly looked thoughtful. "Maybe we could fix it up and it could come and live with us at the chiller factory. I'm sure Melton would like a top motor like this instead of that flea-bitten old nag he likes to ride on." Ned recalled the donkey he had thrown a snowball at during what seemed to be the beginning of this horrendous nightmare. He looked down at Grumpy's broken old van.

"I don't think Melton would lower himself with this type of model. Anyway, it's scrap now."

Top Hat was not listening. Instead he was slapping Bowler across the face to bring him around. There was a protested groan. It was so cold that Ned suddenly shivered and pulled his coat closer to himself. It must be the coldest night of the year, he thought to himself. Everything around is frozen up and I'm beginning to as well.

Ned looked at Top Hat trying to bring Bowler round. The unconscious snowman was cradled in the other's arm down near the front of the car. Top Hat had given up slapping his friend now and was flicking what appeared to be water onto his face. It had the desired effect as Bowler suddenly lashed out and knocked Top Hat over.

"Oi! I was trying to help, you ungrateful bugger."

"That water bloody stings!" Bowler said hurtfully.

Top Hat flicked his hands quickly and let out a gasp. "Oh yeah, you're right, it does sting." He immediately stuck his mitten hand in his mouth and started to suck.

Ned looked on curiously. The area in front of the wrecked van was free from snow. It had melted. Ned walked over and looked at the broken front end. The torn radiator had poured antifreeze-enriched hot water into the snow but it had run down and out into the middle of the road nowhere near the snowmen. Ned was puzzled but the chilly night brought a clearer vision to his senses. His eyes levelled on the broken yellow box. All around, pinkish lumps of grit had been strewn around the vehicle and they were melting the snow. Ned's mind focused and the cold air cleansed his addled brain.

Top Hat pulled Bowler out of the watery area. "That wet patch is making my arse sting." They both rubbed snow on the areas that stung.

It was grit. Good old salt grit; the stuff that was used to clear the roads of snow. The rough textured hard snow murdering shingle that lorries love to pour out at machine gun velocity across the flurries of a pallid winter wonderland. Ned stared at it. He stared so long that an icicle of dribble started to form on his lower lip. It came to him. This was his answer. This was the weapon with which he would fight Melton Mowbray the Third and all his legions.

*

The two snowmen seemed to have forgotten about their stung posteriors and were rummaging around in the back of the van. There were bangs and crashes and sounds of vegetables being thrown around but Ned was not listening. He was still staring at the grit. It lay there waiting like some weapon of mass destruction for his hands to use. He shivered with a combination of excitement and cold. The temperature had dropped even lower as the evening drew on. He had been wrapped in thoughts and had not noticed the Arctic-like freeze until now. In fact, it was so cold that it was freezing the grit into lumps. Ned picked one up and tested the weight. It was about the right size for throwing and a little heavier than a snowball, but to

Ned, that figured on having a greater range and killing power. He looked at the van and smiled wickedly. Should he ambush the two idiots? After all, they were trapped inside a confined space and the grit ball should act like a hand grenade to a snowman in such an enclosed area. He gulped and exhaled his breath into the air, where it fogged and obscured his vision. "Let's do it!" he thought. Then the air cleared and Top Hat's face was staring at him. Ned jumped back and quickly snatched the grit ball behind his back.

"Look!" Top Hat held up a sack. "We found it in the back of the van." Ned looked in and saw what it was full of.

"Hand grenades," Bowler exclaimed.

"They're potatoes, you buffoon."

Top Hat pulled the sack away. "They ain't! They're going to be our hand grenades for the mission."

Ned was about to give into their immature war game plunder when it came to him. It was the spur of the moment stuff and it had to work, but these two had shown their full repertoire of idiocy. "Get rid of them, they're rubbish hand grenades. I've used them countless times and they're crap." And beckoning them forwards, he brought his hand from around his back and covered the grit ball with his other hand. Ned looked directly at Top Hat and Bowler, then then held his cupped hands up to their faces. "Inside here *is* a real hand grenade."

The two snowmen looked in awe at his hands. Ned opened them slowly.

"Wooooow!" they said together.

Top Hat went to grab it but Ned was too fast. "Ah, ah, ah. You can't touch these yet."

"Why not?"

That got Ned. "Er...er...because...I...I...I've got to arm these. And they're...they're special types of hand grenades...so...so...only officers can arm them and give them out..."

There was silence.

"Okay, sir."

Ned was momentarily lost for words. He looked around. Then Top Hat emptied the sack of potatoes, then handed it to him. "Fill her up then, sir."

"Oh…oh yes…of course." He grabbed the sack and turned to the broken grit box. "Right, you two, stand guard while I fill the bag with these goodies. You know, these little beauties have been banned by the Geneva Confection."

"Is that to do with ice cream?" Bowler asked.

Ignoring him and marvelling at the hard grit balls, Ned continued to fill up the sack with the snowmen's downfall. He giggled and finished the weapon stocking. Sixteen grit balls were inside the sack. There was a huge piece of frozen grit left, and though Ned thought it would impress the snowmen if he told them it was an anti-tank mine, he could imagine the idiots insisting they take it with them and use it, so he didn't mention it and turned, then stood to attention. "Right, let's go to the supermarket and get the fish fingers."

Chapter 11

Because the gritting lorries had not been out, the car park was virtually empty when the trio came into it. A shining neon light announced the supermarket's name and Ned led them over to a bike shed where he called a halt and opened the sack. He had decided on the way there that as he did not have the means to pay for the produce, it was going to have to be a smash and grab raid. Hopefully the two snowmen would be slush by the time it was over.

"Right, stand guard and watch the entrance. I'm going to arm these hand grenades now. Do not touch them until I give the order, and that's an order. Okay?" Bowler and Top Hat nodded. Ned continued, "Now, we haven't got any money so I'm going to have to nick the fish fingers. And while I do, you two distract the security guards by throwing the grenades. It'll cause mayhem and we should be—*we should be*—out before you know it. So stick with me and do as I say. Do not deviate from my orders or Melton will hear about it!"

Two snowmen suddenly looked scared, and Ned wondered whether he should have mentioned the old tyrant's name at such a fateful moment, but they nodded again somberly and waited for his next order.

He took one of the pinkish balls out and held it. This was a prototype rushed into service. He had no time for advanced testing, so it was now or never. Top Hat and Bowler would be the guinea pigs. If the plan worked, then battle could be taken to the fortress and Melton. If it didn't, then…Ned shivered and turned to face them.

"Right, open your pockets. I've armed these and will place them carefully inside your pockets for you to throw when I give the order."

"What's a security guard?" Bowler asked.

"You dumb lump." Top Hat snorted.

"Alright then, you tell me what a security guard is then?" Bowler retorted.

Ned pre-empted the bound to happen argument followed by fisticuffs. "They're people who dress in black uniforms and think they're hard and important." He turned to Bowler. "Right, you first." And the snowman held his pockets open to receive the 'hand grenades'. Ned put four in each pocket. Bowler shivered inadvertently. "Ooooh, they tingle a bit. I can feel them through my pockets."

Ned kept a cool head. "Right, you next." Top Hat held his overcoat pocket open and Ned started to put a grit ball in when suddenly the snowman grabbed Ned's hand. A cold sweat broke out on his forehead and he tried to keep himself from shaking. Top Hat took off his glasses and lifted the grit-balled hand to his face. Before Ned could shout out, Top Hat flicked out his tongue and licked the grit. Ned's body shook with terror but his hand remained steady in Top Hat's strong grasp. The tongue rolled around the mouth like someone sampling an expensive wine. His brow furrowed and he started to utter strange noises. Ned was about to scream when the snowman spat a pinkish globule out into the snow where it sizzled and in response. Then Top Hat uttered appreciatively, "Mmmmmmmh. Mmmmmmmh. Not bad, not bad at all. You're right. It's definitely tingly but with a zesty bouquet and a certain tangy aftertaste. You certainly know your weapons, sir." He let go of Ned, who nearly collapsed with relief in the snow. Top Hat winked at him. "Come on then. Fill me pockets up!"

Ned ordered full disguise from the snowmen; glasses on, scarves pulled up and tight, hats down, and coats buttoned up. They looked highly suspicious but he'd rather have them like that than be more open to scrutiny with their features showing. He also thought that their thick clothing might make them prone to melting under the superstore's bright lights and heating system.

The electric doors parted with a hiss and Ned, with two very large, disguised snowmen, walked into the superstore.

They were facing the fruit and vegetable aisle and to their left was a desk.

"Nine o'clock, it's a security guard. Don't look suspicious," Ned whispered.

Bowler looked around. "I'd say it's about seven thirty really, but these dark nights do half mess your brain up."

"Idiot, I mean to my nine o'clock," Ned nodded towards his left and gestured with eyes to the desk.

Top Hat pulled up his sleeve and looked puzzled. "Where's me watch? Oh yeah, I remember now, I don't have one."

Ned shook his head in exasperation. "Stuff the watch. Come on, follow me and don't mess about. Fish fingers, remember, nothing else!"

The security guard looked at them from over the top of his glasses, stared for a while, and with a look of mild disgust returned to a railway magazine he had pilfered from the news stand. It seemed there were a lot of people in and out of the supermarket today that were wrapped up against the cold. Maybe these two big louts were taking precautions against snow-blindness due to their sunglasses. He didn't care as it was much quieter now and soon he'd be home and playing with his model railway.

Ned led them past potatoes, carrots, parsnips, and other root vegetables. They went past pasta, rice, and tinned fruit. He looked quickly behind to see if the snowmen were still with him. There were and were looking in awe at the tins. Both had their mouths open and were dribbling with delight as they walked behind Ned. People, the few that were still shopping, gave the strange trio a wide berth.

On they went along the middle section of the aisles, past milk, past cat food, past special offers and 'buy one get two free', until they came to the frozen food section. Ned did not pause as he went down the long cabinets that were full of frozen lamb, chicken, pizzas, and pies. He saw a sign that told him he was approaching the fish section. Increasing his pace, Ned turned his head slightly so he could see the reflections of the snowmen following behind him in the glass fronted freezers. They were looking in the freezers and commenting to each other on how nice the food looked, but they were still following closely. Ned caught sight ahead of the scampi section. His heartbeat rose and he could feel his heart resounding in his chest. Then he was past and onto the prawns. He stole a glance at the snowmen. They were still talking and with him. Shrimps and fish cakes were at his side now, and there ahead, blazoned with a gigantic special offer sign sticking out over the centre of the aisle, were the fish fingers. Ned walked past it and held his breath. He stole another look at the glass and to his horror saw the snowmen had stopped directly under the sign. Bowler was looking around as if lost but Top Hat was pointing at Ned. "Where the hell are these bloody fish fingers?"

Heart in his mouth, he could not speak for a second and thought that Top Hat was having a laugh at his expense, but then Bowler confirmed that these two snowmen were truly and utterly brainless. "We've been here hours," he whined. In fact, they had been in the supermarket for less than five minutes. "I'm bored and cold and I want to go home."

Some suicidal instinct tried to make Ned point above their heads and announce that the fish fingers were right next to them but he bit his fingers and the hand shot into his pocket in protest. Ned collected his strained thoughts. "We're nearly there and we'll have lots of fish fingers soon." A fine smell of freshly baked bread wafted up the aisle and made his mouth water. "In fact, it's just down here where the fish fingers are made."

And there, at the end of the aisle, was what he had been looking for. Ned had smelt the gorgeous aroma before he had seen it. The bakery was in front of him, so he turned, smiled at the two snowmen, and, putting on as brave a face as he could, beckoned them forwards. "Well, here we are then. This is where the fishy fingers are made."

At the thought of their goal being so near, Top Hat and Bowler hurried forward. They took in all the assortments of bread, rolls, and cakes. Bowler's eyes settled on a basket of French sticks. The coal eyes seemed to bulge in wonder. "Cor! We really could conquer the world with fingers like that!" He went to grab one but Ned stopped him. "Remember, we're here to get loads of fish fingers, not one or two. Now follow me and do as I say."

Ned went past the trays and shelves of bread and as Bowler went to follow him, Top Hat pulled him back. Ned stopped too. He looked at the snowmen in exasperation, hiding the terror welling up inside. "Well…what are you waiting for?"

Top Hat pulled his scarf away from his head. "It's bloody boiling in here. I'm starting to feel a bit flaccid."

Ned thought quickly. "Look, no one said it was going to be easy. This is special ops we're talking about. You two should be used to the risks."

"Yeah, but how are we gonna get all them big fish fingers out of here without alerting the security?" Bowler asked.

From the corner of his eye, Ned saw the security guard passing the top of the aisle. He had not noticed the incursion into the bakery, but it would not be long unless Ned got these two oafs out of sight. He would have to hurry if this was going to work. "You just come on in here where we can't be seen and I'll get the fish fingers."

Top Hat was mopping his brow but then seemed to calm down. "Alright, but hurry up, and I want you to tell Melton how brave I was." Ned nodded. "And me too," added Bowler. He nodded again, then pulled them into the bakery.

There was flour everywhere, it covered the stainless steel tables and tiled walls. It was like there had been a snowstorm in the place, but it had the effect of making the snowmen feel a lot more at ease. Ned looked around for the bakers but they seemed to have disappeared. There was a flour-covered swing door and someone had written into the flour '**Men hard at work. Do not disturb**'. He walked over and rubbed away flour that covered the glass window. Inside there were indeed men but they were not hard at work. Three of them were asleep; two in chairs and one curled up in what appeared to be a dog's basket. Two more were drinking from cans and playing cards. Ned ducked down, scanned the bakery, and quickly found what he was looking for. Near the back were two big ovens that were roasting away. By the entrance they had just come in through he noticed a yellow pallet truck pulled up against the wall. Perfect.

He closed his eyes and prepared himself for action. Top Hat and Bowler were skidding about in the flour and making car noises. Ned gulped. "Let the mayhem begin," he muttered to himself, then startled the snowmen by shouting at them and pointing to the ovens. "Arm yourselves and wait behind those two big things. I'm going for fish fingers and I want covering fire when I retreat." Top Hat and Bowler took off their sunglasses and adjusted their hats. "Woo-ha, woo-ha," the battle cry sounded, and, slapping mitten hands together, they ran behind the ovens. Ned scrabbled to a sink. He rummaged around underneath and found an old mop and ran the hot water tap until it boiled and soaked the mop head. It steamed in the bakery's interior and Ned balanced it under his right arm. Then, like a knight readying himself for a joust, he ran for the door. He hit it full on and it swung inwards. The noise woke the sleeping bakers and the card players looked up to see who had disturbed their game. "Get back to work, you good for nothing lazy buggers!" Ned screamed at them, then threw the mop at the two card players.

The soggy weapon hit the two men and knocked them back off their chairs. The others looked gobsmacked but recovered quickly and roared foul oaths at Ned, who gave them the two-fingered salute, turned on his heels, and ran out of the room. Into the bakery Ned skidded in the flour and shouted, "Security guards coming. Covering fire!" Bowler came from behind the ovens. His movements were slower than usual and Ned could hear the distinct sound of squelching. The door burst open behind him and five angry bakers piled out. Bowler reached into his pockets, ready to throw his grenades. He raised his arm and then, to his horror, saw that the grit ball grenade was melting it. He pulled the other hand out and saw the same thing happening. Panic and dread made him scream out and he tried to escape but the five bakers were forming a line and running at him. They collided with a squishy slap but the snowman carried on moving forwards and fell into a huge stack of fresh crusty rolls. The bakers were strewn across the floor. They were dazed, but one brave fellow managed to get up and crawl to the ovens. One of the card playing bakers shouted out to him, "Hurry, Dennis. For pity's sake, we can't let the fairy cakes burn!" The concussed baker slapped his hand on the door release before fainting. The burst of heat that came from the oven singed Ned's eyebrows. The bakers were on the floor so they missed most of the blast but poor Bowler took the full discharge of heat. He appeared to go translucent, then lose all rigidity. His coal eyes sagged in their sockets and his carrot nose wilted. He had no arms by this stage, only water dripping from the ends of his empty sleeves. But still he tried to walk forward and escape, but the crusty rolls made his feet slip and slide and trip. Bowler tried to balance himself by waving his arms but he had no arms. The sleeves of his coat flapped uselessly like a young fledgling trying to fly for the first time. His unbalanced momentum drove him forwards into the path of the oven. Trip, stumble, slip; the snowman's last trip was over the unconscious baker, and then Bowler fell into the oven. There was a sizzle and a bang and the smell of burning vegetable and clothes filled the air.

Ned looked on in awe. He had inadvertently killed Bowler. Inside he wanted to shout out in triumph, but then he realised that Top Hat was still lurking in the bakery.

A voice boomed out from behind the other oven. "You foul little rat. You've duped us and killed my comrade." Out stepped a very angry Top Hat. His coal eyes narrowed down and he pointed at Ned. "And now I'm going to pull your head off and give it to Melton as a trophy. Come here, little boy."

Others would have cowered, but Ned had gained a first victory [Note: The snowman whose face Ned had slammed the barred door into was not dead but had required a new head transplant performed, under local anaesthetic, by Melton] and the courage of that deed burst forth from Ned. "Not by the hair on my chinny chin chin, you lump of wazz-stained lush." And then he ran.

Top Hat grabbed at him, but Ned was quicker and more solid as the heat had taken effect on the snowman in a similar way to Bowler. His movements were slow and where his melting feet touched the floor, the coating of flour was making him stick partly to the now doughy surface. He wrenched his feet from step to step and then noticed one of the bakers coming to. Top Hat leant down and went to grab him but his mitten hand just squelched over the man's face. Duty and military training were instilled in this snowman, and even though they had failed the mission, the snowman still tried to complete it with some kind of victory. "Where are your fishy fingers?" he asked the baker.

"Get off me with them wet hands. This is a bakery, you know, not a toilet. We clean our hands, then dry them off so no germs get in our mix. Fishy fingers? You mean fish fingers. They're not in here, you big oaf. Try aisle seventeen. Look just down there," the kindly baker replied. Top Hat tapped the baker in a friendly but wet manner and tried to squelch out of the bakery. Ned was out and ahead of Top

Hat. The quest for fish fingered information by the snowman had cost Top Hat time and Ned took it. He had pulled the yellow pallet truck across the entrance in an effort to further slow his pursuer but Top Hat, in a last great effort of strength and solidity, picked up the truck and threw it over the bread stands straight in the direction of Ned.

He heard the crash of metal and before he could look around, the pallet truck had caught Ned in the back on his knees. He was pitched forwards into a neatly stacked pile of baked bean cans. They collapsed all over the floor and covered Ned to his shoulders. Small bruises were erupting from Ned's head but he took no notice of them. What he did take notice of was Top Hat exiting the bakery and coming for him. Trying to extract himself from the mountain of bean cans had the same effect on Ned as the rolls did on Bowler; he could not get his balance and kept falling back down. The clean floor aided Top Hat's steps now that the flour had gone. He knew he was melting and had turned partly transparent in the bright lights of the supermarket, but he willed himself on. If it was the last thing he did then he was going to pull the boy's head off. After that, if he was still complete, then he would get out into the cold dark night and re-freeze and become whole again.

Ned sat down and started throwing cans at the oncoming snowman. Squirts of water spat out of Top Hat where the cans hit him but it was like fending off a bear with rubber balls. Top Hat roared an abominable cry and from around the corner came Mrs Backhouse, a kindly old spinster from Ned's estate. She had braved the weather to get her shopping done while it was quiet. A taxi was waiting outside and had its meter running so Mrs Backhouse was conscious that she had to do a reasonably quick shop or else the taxi fare would be extortionate. One more thing to collect and that was her shop done. Baked beans were around this aisle, she remembered, and that was the last on the list. When she turned the corner, she was presented with a small boy covered in baked bean cans and a very large hoodlum bearing down on him. She had once worked in the military and kept a keen and close eye on all legal and illegal weaponry available to the discerning retired public citizen. Her niece had taught her many new things in modern technology and she had ordered her latest gadget over the internet and now was desperate to try it out.

Top Hat was nearly on Ned. He raised a dripping foot, ready to stamp on the bruised head that had so foully deceived him. Mrs Backhouse opened her handbag and deployed her weapon.

"Say goodbye, little boy!" Top Hat shouted. Ned looked up defiantly, readying himself for the boot. But then he saw two thin pieces of wire stick into the snowman's body. Top Hat saw them and went to pull them out. There was a loud crack and bang, then Top Hat disappeared. One second the snowman was there and the next he was not.

The 50,000 volt charge from Mrs Backhouse's Taser gun had simply vapourized the snowman in an instant. A sheen of microscopic watery mist hung in mid-air like an ethereal cloud. The coal eyes and carrot nose had survived the electric charge and momentarily floated in midair as if defying gravity, then with a soft swish, Top Hat's coat and scarf landed at Ned's feet. His nose and eyes followed quickly.

Ned quickly gathered that he was alive and that Top Hat was not. Someone screamed and he heard the sound of lots of footsteps getting louder. He calmly got up, walked over to Mrs Backhouse, took her hand, and kissed it gently. Then ran as fast as he could out into the night.

Part 2

Chapter 12

In comparison to his earlier adventures, the journey to Ned's house was uneventful. He left the supermarket in uproar, managing to avoid security and the general public. Outside, he quickly disappeared into the darkened side streets and cut a path through the icy streets to the race course and the direction home.

No one, or the very few that were out, took any notice of him. As Ned neared the road that led to his estate, a taxi passed him and he saw an old lady wave at him as the vehicle went by. It slowed and eventually slid to a halt at a perpendicular angle to the road.

The door opened and Ned peered in. Mrs Backhouse peered back. "Would you like a lift, young man?" she asked in a warbling frozen voice. Ned was quite taken aback. This kind old lady was offering him a lift. She had just saved his life, she had confronted an enormous maniac who would—it seemed—have done her mischief and certainly stomped him to jelly, and she had zapped the brute into nothing. All of which she seemed to be taking incredibly calmly.

"Errr...no thank you, it's very kind of you but it is rather a lovely night and I'd prefer to walk, if it's all the same to you," Ned said.

Mrs Backhouse smiled back. "Not at all, young man." And with that, she slammed the door and the taxi skidded off down the road.

Ned put his hands to his mouth and shouted, "And thanks for saving my life back there." Even though it was receding, Ned saw the hand come up again and wave.

He arrived at his street ten minutes later. Snow was churned up on the road and pavement and outside his door it was mashed up as if there had been some kind of fight.

In hope, Ned looked up at the house and expected to see the lights glowing lowly and the television's reflection flickering against the curtains. But there were no lights on, nor any TV. They were not on because his mum and dad were not home; they were captives. The kicked over snow was evidence of a struggle that had gone on. Ned was proud of the messed up snow, as it proved Mum and Dad had not gone down without a fight. He felt a surge of terrible guilt, but it was now tempered with a resolve to fight the dastardly snowmen and get his parents back. He had his weapon, and had he not destroyed two snowmen? Well, no, he had not, the kind old lady had Tasered one into oblivion, but Ned was confident now that he could have killed Top Hat. As he went to the front door, he realised that he did not have his keys with him. So he retraced his steps and headed around the back of the house. Here, the snow was still fresh and unspoiled, and he saw that it had drifted conveniently high against his garden wall. Legs accelerating, Ned ran up the slope only to fall through it with a yelp. He tangled his legs and head in something and, lifting himself up, shook the snow off to find his limbs entangled in a half-dead clematis plant and a broken trampoline. Cursing himself for kicking it over the wall earlier, Ned managed to extract himself from the plant and metal snare. By using the trampoline as a ladder, he climbed over the wall and landed softly in the garden. Immediately, his newfound military senses kicked in, and stooping down—like the former snowmen, Top Hat and Bowler—scanned the garden for danger. There was the sound of revelry, a cat meowed and an owl hooted, but the garden was in itself silent so Ned scampered to the back door. Though he had no keys on him, Ned knew that there was a spare back door key in the hanging basket next to the door. He stretched his legs to the limit and, fumbling in the snow, eventually found the frozen key.

As he returned to a normal stature, Ned's stomach growled in protest. It had not been fed in how long? He could not remember and, entering the kitchen, it howled in protest. It had to be instant. No microwaving, no frying, no boiling, no roasting. His mind in overdrive for nourishment, Ned dropped the keys and then threw himself at the kitchen cupboards. Seconds later he had his meal: nine stale wheat biscuits and a tin of cold tomato soup. Mushing it up, Ned drank the viscous slop eagerly. To anyone else it would be utterly disgusting, but food, in whatever form or matter, gives sustenance and moreover, sustenance helps the mind to think clearly. He finished it with a loud belch and wiped his chin in satisfaction. When this was all over, Ned mused, he must make this delicious meal for his parents. Then he sunk a carton of cranberry juice and went outside again to his dad's shed.

The door was from an old toilet and stained with age. Ned's dad had decided to make the shed himself after watching too many do-it-yourself TV programmes. The project was funded on virtually nothing apart from what his dad could find in the back alleys and the skips around the town. The shed roof was a mixture of old asphalt felt, plastic sheet, and bin liners. An old frosted window from another toilet was the only glazing and during daytime it only let in a miserable trickle of distorted light. Still, Mr Mutton was very proud of his shed and had put it up for a sustainable build award with the local authority. Needless to mention really, it did not win.

Ned pulled on the door handle. It was stiff. In fact, it felt like it was glued shut. He heaved again but the door did not move. Grabbing the handle in both hands, Ned shuffled up the door, eventually spread-legged with one on each doorframe and squatting so that his legs were level with his hands. With that, he pulled at the handle with all his might. It remained shut. He persisted, and sweating and cursing and yanking and kicking with one foot, he pulled and he pulled and he pulled. His face was going purple and veins were pulsing madly on his forehead.

"Come on! Come on! Come on, you piece of crap!" he cried. Then, with the shed shaking like a leaf, something fell on his head and landed in the snow. Ned frowned and suddenly his legs gave way and he landed in the snow. A plant pot was on its side and spewed just outside the rim was something long and slightly rusty looking. Ned reached down and picked up a key. He then smacked himself on the head, called himself something foul and obscene, and unlocked the door.

With the lock released, the contents of the shed erupted out of the opened door. Paint pots, garden tools, boxes, tubes of glue, old furniture, and an exceedingly heavy wheelbarrow engulfed Ned.

To some art critic the pile of detritus could have been entered for a prize, and when the hand suddenly punched its way through like a periscope then the critics would be unanimous in their applause. Ned didn't think much of art and even less at that moment about his father's storage skills. But fate seemed to be on Ned's side, for as he pulled himself from the mess, four things that he required rolled off or banged down in front of his feet: empty cardboard boxes, a large tub of glue, a rusty shovel, and, finally, the wheelbarrow. Silence followed the crashing noise. No cat meowed or owl hooted. No hooligan called. The silence was absolute and Ned craned his head to the myriad of stars where one suddenly sparkled brighter than all the others and he took that as a sign from the heavens that destiny awaited.

The wheelbarrow was left outside with the shovel, glue, and boxes in it. Ned shut the back door behind him and walked through the kitchen to the dining room. As he walked across to switch the light on, his foot kicked something across the carpet. Thinking nothing of it, as his mother and father's and his tidying skills amounted to nothing, he carried on across the carpet. But as he reached the bottom of the stairs, he kicked something else that sounded plastic and hollow. Curiosity aroused, he scanned the floor as he switched on the light.

The dining room was as expected in the Mutton household; table and chairs covered with books, newspapers, opened letters, etc., etc. The carpet was usually kept clear, but what Ned saw was unusual in the sense that there were two empty ice cream cartons lying there.

Now, Mutton Senior loved ice cream, he adored ice cream, he would not give up ice cream. Every other food Mr Mutton could take or leave, but ice cream was his addiction, his Achilles heel. He would not compromise on ice cream. He simply had to have it. But in doing so, he would eat it with a sense of class, he would indulge every minute's worth of flavor. He even had a special bowl, or chalice—as he called it—to serve the ice cream in. Ned would watch in disgust as his father would sit down in front of the TV or at the table studying one of his beloved plastic models and ladle the ice cream on a spoon and then suck it off loudly. After his father had finished slurping the divine nectar, he would take the bowl/chalice, wash it, dry it, polish it, then put it away in the cupboard. And he would never ever eat ice cream directly from the tub. He once told Ned in a moment of ice cream sincerity that to dine directly from the tub was the height of revulsion.

Well now, sitting there on the carpet were two examples of revulsion. Ned knew in his heart that his father would never do this. So what were the two empty tubs doing there? It would not be his mum. She would not touch the stuff for fear of gaining poundage. But there they were.

As Ned bent down to study the tubs, a terrible sound erupted from upstairs. It sounded like a cross between a wail and a foghorn, and the sound was so loud that it shook the framed paintings on the wall.

Thinking it was an earthquake, he grabbed the stair banister. The sound subsided. Then it came in again with an added intensity. There was no dishonour in his next action. He ran from the house, grabbed the shovel, and waited outside the back door. The sound receded, then came on again in gale force decibels. Once, a long time ago, Ned had stayed at his dad's sister's house. She was called Aunty Bill. Why she was called Bill, he did not know, and now was not the time to ponder that, but she had a terrible affliction that kept Ned awake at night. She snored like a hog and the sound he now heard brought that all back to him. It was snoring he was hearing. The relief he felt was palatable but was immediately replaced by fear that someone was snoring in his house and it was not his parents. The dread turned to anger, then rage, and Ned turned on his feet and entered the house again. He kept the shovel in his hand as a weapon, then walked through the dining room and started up the stairs.

They creaked and groaned, but the loud snoring effectively deadened the stair's protest. Not wanting to alert the snorer, Ned left the landing light off, relying on the illumination from the light in the dining room to light his way. He tested the weight of the shovel. It felt good in his hands and he was prepared to use it. In fact, it gave him more courage knowing that he had a heavy weapon in his hands, and so he continued up the stairs.

Tippy-toeing but ready to cause grievous harm, Ned climbed on. Then his eyes fell on another empty food carton on the step above his left foot. He bent down in the dim light and his eyes focused on an empty packet of fish fingers.

Weird, Ned thought. Who would want fish fingers and ice cream as a meal? Then he stopped and the sudden horror dawned on him. "Oh no. No, no, no. It can't be. Surely it can't be?"

His breath became quicker. His heartbeat accelerated and, readying the shovel, he kicked the fish finger packet down the stairs and stepped upwards. His hands shook as he put down the shovel and waited for the next snore. It came suddenly and in the narrow landing sounded like a constipated elephant straining in agony. The horrendous roar was coming from his parent's room on the right. Ned gulped and, picking up the shovel again, he brandished it like a war axe. With his other hand, he turned the handle and craned his head to peer into the room.

The small bedside lamp revealed a figure slouched on his side, fast asleep with mouth open wide. It was a snowman. Ned crept into the room ready to bring the shovel down. The slumbering snowman turned over on the bed and tried to suck his thumb. Ned smiled as he recognised Heinrich. His smile quickly vanished as he saw what sort of thumb Heinrich was trying to suck. It was a fish finger thumb. Heinrich also had four other digits in the shape of fish fingers protruding from his hand. He had not eaten them with ice cream at all but had tried to fit the fish fingers into a rudimentary hand. It was not a good job at all; in fact, it was a dreadful job. The fish fingers stood out at acute angles. One was broken, another was crushed, and another stood out like an erect forefinger, as if in the throes of an obscene gesture. The other hand suddenly came up and Ned saw it was even worse with only one complete finger; the others were broken and crushed. In fact, there were remnants of fish finger all over the bed.

The horror of this attempted DIY surgery made Ned pause, but his subconscious made him lift the shovel/axe ready to strike. It seemed Heinrich was having a nightmare. He had moved over to his front and the snoring had stopped, only to be replaced by groaning and moaning. Then the snowman started to talk in his sleep, then shout out, "Melton", "kill", "swine", "poo", and "pants". Then Heinrich screamed out, "ICE CREAM SUNDAES!" The blood nearly froze in Ned's veins. He went to swing the shovel/axe at Heinrich's head, but the snowman suddenly went silent and rolled on his side. Where he had been laying before was a piece of screwed up paper with what seemed like writing on it.

Again, Ned's curiosity got the better of him and he leant over the bed, trying not to make the floor boards creak. As he balanced carefully over Heinrich, the snowman let out an explosive fart right in Ned's face. His survival instinct kicked in with his finger and thumb closing over his nose. Ned even shut his eyes. The trump was loud, long, and rather wet. But at this moment of heightened tension, Ned could not help but start to giggle. He bit his teeth together in order to stop but then realised that he could not breathe with his mouth closed. He must stop giggling, but he could not. He must breathe, but he could not without taking his fingers and thumb from his nose. Heart pumping in his chest and face turning blue, Ned had little choice; he opted to breathe in through his nose. It was a dreadful mistake. He nearly fainted from the smell and the lining of his nasal passages blistered from the gaseous attack. The volatile mixture of five different flavoured ice creams and whatever else snowmen eat released in a confined space was too much. It certainly stopped Ned from giggling. His head swam as he snatched the piece of paper and staggered. He dropped the shovel loudly and slammed into the door, not caring what noise he made as he tried to exit the room and breathe pure, uncorrupted air. Heinrich slept on without a stir and Ned made it to the middle of the stairs before he took another deep breath. After a minute his breathing stabilized, and Ned listened for any signs of the stinky snowman stirring. It seemed that all was quiet, and, deciding he was safe, Ned flattened out the piece of paper and tried to read it. What was scrawled on there looked like drunken hieroglyphics but as Ned slowly read them he could just decipher the appalling writing. The smell from the bedroom was creeping down the stairs so he descended to the living room and sat at the table, where he extracted a pencil and paper from the drawer. Like some master code breaker at work, Ned wrote down in his own hand writing what the note said:

VERY IMPORTANT NOTICE

Idiot, read this and memorise it. I have tried umpteen times to explain to you and still you do not understand, so read this slowly and properly and when you have finally understood it, destroy this message. You can eat it if you want but make sure the message it destroyed.

My special-forces snowmen have the fleshy swine in their keeping. He (the fleshy swine) is to get the fishy fingers and bring them back to me at the fortress. But he (the fleshy swine) is a devious and wicked boy and I do not trust him. He (you should know who I mean by now) may try to dupe the two special-forces snowmen and escape. I do not want any bother with the law and if they come within a mile of the fortress I will make his parents into ice-lollies. So, to be sure, this is where you come into the scheme of things.

Follow the simple instructions below and you may return to the fortress for fishy fingers and a big kiss from me. Deviate from these instructions and you are slush. So here we go again:

*If the fleshy swine comes back to his house **without** my special-forces snowmen but **with** the fishy fingers then pull his head off and return to the fortress immediately with the said fishy fingers.*

*If the fleshy swine comes back to his house **without** the special-forces snowmen and **without** the fishy fingers then pull his head off anyway. The little swine has broken his word and I will ice lolly his parents.*

If the fleshy swine does not come back to the house then wait until the morning (that is when the big yellow ball is back in the sky) and return to me at the fortress.

If he keeps his word then I am going to turn him into ice lolly anyway, and his parents, come to that. By chance, if you find any fishy fingers in the house you are not to attempt any form of self-grafting as you are a complete idiot.

*One last point: **Do not**, I repeat, **do not** under any circumstances eat ice cream if you find it in the house. If you so much as have a lick I will slush you, Heinrich. Leave it alone and do not touch it. I do not want you drunk on duty and ice cream makes you drunk as a lord, so **do not** eat any!!!*

If you disobey any of these instructions I will have you slowly slushed. I do hope I make myself absolutely clear.

Obliged,
Melton Mowbray the Third

Ned let out a long breath. So Melton was going to do him in anyway, fish fingers or no fish fingers. What a deceitful old bugger, he thought. It did not occur to Ned's wounded pride that Melton suspected him of doing exactly what he was doing anyway. The note was screwed into a ball and thrown across the room. Ned stood. "Right, no more Mr Nice Guy. The gloves are off and it's unconditional warfare from now on!"

In the kitchen he fumbled in a drawer and found an old clothes peg. Ned clipped it over his nose and ascended the stairs to his parents' bedroom. Opening the door carefully, he peered in, seeing Heinrich still asleep on his mum and dad's bed. A tiny part of him admired Heinrich for completely disobeying Melton's instructions and going for it. The snowman was out of his brains on ice cream and damaged fish fingers but he could still be dangerous if woken up. Needs must, and Ned was not going to have his head pulled off by a sloshed snowman, so he entered the room and quietly walked over to the other side of the bed. His fingers searched for something under the side of the bed and in a few seconds he found it. His parents loved their bed, come spring, summer, and autumn they loved lying down on its elegant covers and wonderful mattress. Winter made it cosier, and to add to that, Ned's mum had purchased an electric blanket to keep the bed a comfortable heat in the chill months of the colder climate. Their son now found the controls for the electric blanket in his hand and turned the dial to the hottest setting. That done, he leaned over Heinrich and whispered in the snowman's ear, "Sweet dreams, fart arse." Then he picked up the shovel, took the key from inside the lock, walked out of the room, and locked the door from the landing.

*

At about this time, a military operation was being planned by Beetie in his ops room at Stalingrad Towers. Over the bureau, a map was spread out and Beetie was studying it. Behind him and standing on a chair sipping a cocktail was Fabian. He had his pipe out and was pointing to parts of the map and growing excited.

"Yes, Father, at military studies we re-enacted the Fifth Punic war. Of course, I was Hannibal and the headmaster was Scippio or some Roman corporal chap or some ghastly thing. But he thought he could beat me! When I said I have the lineage of the Vaughan-Abbotts flowing through my veins he very nearly soiled his gusset and buggered off without so much as a doff of the forelock. I tell you, Pater, there's no class these days."

Beetie ignored Fabian and continued to pore over the map. He looked up after a while and withdrew a pocket watch from his waistcoat. His brow creased, then he shouted out irritably, "Where the hell's that loafer Crichton?" Fabian nearly fell off his chair and, in doing so, managed to spill pipe tobacco down his father's neck. It was Fabian's turn to nearly soil his pants but Beetie merely brushed at the irritation and bellowed again about the whereabouts of his batman. As if in answer, there was a knock at the door and a cough.

"Damn and blast, woman, can't you see I'm planning a military campaign!" Beetie exploded.

"Father, I, er...I think it's..." Fabian tried to interject.

Beetie cut him off. "Shut up, boy! It's that damnable woman who professes to be my wife!"

There was another gentle knock at the door. This time, Beetie did not retort. He stomped over to the door and yanked it open. "Hell, woman, can't you hear your master—" He stopped, grunted, turned, and walked back to the map. Crichton was in the doorway. He leaned into the room but waited at the door.

"Well, don't just stand there like a sissy, get in here and show us what you've got!" Beetie shouted.

Crichton entered the room, shut the door, and walked over to the table. With shaking hands, he emptied the contents of two bags over the map. Beetie tutted loudly but gave no further verbal assault.

"Well, did you get them?" the beetroot head erupted.

Crichton doffed a half-dozen forelocks in Beetie's direction. "If it pleases you, sir...I...I got three suits, sir."

Beetie beamed. "Well, well done, my lowly slave."

Crichton did not smile or take the offered praise, and Beetie took this as suspicious. "Tell me, Crichton, you did get what was tasked to you, didn't you?"

The manservant gulped quickly and coughed. "My lord, I did get three...only one is...is a female outfit." He backed towards the door as he finished the sentence.

Beetie's eyes swiveled menacingly. "You did what?"

A high-pitched stammer came out of Crichton's mouth. "I did...I did as...as you told me, my lord, but they had leased the last male outfit and rather than come home short I thought that three would be better than two...if you take my meaning...sir?"

Beetie snatched up what was lying over his map and studied them. He held them up to the light for a long time, then threw one on his chair, one towards his son, and the last violently at Crichton. "You can wear the girly outfit. It'll be befitting to a ponce like you." Crichton caught it and proffered thanks with another doffing of forelock. Beetie walked to the door and opened it. "Now get out of my ops room, the both of you. I need to plan a rescue mission. We meet back here at 22:00 hours, and woe betide any of you if you're late, because if you are I'll tan your hides with the Baron." Crichton ran from the room, followed quickly by Fabian.

Beetie slammed the door, then walked back to the table. He got a pair of dividers out from a drawer and walked them across the map whilst muttering to himself. This went on for some time. Then he folded the map up, poured himself an obscenely large gin and tonic, and sat down heavily in his chair. He seemed to be brooding to himself and was deep in thought. With a quick tip of the glass he finished off the drink and ran his hand along the underside of the bureau until he felt something. His hand squeezed a hidden button and with a sharp crack a secret drawer opened. Beetie smiled and produced an old Smith and Wesson .45 pistol. It was gun-metal in colour and dully shone in the room's light. He released the catch and spun the empty bullet chamber. It whirled in his hand, then came to a halt. Beetie held the gun pistol barrel up to the light and squinted through it. Satisfied it was spotless, he reached in the drawer and extracted a case. From this, he deftly loaded six bullets into the chambers, then snapped the pistol shut. He stood and pointed the gun at the mirror. In the reflection he smiled. "And bang, you're all dead!"

Chapter 13

Meanwhile, Ned was organizing too. He had left the snowman Heinrich to cook on a slow heat and was trying to make his way through the dining room door with the wheelbarrow. It had come through the back door no trouble but when he had slammed the door shut it seemed narrower. He heaved and pushed and kicked, wood creaked and splintered, but he finally managed to shove it through into the hallway. He pushed it towards the front door and then climbed over it so as to open the front door. Ned felt the chilly air and reached out for a coat from the coat rack. He grabbed one at random and threw it into the wheelbarrow, then heaved and pulled it through the door. Wood splintered and cracked again but with a sudden slip backwards, Ned landed on his backside in the snow. The wheelbarrow smacked him on the forehead and he let out a curse, but he was outside with his equipment and his rescue plan was about to start. Pulling the door shut and hearing the lock engage, he set off down the quiet street.

Wheelbarrow in hands, he suddenly remembered that he had better bring a present, as it was near to the time of good will to all men. So he parked the barrow and ran back to the house and searched for his keys. They were not in his pocket because he had not put them there and the spare set were in the lock inside the door. Ned swore again and wondered how he was to get the gift he so badly needed. The plan did not really hinge on this but during his disgraceful time working for Beetie on dodgy building projects he knew that a little added bribe could go a long way. Unfortunately, the bribe he was looking for was in the kitchen cupboard. He ran around the back of the houses again and managed to scale the wall and land with a splat in the yard. Slipping his way to the door, he turned the handle and pushed. It was locked too. Ned swore a third time and kicked the door a few times. Then he stopped. What if the neighbours heard him and called the law, thinking it was a break in? Worse, what if he woke up that drunken sop Heinrich and the idiot came down and pulled his head off? Ned pondered this for a while, then remembered that roughly five years ago his dad had attempted to make some homemade whiskey from potatoes. The experiment had lasted a month and at the end his dad had ten and a half bottles of evil-smelling clear liquid that swam around the bottles like a weapon of mass destruction awaiting to be let loose on an unsuspecting public. Ned recalled a summer's day when his dad happily started to decant a bottle in some plastic glasses; they immediately melted when the liquid touched them. Not perturbed, his dad then tried real glasses, but the first one shattered. After that he put the bottles away, but Ned's mum had used the liquid to clean out a blocked drain and scrub the patio clean. She also had the ingenious idea of stripping 100-year-old paint from the doors in the house. It came off like the skin of a well-barbequed fish, even though there were twenty-three layers of paint that had accumulated over the years. Ned had even heard that a man from the Ministry of Defence called around to see his parents. He had introduced himself as a major in the Bio-Weapons division and had heard a rumour that certain weapons-grade material was being stored in the town. After that, his dad had got rid of the other bottles apart from one that Ned saw his mum shove under a pile of old paint pots in the shed. It was there that Ned now went to, and after a quick scrabble about, his hand moved something that sounded like liquid swashing about. Eagerly, Ned grabbed the bottle and pulled it out. Attached to it was what looked like a very large rat. He screamed and ran into the corner of the shed. Ned looked at the rat but it did not move. He then thought his scream might have awoken Heinrich or alerted the neighbours, so he sat still and waited. There was no sound, so he summoned his courage and looked down at the rat. He could see a thick set of hair, four legs, a snout, but no movement. He found a bamboo pole and jabbed the thing. The rat did nothing. Ned let out a sigh and walked forward. He kicked it again, just in case, then side-kicked it into the yard. He grabbed the bottle and exited the shed.

    Curiosity got the better of him before he scampered over the wall and he went back and gingerly picked up the rat. It seemed to be stuck to a piece of wood. Ned's brow furrowed in question. He held the hairy object to the light and recoiled to see a mangy Yorkshire terrier staring back at him with black bead-eyes. He chuckled, remembering the rat dog his Aunty Bill had. When she passed on she had insisted that when the dog passed on it was to be stuffed and left to Ned. He did not ponder on why he had been left a taxidermied rat dog at the time and he did not now. There were far more important things to worry about. Ned threw the stuffed dog back into the shed and, bottle in hand, scaled the wall.

Four men stood around a burning oil drum warming their hands. The wood spat, fire fairies flew into the dark night, and the men talked of rebellion. Whenever people need something desperately there seems to be a shortage of it. Or someone decides that there should be a shortage of it. It was on this winter's day that salt grit was needed to clear roads, paths, and drives, but the council drivers who manned the trucks that spread the salt had voted to go on strike. Workers' rights had dictated that better working conditions and better pay were needed. So, in the age-old case of strike whilst the iron is hot and inconvenience people everywhere in the town, they had chosen to down tools just as the first snowflakes had started to fall.

"Here, I had some ponce this morning coming up to me telling me I was a no good red and I should be shot!" one of them bemoaned to the rest.

"Oh yeah, I saw him in his tweed suit and wellies. He's a doctor or something." Another scratched his chin and stoked the fire. "Or is he a dentist?"

"No, no." A third striker interrupted. "He's a chir...chir... chiro...chiroo—"

"A chipmunk?" the original bemoaner interrupted.

"No. A chirop—"

"Cheerleader?" the other volunteered.

"Shut up, the both of you. I'm trying to think!"

"How about a chimpanzee?" another guffawed.

The thinking striker took a burning branch from the fire and threatened the others with it. "Shut it! I'm trying to think what the wife called him?"

"How about darling?" the guffawing striker said before backing away from the burning weapon.

There was arguing and shouting when suddenly the burning drum was kicked hard. Sparks and flames shot higher into the chill night and the strikers turned to see a huge man-mountain staring down at them. His features were reflected in the fire and they made him look more menacing than normal. The red glow highlighted a massive brush of gingery hair on a flat, wrinkled head. His eyebrows were furrowed down in a condemning fashion. The eyes were big and bulbous. One looked to the left whilst the other pierced whoever was unfortunate enough to be in its sight. The mouth snarled and stubble grew over the lower face like an unkempt lawn.

The strikers looked at him and smiled anxiously.

"Alright, Mick?" the branch brandishing man enquired nervously. The head turned to where the eye was focusing. "A chiropodist."

"What?" they all said.

"He's a chiropodist," the voice growled slowly.

"A what?" the others said in unison.

"A chiropodist; he's a bloke that looks at your ears. He syringed mine last month and you should have seen the gunk that came out of them. Like sewage, it was. He even said my ears stink and I should wash them out regular like," Mick explained.

There were nods and looks of great approval by the others accompanied by lots of "oh"s and "aah"s and "Well, that explains it then." Mick kicked the drum again. They went quiet.

"There's to be no grit given away for free alright!"

Heads nodded silently and Mick pointed back to where he had come from. They looked to see the doorway of a cabin in the yard open. The light inside silhouetted a figure leaning on a stick. Mick looked back at him, then to the strikers. "The boss insists," he added, and cracked his huge knuckles for effect. The others looked nervous, then one plucked up the courage and shouted, "No grit for the bourgeoisie!" The others took up the cry and shouted it out. Then they turned to the boss and gave a Caesar-style salute. Mick walked back to the cabin, satisfied that no one was going to give grit away for free. The strikers returned to the fire and started an in-depth conversation about collectable postage stamps.

"I had a Penny Black once," one of them said wistfully.

"They're worth a fortune!" the singer of anthems stated.

"Yeah, so I was told," he agreed.

"Well, how much did you sell it for?" the singer demanded.

"Oh, I didn't. I think next door's little boy ate it."

The others sounded outraged. "What did you do with the boy?"

"I didn't do anything. I found him and his mum in my flat. She was ever so nice and good looking too. Came onto me real strong and asked me out but said that if I leave a stamp collection lying about then it isn't her fault if her kid likes to eat stamps." The others looked astounded. The stamp collector took this as concern and carried on. "I said I'd take the little chap to the hospital but she said it was no bother really. Said she goes to the post office and buys him a couple of books of stamps so he can have them in a sandwich." He smiled contemplatively. "Well, I let it go because she said that that old stamp could be full of germs and vile stuff and that if she wanted to then she was in her rights to sue me. I didn't want no trouble so I asked her for a date and let it go."

The others were wordless but then one shook his head in a mystified fashion and managed to ask, "Well, did you see her?"

"Oh no. A few weeks later she moved with her family to a large villa in Spain, so I heard," he explained whilst warming his hands on the fire.

One by one the other strikers' jaws dropped. Then they started to laugh. Soon they were rolling about in the snow howling with delight. The former Penny Black owner was mystified. "What's so funny, lads?" he asked.

From behind, Ned Mutton, with wheelbarrow in hands, negotiated the picket line. He was wearing a bright red welt mark across his forehead where the wheelbarrow had hit him. He also wore his mother's fake fur coat. The coat he had grabbed from behind the door without thinking. It was a nylon style ermine and was very warm. It also blended him in with the snow beautifully, so when he approached the picketing strikers it was comparatively easy to pass unnoticed. It also helped that most of them were rolling helplessly in the snow laughing at their comrade. Ned entered the depot without as much as a challenge. He saw the cabin and from inside an orange glow burned, offering further warmth on this cold, cold night, but again no one challenged him. The snow dampened the wheel's noise as it moved over the natural white carpet but then the axle started to squeak. Ned looked around as if the tortured noise would suddenly alert all the strikers. The picketers were pulling each other up from the ground and still laughing, with the stamp collector still docile in mystified ignorance. Ned's eyes flicked to the cabin. He thought he saw movement and ducked down behind the wheelbarrow. Nearly a minute passed and everything seemed still, so he got up and, quiet as a mouse, pushed the barrow forwards towards what he had spied out earlier. It was a huge corrugated shed and inside was what looked like hundreds of tons of salt grit.

The look of this made Ned quicken his pace. There was the weapon of mass destruction. It was not a myth, it was not something made up by some politician with a maniacal smile and beady eyes to justify an invasion of a country, but it was Ned's weapons-grade material to bring ruin on Melton Mowbray and his minions. A mountain of pinkish grit was there for the taking. Then, suddenly, a hobnail boot slammed down on the barrow's squeaking wheel, Ned cartwheeled over the rusty handles and landed with a thump in the wheelbarrow's body. From above, a horrible ginger-haired apparition lolled over him. "Well, well, well, a pretty little snowman. Where do you think you're going?"

Ned went to get up but a pair of massive hammer hands pulled him out of the wheelbarrow as if he weighed the amount of a sparrow. The hands held him up to a man's face. It snarled. "Well, I asked you a question. Where do you think you're going with that barrow?"

Dangling in the air, Ned thought about correcting the man. His first question was the whereabouts of his going, whereas the second question was the whereabouts of where he was going with the wheelbarrow. The grip tightened, and Ned thought the better of correcting the man's enquiry.

"I've a grandmother who can't get out of her house and she needs a shedload of grit," he offered up.

The big bulbous eyes seemed to swivel on their own axis, then one jumped like a slot machine key and stopped, directly peering at Ned. "Who are you trying to kid, boy? We ain't got no grit!"

Ned's body hung but his head turned to the shed which held the mountains of grit. He pointed towards it. "But you've got loads of grit in there."

Again, the eyes span. This time one landed on Ned, the other on the shed. "That ain't for nobody. We're striking and that means no grit for no one!"

Ned tried to prise the hands away but it was like unclamping a vice. He tried another approach. "Look, in my barrow is a bottle of the most excellent booze your lips could ever taste. It's a fiery blend of...err...pots...malt...err, and the finest herbs in the...land."

The eyes narrowed. "I don't drink." Ned looked at him and could not believe that this man did not drink. His face was ruddier than the freshly painted hull of a ship. His nose was swollen like it had been stung by some mutant bee and the veins of the nose looked like a map of the London Underground.

He thought of the grit and his need to have it, so Ned tried some negotiating skills. "But you *look* like a man who likes a drink." The veined nose sniffed but the mouth remained silent. Ned took this as a good sign and carried on. "That bottle's vintage and on a night like this it would certainly warm you and your friends up. Anyway, aren't strikers supposed to support each other and be in it all together?"

The nose sniffed again and the eyes moved to the bottle and then to Ned, to the bottle and Ned, and to the bottle again. Ned saw that beads of sweat were starting to appear above the overworked eyes. The giant hands released Ned. "Good, is it?" the stubble-haired mouth enquired. Ned took this as a buying sign. "Good? Good? It's marvellous. This isn't your normal bottle of cheapo plonk. No, siree." He put a foot on the barrow and casually leant on his knee. A confidence borne of working for Beetie and dealing with psychotic snowmen grew in Ned. He felt he could talk this man and others into giving him what he wanted. He could steer the conversation to his advantage and fool the others with his quick thinking. This was not the Ned of a few months ago who did not know where South Vietnam was. Oh no, this was the new Ned Mutton; confident, cool, and capitalist, with a casual wit and smart style. Anyway, South Vietnam was off the coast of Canada and he didn't care to go there anyway.

Picking up the bottle, Ned held it under the man's nose. "This is your very best, no nonsense, straight to the spot, high quality booze. My dad bought it from a man who knows the queen and her bloke. It's the stuff they drink at the palace. Look," Ned pushed the bottle right under the nose. "There's the royal seal, see it?" Ned pulled the bottle away before the bulbous erratic eyes could zero on the bottle and put it behind his back. He noticed dribble starting to gather at the stubble-clad mouth. Then it dripped down on his own chin. Disgusted, Ned stepped back but brought the bottle from behind his back and brandished it to salivating mouth. More dribble ran out and the head shook excitedly, drenching Ned's mother's coat in spittle. The hammer hands went to grab the bottle but Ned was faster and he hid the bottle again. The hands went for Ned's throat but he ducked under the huge arms and ran out from harm's way. The man turned and snarled at him. Ned shook the bottle at him. "If you want it, you can have it. Just give me a barrow-load of grit." This enraged the spittle spitter even further and he ran at Ned but slipped in the snow and fell down with a crash, headbutting the wheelbarrow in the process. The garden barrow somersaulted in the air and then landed on its handles. It momentarily swayed there, then fell over the body like a giant metal tortoise shell. There was silence. Ned crept over and listened. Then he carefully pulled the barrow up and found the irate former drinker insensible with a great big welt mark growing at a rapid rate across his forehead. It was just like the mark Ned had when the wheelbarrow had hit him in the forehead. He kicked the man in the ribs just to see if he was not bluffing but there was only a muffled grunt. A smile grew across Ned's face as he uprighted the barrow and made his way to the shed full of grit.

The spotlights in the building illuminated the mountains of orange grit. There was tons of the stuff; enough to melt the snow in the town ten times over. The snow ploughs were parked in there and a huge tarpaulin covered a tracked vehicle that Ned could not identify. He thought it might be a tank, but then his eyes returned to what he had come for. The grit lay in front of him but it was being kept back and hoarded by no-nonsense talking strikers.

Well, some was going to be purloined tonight by Ned Mutton and they would not know a thing about it. So, grabbing the shovel, Ned readied himself for the first scoop of Melton's downfall but then from behind him a voice rang out: "Cease that immediately!" The tone of the voice sounded malicious as it echoed around the big shed's interior. Ned spun around and saw the silhouette of a large person leaning on a walking stick. His knees turned to jelly as he thought he recognised the form. It could only be Melton Mowbray the Third. Then he fainted.

*

He was lying in a puddle of water and a snowman was staring down at him. Ned's eyes moved around and he realised with horror that he was the puddle of water. His body had melted and only his eyes remained. "You are slush now." The snowman laughed and went to step on Ned's eyes. He screamed and woke with a start. There was no snowman and he quickly felt himself and was relieved to find he was whole again and not watery slush.

Raising himself up, Ned's head started to spin, so he lay back down on a rather scruffy paisley chaise longue. He was in what looked like a set from a very camp theatre production. There were velvet drapes hanging down from the walls, a huge gilded mirror, red velvet chairs, a gigantic cactus in a pot, and a large marble fountain which gushed coloured water. Ned shook his head in case he was having another nightmare and in the process managed to knock over a vase of plastic lilies that sat behind the chaise longue. It landed with a thud on the purple shag pile carpet. A door opened and in stepped a man. "We heard you scream. Are you alright?"

Ned looked at the man. He was thin and haggard with grey temples and a fez set upon his head. His eyes looked threatening, his nose red and bulbous. His voice was gruff and tinged with tiredness, yet edged with a friendly tone. White string vest and a grey suit with sandals (no socks) finished his attire. In his hand he carried a long galvanized pipe. Looking at the pipe, Ned started to worry again. A smile grew across the man's face and he stepped into the room. "You fainted when I shouted out. So we brought you in here, or rather Earwax did." The man snapped his fingers and in walked the brute who had been trying to get the bottle from Ned. In an effort to distance himself from the twin threat of brandished pipe and Earwax, Ned crawled backwards on the chaise longue.

"It's alright. We're not going to harm you. Earwax here had a problem with the booze so he gets a bit upset when people offer it to him. He got religion a few months ago and he's quite harmless now, you know." As if to demonstrate the healing effects of religion, he hit Earwax across the skull with his pipe. There was a hollow clunk and Earwax started to sing a hymn. The man ruffled his victim's hair and then spoke again. "Shut up now, Earwax. You're not in the chapel." He turned to Ned. "There, you see, soft as puppy cack. But he can still pulp anyone when I order him to." Ned gulped and nodded nervously. "By the way, my name's Lionel, Lionel Frampton, and I'm the manager of this road maintenance depot." Ned relaxed a bit but still looked uneasily at Earwax and the pipe. Lionel saw him looking. "Oh, the pipe. It's not my walking stick. It's for killing rats. We've got loads down here and Earwax and the boys are scared of them." Ned could not believe that the man monster Earwax was afraid of anything and, uncannily, as if reading Ned's mind, Lionel delved into his pocket and brought out a dead rat. He winked at Ned and then brandished it in front of Earwax, who screamed and ran out of the room. Lionel chuckled to himself and then threw the rat at Ned, who screamed as well, then tried to throw it away and in doing so realised it was made of rubber. He looked at Lionel who was hooting like a donkey now and threw the rat back at him. The pipe came up lightning fast and knocked the rubber rodent across the room to splat on the mirror. "We ain't got no rats really. I just like to keep the boys on their toes so I carry that rubber one about."

Lionel extinguished the last laugh, then sat next to Ned. "This is our healing room. We come here when the public or the hierarchy get too heavy on us." He explained, "Over the years we've collected this stuff from house clearances and skips. It's quite beautiful, don't you think?" A silent nod came from Ned. Lionel rose and started to wind up an old gramophone player. He picked up a record, blew the dust off it and placed it on the turntable, then continued, "We've had an especially hard few days, what with the strike and public opinion not lending itself to our cause, so we come in here and be at one with ourselves." Ned just raised his eyebrows in question. The sound of cracking and scratching emitted from the gramophone's speaker, followed by the random noise of sitars being plucked and bongos being drummed. Just then, a man came out from behind the chaise longue. He was dressed in purple robes and had the toy rat in one hand. He looked at Lionel and shook his head. "Bad karma, man! I nearly attained nirvana when this artificial rodent hit me in my third eye." Lionel's head followed him as he left the room. "That's Roger Parkstone, he's head of legal. Likes to come down here to chill."

Ned found his voice at last. "Oh, does he?"

"Yes, he does," smiled Lionel, then straightened. "Now, you haven't told me your name or why you came down here to steal our grit?"

Maybe it was the room's atmosphere or maybe it was the rhythmical music slowly beating a chant, or the unbelievable strain over the last few days. Maybe it was talking to someone who was human and not made of snow. Or maybe it was the offer to explain—however mad it seemed—to an adult, even though Ned suspected that Lionel Frampton was not particularly sane. Whatever it was, Ned let out a deep breath and barked a laugh. "My name's Ned Mutton and if I told you my story you wouldn't believe it."

Lionel looked hard into Ned's eyes. "Try me, Ned Mutton."

So Ned told his story. Lionel did not interrupt once during Ned's story. He just sat there and listened, nodding his head silently and growling quietly at the mention of Melton Mowbray the Third.

"And then after putting Heinrich on a slow roast I came here to get some grit," he finished. Lionel breathed deeply, then was silent. He seemed to contemplate the strange tale for a long time, then cleared his throat and smiled. Ned thought that he was going to break into a fit of unrestrained laughter. Suddenly there was a knock at the door. Lionel rose and opened it. A man in a three-piece suit was standing there offering his hand to shake.

"Ah, Roger, all changed and finished?" Lionel said. "I must apologise for the toy rat, but it keeps the workers on their toes and I find it amusing." Roger Parkstone shook visibly at the memory of the assault by the rubber rodent.

"Don't mention that thing again, please. I have a psychic stye developing over my third eye." He touched his forehead and shuddered. "What's more, I've got a case on Monday to prosecute a worker who was found stuffing live rats down his pants at the Working Men's Club whilst supposedly clearing drains for the council. It's going to be traumatic, I tell you."

Ned interjected. "For the bloke, he must have been desperate for money to stuff live rats down his pants?"

Roger slapped the air in front of him. "No, no, no. For me, you obtuse fellow, for me, for me!"

Ned leant back on the chaise longue. Lionel grabbed Roger's hand and planted it on his fez. "Don't let these negative vibrations invade your own self. You are at one with the flow of nature and the great life force itself. Beyond this space is a higher plain where we can all wear purple and dance under a turquoise moon and lavender stars."

Roger took his hand from the fez and clamped it to his other as if in prayer. "You, my friend, should be the next Dalai Lama." And with that, he turned and left the room.

Lionel then put his hands together as if in prayer and lightly slapped his palms together. "Roger Parkstone is a former QC and very, very good at being a lawyer. He can defend or prosecute the most utterly hopeless case in the world, but he does think that purple and lavender combined will make him into the next Holy See." He rubbed his palms together, sighed, and then faced Ned. "Now, you come here to me with this amazing tale of walking, talking snowmen who have captured countless innocent people and had then frozen in this 'fool's gallery'. You say that they have kidnapped your parents and blackmailed you into purloining them fish fingers so as they can take their rightful place in this word. And the leader of this great conspiracy is this snowman called Melton Mowbray the Third. Is that correct?"

To hear a man in a grey suit, fez, and sandals recount this story struck Ned as mad. How on earth could anyone believe that this was all true? Mad snowmen, fish finger, parents kidnapped, and he had not even mentioned his time with the Vaughan-Abbotts. It would be too much for anyone to believe really.

So he stood and smiled weakly at Lionel. "See, I knew you wouldn't believe me. Who on this planet would?" As he finished the sentence he had tears in his eyes. "Look, all I ask is that you give me a barrow full of grit. After all, you got mountains of the stuff and you wouldn't miss a wheelbarrow-full would you?"

Lionel walked in front of the door and so blocked Ned's way out. His voice growled low. "Ned Mutton. This chief snowman of yours, what leg does he limp on?"

Ned did not think why but he just recalled in his mind the peg-legged tormenter shuffling about browbeating the other snowmen and Ned. "It's his right leg."

Lionel raised his eyebrows to the ceiling and a smile grew across his face. "And do you know how he got that limp?"

Ned went to push past him. "Look, I know you don't believe me, but just let me go and I'll find some grit elsewhere. You lot are rotten if you won't give me just a bit. Stuff your karma and your purple robes and lavender. I'm off to get my parents back."

Lionel stopped Ned. "You haven't answered my question, Ned Mutton?"

Ned started to get angry now. "No, I haven't. Because you don't believe me and you're just making me look a dimwit. But I can live with that. Just let me go. Stuff your mountain of grit, I'll go elsewhere."

One hand stopped Ned whilst Lionel's other hand rolled up his own trousers to reveal a long scar across the length of his calf. "I got this for giving Melton Mowbray his limp, boy."

Ned stopped and stared at the scar. "Are you taking the—"

But Lionel put a finger to Ned's lips. "No, I ain't! I know what you talk of is true. Thirty years ago, I was in your shoes and I gave the old bugger something to remember me by. Now sit down and listen to my story."

Chapter 14

"I was about eleven at the time. My mum and dad had split up and I was living with my dad. He was a good bloke but liked to drink a bit and would rather be in the pub than at work, hence we never had much money for grub or rent and stuff." Ned was reclined on the chaise longue again and Lionel had taken up the lotus position in front of him. He had his eyes closed while he spoke to Ned, who found this a little disconcerting but was enthralled by the tale of an earlier encounter with the beast Mowbray. Lionel continued, "The old man would nip into pubs and whilst no one was looking he would down someone's pint and then scarper to the next pub and do the same. He developed this idea to greater effect by employing me as a distraction. I was to divert the drinker's attention with my live worm eating act. The pub drinkers loved it but couldn't understand where their drinks had gone afterwards. It worked for ages and Dad got slaughtered every night but it all came to a dreadful end when I spewed worms over the mayor and his wife and they banished me and Dad from all the pubs in the town."

Lionel reached in his pocket and pulled out a plastic bag. Inside, things squirmed and, with his eyes still closed, he deftly reached into the bag and extracted a long earthworm. "Care for one?" he said. Ned remembered Fabian force-feeding him one and the convulsive spewing afterwards. "Er, no thank you."

"You don't mind if I do?" Lionel asked.

Ned shook his head. Lionel's two eyes were still shut but it seemed with his third eye he saw Ned not minding if he indulged, and with that, he sucked the worm into his mouth and chewed. There was a sound of grinding soil, then a gulp. Lionel licked his lips. "Ahhhh, a rare delicacy, and full of protein, you know. Now, back to my tale. So me and Dad had no money, no house, and had to find somewhere to sleep. Winter was around the corner and we needed shelter. So Dad decided that we could live wildly and he tried it out in the local park, but the warden was a mean bugger and he threw us out. We were living off berries and winter fruits; it was rough but exciting in a way. Dad gave up the booze and even got a job as a scarecrow on a local organic farm. We still needed somewhere to shelter in over winter and one day, Dad saw this chiller factory that had been abandoned, so we went in and investigated it."

Lionel breathed deeply and then went silent. He stayed that way for a while until Ned coughed and he opened his eyes. They were edged with tears. Lionel sniffed them back. "Well, we went in. Dad had a torch and I noticed an iron bar outside and took it in with me. You see, I had heard rumours of this place. People were nervous about it and they said strange things had happened there. Folk had disappeared and ghostly white figures were seen there on certain nights. Dad scoffed at the tales. He said it was all the better if people were scared because they wouldn't bother us if we lived there for a bit. Anyway, in we went, through an old broken window and down into the factory. It was so cold in there, and dark too. It was too dark. I kept hearing strange scraping noises and footfalls but Dad dismissed them as my own imagination. We went through the lower levels and up a spiral staircase—"

"I know that one. It creaks like it's going to fall down," Ned interrupted. "In fact, it did fall down."

Lionel took no notice and continued. "We walked for ages and thought we were lost. Then Dad saw a faint light ahead of us and when we reached it we saw an old office. It was alright actually. Dad put down his rucksack, had a look around, then got out our sleeping bags and announced that this was our new home. I wasn't keen but Dad said it would be alright, at least until the spring. I remember him looking into my eyes and smiling, then saying that one day we'd have a proper house with a garden and real beds to sleep in. So I believed him as I got down to sleep on the first night. He said he was just going to have a quick look around to check on things before he turned in as well. I thought I'd not sleep but sleep came to me and I went off before Dad returned."

Lionel delved into the bag again and picked out a handful of worms. He offered them to Ned again before swallowing the wiggling load in one. Munching for a while, as if for comfort, he gulped loudly, belched even louder, then took the tale up.

"Something woke me up in the middle of the night. The light was off but I could sense that Dad was not there. I felt his sleeping bag and it was empty. I started to panic then. It was pitch black in that office and Dad had taken the torch. I stumbled about and knocked things over that seemed not to be there when we had entered earlier. I fell forwards into a table and I put my hands out for support. They landed on something cold and soft. I immediately withdrew them but these things grabbed my wrists and pulled me forward. It was then I felt a cold breath on my face that smelled of ice cream. I struggled to free myself but the thing that had hold of me was too strong. I screamed and then a chill voice came out of the darkness. 'What have we here then?' My mouth was dry with terror. I tried to scream again but was sick instead. I still enjoyed worms and they supplemented my wild fruit diet well, and a hot lava of earthworm à la fruit hit the fiend that held me right in his face. This time it was him that screamed and I got away from his clutches. I remember tripping over the iron bar that I had brought in and, grabbing it, I flayed it around in front of me like a mad man. There were further screams and cries of pain and they weren't from me either. I continued my blind assault with added relish as the cries got louder. But then I made out, in the midst of the cries and screams, my dad shouting at me to stop." Lionel looked down and then with a gulp turned towards Ned with a dreadful look of anguish etched on his face. "Then I realised I had beaten my own father senseless." Ned cried out in sympathy, but Lionel held up his hand to continue the tale of kindred assault. "Yes, my own father I had nearly beaten to insensibility. He lay on the floor groaning and I dropped the bar and ran over to cradle his head in my shaking arms. He didn't move and I feared the worst. I cried out his name but was only answered by the sound of laughter echoing around the room. Then the chill voice started again. 'Oh, my boy, my dear boy, what a killer you are. I could use someone like you in my cause. Come and join Melton Mowbray's new army.' I heard footsteps approaching me and I lunged for the bar and struck out with all my hatred and might. Cold snowflakes hit me in the face and a cry more terrifying and spine-chilling than my father's cut the air. Something lashed me across the leg and I cried out too. The pain cut through me and I started to pass out, but before I did, the last thing I heard was the other scream receding into the gloom. Then it all went black."

Ned was speechless. Here was someone that had encountered a living snowman and that snowman had been none other than Melton Mowbray at that. Now his troubles seemed halved. Now he had a confidante and an ally. His brain re-engaged and started his voice box. "So what happened?"

Lionel looked in the bag for worms but he had eaten them all. He tossed it away and smiled ruefully. "When I came around, the lights were back on in the office and there was no sign of Melton or, worse, of my dad. I started to panic and throw things about, and then I found the note."

"The note?" Ned asked.

"Aye, a note; it was written terribly and I could hardly read it but eventually I made out the scrawl. It was from Melton and in essence it said that he had my father captive and would kill him—'slush him' were his words—if I ever let onto anyone about him or the chiller factory."

Ned gulped back tears and Lionel tried to but did not succeed. Small drops ran down his gaunt face and Ned did something that he did not expect to do. He instinctively hugged Lionel. The effect of being embraced made Lionel pour forth with further tears and moans of self-pity. Ned suddenly felt embarrassed and tried to pull away without trying to make it too obvious. Lionel clung onto him and wailed further. Ned tried to stand but Lionel held on like a limpet. Ned wiggled his hands nervously and tried again to shake off the traumatized road maintenance manager but ended up knocking over the cacti which spilled dry soil on the floor. Trying to escape from its smashed warm home was an earthworm of unnatural proportions. It was massive by earthworm standards and nearly the size of a sausage. Ned thought it was a snake at first, but then leaned away from Lionel's embrace and picked up the worm to offer it to him like some surrogate bird giving food to its cuckoo offspring. The tears cleared suddenly to be replaced by an insatiable hunger for the gargantuan worm. Lionel growled and snapped at the proffered snack and Ned dropped it into his greedy maw and he wolfed it down. Enduring gulps and loud munching noises, Ned was glad when

Lionel finished scoffing and rose up to smile confidently at him. "I must apologise for that moment of weakness. It will never happen again. You hear me, Ned Mutton, that will never happen again. I have never spoken of the incident until now and feel I have released a burden that was causing inflation to my inner purple flame. But I'm going to kill that maimed maniac Melton, if it's the last thing I do!"

Ned did not know what he meant but smiled back anyway. "It's alright, I know how you feel."

Lionel smacked him on the back and chuckled. "I know you do, my friend. I knew that from the first time I set eyes on you. Well, now we have a vested interest in Melton Mowbray and a rescue mission to plan. I've also got something of a secret weapon that I've been working on for the last ten years, and now seems an appropriate time to show you Thaw: the Snow Hammer." His eyes bulged, he screwed his knuckles up and punched the air, then did a quick boxer's shuffle. "I tell you, son, Hitler's Panzer Blitzkrieg will seem like a teddy bear's picnic when this baby rolls out of the grit shed. Vengeance, and I am its deliverer!" He punched the air again and led the way out of the healing room into the night.

Ned followed excitedly. They were going to take the battle to the enemy and it seemed that they were going to use some secret weapon that Lionel had made. As they neared the shed, a thought came to Ned. "Why didn't you ever look for your dad or inform the law?"

Lionel didn't stop but talked as he walked. "The same reason you didn't inform the law."

Ned realised that all those years ago, Lionel was in the same predicament as he was now, only Ned had a plan to work around. The salt grit he needed would be offered now by his new friend and, moreover, he had back-up in the form of this wonder weapon, whatever it was.

"Lionel, what do you think happened to your dad?" Ned asked carefully. He did not want a breakdown again and could see no hope of worms anywhere in the snow-covered vicinity.

Lionel stopped and turned to Ned. "I don't know, son. I suspect that Dad slipped away from that horror's reach. He may have liked the sauce a bit but he wasn't stupid, you know. Dad even tried the army when he was young, but was caught drinking the fuel from a

Chieftain tank. He got a dishonourable discharge for that, he did, but he learnt a lot about survival and all that." Ned groaned inside, thinking that lots of adults and snowmen liked to act as soldiers and be great at soldier things.

Lionel winked at Ned. "Yeah, I think he's well gone and living a dream somewhere. Or that's what I like to think. I can't...or I don't want to think of him trapped down there in that freezing hellhole. Anyway," he continued with a rueful smile. "Fate's brought us together, my lad, and it's time to bring retribution to that evil snowman."

They both entered the grit shed and Ned stared in amazement again at the huge amount that was piled in hillocks inside the building. He could also see the strikers now lined up as if on an army parade ground awaiting inspection and as Lionel approached, they saluted. Earwax marched out and offered a shovel to his leader. "We're ready to follow you to the end, my leader," he shouted and the sound echoed around the shed.

Lionel's head fell back as he laughed out loud. "Ha, ha, ha, ha...my brethren, now the time has come. The prophecy has come true. A child has come. It is just as I told you."

Ned looked at the door and started to worry again about his newfound friend's sanity. Maybe it was not such a good idea to get involved with this lot. He started to edge towards the door but then Lionel grabbed his hand and pulled him back. "Yes, my scabby strikers, now the day of retribution dawns. It is judgment for the white flaked filth."

Ned went for the door but Lionel increased his grip, then spoke quietly in his ear. "Don't worry, Ned, this lot have to get worked up to do anything, even to go to the bog. Lazy buggers all of them, too much union influence and Marxism. But deep down they're a good bunch—misguided, but good." He walked forwards and raised his hands to the men. "Now, boys, let's get it together and fire up Thaw's Hammer!"

Earwax and the boys ran over to what Ned thought was a small mountain of grit. They clambered around the mound and pulled back the green-grey tarpaulin to reveal a tracked armoured vehicle with a gun turret and a snow plough attached to the front. It was camouflaged in grey and white stripes and looked like a wicked weapon of mass destruction. Ned gawped and Lionel let out a satisfied sigh. The strikers jumped onto the vehicle and, opening hatches, climbed in. A sound of thunder broke into the shed as someone inside started the engine. Black smoke and sparks belched from the exhausts and Thaw's Hammer looked like a dragon spewing fire. Then, with a tortured squeal of metal tracks on concrete, the machine moved towards Ned and Lionel. As it came nearer, the snow plough loomed and the turret traversed to point its gun directly at Lionel. Ned stepped back but Lionel stood his ground, and just as it seemed Thaw would crush him, he held up a hand. In that instant, the armoured vehicle halted.

Lionel smiled. "Ain't she a beauty? And Thaw's ready to kill snowmen, Ned. Ready to kill lots of them."

Ned's body still aimed for the door but he was awestruck by the sheer power of the armoured monster. Surely nothing could stop this, not Melton, not snowmen; even the chiller factory would be crushed by the metal might of Thaw. He walked over to it and laid a hand on the steel body. The hand shook as the hull of the vehicle throbbed under the power of the engine. Ned smiled and looked at Lionel. "How did you do this? How did you afford it?"

Raising his eyebrows, Lionel glowed in self-admiration. "Well, you see, Ned, I said it took nearly ten years to build. It's a mixed match of gritter lorries, armoured personnel carriers, main battle tanks' spares, and industrial parts. As for the cost, your mum and dad paid for it, along with all the other tax payers in this town. Council didn't question anything, just kept giving me more money for my department when I asked for it." He chuckled at the thought of a blank cheque being produced on request. "Come on, I'll show you how she works and how to handle her." And with that, he climbed on Thaw, then pulled Ned up onto the hull.

*

It was 21:55 hours at Stalingrad Towers and waiting nervously outside Beetie's study were Fabian and Crichton. They could hear movement inside mixed with loud bangs and curses. Fabian beckoned the retainer forwards and motioned that he should knock on the door. Crichton's eyes flickered with nervous tension and pearls of sweat started to form on his forehead. He hesitated but then Fabian darted forwards and kicked the door loudly, then moved back just as quickly to stand behind Crichton. The door opened violently and Crichton fell through into the room to pile into a snowman.

There was a scream and Crichton recoiled in terror. The snowman helped by pushing him backwards out of the room and into Fabian, who pushed forwards. Poor Crichton fell forwards again into the snowman and was immediately knocked backwards again. He went back and forwards between each tormentor like a human shuttlecock until the snowman got tired of the game and grabbed the poor manservant by his arms and threw him across the room into the curtains. There was a crash and squeal and little Fabian hooted with delight. The snowman pulled off his own head to reveal a grinning Beetie. "Howzat!" he yelled. Then, grabbing his son and pulling him into the room with similar violence, he released him to crash into a rising Crichton. "Game, set, and match I think!" Beetie howled and laughed even louder than his crumpled offspring.

They tried to uncoil themselves from each other but just managed to get coiled further in the curtains and rip them off the rails. Beetie picked up the Baron and started to assault the draped duo. After many yells of anguish and pain, the two crawled out from the now ripped curtain nursing bruises and contusions.

Beetie berated them. "Now is not the time for horse play, you idiots! Get those damn disguises on and follow me!"

The Baron hovered above and so Fabian and Crichton snatched up the outfits. They briefly fought over the male snowman disguise until Fabian landed a wicked kick in Crichton's shin and Beetie also intervened. "Crichton, you are the girlie snowman as I ordered you earlier, so get that little number on sharpish!"

They were still hopping around trying to get legs and arms in when Beetie started to leave the room. They followed, pulling fake heads on, and scampered down the stairs to the back of the house where the servant's entrance was. Beetie undid the door and exited Stalingrad Towers to make his way to the garage. He pushed the button on a remote control and the double doors clattered open. A light was on and parked there was a Rolls Royce, a Range Rover, an E-type Jaguar, and a small red tractor complete with grass cutting blades and a trailer. Without a pause, he walked past the cars and stood in front of the garden tractor. "Right, we don't want to draw attention to ourselves and I'm not taking the Rolls out in this filthy weather." It was then that he noticed Crichton dressed as a snowlady. With big eyelashes, the fullest of red lips, a ludicrous coconut shell bikini top, and grass skirt, Beetie gave his servant a lustful sneer. "Damn my bones, Crichton, but don't you look ravishing!" then he snapped his fingers. "Now start the tractor and drive me and the boy to that miserable little chiller factory. We've got something to rescue."

And he did.

*

It had taken an hour for Lionel to show Ned around the inside and outside of Thaw, and by the finish he was impressed with what the machine could do. Lionel and his workers had spent what seemed like years on the design of it. They had hidden it away in the huge shed and gradually built it up from plans that Lionel fabricated and sweated over night after night to engineer this snow mincing machine. The boys and their boss were justifiably proud, and now they were ready for battle with the snowman and his cohorts who had so cruelly hurt Lionel. With Ned coming, it seemed like fate had come—or at least to Lionel it seemed—to take charge of the future.

Ned stared up at the short gun on Thaw and as Lionel jumped down from the turret, he asked something that had concerned him all those years ago reading exploits of war heroes and making models. "For the size of your 'baby', why has it got such a dinky gun?"

The reaction from Lionel was what looked like barely controlled rage. His face went red and the iron bar threatened the air in front of Ned with a clubbing motion. Before vitriolic frenzy could explode from the manager, Ned interjected his own question. "I mean, in all the books I've seen and read, the bigger the gun the better."

Lionel hit the concrete floor and sparks flew. "No! No! No! You've got it all wrong!"

Ned and the now dismounted crew backed off. Lionel jabbed his pipe in the direction of Thaw's gun. "Damn it all, when I designed her I didn't just build her with no consideration to what she was designed to kill now, did I?" No one spoke, so he carried on. "Tanks are primarily designed to take on other tanks, so they fire armour piercing rounds to kill them. They also fire high explosive shells for suppressive fire and to kill soft skin vehicles, artillery pieces, et cetera, et cetera. My baby is not designed to fight other armour but to destroy those filthy snowmen. So I don't need a big gun, I need a smaller mortar style gun that can fire anti-personnel…I mean anti-snowman rounds. Thaw's gun fires case shot that explodes into tiny little fragments of grit, stones, metal shot, and other nefarious and unpleasant stuff so as to disintegrate all snowmen within a ten-metre area of impact. Are you clear on that?" Lionel finally gasped.

Ned and the crew nodded politely. "Good. Now no more questions, please. We have to plan a search and destroy mission." Lionel snapped his fingers and the crew shuffled into line. He gave them a quick inspection, then started off to his office with them marching behind.

"Hang on," Ned said. "I know you hate Melton and his cronies but if you go blasting in that chiller factory with Thaw then my mum and dad are going to be slushed—I mean murdered—by that old git Melton."

Lionel stopped. "Oh yes, I forgot about that. Bugger it!" He thought for a moment.

"Right, Earwax, you get Thaw ready for action. I want her ship-shape and Bristol fashion and all that. I want a full consignment of ammo and her tanks full to the brim. When you've done that, you and the boys have a glug of that bottle young Ned brought. It'll keep the chill away while we have a military conference in my office."

Lionel unlocked the office door and fiddled for the light switch. He walked in and Ned followed to see a very tastefully decorated room. It was panelled with mahogany wood and there was an internal door finished in the same wood. Gold framed paintings of rural scenes hung on the panelling. A swivel captain's chair and a red leather-topped bureau sat on a luxurious looking carpet. On top of the bureau was a green reading lamp and a few photos but Ned could not see who they were of. This was all illuminated from above by an enormous crystal chandelier. "It ain't much but its mine," Lionel said. "Make yourself comfortable." He sat down and opened a drawer in the bureau and produced a bottle of Chivas Regal. "Want one?"

Ned shook his head and sat down. "Got any milk? I could murder a pint of milk."

Lionel pushed a switch on the leather top and spoke into it. "Hello, my sweet. Can you bring in a pint of milk when you're ready?"

Lionel poured himself a large one. "Now, young Ned, what is your plan for rescuing your parents?"

"Well, I came over here to get a barrow full of grit to make fake fish fingers with them. I was going to box them up and give them to Melton in exchange for Mum and Dad. We get out of there, and when those snowmen fit them fingers on, then they'll melt—or at least their hands and arms will—hopefully," Ned explained, then yawned.

"Damn. That is one good plan but it all depends on whether Melton will fit the fingers on before he releases you and your mum and dad, doesn't it?"

Ned swore. He hadn't thought of that one. For all his planning and growing confidence, this was a major flaw in his scheme.

Lionel slurped the remnants of the glass. "Don't beat yourself up about it, Ned. It still has potential, though we need to rethink a bit. And now me and the boys are on board, you've got yourself an ally in this battle."

Ned started to think again but he was dog tired. He hadn't slept for what seemed like days and his body and mind seemed to be starting to go on strike. Lionel realised this as well.

Then the inner panel door opened and a young girl stepped into the room. She was holding a pint of milk. Lionel turned with a smile so wide he looked like a cat with the cream. Ned looked at the girl. She went red, then Ned screamed. The girl dropped the milk and Lionel was up and out from behind the desk and putting himself in front of the girl so as to protect her. "What is it?" he cried out. "What's wrong?"

Ned pointed at her and then fumbled in his pocket. "It's her. It's her, the girl in the photo."

Lionel's face turned from surprise to suspicion. His brow furrowed and his face darkened. "What photo are you talking about?" he said in a threatening tone.

Fumbling away, Ned eventually withdrew the photo he was searching for. "This one."

Lionel snatched it from his grasp and looked at the crumpled picture. Although creased and cracked, it was indeed a match to the girl in the office.

He stomped towards Ned. "Where the hell did this come from?"

Ned fell back in the chair. Lionel loomed, then Ned found his voice. "It was Beetie...Beetie Vaughan-Abbott who gave it to Melton. He told him to get rid of her."

Lionel hovered over Ned. "Who did you say?" His eye twitched and his fingers squeezed the air threateningly. The girl came over and started to comfort Lionel. She stroked his convulsing hands. He twitched erratically and turned to Ned again. With his face contorting violently and the girl trying to hold him back he stammered a question to Ned. "Who...who...did you say gave...the picture... to...to...Melton?"

Ned sat up in the chair. Hell, he was getting used to dealing with maddened snowmen and he'd had his lot of them but now he was on the receiving end of an unreasonable psychopath who was human. His eyes met the swivelling eyes of Lionel. Ned thumped the bureau top. "It was a self-centred turd of a man that took me in and promised me the world. His name is Beetie, or that's what he likes people to call him. Beetie Vaughan-Abbott and his outrageous, lying, pant-eating son called Fabian, and now you're acting like him too and I've done nothing to this girl or been involved with anything to hurt her, so stick Thaw where it don't shine because I'm off!"

And with that, he went to go. The girl suddenly let go of Lionel and pulled Ned back. "I know you. We've met before. You saved me from a worm supper that horrible offspring of the man that you call Beetie was going to feed me." She turned to Lionel and let go of Ned's hand. "The very man who took my mum from my dad."

Ned looked at her mystified. "Sorry, can you say that again? I don't understand?"

"My name is Elsie Frampton and that's my dad standing there." She smiled quickly. "And the man you call Beetie stole my mum from my dad with promises you've just mentioned." At this statement, Lionel fell into his admiral's chair and started to weep. Elsie ran over and held his head in her arms. She looked at Ned. "You can go if you want but you should listen to what I say. Dad's a wonderful man but he gets emotional when my mum or I are mentioned. When you showed the photo of me to him and mentioned the man he hates most of all to him, it's bound to have a violent reaction."

Ned stood and leaned against the wood panelling. He thought for a bit, then went to say something, then thought again. He eventually started to talk slowly. "Now, you're the girl that I fell over and stopped Fabian Vaughan-Abbott force-feeding a worm to. Am I right?"

Elsie nodded again. She had a sweet smile and nod and her huge green eyes stared into him. Ned carried on piecing things together. "So your dad is Lionel. Yes?"

She nodded.

Ned breathed deeply and pondered. "Then your mum is Simone?"

The smile vanished. "Who the hell is Simone?"

Damn, she's got her father's temper, thought Ned. He tried to get the image of Simone cradling him in her arms all that time ago out his head. "Simone's the woman who's married to Beetie!" he blurted out.

Elsie crossed her arms and stared at him. "Simone is NOT my mother's name. It's Bessie. She and Simone are the same obviously, but Simone is a fake!"

"I don't understand," Ned said.

From behind the bureau, Lionel sat up and tousled his daughter's hair. His voice seemed worn and rough and he smiled apologetically to his daughter. "It shouldn't be up to you to explain the failures of your parents, my love. Sit down, Ned, and I'll explain."

So Ned sat again. He thought of the time and prompted Lionel. "Okay, explain. But I've got my parents to rescue, so please make it quick."

Chapter 15

Lionel held up his hand and laughed bitterly. "Alright, my boy, I'll be as quick as it takes. Simone is the former Bessie, who was my wife, who is Elsie's mum. Bessie and me were happy for a long time but I kept having nightmares about Melton and snowmen. It started to take over my life a bit and Bessie didn't believe in them like me and you do. She said I should go to the loony bin and get sorted but I wouldn't go, so she did."

Lionel picked up a framed picture from the bureau and handed it to Ned. It showed a very natural-looking, beautiful young woman in a polka dot summer dress. It was nothing like Simone, yet as Ned stared at the photo, he could see some resemblance to Bessie's face to the newer Simone. Lionel snatched it back before Ned could stare anymore.

"She started to work for this bloke from out of town; he was an up-and-coming property developer. We got invited to one of his swish parties. It was a fancy dress and I met this Brinsley Vaughan-Abbott for the first time and I hated him. He was so full of himself; he was arrogant and slimy and he was a real toad. But he had an eye for my Bessie. I wanted to go but she wanted to stay. Then this bloke comes up from behind in a snowman's outfit and offers me a drink. Well, I freaked and knocked him flat out. Then everyone freaked and I left. Bessie left me soon after that and moved in with him. She took Elsie with her for a while. Then, one day, Elsie turns up at night on my door and says that Mum don't want her no more. I can't believe that; not even Bessie would abandon her own daughter. I know it's that bugger Brinsley Vaughan-Abbott who's behind it." He grabbed Elsie in a bear hug and held her there. "I won't let you go, my love, and I know your mum still loves you."

Elsie let him embrace her and smiled. "Dad, you're a soft-hearted idiot at times but I do love you. Mum, on the other hand, does not love either of us."

Lionel shook his head. "No, no, no, my dear, I'm sure there's a reason why she hasn't seen you for so long."

Elsie raised her eyes to the roof. "Well, if you believe that, then that's your problem."

Ned interrupted. "Beetie wants rid of Elsie. That's why he gave Melton the photo and said as much."

Lionel's docile loveliness dropped instantly. "Over my dead body. Let's get Melton and his cohorts, then we can deal with that worthless maggot Vaughan-Abbott."

Elsie, Ned, and Lionel put their hands on top of the desk and clasped them together. "Agreed," they said in unison. Lionel switched the intercom on his desk. "Oh boys, are you in agreement with the days orders?" From a little speaker in the room a roar erupted and as in a military fashion, the ranks called out loudly and clearly, "To the death!"

Lionel smiled and returned to his former calm self. "Right, my dears. Let's revise the battle plan."

*

Ned was thoroughly exhausted, befuddled, and crying out for a bed by now. His body moved in protest and he was even starting to hallucinate, so Lionel ordered him to go home and sleep whilst he and Elsie got on with things. The wheelbarrow that Ned brought to the works with him was now wheeling him back to his house. Earwax was pushing it and even before it left the gate, Ned was gently snoring.

It was a wonderful sleep, utterly relaxing and with no nightmares. He woke as someone was pulling back the curtains in his room. A delicious smell of eggs and bacon crept in the room from downstairs and Ned's mouth watered. The sun shone in and a figure stood above him holding a steaming mug.

"Here, it's got ten sugars in. You can't beat a good cuppa tea." Ned recognised Earwax.

"Thanks," he said, then stretched and took the tea. "What's the time?"

"Teatime," Earwax explained happily, and Ned could see he was wearing a pinny.

"No, what's the real time?"

"Dunno, I can't tell it," Earwax said and left the room.

"It's five thirty in the afternoon," a voice shouted from downstairs.

Ned shot out of bed, spilling his tea in the process, and ran down into the living room. Lionel, Elsie, and some of the strikers were sitting around the table eating breakfast. Ned grabbed Lionel. "Come on! Come on now! We've got to go and deliver the fish fingers. Mum and Dad will be frozen if we don't go!"

Lionel stood up and pushed Ned into his seat. "Relax, Ned. I was only joking. It's not eight o'clock in the morning yet." The others started to laugh, but Elsie looked at her father angrily and Ned was not pleased either. "That's not funny Lionel. Not funny at all!"

Lionel suppressed a laugh. "Okay, okay, I'm sorry. Couldn't resist it."

"Is that an apology?" Elsie asked.

Lionel shrugged. "No, but that's all he's going to get. Anyway, boy, relax and have some breakfast. Then we'll explain what we've been doing while you've been sleeping."

From the kitchen, Earwax brought out a huge plate piled with eggs, bacon, and toast. Ned dribbled on the table in anticipation of his first good meal in days.

"You not having any, Earwax?" Lionel asked.

"No, boss. When I put him to bed last night I went in the other room and found a perfectly boiled carrot and ate that. I didn't bother with the two pieces of coal though, not because I don't like the stuff; I used to lick a piece when I was a kid. Now though, with the diet and all, I got to watch what I eat." Lionel nodded politely, but Ned spat bacon and egg all over the table. He started to cough uncontrollably until Lionel hit him on the back with his pipe. Then, when he got his breath back, he looked at Earwax. "Is that all you found in the bed?"

The big man thought. "Yeah, only it was ever so hot in there. Steam was everywhere, so I opened the window to air the room. Why do you ask?"

Ned thought of Heinrich slowly cooking on the bed as the electric blanket gradually got hotter and hotter. So he had knocked off another snowman and all that was left of him was a boiled carrot nose, two pieces of warm coal, and a room full of steam. He smiled at Earwax. "No reason really," he said, then dug into his breakfast again.

*

Twenty-four boxes were stacked onto the wheelbarrow when Ned went out into the yard. He had showered and put on clean clothes that Earwax had neatly ironed while he ate. The air outside seemed to clear his still slightly sleepy mind. The boxes were taped up and on the sides, written in red ink, was 'Bigger Value Fish Fingers'. A knotted rope held the pile of boxes tightly in the barrow.

Lionel took a slurp of tea. "Now, my boy, listen very carefully. Inside these boxes is the instrument of destruction for Melton and his snowmen. I took your idea and added a bit of my own. We've moulded the fish fingers from our grit. This ain't any old kind of grit. No, this is weapons-grade material grit. We've taken the normal stuff and added some turpentine, creosote, bleach, washing up liquid, petrol, and tea. When this stuff comes into contact with snow, it vaporises on contact. Watch." And he took a 'Bigger Value Fish Finger' from his pocket and threw it like a knife at a small snowman that had been made near the end of the yard. Ned had not noticed it before, but he did now. The fish finger hit the snowman's head and it blew apart. Lionel shouted out in triumph. Ned was awestruck.

"Now, you see, when those idiots fit them onto their hands, there's going to be bedlam and lots of exploding snowmen. So you've got to get Melton to hand over your parents before you give him those to fit. And when he does, you get out of the area sharpish-like. We'll be waiting nearby with Thaw, ready for action if there's any trouble. Whatever you do, don't go into the factory with those snowmen or you'll be trapped and Melton will have the upper hand—or mitten, so to speak. You negotiate their release outside the factory where we can see you. Get him to bring them outside and exchange the fish fingers for your parents. They walk to where you are, and you get away from the area with them but leave the barrow of fish fingers, alright?"

Ned nodded an affirmative.

"And one more thing, Ned. Don't lose your temper with Melton. Don't provoke him or any of the other snowmen. Just do the deal there and then. Do not get involved in arguments and don't be too cocky."

But Ned was not listening now. He had the fishy fingers, he had a plan, he had Lionel and his team, and he would have his mum and dad back soon. Confidence was growing in him and the new day would prove to be victorious.

*

The snowman Vincent stood near the perimeter fence of the chiller factory. He had been ordered there by Melton on express orders to look out for the vile child Ned Mutton. On seeing him, Vincent was to report it immediately. But Vincent's mind was not on the orders given to him. Instead, he was on an equally important job—to himself—of trying to extract a particularly huge and encrusted bogey from his carrot nose. Two days it had been forming on the inside of his orange proboscis, and now it was so huge he was having trouble breathing and was starting to feel faint from lack of oxygen. The cold air accentuated the problem by drying the outermost part so that it was like a thick impenetrable skin and, having no fingers to attack it, the caked snot was driving Vincent insane. He had resorted to sticking thin objects up his nose to try to hook or snag the offending bogey but had failed. Now he thought he saw salvation in the form of a winter-bare hawthorn bush. Its jagged thorns stuck out at acute angles and it looked just right to free him from this snotty encumbrance. Vincent tore off a small branch and dislodged an empty bird's nest in the process. He was about to gouge it into his right nostril when a voice shouted out behind him.

"BOO!"

The shock forced Vincent's arm to jerk sharply up and he screamed out as the branch went right up the left nostril and stuck there.

Ned bellowed with laughter. "Some guard you are."

"You little swine." Through pain filled watery coal eyes, Vincent tried to grab at a blurred Ned, who stepped back and let the snowman grab at nothing. He continued trying to grab a blurred image but managed to wander away completely from Ned's general direction. Leaning on the wheelbarrow, Ned watched for a while, then started to shout, "Nowhere near, you're very cold. Turn around. Yes, that's it. Warm…warmer…warmer still." Until eventually Vincent found his way back to Ned and then grabbed him by the collar, the hawthorn branch hovering near to Ned's ear. "You vile little beast. Master Melton told me all about you, and you're going to—"

"Hold up there, friend," Ned cut him off. "Is that any way to treat the person who has brought to you the gift of touch?"

Vincent stopped pulling on Ned's collar. "What do you mean?"

"I've brought Melton his fishy fingers," Ned explained.

"Where are they then?" Vincent asked and looked around. Ned ducked so he didn't get speared by the branch. "I can't see anything through these watery eyes."

"There, right here. Hang on." And with that, Ned yanked the branch from Vincent's nose. There was another scream. Then, as he wiped the tears away, a look of delight appeared on Vincent's face. "Wow. You did it. I can breathe properly now. You got rid of that caked up bogey. You really did it." Then his eyes fell on the wheelbarrow. "And look at those fishy fingers. You did that too!" And he grabbed Ned in a hug. Ned tried to extricate himself from his loving embrace.

"Hey, wait a minute. I know you," Ned accused him. "You're the one who tried to empty my pockets and who gave Melton my address. So you're not having any fishy fingers. No, sir." Vincent let go. Ned stood in front of the wheelbarrow and looked away.

Poor Vincent started to sob. Ned tried to ignore him, but in his experience of snowmen, this softer side of the snowy personality was a new thing to him. Ever since his first encounter with them, Ned had found them to be spiteful and selfish with a great tendency for bullying. He put his mind on the job and again ignored the sobbing.

"Now look. Where's Melton, because he's expecting these and I'm expecting my parents back in return?"

Vincent did not say anything but just pointed towards the factory and continued to cry. Then Ned recalled something else about the snowman. "Yesterday you spotted me in the chiller factory outside Melton's office. You could have grabbed me and given me to Melton but you didn't. Why?"

Vincent glanced at him, then away again, then to the factory, and finally back to Ned, who was getting as uncomfortable with the situation as Vincent obviously was, so he decided on another prompt. "Well?"

Blowing his nose in his hand and then wiping it in the snow, Vincent then looked at Ned with a defiance that seemed to banish the crying white lump that he was a minute ago. He put his hands on his hips. "B...b...because I can't stand it anymore in that bloody fortress and because that old gammy-legged bugger is a bully and because I want to travel and do something different than slopping out after snowmen. That's why!"

Ned's eyes widened in shock and he was silent for a few seconds. He looked up at Vincent and poked the hawthorn stick at him. "Well, well. Damn it all, I am impressed. We got a rebellious snowman here who isn't a bully or a selfish lout."

Vincent looked around with concern. "I shouldn't have said that. Now I'm going to be for it. Just give me the fishy fingers and I can be out of here and chase my dream."

"You want the fishy fingers and to get out of here?" Ned said in realisation. "You want to disobey that nasty old snowman Mowbray and chase your dream, do you?"

Vincent held one hand up to his mouth. "Not so loud, boy. Melton can hear things even around here, you know."

Ned laughed. "Don't be daft. He's not that clever and he ain't got that good hearing."

The snowman shook his head and waved his arms in mute warning to shut up.

"Melton can't hear me or you out here. I know because those idiots from the Frozen Death Squad thought he could. But he can't because," Ned took a deep breath and shouted out, "MELTON'S A MEAN AND CRUEL NASTY OLD FART." He stopped shouting as his hearing registered what he thought was the noise of sleigh bells and so he turned his head to get a better fix on the sound. As he did, Ned saw Vincent's coal eyes widen in abject terror.

"Just give me the fishy fingers now, boy, and I can go."

Ned thought of the plan and his parents and how this strange and different snowman was putting it all at risk. He came out of his reverie. "No, I...I can't...I need my parents back." Vincent dived in the snow and tried to bury his head in it. As he did, Ned's eyes took in the scene heading towards him.

Like Santa Claus being pulled along in his sleigh, Melton was speeding along in a rusty old bathtub. There were no sweet and charming reindeers pulling this metal sledge, but eight tethered snowmen running along on all fours. Melton had the reigns in one hand and a long whip in the other that he was cracking above his charges' heads with great relish.

Ned dropped the hawthorn stick. Vincent tried to bury himself deeper in the snow.

As the sledge came nearer, Ned saw that dangling above the snowmen was a tub of ice cream. It was like the carrot on a stick for donkeys, except these eight snowmen were running in their harnesses trying to reach the tub and in doing so were propelling the bath tub/sled along at an incredible rate. Before Ned knew it, Melton was heaving back on the reins and was level with him. The snowmen collapsed in a heap, the string holding the ice cream tub broke, the bath tub fell over, and Melton stepped out.

"Did you mutter something derogatory about me?" he asked in a mock surprise.

Ned shook his head. "No, not me. I didn't say a thing."

Melton smiled. "But I heard you."

Ned crossed his arms and leant on the wheelbarrow. "Err, no. I told you I didn't say a thing."

Melton limped over to where Vincent was. "But I have a witness." He kicked Vincent, who yelped like a puppy and sat up. Melton studied Vincent with a look of mild disgust. "Idiot. What did that vile little fleshy thing say about me? Answer me properly within the allotted timescale of five seconds and I will take you off slopping out duties and guard duties. Do not and I will give you an ice cream sundae."

The tethered snowmen had found the ice cream tub and were fighting over its contents. They were covered in Neapolitan colours, but suddenly forgot the sweet delights and gasped in horror at the mention of an ice cream sundae. The multicoloured snowmen tried to back away from Melton and Vincent but they were tied together and got tangled up instead. Vincent started to shake and Melton took his walking stick from the bath tub and jabbed the snowman with it. "Yes. You'll be scooped out by my dear pet if you don't tell me the truth." He turned to the others and snapped at them, "And that goes for you lot too if you so much as hit a bump on the way back." They cowered down and held each other.

Ned had had enough. "Leave him alone, you rotten old bully. He hasn't done anything other than to report to you that I've brought your precious fishy fingers." He lifted one leg onto the wheel and gestured to the contents. "There. Fishy fingers for you!"

Melton did a double take and his eyes glowed red at the sight of the prized fish fingers. But bullies don't back down that easily and his pride was at stake.

"Mmmmmh. Jolly good. But you still caused me great offence and he's going to tell me what you said."

"I told you, I didn't say anything rude about you," Ned implored.

"Silence!" Melton shouted. "He will tell me, or else."

"Look, leave it out. I've got what you wanted." Ned tried to change the subject.

"Words were said that sounded like mean...cruel." Melton had trouble talking and saying the words. "And...nasty...oh...and f-f-f-fart. This is utterly despicable and disrespectful!"

Vincent got up and walked directly in front of Melton. He saluted. "My lord, the vile fleshy one said that he could do with a bean and gruel pastry tart as he's so hungry from the getting of the fishy fingers."

Melton was silent, as was Ned. Vincent had lied supremely and no one seemed to know what to say. Melton blinked twice. "Oh well. I suppose my hearing isn't what it was." He looked around as if trying to find something else to be spiteful to or someone to bully, but then he saw the fish fingers again. A smile broke out on his face.

"Well done, you little swine. It seems you have kept your side of the bargain. But where are Jean and Grant?"

"Who?" Ned did not know what the hell he was talking about.

Melton seemed lost and looked around the snowy landscape in desperation. "Where are my special forces; where are my Frozen Death Squad?"

A small pump emitted from Ned's pants as he suddenly recalled his two escorts. One had sizzled into steam falling into a baking oven and the other had been fried by an old lady with her killer electric zapper. So Grant and Jean were their names, and he had never even bothered to ask. Ned saw Melton frowning at him. He thought quickly. "The...the...they went off this morning...yes...this morning. They were pulled away on a...a...an...another special mission. Yes, that's right, another mission."

Melton looked surprised. "Oh they did, did they? And did they say where they were going?"

Ned shook his head, then changed his idea. "They...were...going to...Lapland...to find...Santa...Santa Claus. Yes, they are on a mission to find Father Christmas."

Melton shook his head and leaned against the bath tub. "I mean, they just upped and left me without so much as a please or thank you for all I've done for them. I know they're special faeces and all, but you would think they would consult me first. I could have saved them the trouble of looking for someone that does not exist."

The tethered snowmen turned to Melton at the mention of Santa Claus. Vincent had a strange look on his face also. It was a look of disbelief matched with forlorn hope. Ned looked at him and the others and he saw an opportunity to change the awkward subject of Grant and Jean and cause some underlying tension between master and servants.

"Santa does exist," he stated loudly.

Melton chuckled. "Oh no, he does not."

Ned inclined his head and looked at the snowmen. As they looked at him they smiled, and as they looked at Melton their faces took on a disappointed look. Ned pointed at Melton. "Oh yes he does."

Melton shook his head. "No, I think you'll find he does not exist at all."

Ned retorted. "I think you'll find he does."

Melton clucked his tongue loudly. "Oh no he doesn't."

Vincent and the snowmen looked on like spectators at a tennis match as Ned and Melton batted the ball of argument stating the existence and non-existence of Father Christmas between themselves. Eventually, and true to his nature, Melton lost his temper, picked up the whip, and cracked it loudly over Ned's head. It was so close that the whip end cut a furrow in his hair so that it looked like he had two bunches of hair on either side of his head instead of one big hedgeful. Melton whooped in delight and the snowmen, who seemed to have forgotten about whether Santa existed or not, started a round of applause. Melton bowed to them in theatrical gratitude. Ned touched his scalp. It was still hot from the whipping and he was not pleased. "You mad old bugger! You could have taken my eye out with that." Melton turned to him and then started to laugh hysterically. So did the others, apart from Vincent, who looked around and, spying something in the snow, went off to get it. Melton was on his knees now and tears of laughter were coming from his coal eyes. He was hitting the bath tub in an effort to stop but every time he looked at poor Ned he became hysterical again. "You…you…look like some kind of heffalump that's had its trunk cut off." And with that, he fell down in stitches of laughter again. Ned rubbed his violated head. He had lost most of his dignity in the last few days but this was the end of it. His anger overcame him and he picked a box of fishy fingers and walked over to Melton. "Think it's funny, do you? Well, have this from Nelly." He threw the box down on Melton's head. There was a loud thud and the laughing stopped instantly. Ned's anger seemed to fly away with the sudden halting of Melton's insane giggling and reality hit him. He backed off as the snowman started to rise. Steam was issuing from his eyes. He was breathing hard and flexing the whip. Ned backed into the wheelbarrow and closed his eyes, ready for a lashing. Instead, he felt something scratching and prickling his head and opened his eyes to see Melton had dropped the whip and was staring curiously at him. Ned's eyes looked up and around, then he felt where his bald cranium was. Only now it was not bald but covered with something that felt like moss and twigs. Ned grabbed it and pulled the thing off, and as he did, he saw Vincent smiling at him. He looked from the snowman to what was in his hands. It was a bird's nest.

"It's not a perfect match but if you take off the moss then the colour is very similar to your own. A perfectly natural 'syrup' for you," Vincent explained.

Ned was perplexed but grateful all the same.

"What are you telling him, idiot?" Melton shouted.

Vincent raised his eyebrows at Ned in amusement and turned to his master. "I said, lord, that the bird's nest makes a fine 'syrup of figs', so to speak."

"A what?"

"A wig, sir. Syrup of figs, Irish jig, or toupee for the more discerning person."

Melton shook his head and looked at the box he had been assaulted by. It had not broken open and Ned was thankful for that. If the fake fish fingers had hit Melton and started to melt him then the game would be up and Ned, with his mum and dad, would be dead. "Consider yourself fortunate, boy, that today I'm in a forgiving mood. No one has ever assaulted me and got away with it before. But today you may have...or maybe you have not. I haven't decided yet, but you have achieved the mission that I tasked you with. So come, all of you. Today we change the world. Today we will have fishy fingers; by tonight, we will be the new master race." He slapped his hands together and the sledge crew readied themselves.

"Idiot," Melton addressed Vincent again. "For your disobedience today, you will escort the boy back to the fortress whilst carrying the wheelbarrow of wonder weapons." Vincent saluted.

Ned was suddenly horrified. In the back of his mind was Lionel's voice repeating to him not to go into the factory whatever happened. The plan was to make the fish finger/parent exchange out in the open, not away from where Ned could be seen. But the plan was falling to pieces. If only he had kept his mouth shut and not lost his temper.

"Wait a minute! We had a deal here. Fishy fingers for my mum and dad. I want them here now before I let you have them fishy fingers." He tried to sound confident but it came out in a pleading manner.

Melton grabbed the reins and flicked the whip. He looked back at Ned. "You are not in a position to negotiate after your violent and abusive outburst towards me. You will accompany that fool into the factory and then I will let you…" He thought of the right words to use. "How shall I put it? Join Mummy and Daddy again. Now hurry up!"

Ned panicked then and laid his body in front of the wheelbarrow. "You'll have to squash me first. Those fishy fingers are staying here."

Melton was not impressed with Ned's bravado. He smiled evilly at Vincent. "Idiot, run him over and squish him."

Vincent pushed the barrow forward and Ned quickly scrabbled out the way. Melton laughed. "What a wretched little cowardy custard you are. Once we have the fishy fingers on, the human race is on borrowed time."

Ned screamed at him. He still had the bird's nest toupee in his hands and he flung it uselessly at Melton. The whip cracked and cut the little nest in two. Ned collapsed in the snow and started to sob. A cold hand lifted his chin up and Ned stared into Vincent's face. The snowman had a gentle smile on his face and he winked at Ned. "Come on. It's not over yet."

"Yes it is. I had a plan and now it's in ruins because I couldn't keep my mouth shut or my temper down. Melton's not going to keep his word anyway. The plan's completely ruined."

Vincent just looked at Ned, then took his hands in his. "Then make another plan." He lifted Ned up, hefted the weight of the barrow, and started off towards the fortress. Ned looked around for any sign of Lionel and his team but saw nothing. Then he turned and hurried after Vincent.

Chapter 16

Earwax crawled back down from his lookout position. In a hollow, and camouflaged with stolen white bed sheets so as to blend in with the snow, was Thaw. Lionel, Elsie, and the others were sharing a flask of something hot when Earwax slid to their feet.

"What's up, Earwax?" Lionel asked.

"Plan's gone to crap, that's what's up." He looked up as Lionel nibbled on a worm. "The boy's gone into the factory."

"He's done what?" The half-chewed worm was spat in Earwax's face. Lionel led and they all scrambled and slipped up from the cover to look.

Just as they reached the top, they heard the faint low noise of a steel door slamming shut.

"Oh no! The little fool's gone in," Lionel shouted in fear. Earwax and the others started to roll and run around in panicked movements. One even fainted. Elsie brought them out of the mass panic attack. "Quiet! All of you! This is no time to lose your minds. We must re-plan quickly and take action."

They stopped their fright-filled frolics. Lionel looked proudly at his daughter.

"Chip off the old block, boss. Ain't she?" Earwax said.

Lionel sat up in the snow and dusted himself off. "She sure is that. Now, let's think." He looked at his men. "No, maybe we'd better not all think. Me and Elsie will think for you lot. You lot stay here and keep a look out. We'll reassess the tactical situation."

"If we pile in there," Lionel said. "Without knowing where young Ned is, then he could be slushed before we find him. I know, because that place is a maze. Even in daylight it's nearly impossible to find your way around."

"But we can't abandon him!" Elsie said.

"I know we can't, but I told the little fool not to go in, didn't I?"

"Dad, something has obviously gone wrong. Ned said he wouldn't lose his temper or be cocky," Elsie pleaded. "Someone needs to go in there and help him."

Lionel scratched at his stubble, trying to think. After a while he stood and, holding Elsie's hand, descended to where the others were. "Okay, we're going to have a group meditation here. Everyone get in a circle and take up the lotus position."

Elsie was horrified. "Dad! There's a boy gone into that chiller factory and who knows what horrors await him? He needs rescuing now!"

Lionel held up his hands. "Now, now, Elsie, I've told you time and again, haste leads to waste. If we combine our cosmic energies, then the right answer will present itself. Come and take up your position like a good girl."

She stamped the ground and then stomped down to the circle.

All the group sat cross-legged.

"Do you want me to sing a hymn, boss?" Earwax enquired.

"No, Earwax. Not yet anyway. Now close your eyes and find your inner self," Lionel calmly offered.

They all did and started to chant a rhythmical mantra. Two minutes into this, Elsie opened her eyes and crept off towards the chiller factory.

*

As they slowly followed behind Melton's sleigh, Ned's mind was awash with trying to form another rescue plan. Lionel was somewhere out there with Thaw, but he could not count on him attacking now for fear of Melton killing his parents. But there was another possibility. Could he trust the snowman, Vincent? He had, after all, said that he hated Melton and the fortress and wanted out. He had openly defended Ned even though threatened with an ice cream sundae, whatever that was, and had said that Ned should think of another plan. Again, he thought if he could trust a snowman? Every one of them so far—bar Vincent—had shown immediately that they were cruel bullies out for themselves and no one else. The similarities between Melton, his snowmen, and Beetie and his lot were strangely similar, Ned thought. In fact, all grown-ups he had met over the last few days seemed slightly deranged with violent, war-like tendencies. But Vincent; was he a spy deliberately put here to find out about Ned's plan, or was he genuinely a nice snowman?

Ned could now see the door at the chiller factory getting nearer; the door that he had left with Top Hat (Grant) and Bowler (Jean) in what now seemed like an age ago. His head was beginning to hurt and he had to find out more before he was inside the factory.

Vincent was whistling softly as Ned caught up with him. "Erm, I don't know your name. Melton called you Idiot and I don't want to, so what is it?"

The whistling stopped and the snowman turned. "My name is Horatio Cornwallis Banrock Moritz the First."

"Damn, that's a mouthful," Ned mumbled.

"But you can call me Vincent," the snowman said.

"Okay...Vincent. That's a nice name and easier to remember. Why did you defend me back there and tell Melton that I wanted a...?" Ned could not remember.

"A bean and gruel pastry tart," Vincent answered. Before Ned could continue, Vincent explained. "I work in the kitchens at the fortress—or I used to, before he put me on slopping out duties. Not that Melton lets us have anything other than jelly and ice cream, but I like to cook. Just think, all those lovely ingredients, spices, poultry, fish, meats." He looked up dreamily at the sky. "I found a couple of old cookbooks in the kitchen cupboards a while back; Women's Institute's *May I Have the Recipe* is the best, I think. Lovely pictures. Still, if I went near a cooker I'd have to be careful, wouldn't I?" he chuckled. "There was a book on cockney rhyming slang as well. I thought it would be amusing to teach my fellow snowmen some of the sayings. That way, they could say things to Melton without him or them knowing the real meaning. I used to have a right giraffe when I heard what they were calling Melton to his boat race."

Ned tried to make out what the words meant when it dawned on him. "You can read too?"

"I'm the only one in that bloody fortress who can read apart from old peg leg." Vincent corrected Ned. "He doesn't want any of them to read. When you can read then you can learn and if you learn then you can find out the truth and be your own person. Melton doesn't like that sort of thing happening. Although I did hear him trying to teach Heinrich to read once and that was agonizing. It was a hopeless cause."

"But Top Hat, I mean, Grant and Jean could read. They told me."

Vincent put the barrow down. "Those two cretins couldn't read. I tried to teach them but all they wanted to do was play war. So I read to them and thought I'd have some fun at Melton's expense. I encouraged them to pretend to be members of an elite squad of special forces snowmen. They couldn't even say the word, mind you, neither can peg leg. He refers to the special faeces. Do you know what that means?"

Ned shook his head.

"Well, it means poo." He suddenly changed the subject. "Where did they go really? Grant and Jean were helpless outside of the fortress. They used to get lost trying to find the toilets, and I know there's no hope of them trying to get to Lapland."

Ned's mouth went dry. He could either lie again or tell the truth, but if he did, what would Vincent do? He kept quiet.

"Well, that's a sign of guilt if ever there was one," Vincent laughed. He pointed to the door. "We'll be overdue if I don't hurry and Melton will become angry with me and you. Now, you don't know whether to trust me and I don't know whether I can trust you, but we have a mutual problem. We both want to get out of that place. You do with your mum and dad well, and I do with my cookbooks. So you tell me what happened to Grant and Jean and I take that as a positive step towards escaping from here. Also, you keep looking back towards where we came from. Are you planning a rescue mission?"

If Ned told what really happened to Grant and Jean and Vincent was Melton's mole then he would be for it, but Ned still would have the satisfaction of not telling the whole story. The fish finger surprise would melt the foul race of snowmen even if Ned was not there to see it. So he figured it would not hurt to tell the truth. Anyway, he could deny it and tell Melton about Vincent's name-calling and his cookbooks. So Ned went for it.

"Jean was melted in a bread oven and Grant was vapourized by an old lady's stun gun."

Vincent looked mortified. "Damn. That means I'll melt if I go too near an oven."

Ned was relieved by his reaction. "This was an industrial baking oven, not a standard kitchen one, Vincent. I think you may be alright if you use mittens."

Vincent started to laugh. "Look, I've got mittens already," he said, and held up his hands. Then he leaned on the barrow. "Well, I'll give it to you, boy. You have been more of a soldier than those two thick buggers. Still, I'll miss them all the same."

"So, you're not going to tell Melton, are you?" Ned asked.

Vincent chuckled. "No. Don't worry, er...I've forgot what your name is?"

"Ned. Ned Mutton."

"Damn. That is a mouthful," Vincent said. He lifted the barrow and started to walk towards the door. "Now let's do a deal here, Ned. I'll help you get your parents out of the fortress if Melton does not keep his word, which in all probability he won't. I've been excavating an escape tunnel for the past two years so you, me, your mum, and your dad can get out. After that, you can help by giving me what I want."

"Which is?" Ned asked curiously.

"Well, you remember all that business with Melton saying Santa doesn't exist, yes? Well, I think—no, I know in my heart—that he does, and I want to see him. Can you fix that for me?"

Ned thought. What could he say? What could he tell Vincent? This was too good an offer to turn down and the lives of his mum and dad depended again on what he said. He nodded to the snowman. "Okay. It's a deal."

Vincent put down the barrow and offered his hand. Ned shook it. "Come on then. Let's get this thing over and done with. Old peg leg's expecting fishy fingers, and in truth, I'm looking forward to getting mine too."

Ned's stomach turned as he thought of all the snowmen melting or exploding whilst he was in the factory. And Vincent, who he had just made a bargain with, was going to be one of these if he did not tell him now.

"Vincent, wait! There's something else."

Just then, the door burst open and Melton called out, "You two are holding up proceedings. Hurry at once, or I shall sundae the both of you!"

Vincent seemed to ignore Ned and offered a putrid smile to his Melton. "Forgive me, master. The wheelbarrow's handles were very coarse on my poor mittens and the little fleshy one needed the toilet."

Melton glowered at Vincent. "You nincompoop. I'll have to send you on hard labour duties to toughen up those spongy little mittens of yours. As for that fleshy swine, you should have let him wet his pants. Our destiny comes before any water closet relief. Now schnell, rapido, hurry!"

"Vincent!" Ned said loudly from the corner of his mouth.

"It'll have to wait until after the fishy finger presentation, Ned," Vincent said, and he entered the door.

Ned followed. In here, he had no back up apart from Vincent, and if he were to trust him then he had to stop him from putting on the fish fingers. But his thoughts changed as he now saw not the dreary room dimly lit by a grimy bare light bulb that he had seen before. Now the area was huge. It seemed that the inner walls had been removed and multicoloured lights shone down to reveal a room set for a party. Bunting that was mildewed and faded hung above rows of benches that were arranged one behind the other. Spoons and Christmas crackers were placed on these and on the centre table was the half-dead Christmas tree that Ned recognised from Melton's office. At the head of the benches he saw a damaged amplifier leaning against what looked like a church pulpit. A loud sound of static erupted from the speaker, followed by the jolly sound of carols. Ned saw that Vincent had a look of utter delight on his face. He moved over and tugged at the snowman's arm.

"Vincent!" Ned whispered. But he was cut off by another voice behind.

"Just because I don't believe in Santa Claus doesn't mean that we can't celebrate Christmas," Melton sniggered. He had a stove pipe hat on, a reindeer embroidered waistcoat, and a novelty Christmas cake tie around his neck.

"Christmas is over a month away," Ned corrected him, then remembered to stop being cocky. Get the job done. Parents, Vincent, escape tunnel, and away. "But it's a nice idea, Lord Melton."

Melton looked at him suspiciously. Then his eyes moved to Vincent. "Over to the table in front of my dais with the fishy fingers, and then go to the very last table at the back and be quiet. One word out of you, idiot, and Mr Sundae comes to visit."

Vincent pushed the barrow to the bench and started to unload the boxes onto the table. His wicked master seemed to follow his every move.

Ned coughed to get Melton's attention. "Ahem...now you've got the fish fingers, can I get my parents back, please?" Melton was fitting his gold monocle into his right coal eye and staring at Vincent as he moved to the last table. "And can the idiot Vincent show us out of your fortress?" he added.

Melton turned on Ned. "What?" He looked around, then back to Ned. "No, you can't. You can savour our moment of triumph by watching my glorious minions insert their new digits."

"But you promised!" Ned shouted.

Melton seemed distracted. Ned had to think quickly. "Look, sir, I've had a terrible few days and all I want is my mum and dad back. You don't want me hanging about. It's your day now, so please?"

Melton fumbled in his waistcoat but could not fit his huge hands into the tiny pockets. Ned fished inside and brought out what he was trying to reach. It was an antique pocket watch, and quite beautiful. Engraved on it were scenes of snowmen carrying spears and other weapons and above them was a wondrous and intricate crown that seemed to shine brighter in the multicoloured light.

Melton snatched it. "Get your filthy, fleshy hands off my timepiece. This is a family heirloom, and not to be handled by mere mortals."

"Sorry." Ned emphasized the word. "I was just trying to help."

Melton looked at the time. Instead of hands, the watch had stars moving around a black face. Ned could not tell anything from this type of pocket watch, but it seemed Melton could. "Where's that lump of a servant Heinrich? Late as usual; he'll be for a sundae as well if he doesn't hurry." Ned coughed in shock. He could not catch his breath as he remembered cooking Heinrich on the electric blanket.

Melton hit him on the back. "Stop coughing in my presence, you irritating little turd." He did not allow Ned to recover but carried on talking. "Why you want that idiot snowman to escort you, I don't know. He's a trouble maker and he's going to get a sundae instead of fishy fingers." Ned started coughing again but managed to splutter and ask, "What…what…is a sundae anyway?"

Melton hit him again. "A sundae, my little pink-tissued sapien, is what I order to be administered to disobedient snowmen. And that idiot sitting down there is one of the most disrespectful oafs that I have ever met." He limped to the dais and Ned followed, the coughing having finally stopped.

"Yes, but what is it?" Ned was intrigued, but more concerned that if Vincent had it done then would it affect their escape plan.

On top of the lectern, a stick was attached, and on this a microphone was taped. The sticky tape was peeling and hanging down limply. Melton covered the microphone with his hand and whispered to Ned. "In the bowels of this fortress is a mutation that I reared especially for the purpose of carrying out an 'ice cream sundae'. It's like a lobotomy, but done with an ice cream scoop, and the creature does the act with great enthusiasm. Down in the dungeons are countless Sundaes that I will use for cannon fodder for the up-and-coming struggle." He smiled evilly at Ned.

"That's horrible!" Ned said.

"Sssssh!" Melton said. He obviously didn't want his voice amplified across the room, announcing the part brain removal. "And no, you can't get Mummy and Daddy now. You're going to have to help me out one last time. That klutz Heinrich has let me down again, so you'll have to take his place."

Ned looked shocked. "I don't want any fishy fingers. I've got my own, thank you."

Melton's walking stick was leaning against the dais. He picked it up and swiped it at Ned. "You're not getting any of them, you little fool. You're going to hand them out to my troopers. Anyway, it's probably better all round. After all, you can count and Heinrich can't, so unpack the fishy fingers and I want..." he paused. "Oh, I don't know. I'm under so much pressure I can't think easily. You work out how many are needed per bench if there are two snowmen at each. You can discount three because Grant and Jean won't be joining us, and even if that swine Heinrich turns up, he's not going to have any. Also, if I'm going to sundae Vincent then I'm not wasting precious fingers on him."

If Ned handed out the fish fingers, then waited near to Vincent, they could try to make a run for it before the place went wild with exploding snowmen. It was worth a try after all and it seemed his only option in this ever-changing life or death struggle.

"Okay, I'll start now," he told Melton, who was now studying some notes he had on the lectern and not taking any notice.

"I said, I'll—" Ned started to say, then stopped. Seeing Melton engrossed in his notes, he saw an opportunity. Backing off, he tiptoed over in Vincent's direction. Halfway across the floor and between the centre benches, the carols stopped and a voice boomed out.

"Today our destiny has been delivered to us by this foul young fleshling." Ned jumped out of his skin. He looked around and saw Melton speaking into the microphone. He was practicing a speech. "It is time to take our rightful place at the head of society. We are no longer slaves to society, for now we will be able to open doors properly. We can hold a cup and saucer with aplomb. We can push buttons, undo buttons, open sweet wrappers, paint things properly by holding a brush correctly. Today we become independent. Today we celebrate our non-dependence day! Now my troopers, or shall I say, my super-duper troopers." He was building himself up to a fury when there was a sudden bang and Melton's voice sounded normal again. Ned saw smoke rising from under the lectern.

Melton spied him. "What are you doing down there?"

"I...I...just needed the toilet?" he said weakly.

"We don't have toilets!" Melton shouted. "Now get back up here and fix this microphone."

"I'm not an electrician, you know!" Ned shouted back. "Perhaps you should call one and get them to come and fix it."

The walking stick slammed down on the wood. "Get up here now!"

Vincent was standing up and looking concerned.

"You go and get the others," Melton ordered him. "Bring them in here and tell them to sit down at their allotted places."

Ned and Vincent's eyes met. The snowman winked and set off. As he passed him, Ned grabbed his arm. "Vincent, don't—" but Melton interrupted yet again. "Stop that now, you idiot. Go and do as you're told. Both of you!"

Vincent bowed to Melton and walked away. Ned cursed, then stomped up to Melton.

"Under the lectern is a fuse box. The one that feeds the microphone has blown and needs resetting, so get down there and do it."

"If I can go and get my parents first," Ned said.

"No!" Melton bawled, then calmed down. "Look, this is the last time I'll ask you to push buttons or switch switches, so just do it! After that I'll reunite you with your parents." Ned went to look under the table and, as he did, saw Melton trying to suppress a laugh. Gritting his teeth in anger, Ned saw the fuse box. It looked lethal; the wires going into it were bare, a loose screw held the cover down, and smoke seeped from one corner of it. He thought if he touched it then he would be electrocuted. Tentatively, he put a finger towards the box. He paused, then, suddenly, "Ouuuuuch."

Melton had kicked him.

"Reset the damn thing! I've got an audience arriving shortly." There was a shuffle from above and a groan and Ned got another kick. "They're here now, damn it. Throw the switch, boy. Throw it!"

Instead, Ned stood up. He saw all the snowmen filing into the room. They looked very excited and beamed in anticipation at the fitting of fishy fingers.

Melton looked at them. "Yes, yes, very good. Let's calm down and take our seats. We have a minor setback. Please remain quiet whilst I fix it." He turned on Ned. "Get back under there and fix it!"

"No way! All the wires are bare and it's still smoking. Only an idiot would have wired something up like that."

Melton took on an affronted look. "How dare you? I wired that up."

"Oh, well then that explains it!" Ned retorted and ducked under the lectern before he was hit. Instead, Melton poked at him with his stick. "Fix it, boy, or else," he demanded.

Ned winced at the thought of touching a very dangerous and highly botched electrical box. "Got any rubber gloves?" he asked.

"Damn the gloves. Fix the blasted fuse, boy!"

Ned grabbed Melton's stick and jabbed at the box. There was a violent bang and sparks exploded all around him. He thought he may have died as he was in near darkness. Only his clothes offered a tiny glow of amber light as they smoldered gently. He patted himself down and tried to stand. He could hear bangs and crashes all around, followed by scuffling, and then a beam of light fell on him. Is this heaven? Ned thought briefly, and then realised it could only be hell as the face of Melton loomed down at him. "Imbecile. You've gone and fused the whole bloody room now!"

Still shaking, Ned crept out from the dais. He heard the sound of crying and jibbering. Melton grabbed him by the collar and lifted him up. "Right, dotard, you can go down downstairs to the mains and switch the power on again."

Ned was angry. "You get stuffed, I will." Then he thought about it. Downstairs was where the gallery of fools was situated, where his parents were. He could try to get them out whilst these lot were preoccupied. Then escape!

"Oh, alright then. Where is it?"

"Good," Melton said, and in the torch light he turned towards the seated snowmen. "Now stop your crying, all of you. There is no need to be afraid of the dark and the lights will be back on soon."

"How do I get there?" Ned asked eagerly.

"Go out of here. Take the first left, then second right. You'll find some steps. Go along them, count fifty steps, then turn left, left again, then right. Go through three doors, then take the second spiral staircase and at the bottom turn around, go back on yourself, turn right twice, then there's the fuse box on the left-hand wall. Got it?"

"No!" said Ned. "You can't expect me to remember all that and find it in the dark."

"Oh, well in that case I'll have to get you an escort, won't I?" Melton chuckled, as if reading Ned's escape intentions.

Ned swore under his breath. Damn it. That would have been a golden opportunity if he had only remembered Melton's instructions. He kicked the dais in frustration. Which bully was Melton going to lumber him with to go and switch on the mains again?

The torch shone out over the seated snowmen. Melton was muttering to himself. "Where are you, where's he gone?" The torch settled on a bench.

"Simpleton, get up here now and escort this little fiend to the main fuse box."

There was the scraping of a chair, then footsteps. Ned looked down and saw a snowman wearing a pink wooly hat. His head was bowed.

Melton pushed Ned aside and snatched the pink hat. "No one wears a hat in here except me." And he threw the hat away. The abashed face stared up at Melton, who sneered back. Ned saw the face and gulped. Then he held his hands behind his back to stop them shaking. He was staring down at Vincent. "Oh, you beauty, Melton," Ned said to himself. The maimed tyrant spoke to Vincent. "Right, go down and fix the lights. On the back of the door is another torch, so use that to see with. Make it sharpish, both of you!"

Vincent took Ned's hand and led him. Melton kindly lit their path with his torch. They found the torch. It was rusty and had a cracked lens, but after a couple of hits its beam flickered into life. They left the room as Melton addressed the crowd. "Now there will be a short interlude whilst the luminaries are fixed. Soon you will have the fishy fingers and soon we shall pull crackers and eat ice cream." There was a roar of delight from the darkness. "In the ensuing time, though, I shall entertain you with an exciting demonstration of my skills with the whip. Can I have a volunteer?"

The sound of scraping chairs and suppressed panic was audible in the darkness.

Chapter 17

Vincent was striding through the darkened factory. The torches' beams wobbled and jumped as he went. Ned was trying to keep up. "We've got to get to the gallery of fools, get Mum and Dad, and get out of here before those lot start fitting their fish fingers."

"Okay," Vincent said. "But I was really looking forward to a pair of proper hands, you know. Just think of all the things I could do with them." He started to list them. "I could take up origami, I could take up smoking a pipe and hold it in the correct manner and point it at things, then comment on them whilst emphasizing a certain matter. I could—"

"No, you couldn't, Vincent," Ned interrupted him. "They'd melt you or you'd explode as soon as you touched them."

"What?" Vincent stopped and turned on Ned.

"I didn't get real fish fingers. I...I mean, we...Lionel and his lot made them. They're fake fish fingers made of grit mixed with other stuff that's deadly to snow."

"I don't understand. Who's Lionel, and what's grit?"

"Look, it's just as well we got away now. You don't want any of those fish fingers, and anyway, Melton told me you weren't to have any and that you were going to get a sundae."

The torchlight reflected off the wet floor and Ned could see Vincent's face turning angry. He suddenly lashed out at the wall with his fist. "Damn that evil old viper. I'm going to get him one day. I swear it. I'll give him yellow snow to eat, you wait. You just wait!"

"Look, Vincent, when we're out of this place and back home with my parents, I'll get you your fish fingers. I promise I will. Now, can we go and get them please?" Ned was aware that killing other snowmen could anger Vincent, but the snowman didn't seem too concerned with that. His reaction to Melton's potential sundae was understandable but Ned had to get him to calm down and onto their escape plan.

Vincent nodded. "Come on then, it's this way. You can fill me in afterwards about the grit and that bloke." He started to chuckle as he went. "Exploding snowmen, eh? I'd like to see that. Especially Melton, oh that would be good."

They ran through the complex. Vincent knew the place well, and panting, they arrived shortly outside the gallery of fools.

"No time to lose. I have a bad feeling about Melton and those snowmen. Do you think they'll start trying to fit them in the dark?" Ned asked. He kept cocking his head trying to catch any sound of screaming or of exploding snowmen but the only sound was his and Vincent's breathing.

Ned hit the red button. Nothing happened.

He hit it again. Nothing.

"Here, let me try," Vincent jabbed the button. Still nothing.

"Your hands are too big, just like Melton's. He couldn't do it either." Ned was starting to panic.

"Hang on," Vincent said. "The power's down, isn't it?"

"And from what Melton said it's a right journey and a half to the main fuse box." Ned's voice was rising further in fear.

Vincent looked questioningly at Ned. "No it isn't, it's just along the corridor in a recessed compartment."

"But Melton—"

Vincent cut Ned off. "Melton said it to confuse you, so that he could send an escort down to accompany you. You're lucky he chose me, eh?"

"Oh, right," Ned said meekly.

"You wait here. I won't be a minute." And Vincent scurried off. Ned could not keep still; his nerves were shredding and he paced up and down in front of the door. Were his mum and dad still alive behind there or had the wicked old snowman broken his word and froze them? With the power back on, the door would open and he would see. But then it struck him. With the power back on, the lights would come on and the fish finger applications could begin upstairs. The dilemma was terrifying but one could not happen without the other. Ned kicked the door and he heard a muffled sound of something. He hit it again. It sounded like someone or something struggling or in pain. Was it his mum and dad struggling to free themselves? Ned kicked harder on the door. There was a bang and it seemed to give slightly. He kicked it again. It gave a little but there was no bang this time. Lifting his leg and readying to give the door an almighty boot, Ned heard another bang. Then the lights came on, the switch glowed red, and Vincent came running around the corner.

"Did you hear that? It's started; they're fitting the fishy fingers and they're exploding!"

Ned hit the button and the door groaned open. Before it had swung fully inwards, Ned had scrambled through and was running down the line of tanks towards the one that held his parents.

He looked in. The glass was covered in condensation so he rubbed it away and saw two figures covered in ice and motionless.

"NO!" Ned screamed and started to hit the glass. Vincent came up behind him and stared in.

From inside the tank two sets of eyes opened and, at the sight of the snowmen, bulged in terror. Ned's dad let out a scream. Ned's mum strained at the ropes that held them and swore loudly at Vincent.

Ned started to laugh. He slapped Vincent on the back. "They're alive, they're alive, they're alive," he kept repeating.

Vincent pulled him away. "This place is thawing out. The power's not back on in these tanks. Stand back." He made the shape of a fist and brought it down in the centre of the glass. It shattered into a thousand tiny pieces and Ned's mum's swearing was suddenly deafening.

Ned jumped in and embraced them. His mum allowed him a kiss on the cheek, then continued her vocal assault on Vincent. Ned held up his hands. "It's alright, Mum. He's a friend. He's with us. His name's Vincent and he's going to help us escape!"

She stopped swearing and strained to look at her husband. "Did you hear that, Geoffrey? Ned's got a new friend and he's a snowman." Then she did a double take. "What on earth have you done to your hair, dear?"

Ned rubbed his head and remembered that Melton had sliced the top of his hair off.

"Yes, Audrey, dear, I heard it. Now give it a rest with the swearing. I've gone deaf in one ear with all your shouting." He looked at his son. "Well, son, that's one bad haircut. Are you going to undo our bonds and get us out of here?"

Ned was just smiling at them now. Vincent was patting him on the shoulder and smiling too. Then Vincent cocked his head and listened. Ned heard it also. Voices and shouting. It was getting louder.

"Come on. Let's go." Vincent pulled the chair apart and the ropes fell away in coils.

Geoffrey looked at Vincent. "Handy friend to have, Ned."

Vincent hit the button on the other door. Nothing happened, so he kicked it open.

"Follow me," he said, and started to run. With the lights on they made good time but instead of heading towards the entrance, Vincent appeared to be leading them deeper into the complex.

Ned spoke up. "Is this taking us to where the escape route is, Vincent?"

"Yes, I just want to get my cookbooks first and then we're out of here," he replied.

Ned's parents were breathing heavily. "He wants what?" Geoffrey asked between breaths.

"Cookbooks, Geoffrey. Are you deaf?" Audrey replied.

"No, I'm just concerned that we should be getting out of here rather than going on a book hunt."

"Dad's right, Vincent, we should get out now before Melton comes and finds us," Ned said.

Vincent carried on the pace. They came to a section that was much lighter and cold, chill air blew down on them. Ned saw that they were in a large corridor with passages that branched off left and right. Snow blew in from a large hole in the roof high above them where it had piled up in drifts along the floor.

"Can we get out there?" Ned said, pointing to the roof.

"No, there's no way to reach it. Anyway, I've got to get those books. They've been like a companion to me during all this time down here in the fortress. It won't take long and it's on the way. They won't get here that quickly anyway, not with peg leg limping along at a snail's pace."

Ned was slightly reassured but then they turned a corner and came face-to-face with three snowmen.

Vincent's eyes widened. Ned's mum and dad looked on in confusion. Ned saw what Vincent was smiling lustfully at. It was not a snowman that was standing in front of Vincent, but a snowwoman.

"Well, hello there," Vincent uttered smoothly.

The snowman behind pushed the snowwoman aside and pointed a pistol at them. Ned, Audrey, and Geoffrey huddled together. Vincent looked outraged.

The snowman holding the gun advanced and they pressed back into the snow-covered corridor. Ned looked at the snowman. It had very strange skin, looking more like cheap fur or dyed nylon than snow, and it was filthy too. The other snowman was tiny by snowman standards, being only about Ned's size.

The pistol-packing snowman held his gun at them with one hand and with the other pulled at something on his neck. He moved his hand and then pulled off his snow head.

"Well, well, well. The Muttons, I assume?" The face was red as ever but showing a bald head this time. Ned growled with anger as Beetie Vaughan-Abbott stared back at him.

"What on earth are you doing here?" Ned asked.

"I could ask the same," Beetie growled back at him as he pulled his sweaty wig from the outfit's head.

The other two had followed him in. The tiny snowman tried to pull his head off but struggled as the zip jammed. There was a panicked cry from inside the nylon head and the sound of weeping.

Beetie kicked the snowwoman. "Crichton, go and help Fabian out of his suit."

Ned touched Vincent. "Would you like my friend here to help pull your son's head off?"

Beetie cocked the gun. "Now, now, Mutton Junior, your time will come sooner than you think. I played you the fool and you took it all in and more, so all the evidence is piled up against you. What with the killing of a protected species, blatant vandalism to a historic monument, and lastly, but not leastly, vandalizing this said property that belongs to me."

"What's this?" Geoffrey and Audrey said together.

"Oh, didn't little Ned ever tell you what he was doing these last few months?" Beetie offered innocently.

"I can explain," Ned said. "He's the one who organised to have all them people frozen in the tanks. It was him and Melton!"

"You interfering whelp!" Beetie slapped Ned across the head with his hand.

"Get your hands off my son!" Geoffrey shouted and made a move forward but Beetie brought the gun to bear. "Freeze or the boy gets it."

Just then, Fabian collapsed in the pile of snow and stopped struggling. He let Crichton exert himself in an attempt to pull his head off.

Beetie turned on them. "Well hurry up, damn you. I need to get what I came here for and this place gives me the creeps."

Ned stepped forward. "You fat, over-inflated, syrup-wearing pretend ponce. You'll never get away with it. Not in here. You might shoot me but your friend Melton and his lot of snowmen are coming around the corner soon and he's really, really angry. I've just given him exploding fish fingers and his minions are going off like Christmas crackers. You see, you were such a good teacher and mentor that when Melton tasked me to get the fish fingers, I thought, what would Beetie do? Being such a war hero that you are. I thought, he'd make booby traps out of the fish fingers. So when I did this and brought them here, I told Melton it was all your idea and that you got them for me. When he gets here he's going to be well peeved that it was you. He won't like it that you've betrayed him. In fact, he'll probably give you a sundae."

It was a fine bluff. Ned thought the fear of being trapped down here would outweigh the fear of exposure as a cheating, law breaking property developer and kidnapper to boot.

"Rubbish. The last desperate imaginings of a little fool," Beetie scoffed. Then he heard a bang and turned to see Fabian and Crichton hopping around and patting out burns on their disguises. Fabian then started to grab at handfuls of snow and rub them into his suit and down inside it. Crichton was helping him and doing the same to himself.

Standing across from them was a girl.

"You?" Beetie went purple and lifted the gun towards her.

In her left hand she held a ball of grit that resembled a hand grenade. Her right hand was in a satchel that hung from her shoulder. "I've got sixteen of these. They're made from the same concoction Ned said the fish fingers are made from and they do like to go bang when they hit snow." She took another one out of her bag and started to juggle with them both. "Brinsley Vaughan-Abbott, observe what your son and your retainer are covering themselves in. I know from your nature that retainers are two to a penny, but little Fabby here should be of value to you, surely."

Beetie looked. Fabian was covered in snow and his suit was bulging at the seams where Crichton had stuffed it in. "Crichton. Attack the girl and gets those things off her."

"One move from you or Crichton and Fabby goes boom," the girl said calmly.

Beetie's hand was shaking and he roared at his servant. "You will disarm the girl this instant!" He turned the gun on him. "Crichton, if you don't then I will shoot you."

Crichton did not move. Beetie shot at him. The bullet passed between his legs and ricocheted off the walls. Everyone ducked, even Beetie, but when he got up he was staring into Vincent's eyes. The snowman disarmed him in one move. Beetie squealed and tried to back away. Vincent grabbed him by the collar and dragged him over to where his son was whimpering.

Audrey picked up the gun, checked the chamber, and strode over to Beetie. "If you ever touch my son again then I'll put one of these bullets through that beetroot head of yours. Do you understand me?"

The beetroot gulped and nodded slowly but did not say anything.

Ned had learned much these past days and suddenly he recalled Top Hat and Bowler. Remembering their actions, he ran over and kicked Beetie hard, and then did the same to Fabian, who squealed like his father. Crichton ran off up the way they had come in. Beetie stared at them with silent hatred, but then he pulled at his son and ran off after Crichton.

"Damn, Mum, I never knew you were such a real bad mutha." He hugged her, then went over to the girl and laughed. "Hello, Elsie. What on earth are you doing in here?"

"Come to help you. Earwax saw you come in here and all Dad did was call for a group meditation. They're probably still doing it now. So I thought I'd help. By the way, Ned, that's some haircut you've got there." He groaned and she tossed one of the grit grenades in the air and caught it. "They're good, aren't they? I made them while you were snoring in your bed." She caught it and looked at Vincent. "He's one of us then, so to speak?"

Laughing again, Ned beckoned Vincent over. "Yes, he's my friend." The huge snowman towered over Elsie. "Vincent, this is Elsie Frampton, a friend of mine. Elsie, this is…I can't remember his real name but you can call him Vincent."

Vincent bowed to Elsie, then took her hand and kissed it, being careful to avoid the grit grenade.

"And this is my mum and dad, Elsie," Ned pointed to them.

"Hello, Elsie, and thank you," Geoffrey said.

"Very pleased to meet you, Elsie, dear," said Audrey.

"Elsie, how did you get in here without being seen?" Ned asked.

"I found a trap door near to where a donkey lives. The door was open so I thought I'd have a look and ended up in here."

"I thought I'd shut that the last time I went out," Vincent said.

"What?" Father, mother, and son said together.

"That's my escape tunnel," Vincent said, then added sheepishly. "I'd finished it a few days ago and decided to go out and get a new hat. You know, that pink one Melton snatched off my head. But I swear I shut it."

"Why didn't you do a runner, Vincent? Why stay in the fortress?" Ned asked.

"We were all eager when Melton mentioned he was on the verge of attaining the one thing we as a race lacked: fishy fingers. So I thought I'd stay around and get some. Also, I was going to help a few victims of Melton's bullying to escape."

"Bloody hell, Vincent, you ran a risk." Geoffrey interjected. "That's either very brave of you or very stupid."

"I think the latter!" a wicked voice cut in.

They all turned to see Melton and his minions crowding into the corridor. He had got rid of the stove pipe hat but still had his waistcoat on and now added were a pair of black evening gloves.

The fingers and thumbs of the gloves hanging down like tassels on the end of his mitten hands. A bang suddenly shook the place and covered them all in a pinky slush. Ned's group turned to Elsie, who shook her head. "It wasn't me."

Melton railed at his snowmen. "Cretins, will you stop trying to fit the fishy fingers in? They are not real fingers but explosive devices. We have had countless casualties now from them and you dunces are still trying to fit them in. Now stop it! Who was that anyway?" he added with a concerned air.

"I think it was Wayne, sir?" one offered.

"No, it ain't. I'm here. I'm Wayne," the snowman Wayne corrected them.

"Was it Chesney?" another asked.

"No, Chessy's had a head transplant and he's recovering in the sickbay," a slightly charred and blackened snowman explained.

"What about Heinrich? Exploding himself is the sort of thing he'd do."

"He's gone AWOL. So it ain't him," the blackened snowman droned at them, then suggested, "What about what's-his-face?"

"What about him?" three snowmen said together.

"Well, was it him?"

"No. It weren't him. He don't do stupid things like that," the largest one of the three said. "But I tell you who would though…"

"Who?"

"Dennis, he would!"

"Dennis is in Iceland eating lemmings, so it weren't him either," Wayne concluded.

"So, who was it then?"

"It was Clive, it was," another suggested. There was no comment to the contrary, so they started to call out this name.

Silence followed.

"There you go, sir. It was Clive after all," a quicker-witted snowman volunteered.

Melton had been pushed to the back of the crowd as they argued and contradicted themselves. He hit his way through to the front and looked at the corridor. It was empty.

His ears sizzled and he turned red. "You absolute utter bunch of pond life. Look, they've got away!"

"Oh yes, sir, I saw them go," Wayne said happily.

Melton grabbed a fishy finger and pushed it into Wayne's head, which promptly exploded and showered the snowmen in another glut of pink goo.

They wiped it off and cleaned Melton down with the drifted snow. It brought precious time for Ned, his parents, Vincent, and Elsie.

"Which exit did they take then?" Melton asked as he was being cleaned.

"I dunno, sir, but Wayne does," one of them said.

"Wayne did," Melton corrected him. "Do you mean no one else apart from Wayne saw in which direction they went?"

There was silence and shaking of heads. None looked at Melton.

"Right, you bunch of loafers, it's time to call in the reserves. You lot go back upstairs and cover all the escape routes." Melton thought about his order, looked at his snowmen, then sighed in despair. "Look, just go upstairs and wait outside the doors. I mean outside the doors, not inside, alright? Get it right because your very survival depends on it." No snowman moved. Melton smiled at them. "Oh, I forgot to tell you the reason why. You see, I'm going to unleash the Ice Cream Sundaes, and you don't want to be locked in the fortress when they go hunting, do you?" The snowmen launched themselves down the corridor. They screamed and cried out as they shoved each other out of the way in order to get escape quicker. "And someone prepare my steed," Melton called out as they disappeared.

Chapter 18

"Come on. It's a fair track," Elsie said as she led them along a darkened passageway. It was about as high as a man and poor Vincent was running along on all fours so he would not bang his head. He suddenly stopped. Ned turned and the rest followed.

"Vincent!" Ned pleaded. He knew why he had stopped. "Forget the cookbooks. Mum and Dad have got plenty anyway." He turned to them. They were panting and probably glad of the stop.

"Yes, Vincent. Audrey's got a bookcase full of them which she never reads. My wife's the only person who can burn a salad."

That earned Geoffrey a rebuke followed by an elbow in the ribs. "I'm not that bad, surely?" she asked.

Ned looked at his dad. They made painful faces to each other. Ned took a deep breath. "You're not that good either, Mum." She looked upset, but Ned added, "Vincent here is a real master in the kitchen and he can help when we get out of here."

Geoffrey's face lit up at this.

Vincent was undecided. He kept looking back down the tunnel, then asked, "You don't happen to have a copy of *May I Have the Recipe* by the Women's Institute, do you?"

"No, dear, I haven't," Audrey replied. "But my mother does, and I'm sure she can lend it to us."

"Alright then." And Vincent shuffled up to the front. "I'll lead the way from here, Elsie. You don't know what's around the corner."

"I'll take the rear," Audrey said.

"No you won't, I will." Geoffrey walked to the back. "And give me the gun just in case." He went to take the pistol, then stopped and turned his head. His brow furrowed in concentration and as Audrey went to speak, he put a finger to her lips and a warning hand up to the others.

"Can you hear that?" he whispered.

Ned strained his ears. Elsie put a hand to hers, Audrey did the same, and Vincent put his ear to the floor. He pushed his head down and listened, then Ned saw his eyes widen.

"What is it?" Ned asked. "What can you hear, Vincent?"

But Elsie answered for him. "We can hear running mixed with screaming."

"It's Melton's lot coming! They've caught us up," Ned shouted.

Vincent stood as best he could, looking worried, and said, "It's not Melton. I know a snowman's scream when I hear one."

Ned's eyes and the others were bulging in fear now. "Then what is it?"

Vincent shuffled past them and pushed Geoffrey towards the others. "You get up the front. Elsie, lead them to the tunnel. I'll hold them off."

"No you won't!" they all said.

"We're a team and we stick together," Elsie said courageously.

"What the hell's coming, Vincent?" Ned sounded terrified.

"Melton's released his Ice Cream Sundaes and they're coming this way," Vincent finally explained.

"What are they?" Ned's mum asked.

"Lobotomised snowmen," Ned answered.

"What?"

"Melton's got a creature in the very catacombs of this place that does the act with an ice cream scoop," Vincent explained. "I've never seen it but I have seen the Sundaes. They're fearless, deranged, and do Melton's bidding without question. He only allows them out once in a while just to scare us and keep us in order."

"How many are there, Vincent?" Geoffrey ventured nervously.

"Too many. Probably about three hundred in all. Now go!"

"Not without you," Ned shouted.

Geoffrey spoke. "Then we'll all stay here with you." He pulled out the gun and sat down, followed by Audrey, Ned, and Elsie.

Vincent looked at them. "Please go. If they get hold of you, you'll be torn apart, and I don't want to see that happen."

"Well, we don't we want to see that happen to you," they all said.

Vincent looked angry but then put his ear to the floor again. His face twisted as he listened. After a brief time, he smiled. "I think they've gone in another direction. Okay, let's go."

They set off again, fast, Vincent running like a blood hound in front and the others hurrying after him.

Geoffrey kept looking back. "How far now?"

"At the end of here we turn right. Then there's a choice of three passages and we take the centre one. After that it's up some stairs and into the maintenance room, then through an access door and up the escape passage." Vincent explained. "I tell you this in case you become separated from me or Elsie."

Before they knew it, Vincent was turning right and relaxing the pace as they came to the junction. Here it was double the height of the passage and lit better. The three exits that Vincent described were ahead of them.

Out of the right-hand passage a snarling, dribbling, and growling group of Sundaes advanced. Ned stared in horror at them and red coal eyes stared back. Withered and mildewed noses hung from their faces. They stooped and jerked uncontrollably as they walked; others were shuffling around on all fours. Each one had a single round cratered wound on different parts of their heads.

Blasting out of the left passage came Beetie, Fabian, and Crichton. They stood in shock for a moment, saw the Sundaes and Ned's group, then ran up the centre passage. Vincent grabbed Ned and Elsie. He tore the satchel off her. "Go!" he shouted and hurled them across the floor with such force that they shot up the passage that the Vaughan-Abbotts had gone. Geoffrey pulled the gun out. "Come on, quickly." He pulled his wife's hand and marched into the room. As they reached the centre he stopped and pushed his wife towards the exit. Dropping onto one knee, Geoffrey took aim with the gun and gripped a grit grenade. He kept his eyes on the advancing Sundaes but spoke calmly to Vincent: "Come on. I've got them covered."

Vincent came running out. As he neared Geoffrey, he threw the satchel into the Sundaes' tunnel and grabbed him. The bag fell apart as it flew and the contents rained down on the mutated snowmen. Bangs and splats followed, mixed with howls and screams. The tunnel turned pink. Red coals and pieces of rotten carrots flew into the room. Vincent rushed past the snowman shrapnel with Geoffrey under his arm and jumped into the tunnel.

They ran up it and found Ned, Elsie, and Audrey.

"When we heard the explosion we feared the worst," Audrey said as she hugged Geoffrey.

"Now's not the time for that sort of girly stuff," Ned said in a disgusted tone.

"He's right. That was only a small group and there's more coming or I'm not made of crystallized water," said Vincent.

"Where did the Vaughan-Abbotts go?" Elsie wondered aloud.

There was a cough and then someone cleared their throat. "Erm...we...we're here."

There was a long hosepipe locker set in the wall. The door open and out fell Beetie and Fabian.

"Bad pennies always turn up," Elsie said. Ned said something worse about toilets not flushing properly and his mother glowered at him but Vincent laughed.

"Where's is your manservant, Beetie? Have you sacrificed him for the greater good?" Ned asked.

"I'm up here." a voice whimpered from behind the ceiling. Vincent hit the ceiling tiles and a section fell down with Crichton in it. His snowwoman's head was caught up in the ceiling's grid and his own head doffed low at Vincent.

Beetie got up and dusted off his outfit. "Now look here. Let's say bygones are bygones. I am prepared to reward you all handsomely if you lead us out of this infernal place. How does that sound?"

No one spoke.

Vincent started to walk off. Ned followed, then Elsie. Geoffrey tutted loudly at the Vaughan-Abbotts, but Audrey did not follow.

Beetie took advantage. "Please, my dear. There'll be a widow weeping for her lost loved ones if you leave us here. Think of the lad." He pushed Fabian forward and, pinching him hard, Fabian started to sob.

Elsie shot back and kicked Fabian, then slapped Beetie around his head with a grit grenade. "Don't even go there, you hear me? Don't ever say a thing about your new wife in front of me." She stormed off.

Beetie shrugged and put on an innocent look.

"Can't we take them with us?" Audrey asked.

Vincent looked at Ned, who looked at his dad, who looked at Elsie.

She jutted her jaw out and crossed her arms.

Ned spoke up. "Ah, go on then." Beetie and Crichton let out a small cry of delight. "But they can cover the rear as we go, and remember, if it gets tough, then we can always sacrifice them. You know, Beetie, last stand and all that."

So the five became eight and they set off along the tunnel. Fabian was still weeping and would not stop until Ned threatened him with a grit grenade down his pants. The sound of dripping water heralded the approach to the stairs. It seemed like it was thawing inside the fortress. As they walked up the stairs, water dripped down from above. It was cool and refreshing after the terrifying journey they'd had.

"Top of these, then we're nearly home and dry," Vincent smiled at Ned.

"What are you going to do when we're out of here, Vincent?" Ned said.

"Well, you're going to keep your promise I hope and show me Santa," Vincent reminded Ned. "Then I think I fancy getting a little café or restaurant."

"Bloody well melt, you would, if you did that," Beetie cut in. They turned on him. It had not taken long for Beetie to get back to his coarse self-arrogance. But he cowered at the sight of Vincent bearing down on him. "Wonder how long it would take you to melt if I held you over a gas hob?" Vincent said.

"No, he's so full of gas he'd explode the minute you turned it on!" Ned laughed.

Crichton came running up. "I hear you want to become a restaurateur. I can proffer some good advice on menus, table manners, choice of wine, et cetera."

Beetie shoved him aside. "Damn it all, Crichton. Can we get out of here first before you start licking the snowman's backside?"

"Err...no. There are noises coming from down there and I want to be near him."

Crichton shoved Beetie aside this time and clung to Vincent.

"What noises?" said Ned.

Vincent shoved Crichton off and leaned over the stairs. Beetie ran past them and Fabian shrieked after his father. Geoffrey and Audrey let them pass but Elsie tripped them as they swept past her. Father and son cried out and landed with a thud on the top step.

Vincent looked up. "They're coming. Sounds like hundreds this time." Crichton grabbed onto the snowman's leg, and try as he might, Vincent could not shake him off. Then the retainer got his legs around the stair rails and was locked solid with fear.

"Let go, Crichton!" Ned said as he slapped him around the head. "Vincent here needs to lead us out and he's the strongest person among us." But Crichton was experiencing a panic attack and was as immobile as the stairs that his legs clung to.

The sound of growling and yelping grew louder. Ned craned his neck over the rails. There were masses of Sundaes at the bottom of the stairs.

"Come on!" Ned said desperately. Audrey and Geoffrey were attacking Crichton now. He was pulling at the legs while his wife had taken off her shoe and was joining Ned in beating Crichton around the head.

Then a shot rang out. They stopped tugging and hitting Crichton and looked up. Elsie had taken the gun and had it pointed at Beetie's head.

"Crichton, if you don't let go I will shoot your master through his pea-sized brain."

Crichton looked at Beetie and then the gun. He shook his head, then let go and instantly ran up to his master. He pushed the gun aside and started to lick Beetie's hand, who in turn shouted at him to cease the effeminate activity.

Elsie blew the end of the pistol and handed it back to Geoffrey. "Born to serve, that one," she explained. "Being told he is of an inferior social class is ingrained in him and of course he suffers from the master/servant complex, so he only knows how to be subservient."

"Come on then." Vincent started up the stairs. Geoffrey, Elsie, Ned, and Audrey came to the top of the stairs to see Beetie was holding Crichton in front of him and his son and staring into the open door of a maintenance office.

Vincent and Ned barged passed them and looked in.

Chapter 19

The room was bare inside apart from a single, dented filing cabinet. "Hello again, Ned Mutton, and Vincent, you traitorous swine," Melton said in a very welcoming voice. He looked past them to see the others. "And Mr and Mrs Mutton, and hello, little girl, I've seen you before somewhere, haven't I? Oh, and Beetie, how are you? Who's this little snowman? And I take it this is your manservant? Well now, let me introduce you please to my friend, Ice Cream Sundae." Melton smiled, then stepped back, and a huge mutation stepped forward.

Vincent held his hands out to cover the Muttons and Elsie. Beetie held Crichton forwards to cover himself. Fabian whimpered at his knee.

The creature looked at them through a single coal eye. The other was scarred over and closed. The mouth showed a few teeth of which two bottom ones were pointed. The nose was bulbous and scarlet coloured. Its body was huge with hardened leathery skin and knotted muscles. One arm looked human but had long sharp nails on its hand; the other was finished at the wrist by a razor-sharp ice cream scoop. An old set of breeches clung to its legs which were held up by braces made from intertwined leather. On its feet were a scuffed pair of cowboy boots. The feet moved forward and the ice cream scoop sliced in the air. It roared at them and went to grab Crichton.

Everyone heard the scream that built up until suddenly something came spilling into the room through an access door in the wall and landed at Melton's feet. Before the maimed snowman could react, a man had uncurled himself and shot upright. He delivered a mocking bow to the despot.

"Melton Mowbray the Turd, I presume? I am your nemesis." And in a fluid movement, the galvanized pipe he held swung down and crashed into Melton's head.

He took a rubber rat out from his trousers and threw it at Ice Cream Sundae. The creature howled in fright and ran to the door.

Everyone moved aside for it as it passed them and escaped down the stairs.

"Works every time," the man said.

"Dad!" Elsie ran over and jumped into Lionel's embrace. He kissed her, then put her down. "Followed your tracks in the snow, we did. Hang on, darling, I won't be a minute." Lionel spied Crichton and looked past him. He walked over and moved the servant to a chair. Then, smiling, he turned to Beetie.

"My, my, what a glorious day for revenge; first Melton the Maimed, now Brinsley Vaughan-Abbott the soon to be maimed." And, holding the pipe like a golfing iron, Lionel swung it like a professional. "Fore!" he shouted as he landed Beetie an almighty smash on his jaw. He fell into Melton, who came out of his unconsciousness and pushed the big man off him.

There was another scream and someone else landed in the room from the access door.

It was a woman and she uncurled herself in the same manner. Ned stared. So did Elsie. It was Simone. She had a pack on her back and unstrapped it, then threw it to Lionel. Ned went to say something but Elsie got there first. "What on earth are you doing here?"

"Not now, sweetheart. I'll explain later." For an instant, Ned thought she was talking to him, then realised that she was in fact addressing Elsie. He momentarily felt sad but then turned to see Lionel produce a lighter from another pocket and untie a fuse from the pack. Flicking the lighter, he held the flame to it, which fizzed and sparked and started to burn.

"Excuse me," Lionel said and pushed past Ned, Vincent, Geoffrey, and Audrey. On the stairs he held the pack out and shouted, "Fire in the hold!" Then he dropped it and calmly walked back into the office. An instant later, the room shook as a colossal explosion tore through the stairs.

"I think that's sorted that," Lionel said, then looked at Ned. "Bad haircut there, Ned."

"Dad, why is she here?" Elsie screamed at Lionel.

He dropped the pipe, walked over and took her hand, then led her to where Simone was. "Your mum was worried sick when I told her you had gone down here."

"She doesn't worry about us."

"When we were up there," Lionel pointed to the roof, meaning the hollow where they had gathered with Thaw. "I tried to brew some magic, you know, get our karma going and get advice from the all-seeing eye, but the mantra didn't work and when I stopped chanting and opened my eyes, do you know where they settled on?"

Elsie just shook her head.

"Well, let me tell you, sweet thing. My eyes opened on Stalingrad Towers and I thought it was a sign. It was time to go and see our Bessie and tell her what was going on. When I looked around you were gone so I knew your mum had to be told and when I did, she would come and help. We tore through an electric fence to get her and I talked with her and she decided there and then to come to you when you needed her."

Elsie glared at Simone. "Well, there's a first time for everything!"

Simone went to comfort her but Elsie drew back. "She stopped seeing us months ago. She never turned up when she said she would. She doesn't care about me or you."

"That's not true," Simone said defensively. "I did try to see you, you must believe me. I really did."

"Then why didn't you turn up or ever come when you said you would? Why?" Elsie cried out.

Simone walked over to where Beetie was laying. Her face showed utter revulsion. Melton moved aside in haste. She looked at him, then back to Lionel. The distasteful looked turned to a mystified one. "Is he real?"

"Oh yes," Vincent answered. Simone noticed him for the first time. She screamed quickly, then recovered herself.

Moving to where Melton sat, she grabbed his head and started to pull. Melton protested loudly and then Ned laughed. She tried one last huge pull, then gave up and turned to Lionel. "So it's true. Snowmen live and breathe. Who would have believed it?"

"You didn't," he said mildly.

"Back to the point in question Simone!" Elsie demanded.

Simone looked at her and tried a smile but received a glaring silent stare in response. So she walked over to Beetie, grabbed him, and shook him by the collar. "Because this worthless, jealous, money grabbing, insecure liar deliberately made a plan of stopping me seeing you." She dropped him on the floor. "That's why! Every time I did organise to see you or wanted to call around, he'd make sure Crichton, his servant, deliberately sabotaged the plan. The fool wouldn't let me out without Crichton. He'd get lost and blame the satellite navigation or drive me near to your dad's house, then shoot off saying the throttle stuck or the brakes weren't working. I couldn't phone you because Brinsley intercepted the calls. I tried to sneak out but he or Crichton or that little beast of a son of his was always watching. I was a virtual prisoner. He even got that electric fence installed because of it." She started to cry. "I'm so sorry, Elsie. I shouldn't have left you and I'm so very sorry that I did."

"So why did you?" Elsie shouted, though this time she was calmer and less anguished.

Simone leaned against the wall. She took a deep breath and let it out slowly. "I needed some sanity, I suppose, and your dad's days were filled with making a bloody tank or eating worms and telling me that snowmen live and breathe." She looked at Lionel and mouthed a sorry to him. "I promise I'll make it up to you when we get out of here, my petal."

"Well, alright then. I forgive you, Simone," a bleary voice uttered. Beetie had just come around and heard the last sentence.

If steam could issue from a human then Ned swore he saw it jet from Simone's ears. She strode over to Crichton and went to hit him with a clenched fist. He fainted before the blow struck. Turning to Fabian, she slapped him. "I know you're in there, you little ponce," she screamed at the disguise. "And when this is over, you're going to get your comeuppance, I swear it. As for you!" She turned and jumped on Beetie, then pulled off her wig, then started to beat him around the head with it. "I'll give you Simone, you toy soldier, you! Never been in the army, have you? Just another lie. I know, I've done some digging. And I know all about your tax evasions and your property scams. Blaming small innocent boys for it, eh? Well no more. You're going down with that brat of yours. You can chew on that. No, hang on. Chew on these." She broke off her nail extensions and started to feed them to Beetie. "And as for these," Simone went to pull up her shirt, then stopped with a look of embarrassment. "As for these, well, I'll keep these." Then she continued the assault by forcing him to chew the coloured nails and smacking him with the wig at the same time. "I did this, all of this, all these vain cosmetics, so I could put you off thinking I still cared about my little girl and only cared what you think but..." She started to sob. "But it didn't work, did it? You were still too possessive of me and jealous of that little girl. I became Simone to appease you. But it still didn't work." She gave up the beating and Lionel lifted her up and hugged her. Beetie's eyes span and he spat coloured nails out. She still looked at him and shouted down. "I'm not Simone anymore. Never again! My name is Elizabeth." She looked at everyone in the room as to challenge them. No one spoke. "I'm Elizabeth again!" She cried. Then a sad smile appeared on her face. "But you lot can call me Bessie."

The air seemed to clear and Bessie, formerly Simone, exuded a calmness that Lionel and his strikers would have been proud to achieve.

He stole a quick glimpse at Elsie and motioned her over to him and Bessie. She took a few uncertain steps, then ran over and hugged them both. The calmness cracked and Bessie burst into tears.

Melton leaned on his elbow and coughed. "Excuse me...er...Bessie, but that was a formidable display. If you're ever in need of employment then I could do with a sergeant at arms of your calibre."

The sound of rumbling and shaking struck the room. Ned thought that someone was laughing loudly but then Lionel looked at the roof. A crack started to appear followed by a crash as the light fell down.

"What is it?" cried Geoffrey.

Lionel sniffed the air. "It's Thaw. I'm sure it's Thaw." He gently let go of Bessie and Elsie.

"It's who?" Geoffrey, Audrey, and Vincent said together.

"My baby. Ned knows." His eyes darted to Ned, who flinched as a piece of plaster and some bricks fell down. "It's his armoured fighting vehicle." Ned explained. Lionel looked at him proudly, then took up the explanation further. "For years I've been working on this vehicle. It's designed around the principles of the main battle tank but refined to kill or maim snowmen or snowpersons. In fact—"

"How much does it weigh?" Vincent interrupted.

"No idea. Never had it on the weigh bridge but I reckon in excess of thirty tons."

All eyes crept to the roof. "Vincent, how deep down are we?" Geoffrey asked. They all walked back from the centre of the room.

"I think about twenty-five feet," he answered.

"We are approximately fifteen feet from the surface." Melton corrected him. "We are in a subterranean extension that was built around fifty years ago, and not, may I add, with planning consent."

Everyone put their backs against the wall as if it offered some illusion of safety.

"Lionel, are you in communication with your men?" Audrey enquired nervously.

"Hell yes. I wouldn't let them loose on Thaw without me being able to speak to them," he said smugly.

"WELL GET THEM TO MOVE FROM ABOVE WHERE WE ARE THEN!" Audrey screamed like a banshee at him.

"Oh, right," he said tensely and fished in his pocket, bringing out a brick-like mobile phone. "Alpha Dog to Tiger One, do you receive, over?"

There was the squeal of static. Lionel repeated, "Alpha Dog to Tiger One, come in, over?"

Static sounded. Then, "Who's that?"

"Tiger One, this is Alpha Dog, over." Lionel looked at them and smiled in triumph, then added, "Please use correct RT procedure at all times, Tiger One."

"Did you order a delivery, Earwax?" the response came.

"Alpha Dog—" Lionel started but the static came again. It cleared and voices were heard. "Ere, I ordered chicken fried rice, sweet and sour pork, and prawn crackers. What did you order, boys?" The voice cut out and the line went horribly dead.

Lionel looked apologetically at them, then the ceiling. "Providence would tell us to get out of here now."

At that, the ceiling started to fall in. Vincent moved Bessie, Elsie, and Audrey to the electric box. "Climb in. It's quite wide and you'll be alright. Head upwards and you'll be at the surface before you know it."

Elsie and Bessie looked around at Lionel. He grinned at them. "Go on, I'll be along shortly." Then he pushed Ned and his dad towards the snowmen. "You next."

Bessie went to go back but Vincent stopped her. Elsie ran but Bessie grabbed her. "Look, just go now before the whole room crashes down." He pointed at Beetie, Crichton, and Fabian. "I'm going to bring these reprobates up before I come."

"We should leave them here to rot," Bessie told him.

He shook his head. "No. It's bad karma to leave a life to rot. Anyhow, they've got to stand trial for all they've done."

"What about me?" Melton said.

"I'm talking human life here, Melton." Lionel moved his eyes to Vincent. "No offence meant, my friend."

Vincent shook his head. "None taken, my friend."

Bessie grabbed at Geoffrey's belt. "I don't trust him," but she was pointing towards Beetie. "So take this." And Bessie threw the pistol at him. "Do hurry up. I want to see you at the top so we can start being a proper family again."

Amidst watery eyes, Lionel caught the pistol and waved them goodbye. Elsie held back. He wiped his eyes. "Go on, love. Follow your mum. I'll be out soon."

They smiled and climbed into the tunnel. The room shook again. Vincent pushed Ned and Geoffrey in. He looked back. "I should stay with you."

"No you shouldn't. They'll need a tough nut at the top. I somehow think there'll be trouble waiting and you can handle it while I'm coming."

Vincent nodded curtly. "Alright, but hurry." He pointed at Melton. "And don't listen to anything that old fart says to you."

"How dare you talk to your master like that?" Melton uttered.

"Shut up, peg leg," Vincent said, then winked at Lionel and shoved himself into the tunnel.

Chapter 20

Lionel dodged another downfall from the ceiling and cocked the gun. "Right, you lot. Up that passage and make it fast," he looked at Melton. "Any funny business and the snowman gets it!" Then he started to laugh. Melton sniggered too, which made Lionel uneasy.

Beetie got up rubbing his head. He looked redder than ever and bruising was swelling his cheeks where Bessie had slapped him and his chin where Lionel's pipe had hit him. Also, the wig was tangled in his suit so he ripped it off and threw it at Crichton. "Come on, you failure, and bring the boy." Fabian ran to the opening whilst Crichton sneaked a quick look sideways, then pocketed the wig.

Melton did not move. "Well, the mighty Beetie defeated," he said with a sarcastic relish. "Going to his fate with head hung low. I congratulate you, Mr Frampton. You have tamed the beast."

Beetie picked up a piece of plaster and threw it at Melton. The snowman ducked out of the way easily. Lionel was looking at him. "For someone who is about to become slush when the ceiling collapses, you're certainly acting with admirable calmness."

Melton sat up and his coal eyes stared back at Lionel with an intensity that unnerved him. "Oh, I don't think I'll die down here on my own when the end comes."

"No? Well like all bullies, dictators, and despots, your end comes quicker than you know it." Lionel said in a manner that was meant to intimidate Melton, but he just smiled back. "If I'm to get squished then allow me a few more minutes to express my happiness at your recent family reconciliation."

"My daughter and wife will be laughing and enjoying their lives as yours drips its way down the drain," Lionel chuckled. He slapped Melton around the face, then pushed at Beetie. "Come on, Crichton, then Junior, then you. Move it."

They made a start into the escape tunnel. Beetie was climbing in when Lionel turned to Melton and pointed the gun at him. "I should shoot you for what you've done."

Melton did not flinch at the prospect of being shot. "You would shoot me for helping you reunite with your family?"

"You didn't do that, you old bugger. I did that. Bessie, Elsie, and me will be fine, no thanks to you."

Melton took on an apologetic look. "Oh, I wasn't taking about your daughter or your former wife. Why, no. When you came in, I recognised you from all those years ago; young Lionel Frampton, eh? You certainly have your father's nose."

Lionel pushed the gun into Melton's temple. "What do you mean?"

Melton gently pushed the gun aside. Lionel's curiosity allowed him, so Melton smiled. "Well, I mean to say that you are just like your dear father."

The gun returned to his temple. Beetie was taking an interest now and stuck his head back out of the tunnel, trying to avoid the falling masonry. Lionel saw him, aimed the gun in his direction, and pulled the trigger. The shot slammed into the door and the red head shot back.

"Next one's for you, Mowbray!" Lionel said manically and clicked the firing hammer, chambering the next round. "Unless you tell me quickly what you mean?"

Melton held his hands to the gun as if in prayer. "Why, Lionel, I was just about to tell you that although you may think your dear father perished all those years ago or that he ran off and abandoned you for a better life, I can tell you he did not. Indeed, you met him recently and dropped a bomb on his head."

"That's it. You're going to be snowflakes now," Lionel said, squeezing the trigger.

"Wait!" Melton shouted, and with surprising strength pushed the gun away. "You may shoot me if you want but your father is wandering about down there." He pointed to the stairs. "And he's probably wounded and scared after that bomb explosion. These days he hasn't the strength he had all those years ago and he's developed a fear of rats that you so unkindly accentuated by throwing that rubber imitation at him."

Lionel dropped the gun to his side. "No?"

"Oh, yes. I'm afraid to say that, you see, my boy, the creature Ice Cream Sundae is in fact your father."

Lionel swayed. His recently blooming world of reconciliation and returning wife rocked uncontrollably as Melton's words sunk in. The night his dad had disappeared came back to hit like a hammer blow. The note from Melton; the hope upon hope that he had in fact escaped and was living a dream was brought down like the ceiling now collapsing above him. The father that he had was now the terrible creature that Melton commanded to lobotomise disrespectful snowmen. He saw it when he entered the room through the escape hatch. He had seen the monster and with what seemed an easy contempt had made the horrible thing run away with the aid of a fake rodent. But in that fleeting glimpse, Lionel had recognised something that had been buried in his subconscious for years. He had seen the family nose, and for generations of Framptons, there was no getting away from that. Blood was blood and family was family.

"DAD!" he screamed in anguish, then bolted for the stairs, picking up his galvanized pipe on the way.

Melton watched him go, then dusted himself off and stuck his head up the escape hatch. "Beetie, one last proposition to make, if you're so inclined."

The red cranium came through the door. Beady eyes looked around. "Where's that psychotic gone?"

Melton pulled a drawer open from the filing cabinet and produced an umbrella which he opened out to stop the dust and broken plaster falling on him. "He's gone for another family reunion. Now, it seems that I have played the advantage, so to speak." He walked to the escape door. "I suppose you came here to rescue the boy's phone that incriminates you?"

Beetie nodded.

"And I suppose you didn't get me the Austrian ski instructor?"

"Well, you never froze that brat Ned Mutton or that madman's daughter." Beetie's arrogance had returned but Melton ignored it.

"Obviously," Melton said flatly. Then, with ease of a teacher explaining some rudimentary sum, he continued, "If you go up that tunnel, then you go straight to jail, Beetie. If you follow me then you can escape from here. There will be the matter of giving me vast amounts of your ill-gotten gains, but I think you'd rather do that than indulge in a custodial sentence." He grinned and clinked his tongue. "Your love's competition has gone to seek lashings of his father's embraces, but he will fail. Ice Cream Sundae is a monster. I know, I made him what he is. Anyway, all of Sundae's victims are running amok down there, and Lionel's life can be measured in seconds the minute he reaches the bottom of those stairs."

Melton pulled Beetie out from the hole. "So, come on, my former business partner. Times change and people, or snowmen, have to change with it."

Beetie looked at Melton with much ingrained suspicion but he saw an opportunity when one was presented so he pulled Fabian back. He shoved his hand up again and tried to grab Crichton. There was a squeal, then Beetie withdrew his hand. "The swine bit me!"

Beetie tried again and this time Fabian helped but all they got was another bite and a kick. Then they heard Crichton scurry up the tunnel.

"The damn rat has betrayed me." Beetie bellowed.

"Never mind that, we'd better go," Melton said as he limped out of the room and started to descend the stairs.

"What about the mad snowmen and the freak?" Beetie said, as he yanked Fabian to the top of the stairs.

"Stop whittling. We haven't started yet and you're bothering me with trivial details," Melton snapped.

"I'd hardly call deranged snowmen and an ice cream scoop-wielding fiend a trivial detail," Beetie countered.

Melton stopped on the stairs and pulled his hand away from the rail in disgust. It was stuck with goo. "Urgh…disgusting. Somebody's brain I think." He wiped it on Fabian, who screeched. Melton gave him a withering look, then continued, "Listen to me. Do you think I have achieved all my great triumphs by not planning properly and being particular about dastardly details?"

Beetie grunted something but Melton chose to ignore him. "That thing you call an ice cream-wielding freak answers to me and me only. He will do as he is told, should we bump into him. As for the Sundaes, they are fanatically loyal and will lay their lives down for me, should it be required. And anyway, I know a short cut, so come along and follow me."

"Alright, lead the way, but we get the phone first, you understand. We get that first," Beetie insisted as he followed Melton.

*

The tunnel was well-made and went upwards at a slight incline. It was enclosed with wood panelling made from old sardine boxes. As the group of escapees went deeper up the tunnel, the smell of fish became worse. Still, Geoffrey, who had taken the lead, marvelled at the finish and dedication Vincent had put into it. "This is very well done, Vincent," he said and knocked the wooden cladding. There was a hollow thud, then earth came in and the area started to shake.

Audrey flinched. "You were saying?"

"It's not my tunnelling skills that are at fault, it's that damn tank. Can't you feel it? It's moving alright, but it's following us." As if to endorse Vincent's theory, that practically came into being when the wooden planks above them started to splinter.

Just then, Elsie stopped and held up her hand. "Wait. Be quiet. I thought I heard a shot?"

"That's just the wood breaking," Ned said in an urgent fashion. He was dreadfully scared of enclosed spaces since he had been caught in the mound of donkey dung.

"No. It was a shot from a gun," Elsie insisted.

"Are you sure?" Bessie said. She had stopped and was now trying to pull her daughter up the tunnel.

Vincent looked back. "There's someone coming now. It must be Lionel. He's moving like the clappers." The snowman pushed them upwards. "Come on, he'll catch up. We've all got to get out of here before the whole tunnel collapses.

Elsie took a look back, then let Bessie pull her forwards. "He'll come, don't worry. Your father's a survivor."

Geoffrey came to the opening first. He slowly peered out and, seeing no lurking snowmen, pushed his head out to scan the whole area. He became aware of the noise first. It was a terrible sound of squealing and clanking. The ground shook and his vision blurred as he saw something coming towards him. Snow blew at his face from the surrounding chiller factory and the smell of donkey manure hit him. Instantly it took him back to his childhood where he had grown up next to a donkey sanctuary and he breathed the smell in happily. Then the clanking thing interrupted his nostalgia and at the last second he ducked back in the hole as the huge caterpillar tracks of Thaw narrowly missed crushing his head.

"What a stink!" Audrey said as she pushed past him. "Have you done something?"

Geoffrey turned on his wife. "No, I have not! It's donkey caca, and in case you didn't notice, a bloody tank nearly smashed my head in."

The shaking stopped and the sound receded. Geoffrey took a tentative look, then climbed out. Audrey followed, then Bessie, who then pulled Elsie out. Ned came next and was immediately relieved by the cold air and light on his face. He got a huge whiff of donkey muck and gagged. Vincent pushed Ned out, then himself, and turned to poke his head back in the tunnel.

"It's collapsed, but here comes somebody." He leant in and pulled at the figure.

"Ouch!" Vincent pulled his hand back out quickly. "Does your dad usually bite people?" he said to Elsie.

"No. He sticks to worms."

"Well, something bit me."

"I apologise," a weak voice said from the tunnel. "Please don't beat me."

Bessie looked horrified. "I know that feeble warbling anywhere. It's Crichton." And the servant's head came out of the hole. He smiled nervously and flinched at the sight of Bessie.

"Where's Lionel, you timid little twerp?" she shouted.

"He…he…the nasty snowman said the creature Ice Cream Sundae is his father, and he shot off to find him, my lady." He doffed a good dozen forelocks and climbed out of the hole.

"Oh bugger!" Ned said for all of them.

Chapter 21

Lionel ran and slipped down the stairs. Everywhere was covered in gooey pink slime mixed with pieces of coal and crushed carrots; evidence that his satchel charge had done its job well. It was so thick on the last two sets of stairs than he mounted the metal banister rails and slid down to the floor. As he went, he looked for parts of Ice Cream Sundae; clothes, boots, and the metal scoop, but he found nothing. In his heart he was relieved, but the thought of going into the maze of passageways again, with no doubt more Sundaes on the loose and his father, who may attack him, did not fill him with confidence. But he had to try to find him. He had to see his father, even though he was a freak of unnatural nature. So, with pistol and pipe in hand, and tiptoeing across the mess of exploded Sundaes, Lionel ran up the passage.

The light was worse here. It seemed as though the power to the fortress was on the blink. Lionel slowed when it faded to a dim grey and then stopped to listen. He could hear the sound of water dripping and footfalls splashing in the distance. Laying his back against the dented metal-cladded walls, he waited to hear if the footfalls were getting closer. He looked at the metal pipe, then the pistol, and checked the chamber to see how many bullets were left. Only four. Still, he had the pipe, and that was a weapon in itself, but Lionel knew he shouldn't have shot at Beetie. But he just could not help himself. To see that idiot duck out and cower had been worth it but now one more bullet could mean the difference between life and death. He shut the chamber with a snap and listened. The splashing was getting louder and was accompanied by howls and grunts. Lionel looked around. Panic was rising in him. He went to run back up the passage but then noticed a hosepipe locker opposite him with the access door ajar. It looked long enough and wide enough to allow a person to hide in. There was little time now as he saw shadows moving towards him in dim light. Crawling into the space, Lionel put the pipe down but kept the pistol in one hand. He pulled the door shut and held it there. His hand was shaking and he feared it would attract the things that had now stopped where he had been half a minute ago.

Through a wire re-enforced glass window, Lionel stared out at ten Sundaes who were looking around with erratic, jerking movements and sniffing the air. He gulped. A face was suddenly in front of his and the Sundae's breath frosted the glass. Lionel breathed out very slowly. All of a sudden, one of them looked up at the ceiling and barked. The others started to jump up and down and a fight started. Lionel looked out and up, and as the glass cleared, he saw one of the group jump higher than the rest and pull something down from the ceiling. Dribbling heads looked at the thing dangling from one of their hands. It was the snowwoman's head that Crichton had worn until ripped off when Vincent had knocked the ceiling down. They sniffed it excitedly, then let out a cry and shot off up the corridor.

Lionel gave them two minutes before he pushed the door open and climbed out. He listened briefly, then quickly walked in the opposite direction.

Coming into a larger room, he saw that there were more exits on either side of him. They seemed to go back in the same direction that he had just come, so he ran across the room and entered the passage opposite. He needed to find his father but also needed to get as far away from the Sundaes as he could, and this seemed to be the right direction to go in. With a brief look back, he started to jog along it. As he went the passage grew darker and at times the dim lights flicked on and off. He saw or heard no one, but he kept going and eventually the light grew and grew to reveal a large corridor ahead. Lionel slowed and looked in. The brighter light was coming in through a section of roof that was open to the elements. Snow covered part of the floor and standing in it was Ice Cream Sundae. He was staring up at the hole in the roof. Small flakes of snow were gently drifting down and settling around and on him. The lines on the dreadful face cracked into a beaming smile.

Lionel looked on and he smiled too. "Dad. It's me, your son, Lionel." And he walked in. The smile turned to a look of rage. Ice Cream Sundae growled. The scoop clicked loudly, its blade slicing a spine-tingling sound of metal on metal and he ran at Lionel.

"No wait, Dad. It's me. I'm not here to hurt you!" Then Lionel realised that earlier he had tried to blow his father up, so he had another try. "Dad, I won't hurt you this time. I'm sorry. I didn't know who you were." Ice Cream Sundae was close now and did not look like he was going to stop. Lionel took the gun and pointed it. The monster stopped suddenly but continued to growl.

Lionel stepped forwards hesitantly. "Look, Dad, I'm not going to hurt you, see." He threw the pistol to the side, dropped the pipe, and held up his hands. Ice Cream Sundae blinked once, then jumped at Lionel. The speed of the attack nearly had Lionel, but he jumped aside and grabbed his father in an embrace across his arms. Ice Cream Sundae went mad. He threw himself into the walls and onto the floor, but Lionel held on like some bucking bronco. He managed to shout into his father's ear in between getting winded from the crashing and smashing. "Da...dad...urgh...Dad...it's...ouch...it...it's...you...your ...only...aaagh...son. It's Lionel. Plea...plea...please...ow, bugger that hurt...please stop."

The rolling fight continued until Ice Cream Sundae succeeded in throwing his son off. Lionel landed hard against the metal wall and a section broke off to reveal rich brown earth underneath. He lay winded and the man monster came at him. It clicked the scoop wickedly and grabbed Lionel by his head with his clawed hand. Turning to get a better grip, Ice Cream Sundae squatted and moved his son's head, ready for the 'Scoop de Grace' with the ice cream scoop. Lionel looked sadly into his father's eye, then noticed something out of the corner of his own. An earth worm had fallen from the earth and Lionel, realizing this was his final meal, picked it up and ate it. The scoop rose to perform a frontal lobotomy. Then it stopped. The grip relaxed on Lionel and Ice Cream Sundae breathed out a sigh of immense relief. The one eye blinked and Lionel saw moisture around it and a single tear fell onto his face.

Lionel finished the worm and hugged his dad. "You remember. You remember that worms are my favourite food."

Ice Cream Sundae got up. He inclined his head and stared at Lionel.

"The last time we saw each other was all those years ago, Dad. I...I...would have looked for you but Melton left a note. A note saying that if I did, then he would slush you or whatever it was, but I was so scared he would kill you that I scarpered." Ice Cream Sundae just looked back blankly. Lionel wanted, no needed, to explain this to his father. "I thought that you'd escape and live the good life like we had before...before all this happened." Lionel started to sob. His father kept staring at him. "Dad...oh, Dad, I tried, I really did, but I was only a kid."

Suddenly, Lionel was pulled into an embrace and held there until he nearly passed out. He could hear his father growling lowly and gulping as if trying to clear his throat. Then Lionel was pushed back and held at arm's length. The single eye stared at Lionel. "Mmmmmaaaaeeey...sonnnnn." The voice spoke for the first time in more than twenty years. The deep sound was dreadful, yet the most beautiful thing to Lionel, who burst into tears and kissed his father's cheek. "We've got so much catching up to do. You can," he jumped up with excitement and kissed his dad's forehead. "You can come and live with me and...oh yes...and...I haven't told you, but you've got a granddaughter. Her name's Elsie and she'd love you." He was so excited that he nearly wet himself. "And maybe me and Bessie will get back together and we'd be a proper family; you, me, the missus, and our young one." He wiped the tears from his eyes and smiled at him. "Come on, let's get out of this hole and start to live a proper life."

Ice Cream Sundae smiled back, then shook his head sadly.

Lionel looked shocked. "What do you mean, no?"

There was a noise from the tunnel and Ice Cream Sundae turned to see Beetie picking up the discarded gun. Fabian scurried in, followed by a joyous looking Melton.

"There you are, my pet," Melton said happily. "I've been looking all over for you, and here we find you." He limped forward. "Now, come to Daddy and we'll make everything better."

Ice Cream Sundae did not move. Melton looked affronted. "Come to me now. I order you to come here."

Beetie stepped forwards and levelled the gun. "It all seems so familiar. Indeed, if you look carefully, you can see the impact over there of my first shot. I was trying to kill my butler but now, for the sake of humanity and nature, I'll kill that freak and then I'll kill his weirdo son."

"You will not!" two voices said together. Lionel finished shouting at the same time as Melton. He looked in shock at Melton. So did Beetie, who turned on him. "You want to save that abomination's life?"

Lionel pushed his way in front of Ice Cream Sundae as Melton hobbled over and stood beside him. The snowman looked at Lionel with contempt. "I've never forgiven you for giving me a gammy leg." He turned to Ice Cream Sundae with a look of beatific sweetness never before seen in such a wicked snowman. "I created him, and no one is going to uncreate him apart from me." He patted his creation's arm. "It'll be alright, it'll be just me and you when this is over."

"Get out of the way, peg leg. I'm going to shoot the horror," Beetie said.

Melton took a deep breath and his eyes sizzled. "No you will not, Beetie. I have kept my part of the bargain thus far. You have the phone and we wish to depart from here." He put his arm around Ice Cream Sundae. "You wish to escape with your son, as I do with mine."

Beetie burst out laughing at that. Lionel's jaw dropped in shock. Here was the most unscrupulous, vindictive, foul, and unmerciful snowman ever moulded, who was now expressing love for a would-be adoptive son.

Beetie cocked the trigger. "Oh well, if that's the case, then you can all die." Melton stood his ground and stared back seemingly past him. "You'll regret this, Beetie." Then Melton turned his head to Ice Cream Sundae and spoke, but his eyes focused on Lionel. "You know I invited him to visit you, but he wouldn't come."

Lionel exploded. "You're a liar!" He turned to his father. "Dad, he's talking rubbish. That old brute never invited me, never, ever, ever, ever."

Melton glanced past Beetie again. He was standing with a look of assured victory and guffawing loudly. The snowman sneered at Lionel. "Oh yes, and when he finally does turn up, this only begotten son, what does he do to you? He drops a bomb on your head. I'd hardly call that a reconciliation."

Lionel went to hit him but Ice Cream Sundae turned on him.

Lionel looked heartbroken and gulped. "You'd take his side over mine?"

Beetie slapped his thighs and laughed out loudly. "Look at the pair of you, arguing over the feelings of that freak."

Melton looked at Lionel, then raised his eyes and smiled.

"Don't you smile at me, you lying old piece of—" Ice Cream Sundae blew a loud raspberry in Lionel's face. He caught his son's eyes with his stare and indicated with his one eye to where Beetie and Fabian stood. Then the single eye winked.

Lionel's eyes followed and saw a score of Sundaes creeping up behind Beetie.

Oblivious to the fact that a deranged party of snowmen were less than spitting distance from him, Beetie continued to laugh. Fabian laughed too, though it came out muffled through the zip-knotted suit.

Melton coughed politely. "I'll give you one last chance, Beetie, to mend your ways and help me and my son."

"Get stuffed, you old cripple. I've helped you out for too long now. You can melt down here and I'll see to it that you're not alone. You can have your so-called son and his son to keep you company." He pulled the trigger and the sound of the shot echoed around the space. Lionel flinched, felt himself for injuries, then grabbed his dad, feeling him all over. Ice Cream Sundae protested and went to catch Melton, who had fallen backwards.

"Ha! Got you," Beetie laughed. Fabian, with some primal instinct for survival, turned. What he saw made him scream and run. Beetie looked around and screamed too. He fired off the last shots, then scarpered. The Sundaes went to go after him. Then their eyes fell on Lionel. They advanced with dribbling and gnashing teeth. Lionel looked on in terror. Melton had passed out.

One of the pack of Sundaes opened its mouth and drooled saliva. It screeched and dived on Lionel, but an ice cream scoop shot out and took half its head off. The others, seeing what had been done to their fellow Sundae, ran at Lionel and his father. Ice Cream Sundae brought his hand up and caught one by the neck. He squeezed hard and the neck squished, then he threw the body onto the others. Lionel ran to pick up his beloved galvanized pipe and went to work on the Sundaes as well. Three were now on his dad and were trying to bring him down. The scoop flashed and a head fell away. Then another fell into the grip of Ice Cream Sundae and he threw it off, right into Lionel's path. Screaming with rage, Lionel swung the pipe and the Sundae was sliced right down the middle of his body. It fell forwards and started to walk but the two sides of the body fell apart and went their separate ways. Another Sundae charged Lionel but he brought the pipe down and disarmed it. The attacker ran on without his arms. Ice Cream Sundae started to attack now. He swung the scoop with such speed and efficiency that four more of the Sundaes had no heads by the time they fell. Lionel swung the pipe viciously and another two were cut down. Father and son brought mayhem to nearly half the attackers. They retreated but then more came snarling down the passage. The new Sundaes waited at the entrance. They could see what had been done to their own and wavered momentarily. Melton was still unconscious so he could not call off the attack. Ice Cream Sundae grabbed Lionel and pushed him backwards.

"Goooo!" he cried.

"No. I'm not going to leave you," Lionel pleaded.

Ice Cream Sundae took the pipe off Lionel. He embraced him. "Gooooaa noww and be a gooood father and giiive my graaanddaughter...a beeeeg kisss from her grandfather." He slapped his son's back, then turned. With scoop and pipe ready, he roared a challenge at the Sundaes.

Lionel bowed his head in reverence, then ran. He went along a new passage until he came to a door that was open. Here, he caught his breath. He'd left his dad down there. After countless years of wondering where he was and what happened to him, Lionel had found him here. In the middle of this rusted broken complex he had found his father, only to have him taken away again all too briefly. Lionel sank to his knees and wept. He waited with an empty feeling inside him. Then he heard in the distance the sound of the Sundaes again. Their howls and growling did not frighten him anymore. He sat and thought how it would be when he was reunited with his dad again. It would not be long now, and it would not be so bad. Lionel barked a laugh and saw his dad's face. Though broken and misshapen, hard and deformed, the thought of it was wonderful. He saw the scarred face smile and then the words came to him: *go and be a good father to your daughter.* Those words would be forever etched in his heart now. A new spirit flowed through him. He would not die down here. He would do as his beloved dad had asked. He would be there for Elsie.

The growling was becoming louder. Lionel knew they were near. He lifted himself up and stepped through the door. Broken glass lay on the floor and he looked into a small room. A chair was on its side and ropes lay on the floor. Walking along, Lionel saw that glass windows covered other rooms but that condensation had misted the view inside all of them. Recalling Ned's story, he realised he was in the gallery of fools.

A snarl made him turn. Through the door, he saw a Sundae enter. It looked around and sniffed. Lionel backed off. He subconsciously went for his pipe but remembered that his dad had taken it for a last stand against these creatures. Walking backwards, he tripped and cried out. The Sundae's head snapped around at the noise. It snarled and walked towards him. Others piled in through the open door. Lionel ran to the end of the room. There was a door. Above it a dull red light glowed and below that was a button. Lionel punched it but nothing happened. He punched it again but the door did not open. He saw the Sundaes approaching and realised there was no escape now. Lionel spat at them and put his fists up readying himself for a fight. Closing his eyes for a last few seconds of peace before they pounced, he leaned his head against the nearest glass window. The moisture felt cool on his skin and he opened his eyes to see another pair of eyes staring back. Lionel yelped and jumped back as the glass shattered and a man in a tweed suit jumped out. He looked around mystified, then saw the Sundaes approaching. With a face turning purple with rage, the man took a pair of binoculars from his hand and swung them around his head like a sling shot. He screamed out in a pitch so high that the other glass windows shattered and out jumped the strangest crew Lionel had ever seen. There were two roofing contractors, a postman, two more surprised and hate-filled men, and through one came a family of four; the father of whom spied the Sundaes. "Kill them. Kill them. Kill them all!" He threw down his cucumber sandwich and ran for the snowmen. His family followed, as did the rest. The Sundaes took one look at the frenzied people and ran.

Chapter 22

The silhouette of a door frame could be seen up ahead. Sunshine broke around it and filtered into the space. Beetie and Fabian headed towards it. They were in a large room where tables and benches were set out. Some daylight seeped in through cracks in the roof but the door's outline offered a light at the end of a very dark tunnel. Bunting lay across the floor and a lectern was on its side.

"Come on, boy. We're nearly home," Beetie said, pulling his son forwards. As they got nearer to the door, Fabian could see that there was a loop of electrical wire on the floor. He thought it odd, but then, looking at the state of the room, dismissed it from his attention. In the gloom, he saw a latch on the door. Beetie reached for it and pulled it down. As he did, something dropped and the sound of a reel pulling in cut through the darkened room. The electric flex caught them in a noose by the ankles and a counterweight pulled them off their feet. They shot backwards and were reeled high in the air to swing upside down uselessly. Beetie's wig peeled off his sweat-soaked head and landed on the floor below.

*

"We've got to find Dad!" Elsie cried out. She took hold of Vincent's arm. "Where's the nearest entrance?"

"It's near to here," Ned answered as he remembered where he was. The large pile of donkey manure lay nearby, the very place he had dived into and hidden from the two men that hunted him.

"Okay. But we'll need weapons if those Sundaes and others are about," Vincent said.

That silenced them. The only weapon they had was the pistol and Lionel had taken that. The grit grenades had been used in that one big explosion on the stairs.

Geoffrey started to look around. "We'll have to get primitive weapons. You know, sticks and branches, pieces of wood and bricks."

"How about some donkey cack too, Dad?" Ned put in sarcastically. "You'll see there's plenty of that about."

"What about Thaw?" Bessie suggested.

"You heard what they were saying. They're more interested in a bloody takeaway than rescuing us," said Audrey. "And who's got Lionel's phone anyway?"

Bessie answered for them. "Lionel has. In the panic, no one asked him for it."

Vincent stood up. "I'll go in. I know the place like the back of my hand anyway."

"No. If you go in then you'll get squished or sundaed or whatever." Ned went and pulled the snowmen back.

"Look, let us think about this," Geoffrey tried to calm the situation. "We need to go in and get Lionel but we can also do with Thaw. I'll go in with Vincent." He pointed to Ned and Elsie. "You and you know the crew, am I right? And Bessie and Audrey had better go with you two."

"Can I go as well?" Crichton croaked.

"Yes, please take that worm of a thing. Maybe he'll suddenly become a hero and save the day," Geoffrey said dryly.

Vincent spoke to the others as Geoffrey went to look for suitable weapons. "We'll go in at the front entrance. You lot find Thaw and get in there quick. Ned, you know where I'm talking about, the door where we came in with the fishy fingers, yes?" He nodded.

Geoffrey returned with a spiked pole and a rusty scythe. He held them up and made a ghastly face. "Then I looked and saw a pale horse. Its rider's name was Death and Hades followed close behind…"

The group looked back in horror at him. Elsie stifled a tear. Vincent looked mystified.

"Now isn't the time for apocalyptic verse, Geoffrey," Audrey said sternly, then smiled at her husband. "Be careful in there, dear. We're all counting on you and Vincent."

Geoffrey gave the spiked pole to Vincent. "I'll keep this one." He hugged the scythe and they went.

Bessie took Elsie's and Audrey's arm. Ned gave a light kick to Crichton. "Right, let's follow the tracks and hope they're still here."

The tracks from Thaw had left deep furrows in the snow. They could see torn and marked concrete underneath where the tank had turned. Mounds of thrown up snow lay either side. Diesel fumes still hung in the air but the sound of the engine could not be heard. Through the inner complex of buildings they went and were near the steel skeleton of another when Elsie called a halt.

"Look at these," she said. Everyone saw that the snow across the path of Thaw's tracks had been overturned with what looked like hundreds of round footprints that led off in a strange confused pattern.

Ned bit his lips and looked at them. "Snowmen, and a lot of them too by the looks of it."

"Maybe they ran off though the park?" Audrey said hopefully. They quickly scanned the fence and saw no gaps in it. The place was silent and an uneasiness came over them. A rook called out from somewhere and they instinctively formed a defensive circle as if in fear of the bird's cry. The sound of falling bricks brought their attention back to the building. Everyone looked around. Through the rusted steel beams of the structure a large group of snowmen appeared. These were not Sundaes but Melton's own lot that had been promised fish fingers and got exploding grit imitations instead. One of them saw Ned. "That's the one. He's the beastie that tricked peg leg...errr, I mean our master." His fellow snowmen gave him suspicious glances but he ignored them. "Well, don't just stand there. Get him!"

Crichton was off first before anyone could stop him. Bizarrely, he pulled on Bessie's former persona's wig as he did. Ned went to call him something foul but his mum grabbed him and they all ran back the way they had come.

Elsie and Bessie were in the lead. Audrey had Ned but he had the stitch. They slid and slipped through the snow. Although it was fresh it had frozen overnight, and at the speed they were running, their shoes could not keep their grip. Ned's stitch was killing him now. He had to stop, but his mum pulled him on. Then, as they came to the pile of donkey manure, Bessie's foot caught in some twisted steel rods. She went down and the rest fell over her. As she moved to get up, pain shot through her foot.

Elsie screamed, pulling at her mum's wrist. "Come on!"

"I can't. You go," she cried back.

Ned and Audrey got up and tried to lift Bessie but her ankle was caught and the pain made her wail. Gritting her teeth, she looked at them. "Go now and take Elsie. Get her out of here!"

But they had nowhere to go. Ned looked back where they had come from. There were no snowmen. There was no pursuing mob, just silence and emptiness. Heads looked left, right, front, and rear, quickly. The harsh cry of a rook broke the uneasy silence. Elsie looked at Ned with a bewildered expression. Bessie gave a gasp as she managed to free her foot.

"Did we all have a mass hallucination?" Audrey asked. The rook called again. Then they heard it. A scream of delight and terror mixed with the sound of an engine running at full throttle. All eyes strained in the direction of the unholy racket. Something red appeared through a growing blizzard of beaten up snow. The screaming grew louder, then the engine's noise, and out of the haze grew the image of a grass cutting tractor being driven by a snowwoman. Hair and a grass skirt billowed as she passed the group. The snowwoman had a man's head underneath a wig. He doffed a quick forelock to Bessie and shouted above the engine. "Get out of here! They're following me and they like what they see!" They saw that it was Crichton. He gunned the throttle and shot off quickly in a storm of white flakes followed by a small army of snowmen. As they passed they did not glance once at the group. They were totally and utterly committed to the chase of the first snowwoman they had seen in years.

Ned was amazed. "Well, Dad was right. Crichton has saved us."

Bessie was shaking her head. The shock of seeing Crichton's heroics had momentarily stopped the pain in her ankle. "I would never have believed that in a million years."

Elsie stood up and cheered. Then they all joined in. "Ned, look over there and see if you can find something to help me walk,"

Bessie said. She hobbled upright and started dancing on a single foot as he went to look. "Crichton might have saved us for the moment but when they find out he's no snowwoman then they'll be back." Elsie and Audrey came over and helped her to walk. "And we've got to find your dad too, and Geoffrey and Vincent."

Ned came back with a discarded, rotten-looking mop. It had grey mop tendrils that looked like a dead octopus. He held it up in jubilation. "Look, the perfect field crutch."

Bessie's faced turned sour. "That thing is going nowhere near me."

"Beggars can't be choosers," Audrey said.

"Mum, it's a temporary walking aid. Just use it, please," Elsie added weight to the argument.

She sighed. "Oh, alright. Give it here."

Ned went to pass the mop when they all heard the screaming engine and snowwoman noise again. It was interjected by loud explosions this time. A screaming, like some murderous choir, rose above the singular voice as the sound got nearer. They stared in the direction of this and were rewarded by the sight of Crichton again, still being chased by the snowmen who now were catching up with the tractor. Some had even passed it and did not even bother to look at the voluptuous curves of the driver. Ned thought that they were more intent on getting away this time. A group of snowmen to the right of the tractor veered off in the direction of the fence and were suddenly obliterated by a huge explosion. Crichton passed without doffing this time. "Help!" they heard him cry above the scream of the little tractor engine. The ground started to shake and a thunderous reverberation drowned out the retainer's plea. Snow billowed in huge clouds as out of the white storm came Thaw. Its tracks squealed louder than Melton's retreating army did. Awestruck, Ned and company looked on as the tank halted. Its turret traversed quickly, following a group of snowmen that had tried to double back on themselves. The main gun tracked them, then roared, and the tank rocked on its suspension. The snowmen disintegrated in a powder of pink mush. Thaw's gun slewed round again and they watched the cupola hatch open. Smoke billowed from inside and silver takeaway trays were thrown out. Then Earwax appeared. He saw them, waved, and beat on the turret's roof. Instantly, Thaw's left track locked, the right turned, and then both tracks drove the armoured beast forward. Earwax hit the turret roof with his fists and Thaw came to a grinding halt in front of them.

"Afternoon, all," Earwax greeted them cheerily. He stuck his finger in his mouth, trying to find something, then rolled his tongue about and spat a piece of gristle on the gun. "Should have asked for chicken breast instead of the usual claw meat. How goes it, and where's the boss?"

"Stuck down in that factory while you've been scoffing a takeaway!" Elsie shouted at him.

"Oops, sorry. We got a bit hungry waiting about," Earwax mumbled apologetically.

"Well get down here and help…" Unfamiliar with the words and slightly embarrassed, Elsie paused, then looked at Bessie. She swallowed her pride and thought of her dad's feelings for her mum and her own growing affection that had been shut away for so long. Clearing her throat, she snapped her fingers at Earwax and continued, "Get down here and get Mum up on Thaw." He jumped out of the turret and lifted Bessie up in a fireman's lift. She squealed in a Simone-like way, then let Earwax sit her down on the rear of the turret. Elsie looked at her mum. "Please don't squeal like that again, Mother." Bessie looked embarrassed but did not reply. Ned and Audrey grabbed Earwax's proffered hands and climbed aboard as well. Elsie jumped up and tapped Earwax on the shoulder. "Advance to the factory."

He saluted, then jumped down inside the turret. "Alright, you heard the young miss. Let's roll!"

The engine revved, a cloud of diesel fumes billowed, and with a jerk, Thaw turned on its tracks and headed off.

*

Beetie came around first with a thumping headache. He felt dreadful and realised he was hanging upside down. With his free leg he managed, after ten attempts, to kick Fabian.

"Oh, Father, where are we?"

"Shut up, boy. I've got to get out of here," he shouted.

"Let's call for help." And before Beetie could stop him, Fabian screamed, "HELP!"

Beetie aimed another kick. "Shut up, you little fool. There are things in here that want to kill us."

Then the flex started to quiver and Beetie felt himself descending.

"See, I told you it would work," Fabian said as he saw his father disappear below.

There was the sound of a metal scoop scraping, quickly followed by a low, deep laugh.

"Naughty Brinsley. I've got your phone that you lost, so here it is. Now you and your son are going to have a sundae. Will you have one scoop or two?" Beetie screamed and Fabian, still upside down, wet himself. It ran all over his face.

Chapter 23

Vincent and Geoffrey crawled through the snow to a ruined wall that offered some cover from the factory door. They lay there briefly, then put down their weapons.

"Stay still, I'm going to have a look," Vincent said and stuck his head up above the top of the wall. He ducked down again in an instant. "Damn!"

"What is it?" Geoffrey asked as he repositioned himself.

"Bucephalus. That's what." He had a look of deep concern and fear etched on his usually honest round white face.

"Bu...what?" Geoffrey asked in a puzzled tone, then poked his head up. It was down again quickly, then back up again, then down again. He looked at Vincent.

"It's a donkey?"

"It's Bucephalus, and it's not any old donkey. That thing's evil. Melton found it and trained it to be his steed, or his warhorse, as he likes to say."

Geoffrey started to laugh but Vincent shoved his hand across his mouth. "Look, it's not funny. Any snowman gets near that thing and it'll bite his carrot nose off. As for getting too close to its rear, then you'll get kicked in the taters or kicked into next week. Only Melton and that clot Heinrich could get anywhere near it without the risk of severe damage."

As if not believing what Vincent was telling him, Geoffrey stole a quick glance up again. The quick look turned into a longer one. Then he ducked down again to look at Vincent. "There's a group of snowmen playing with it, so it can't be that dangerous."

Pushing him aside, Vincent stuck his head up. There were three snowmen leaning down and sticking their carrot noses near to the donkey's mouth. Every time it tried to snap its teeth at the noses, the snowmen would move back out of range quickly. Meanwhile, at the donkey's hind quarters another two snowmen were tentatively trying to touch or pull its tail before it could land a wicked two-hoofed kick at them.

Vincent groaned then moved back down. "Idiots. They're playing Russian roulette with Bucephalus. It'll end in tears."

"What are you talking about?" Geoffrey asked.

"Three dimwits are tempting Bucephalus with carrot noses while the other two idiots are seeing if they can pull his tail without getting a kicking."

"Well, we've got to get in there and rescue Lionel, haven't we?" Geoffrey said.

"I know we have but we've got to get past those idiots and that four-legged fiend."

Just as he finished saying this, there was an angry neighing and the sound of heehaws. Geoffrey and Vincent looked up to see one of the rear end teasing snowmen scream as he was launched into the air by a double-hoofed kick. The other four snowmen fell about laughing but were careful to avoid the same treatment as Bucephalus started to turn around and kick at the air. Vincent pulled Geoffrey back down as the flying snowman landed with a crunch into the wall where they were hiding. Bricks and mortar flew and the snowman's head appeared through it to stare point blankly at Vincent. Coal eyes span and dribble drooled from the mouth. Then, with a moan, the eyes closed. Vincent let out a sigh of relief. Geoffrey darted a quick look at him. "Is he dead?"

Vincent shook his head, then looked through the broken section of wall. The other snowmen were getting up. He feared they would come over to help their comrade, but instead they started the baiting game all over again and left the dazed snowman.

"If Melton knew what they were doing to his beloved steed he'd..." Vincent started, then stopped. "Of course, Melton! That's it. Come on!" He pulled Geoffrey upright into full view of the snowmen.

"What are you doing?" Geoffrey snarled between gritted teeth.

Vincent pushed him forward towards the group. "Don't worry, trust me. We'll get past them and into the factory. Just do as I say."

Bucephalus noticed them first. Then the snowmen looked. They forgot the game and the donkey nearly snapped a carrot nose as they tried to line up in a smart military fashion.

"What the hell are you doing teasing Master Melton's prize warhorse?" Vincent shouted. They looked scared and confused. One went to speak but Vincent cut him off. "You oafs are in big, big trouble. If he hears about this, you'll be for a sundae. And I've been risking my neck going undercover whilst you play about!"

One of them plucked up courage. "Melton…I mean, our master, said you were a traitor and you were seen with the brat and the other fleshies."

"Idiot!" Vincent did a fine impression of Melton. "Idiot, Master Melton gave me the honour of infiltrating the fleshy boy and his family. He did not trust the swine and got me to gain his confidence and become his friend. Did you not see me go with the boy earlier? Do you think I like being in the vicinity of fleshies?" Vincent gave Geoffrey a disgusted look and snorted loudly. "I worked under the covers for weeks. Master Melton tasked the little swine to fetch the fishy fingers and I was tasked to track the boy and see that he does not betray us."

"But he did betray us!" another said as he found his voice and brain.

"Yes he did. And it was me that found it out and it is me who brings the father of the vile child back to our master now." He pushed Geoffrey forwards, who nearly fell over, and looked back at Vincent with a new uncertainty, thinking that either the snowman was a great actor or that what he was saying was in fact true. Vincent grabbed him and pushed him again, this time into the snowmen. "I'm bringing Daddy to the fortress so that the son will come and get him." They looked back at him with bemused frowns. One held up a hand and was counting off things in the air as if trying to follow what Vincent had just explained. His hand stopped and went to his head to scratch it. "Can you start at the beginning again? I don't follow you." Vincent shoved him aside and bellowed. "I don't have time to explain our master's plans to dotards. Now get out of my way!"

Bucephalus neighed behind them. Geoffrey's paranoia grew to an unstable level. He mind flipped and he was convinced that Vincent was a double agent, a turncoat who had planned this all along and who now, at this very moment, was betraying him to Melton. His legs went to jelly and he started to jibber. Then he saw his salvation in the form of Bucephalus. Before his legs gave out, Geoffrey lunged at the donkey and with all remaining strength smacked it hard on its rump.

As would be expected, the evil-tempered donkey went mad. The rear legs bucked in the air and the iron-shod feet kicked two snowmen into the steel door with such violence that they splattered into a liquid pinky mush. Their coal eyes ricocheted off and their carrot noses span in the air, revolving down close to Bucephalus, who crunched them to pieces with his great teeth. This quick snack brought Vincent an instant and he pulled Geoffrey out of the target area. The other two snowmen were not so lucky. They went to run but the donkey's hooves decapitated one. Its body still ran but with no head, it collided with the other one, tripping him up. By the time he had untangled himself from his headless companion, Bucephalus faced him. The snowman fell to his knees and tried to beg for mercy. But snowmen cannot speak donkey dialect and Bucephalus' backside still smarted from Geoffrey's hard spanking. The donkey moved forward as the snowman cried tears that were turning to icicles. Their dark eyes met; one set wide with fear and glistening with formed ice, the other dark, cold, and pitiless. Bucephalus bit down and snapped off the carrot nose. The victim squealed horribly as the merciless donkey turned and, with another double-hoof smash, launched the wailing snowman high into the air.

Vincent looked on in horror as Bucephalus now cantered towards them. Geoffrey's legs were solidifying, and with a burst of heroic vigour, he stood up and ran towards the oncoming donkey waving his hands in the air and shouting like a madman.

"Come on, you old nag. I've got two slappers that'll redden your rump raw!" The donkey's eyes bulged in terror. With a loud heehaw, it turned around and galloped off.

Geoffrey stopped running and clapped his hands in triumph. "Stupid old nag." Then he stopped and saw what was approaching and what had actually stopped Bucephalus charging.

Coming towards him was what looked like a very badly choreographed motorcycle display team show. Only this was a tractor and not a motorcycle that roared into view. About thirty snowmen were clinging onto the tractor in a pyramid formation. Under these, Geoffrey could make out what looked like a snowwoman, only she was facing backwards in the seat. How it was being driven, he could not tell. The unstable pile of snowmen were swaying back and forth and were continuingly climbing up and over each other as if trying to escape from something. The whole mass of beings and machinery was coming on fast. Vincent ran and tackled Geoffrey to the floor where they rolled in the snow and landed near the wall. A wail of screams came from the moving mountain of snowmen as they swung forwards towards the wall.

There seemed no escape for Vincent and Geoffrey as the tractor and its stunt team came on. Then, the mountain of snowmen burst apart as Bucephalus' last victim succumbed to the effects of gravity and bombed into the pile. Like shrapnel from an immense snowball bomb, they crash landed all around Vincent and Geoffrey. Then the tractor hit the wall and Crichton fell backwards to land on top of the snowman that the donkey had kicked there earlier. He coughed and smiled, then passed out. The engine of the tractor wheezed a last choke too as the ruptured petrol tank dripped its last lifeblood into the snow. Silence followed, and as it did, snowmen started to stagger to their feet. They saw Vincent, Geoffrey, and Crichton and walked unsteadily over to them.

"A cross-dressing fleshy snowwoman, another fleshy, and a traitor. Let's get them, boys!" And the group of snowmen congregated in a circle around them. Vincent stood up. "Fools. I explained earlier too—" But he was cut off by a strangely distorted voice. "Coth of im Meltonth's teed ate me 'ose." It was the snowman that had his nose eaten by Bucephalus and had crashed into the others. "Tho et's get em!" Vincent knew he had lost the bluff, so he put up his fists, ready to fight. Geoffrey rose with the scythe and readied himself for the attack.

"But what about the steel monster that's chasing us?" another snowman asked worriedly. "We lost it for the time being, but we'd better scarper before it finds us again."

"We've got time to give these a quick kicking," the one nearest to Vincent assured his comrade.

"Yeah, grab them and then hold them down. We'll duff them up, especially that traitor." One behind pushed the other into Vincent's field of fire, who landed a sharp punch on the snowman's nose, so much so that the orange vegetable sank into his face. There was a distorted scream and the rest backed off. Then a loud bang rang out as the factory door burst open and out ran the Sundaes. The snowmen looked at them, forgot about Vincent, Geoffrey, and Crichton, screamed, and ran away in the direction they had come. The Sundaes ran after them. Then, from inside the factory came a chant. It grew and grew until a few seconds later the roar of "Kill! Kill! Kill!" resonated around the factory space and the prisoners from the gallery of fools ran out in hot pursuit of Sundaes. They swept past, intent on extracting severe retribution on the Sundaes. One of them, dressed in tweeds, noticed Vincent and ran with outstretched hands towards him. His fingers were ready to throttle but Geoffrey calmly stepped in front and wielded the scythe. "He's not for slushing. Go and find easier prey." The deranged man skidded in the snow and turned after the others. Bucephalus was swishing his tail in ease whilst munching on the carrot nose of the decapitated snowman.

Geoffrey leant on his scythe and Vincent looked to where the snowmen were heading. He saw them suddenly skid to a halt, wave their arms in terror, and start running back in the direction of the oncoming Sundaes and former prisoners. Just as the whole bunch met there was a huge flash of exploding grit and a nanosecond later the sound exploded across the factory. The ground shook and some steel sheeting dislodged itself from the roof to fall around them. Crichton woke up screaming. Geoffrey indicated that he should be quiet, otherwise he would slice off Crichton's head. Vincent steadied himself and saw Thaw clanking through the debris of snow and grit. It changed to full power and two snowmen and a Sundae were splattered under its tracks as its speed increased. The prisoners, concussed and wobbly but unharmed, started to run after individual snowmen and Sundaes who had escaped the large calibre shell and were now trying to evade the next.

Vincent smiled and Geoffrey slapped his back. Crichton had stopped screaming and raised himself up. "That thing's coming up too quickly. Do you think he knows who we are?"

Geoffrey raised his arms and waved them in the direction of Thaw. "Stop! Stop! Stop!" he yelled. And Thaw did stop. Then they saw the gun barrel depress and point directly at them. There was no need to shout. They all scrabbled under the steel roofing sheets as Thaw fired another round. This one was an air burst and the shell exploded above them to rain white-hot grit down. It clattered on the sheets with such force that the steel was gouged and dented. Vincent threw his off and looked out. The snow around him was hissing and Thaw's gears crunched as it came forward. Poor old Bucephalus had taken a peppering and ran off kicking and neighing in pain.

"Into the factory!" Vincent yelled and grabbed at Geoffrey and Crichton. They all fell back towards the door, taking a steel sheet apiece and holding them up like knights' shields. Keeping their eyes on Thaw and shuffling backwards, they failed to see the door swing inwards and a figure step out.

*

"Wow. That last round was virtually nuclear!" Earwax shouted excitedly. He had his eye squeezed tightly to the gun sight and had the clearest view of all in the turret. Ned was gasping for breath as the fumes from the round swamped the interior. He had decided to go inside the tank and see her in action whilst Bessie, Audrey, and Elsie sat on the engine deck. The noise inside Thaw was terrible. With the engine roaring, the tracks squealing, and then the main gun going off, everyone had to shout to be heard.

"Halt. Turret: twelve o'clock. Target: snowmen. High explosive. One round. Airburst." Earwax issued the order. Thaw stopped and swung on its tracks as one of the strikers selected a new round and slammed it into the breach of the gun. He slapped Earwax on the shoulder and the mad gunner adjusted the range and felt for the firing lever. Ned climbed up to the commander's seat and opened the turret just as Earwax fired. The back blast nearly tore the skin from his face and he fell backwards onto the engine deck to find Bessie shouting at him. Audrey and Elsie were jumping up and trying to get inside Thaw. Ned's ears were still ringing from Thaw's combined assault of engine, tracks, and gun. But he shook his head until he could make out the words "Vincent", "father", and "out there".

Audrey was inside the turret now and slapping Earwax around the head. Elsie was next and started pulling at his big hands that were on the firing lever, but the blood lust was on Earwax and he would not relent. "There's still two out there skulking behind them corrugated sheets. I'm gonna kill them!"

Ned looked at the factory and saw Vincent's large frame sticking out from behind a sheet of corrugated steel. He saw his dad's head peer out from the side of another and Crichton's wigged head peep out from the third. Jumping up and diving into the turret, Ned started to shout to cease fire. But Earwax was still intent on killing. Ned threw himself at him and with Elsie tried to get his hand off the lever. Earwax suddenly awoke to the combined assault and turned on them. "Ger off!" And, grabbing the nearest person—Ned—started to throttle him. Now Audrey and Elsie grabbed at Earwax's hands that were locked around Ned's neck. The crew realised their tank commander's error and pulled at his arms as well. Earwax's eyes bulged with madness as Ned's eyes bulged in asphyxia. As he started to turn blue, something landed on his chest and Earwax's eyes changed from deranged madness to utter horror. He screamed and let go of his grip. Ned fell backwards, gasping for breath, and a toy rat flopped down in front of his face. Earwax shot out of Thaw faster than a grit shell leaving the gun barrel. He was quickly followed by his crew. Breathless from the exertion, Elsie and Audrey went over and helped Ned to sit up.

"Works every time," a voice said from above them. They all looked up to see Lionel staring down at them. Bessie moved over and out of the turret. As she passed Lionel, she gave him a quick kiss on the cheek.

Lionel went red and his legs went to jelly. He fell into the turret, then gathered his dignity and looked around the interior. He smiled again but did not go red. "So, she performed well?" he said, patting the gun's breech. Ned was about to reply when they heard the crash of metal and brick.

"Lionel, quick!" Bessie's voice shouted from the deck of Thaw. He pulled himself up and stared.

An ancient and dilapidated ice cream van launched itself out of the factory, just narrowly avoiding the huddling Vincent, Geoffrey, and Crichton. Its paint was faded and chipped. Green mildew covered the sales hatch and a huge cracked fake plastic ice cream surmounted the roof. Emblazoned on the side in discoloured black paint were the words 'Grampy White's Runny Delights'. Lionel saw who was driving it and dived back into the turret. He jumped into the gunner's seat and pulled a lever. With a mechanical whine, the turret traversed to follow the van. Lionel's eye was squeezed against the gun sight and he depressed the gun with another lever to target the moving van.

"What is it?" cried Ned.

"Melton," Lionel answered. "He's trying to escape in an ice cream van."

The van lost traction in the snow and the old tyres struggled to get a grip. The gun found its target and Lionel went to pull the firing lever. His eye had lined up the crosshairs of the sight with the passenger side of the van. The van was magnified three times on the gun sight optics, and then Lionel saw an arm come from the window and wave. Grafted on the end of the arm was an ice cream scoop.

"Dad," Lionel whispered. He eased the pressure off the firing lever and smiled to himself. The van's tyres eventually ground through the snow to find a purchase on the concrete below. It was enough to drive it forwards in an unsteady motion and gradually, gaining speed, the van slew around the corner, scattering the former gallery of fools in the process, and disappeared out of sight.

Chapter 24

In the months after these strange events many things happened. Stalingrad Towers was returned to its former glory. Out went the stone cladding, UPVC windows, and satellite dish. In went repointed original brickwork, stone window frames, and a historical coat of arms. Inside, more changes were made. The marble floor was torn out, as were the shag pile carpets and lilac chaise longue; in went mosaic tiled floors, period wallpaper and curtains, and lush, deep, comfortable sofas. It was renamed Linden Lea by Bessie, and Elsie was living there when Ned called around one afternoon. He'd had a new haircut that made him look more of a young man than a young pachyderm. The electric fence was gone and workers were planting bushes all around the perimeter. He carried a small cool bag and was sweating by the time he reached the front door. Bessie answered the door and showed Ned into the new Linden Lea. She was project managing the restoration and some of Lionel's men were helping out. They greeted Ned with good-hearted jeers and whistles. Earwax came down from a ladder and grabbed Ned in a headlock that made his face go red until Bessie slapped the big man around his own head with a trowel and he relinquished his hold. Then Bessie gave Ned a peck on the cheek whilst explaining that she had to keep an eye on Lionel's "lot" as she did not trust them to work alone, and that the period wallpaper and flooring were very expensive.

"Why don't you give Ned a tour of the house and gardens while I keep an eye on Lionel's oafs?" Bessie suggested to Elsie.

"Where is Lionel anyway?" Ned asked.

"He's been overseas but should be back later tonight," she shouted over her shoulder as she kicked Earwax back up the ladder.

So, Elsie showed Ned what they had done to the house.

"I thought your mum was responsible for the first changes, when it was called Stalingrad Towers?" Ned asked. He recalled the first time he had seen the house in its entirely foul makeover. "Fabian said it had been your mum's idea!"

By the look Elsie gave him, he knew he had asked the wrong question. He held up a hand apologetically but she slapped it down.

"That foul little oaf lied all his life. My mum did a history of fine arts at university before she met Dad."

"But?" Ned managed.

"But nothing, Ned Mutton." Elsie shut him off. "She must have had a breakdown or something when she went off with that…that…" She was getting angry now. Ned backed off and offered a disarming smile that seemed to have the desired effect. She sighed. "Yes, well…she's better now and I don't want you to mention her former persona, Simone, again. Okay?"

"Okay," Ned agreed. "But tell me what's been happening and how you've managed this?" He gestured at the richly carpeted floor and the framed pictures on the wall. It was a far cry from when he had been on the first floor before, waiting to go into Beetie's study all that time ago.

Now Elsie smiled. "Well, it seems that Brinsley Vaughan-Abbott was a very greedy, tight, and paranoid man. He saved all his ill-gotten money because he feared the tax man would get his hands on it. Brinsley," she emphasized the word with a theatrical mode. "Put it all into an account in my mum's name."

"What?" Ned said. "How much?"

"Enough," was all Elsie would say.

"But how did you get all this, and what's happened to the Vaughan-Abbotts and things, and—" Ned started to say, but Elsie cut him off. "Go in there and all will be explained."

The door to Beetie's former ops room was open. Ned peered in and was taken aback by the change. It was purple. Purple wallpaper, drapes, carpet, chairs, purple everything, except for a man in purple paint-stained overalls who turned to greet Ned and Elsie when they entered.

"Good afternoon, Ned Mutton," he said, and putting down the paint brush, walked over and shook Ned's hand.

Looking at the painter, Ned had trouble placing him. The face was familiar but the attire was alien. Then Elsie spoke. "You remember Roger Parkstone, don't you, Ned?"

He thought about it but was still no clearer. Then Roger gesticulated with his hands at the room. "Purple," he said with enthusiastic relish.

Ned's mind went back to when he was in Lionel's healing room at the council depot and the man who was struck by a rubber rodent as he was meditating.

"How's your psychic stye?" Ned asked with a smile as he recognised the lawyer.

"It is nearly healed, thank you." Then he went over to a sofa that was covered in a dust sheet and gestured Ned to sit.

Elsie sat first and Ned followed. Roger undid his overalls to show a purple toga underneath, which he carefully pulled down so as not to reveal anything naked underneath. Ned looked away. Elsie giggled.

"Now, young man, I believe you have some unanswered questions and I am here not only to spread the joy of the colour purple but to respond to these queries. I am Elizabeth's lawyer now, so ask away. Would you care for refreshments?"

Ned had a deal of questions to ask and, as he had walked all the way over to Linden Lea, was getting thirsty. "Err, yes. Please could I have an ice cream?"

Roger Parkstone looked decidedly worried. "You want an ice cream? After all you've been through at the chiller factory, and those unscrupulous snowmen?"

Ned smiled apologetically. "Well, yes I do. You see, I see it as a form of irony."

Roger and Elsie looked at him with wonder. "I've been doing my schoolwork a lot more now and studying grammar and stuff," he said with a tinge of embarrassment.

Roger nodded approvingly and rang a sash cord on the wall. He turned to Ned.

"Well?"

"Oh, right you are. Vanilla, please."

The look of approval vanished. "No, no, no. What questions do you have for me?"

Ned thought then there was a tap at the door and in came a man wearing a huge peroxide bouffant wig and a floral twin-set and pearls.

"You rang?" he asked in a high-pitched voice. Ned's eyes widened. He did recognize this person. "Crichton!"

The former valet bowed to him, then rose. His wig quivered as he did this, so he grabbed it and readjusted the blond mass. "No longer, my dear master Mutton, I am now Mandy the maidservant, and at your service."

Roger smiled politely. Elsie had a look of strained courtesy and Ned was biting his bottom lip in a desperate effort not to laugh. Roger broke the silence. "Mandy, can we have one vanilla ice cream?" He looked at Elsie, who nodded. "Make that two, and a medium blackcurrant juice, please."

Mandy bowed again and left the room. Ned could not contain himself. "What was that?"

The lawyer held up a warning hand. "Now, now, Ned, we must respect people who decide to change their gender."

"No. No. I don't care if Crichton wants to be a woman," Ned retorted. "I mean, how is he…err, I mean she, working here again?"

Elsie answered. "Well, he did rather save the day back at the chiller factory and lead all those snowmen and Ice Cream Sundaes away for us, didn't he?"

"I suppose so," Ned agreed.

"And he admitted under pain of death that all he did was in fear of Brinsley Vaughan-Abbott's retribution if he did not," she continued. "Also, he is a superb cook, a magnificent cocktail maker, and has offered to turn state's evidence against his former master in the courts."

"He has also, how shall I put this?" Roger Parkstone said, looking for the correct phrasing. "Found himself, in the form of Mandy the maidservant, and who are we to deny him that?"

"Hear, hear," Elsie agreed.

"But I thought your mum hated him?" Ned said.

"Oh, she did. But after his tears and explanations, and after thinking what she had gone through, she decided to forgive him. She also gave him her complete former wardrobe and he has sworn fealty to her for life."

Ned was silent for a while, then asked, "Well, what about Beetie?" He looked at Elsie and mouthed an apology. She nodded stiffly in acceptance. Ned continued, "And Fabian, and all this?"

There was a slight tap on the door and Mandy entered with the refreshments. She served them and gave Ned a wink before leaving. He licked his ice cream and put the wink out of his mind. Elsie studied hers and Roger took a long draught of purple juice, then crossed his legs and adjusted his toga. "After all of you escaped from the chiller factory, Lionel immediately employed me on his, Elizabeth's, Elsie's, the workers', your mother and father's and," he pointed at Ned. "Your behalf to defend you and the said party against accusations of unlawful events."

"I didn't know that?" Ned admitted.

"You were not supposed to, Ned," Roger said. "The enquiries by the police brought up a lot of questions that needed answering, and moreover, needed a guilty party to be found. Fortunately for us, there were certain individuals who fell into that category. You see, with the release of the prisoners from the fool's gallery, the police had sworn evidence of 'snowmen' kidnapping people. But all the snowmen—bar two we can think of, and one of them being a mutation—were destroyed by the former prisoners and the vehicle Thaw. Also, who in their right mind would believe in living, breathing snowmen?"

Ned could certainly agree with that. He then thought. "Hang on. You said two had escaped, I suppose that's Melton and Ice Cream Sundae, but what about—" He was going to say Vincent, but Elsie kicked him in the shins. "Ouch!"

She looked at him apologetically. "Sorry, must be the paint fumes."

Roger gave them a suspicious look but carried on. "These are strange times, Ned Mutton. The release from captivity of the prisoners served us well. They ran amok through town afterwards, smashing anything that looked like a snowman." He pointed his glass at Ned. "So your little snowman trashing exercise through the estate you live on was blamed on them." Ned looked ashamed but relieved.

He started to say thank you, but Roger waved it away before he could. "So what do we do with a group of vitriolic prisoners who all swear that living, breathing snowmen had kidnapped them, put them in freezing glass tanks, and induced a state of trance on them for years?"

Ned shook his head. Roger Parkstone smiled. "You forget your original question. What happened to Brinsley and Fabian Vaughan-Abbott?"

Ned felt as though he was on the stand giving evidence. "I did?"

"Nobody thought to look for them after the events of that day. All assumed that they had escaped. Lionel says he found Brinsley Vaughan-Abbott's toupee near the exit but heard nothing else of them. It was the police that found them later in a cell down in the catacombs of the factory. They were both incoherent and deranged and it seems that someone or something had performed a do-it-yourself frontal lobotomy on both of them with what appears to be an ice cream scoop."

Ned spat ice cream out with such force that it splattered new purple walls.

"Oh, glory be," Roger uttered in disgust.

"It must have been Melton and Ice Cream Sundae!" Ned managed to say, ignoring Roger's outrage at his purple room being corrupted by vanilla. He rose and wiped away the ice cream with a corner of his robe, then turned enthusiastically. "One would assume so, but where were they?"

"They left in an ice cream van," Ned said excitedly.

"I know they did, but the police did not, and they needed to close the case. So we have two people dressed as snowmen who cannot talk or recall anything, nor who can summon up any form of defence for the crime. Brinsley and Fabian also have a catalogue of unscrupulous business undertakings and illegal holdings. Add to that bribery, exploiting underage workers, vandalism, et cetera, et cetera, and they do not have any hope. And the coup de grâce was that your mobile phone was found inside the pocket of Brinsley Vaughan-Abbott's outfit. The police found a video clip of him admitting that he would kill for that factory site."

Ned smiled. It was a long and satisfying smile. All that he had been through, all that he had dragged his family through and his new friends through, was, it seems, coming to an end.

"So they'll get banged up in prison for it?" he asked.

"Oh no," Roger corrected him.

Ned's smile stopped.

"They will be sectioned at the local insane asylum."

Ned's smile returned and he laughed out loud.

"There was one person who was willing to swear to seeing snowmen alive in the flesh," Roger added.

Ned stomach turned. "Who?"

"A greengrocer by the name of Gordon Giles. He swore that he was attacked by snowmen and a young boy whilst delivering his vegetables. But, unfortunately for him, he will be joining the Vaughan-Abbotts at the insane asylum after he attacked the judge with a marrow when my learned friend did not believe him," the purple lawyer concluded.

"Whoopee! Christmas has come early this year," Ned shouted.

"And what with Brinsley Vaughan-Abbott putting all his money in Mum's name, we're going to be alright." She leaned over and landed a kiss on Ned's cheek.

Roger coughed for attention. "There is one more point that needs clarification. It would appear that not only did Mr Vaughan-Abbott have his major accounts in your mother's name, but he also had this house in her name. Ergo, it would seem young Ned is right, and that Christmas has indeed come early to you and your mother."

Ned and Elsie cheered, and even the normally reserved Roger Parkstone clapped his hands together in the spirit of the moment. A tap at the door interrupted the celebratory mood.

"No more refreshments, please, Mandy," he said and rose. "I must be going now. I'll finish the temple off tomorrow."

The door opened and in walked Lionel. He was in a new pinstriped suit with shirt and tie. No fez sat on his head. "Dad, you're back early!" Elsie ran to embrace him. Ned got up and held out his hand to shake but Lionel grabbed him and crushed the two of them together in a hug.

Roger passed Lionel. "Will you be requiring my services for the contract rights, Lionel?"

"I will indeed. Can you call me later?" Lionel said.

"Of course. Do you like the temple?" he asked as he eased himself past them.

"Roger, I think it's truly wonderful. It is an amethyst shrine leading to a purple paradise." The lawyer put his head in one hand and seemed to weep. The other hand patted Lionel's shoulder. "You are a true believer," he said between sobs, then left the room.

"So he's still into purple big time then?" Ned asked, though from the surroundings he knew the answer already.

"Oh yes," Lionel said. "This is his fee; his payment. A room, sorry, a purple temple, where he can be at one with himself."

Elsie jumped on the sofa. "How did it go?"

"Very well, thank you. The trip was worth it and I'm about to sell the manufacturing rights to the United Nations," Lionel beamed and sat next to his daughter.

"What rights?" Ned asked in some confusion. Lionel clapped his hands together. "Thaw; the UN want to manufacture Thaw. They say it's the best armoured vehicle they have seen in years. It can be used for convoy patrol, riot control, offensive operations, anti-personnel engagements, well, the whole lot really. Roger will go through the contract details with me but it means no more council work for me and the boys."

"Is it a lot of money?" Ned asked.

"Damn right it is. Elsie," Lionel put his hands on her shoulders. "We can tour the world with your mum." He turned to Ned. "And you can come too, Ned." He rose and paced the room. "I want to see the boys alright too. They expressed an interest in getting a fruit and veg shop and it looks like one's just come on the market. Mandy can look after Linden Lea whilst we're away, and that leaves your mum and dad, Ned," he chuckled. "Well, they can come too if they want."

"They're on a short break at the seaside right now," Ned said.

"Well they can come on another longer break if they want, can't they?" Lionel suggested.

"And Vincent?" Ned and Elsie said together. Lionel shook his head. "No, I'm afraid he can't unfortunately. Where we're going it will be too hot for a snowman. The sun would melt him."

"But—" they said again together.

"I've thought of this and it's best we go and see Vincent. Come on."

Ned picked up his cool bag and they left the room and went downstairs. Bessie was up a scaffold repointing some covings and the boys were looking at a book of vegetables, murmuring to themselves and playing 'guess the vegetable'.

Chapter 25

They headed for the garage that had housed Beetie's collection of cars. It had been refitted with pine timber cladding and opaque glazing. Where the large doors had been, there was now a single one. Lionel rang a bell on the frame. Nothing happened. Then there was a scrabbling of keys, a muffled apology, and the door opened. A blast of cold air hit them and Vincent appeared.

"Good morning all," he said with a huge smile. "Come in, do."

They walked in. Ned shivered and Elsie rubbed her arms. Lionel did not seem to notice but Vincent did. "I can turn the chill down a bit if it's too cold?"

"No. It's alright, Vincent," Ned said. The snowman looked at Elsie but she shook her head.

"How about a drink then?" he enquired. "Hot chocolate?"

They all nodded and Vincent pulled a sash cord very similar to the one in the purple temple, apart from that it was cream in colour. "Crichton, I mean Mandy, will bring them."

They opted to walk around the building rather than sit and shiver. It was wonderfully built. Vincent and Bessie had designed it and the walls resembled the interior of a cave, with small recesses for lighting and alcoves for pictures and pottery. The lounge had two huge sofas set to overlook the rolling grounds below Linden Lea. The floor-to-ceiling glass that spanned the length of the wall was made so you could see out clearly but no one could see in. Ned could see a paddock in the grounds and saw someone riding a donkey. He strained his eyes and recognised the rider, then turned to Vincent. "I don't think we'll be getting hot chocolate; Mandy's down there riding a donkey." They all came over to look. "He's training Bucephalus to be better behaved with people. I don't think it's worth it really, that animal is too unstable, but Mandy does seem taken with it and he's very patient as well," Vincent explained. They followed him through to the kitchen which was clean and white and even had a cooker. There were rows of cooking books and cooking implements. It all looked very professional. Behind this, a wide corridor led off to two bedrooms. One belonged to Vincent, with a huge chest freezer as a bed. The room had dimmed blue lights and low ambient music coming from some hidden speakers. The other was the guest bedroom and Ned went in and put his cool bag down on the bed. This room was different to Vincent's room because it had heating, a large bed, small fridge, and a TV. It also had a colossal fish tank near the bed which held lots of pond weeds and a small plastic castle, treasure chest, and other fish tank tack. Swimming between these where a group of great crested newts, and as Ned tapped on the glass, they all seemed to head towards his hand.

Vincent poked his head in. "The refugees from your little adventure at Fulwood housing development are quite happy in here."

Ned chuckled. "Yes, we'll have to wait until some other greedy developer decides to build where it's not needed and release a few of them."

Lionel and Elsie walked in and looked around the room in approval. He fished in his pocket, brought out a worm, and, looking briefly abashed, swallowed it. "Don't tell your mum," he said to Elsie. "She thinks I've given them up."

"Did you get those through customs?" Vincent asked.

Lionel gulped. "Yeah, no sweat. Oh, yeah, Vincent, we've something to ask you?"

"What?" he said the sitting down on the bed.

"Did you enjoy meeting Santa when Ned took you the other day?"

Vincent's gave a look of mixed feelings, a slight smile combined with a frown. "Yeah, I think so. Only he wasn't what I really expected him to be like."

Ned looked away and made for the door.

"Come back here," Lionel ordered Ned and then turned to Vincent. "Go on telling."

Vincent put his mitten hand on his chin and thought. "Well, I thought he lived in a wood cabin in a snow-covered forest in Lapland, but he lives in a department store in town, so Ned said. I thought he had lots of little helpers, but there were loads of screaming kids there instead." Lionel and Elsie's heads turned to

Ned. He shrugged his shoulders and offered a very bashful smile. Vincent continued, "Also, from what I've seen of him in the books he's plump and jolly, but this one was thin and scruffy. I think he'd been on the drink a bit as well because he kept slurring his words and falling over when I was talking to him."

Lionel took Ned by the shoulders and sat him next to Vincent. "Where did you take him?"

"Look...I said I would take Vincent to see Santa but, well...with all that's been going on and," he indicated that Lionel should come closer so he could whisper in his ear. He did so. Ned whispered, "How can I take him to someone who doesn't exist? I thought that Mangy Parsons, the department store's Santa Claus, would be sober. After all, I took him at ten a.m. in the morning, but the old bugger had been on the communal wine earlier in the morning during the church service!"

Lionel looked disapprovingly at Ned, then cuffed his hair. He stood and faced Vincent. "Santa's not been feeling well of late, Vincent, and by what you describe of him, he looks even worse. Now I know he's gone back to Lapland to rest and get better after all the work he has been doing. It's a busy, busy time for him, but I have a plan." He pulled out a bag of worms from his pocket. "Oh, wrong one, sorry." He delved into his other pocket and brought out two travel tickets. "Now, these are tickets for you and Ned to go on a cruise around the fjords and also tickets for a trip to see the real Santa...or, I mean, the really rested Santa at his home."

Vincent jumped up from the bed with delight, then landed with such force that Elsie, Lionel, and Ned were thrown into the air to land in a pile on the carpet. "Wow! That's brilliant. Thank you, thank you thank you," he hugged them all and wiped a tear from his coal eye. Lionel leant down and whispered to Ned. "I've cleared it with your mum and dad. We'll drive you to the port tomorrow."

Ned started to panic. "But—"

"It's all arranged. Your suitcase is packed and in the back of my car. Anyway, everyone agrees that you deserve a holiday, after all you've been through."

The panic subsided and the idea of a holiday with his best friend started to wash a warm glow over him. Ned let out a deep, satisfied sigh, then remembered something. He rose from the carpet and got the cool bag from the bed.

"Close your eyes, Vincent," he said.

"Why?"

Ned feigned impatience. "Just do as you're told."

"Okay," Vincent shrugged.

Ned put a long, thin cardboard packet in his mitten hands.

"You can open them now."

Vincent looked down at what Ned had given him. "Are these what I think they are?" he could not help but smile. Neither could Ned, Elsie, or Lionel.

Ned took the packet and tore it open. "Yes, they are. But these are the real thing. Now give us your mitts."

It took ten minutes of careful surgical work, but when Ned had finished, Vincent's smile was so bright it could have outshone the full winter moon. He held up his hands in front of him and flexed his new fingers. Like a newborn baby that has just discovered its own digits, Vincent stared at his own fish fingers in wonder.

"My own real fish fingers at last."

*

Approximately forty-eight miles away at a dreary seaside town, and enjoying a thoroughly wet weekend in a leaking caravan, Audrey Mutton was hitting the television with a bamboo stick she had found in the cleaning cupboard.

"That's it, that's it," she said as the picture on the television stopped flicking and reset on the so called 'talent show' she was watching. Audrey sat back and slurped a mug of tea. "Will you sit down, Geoffrey? You'll disrupt the signal again."

Geoffrey Mutton pulled the net curtain aside and looked out in the drizzle.

"It looks like it's going to clear. I think I'll go for a walk."

Audrey ignored him, so he put on his anorak and left the caravan.

The wind blew hard and pushed him sideways down the maze of well-attended caravan gardens. As he passed the crazy golf course, he heard a noise. It was a sweet sound that brought fond memories flooding back from his childhood. Days of warm summer sun on the south coast, of sandcastles, swimming, and moreover, of ice cream. Audrey had not packed any for their holiday. She had told him no when they had walked along the pier and passed countless little shops selling all sorts of the delicious flavours. But now he was alone and there was no one to stop him. He deserved one, after all that he had endured, and was enduring, on their holiday. He had to have one, and damn it, he would have an ice cream!

The sound of the ice cream van's music came and went with the wind. It was like a tempting nymph's song to him. He walked to where he thought the noise was but there was nothing. He looked left and right and then caught a glimpse of the van. Now, he ran. Through puddles and gardens he ran. He ran until he saw the brake lights glow and, with relief, he slowed his pace and caught up with it. The van looked old and dirty but he did not care. He walked to the side of it. There was a scrape of glass on metal as the serving window opened. Geoffrey looked at the pictures of ice creams and lolly pops on offer.

"My, my, I haven't seen these flavours in years," he said with relish. He scanned back and forth and was so excited; all these sorts, but which one to choose? Geoffrey glanced quickly back in the direction of his caravan to make sure Audrey was not spying on him. Quickly, he brought some money out of his pocket and looked up to the name of the van.

"Grampy White's Runny Delights, eh? Well, Grampy, I think I'll just have one of your traditional ice cream cones, thank you."

From inside the van, Lionel heard the metallic scrape of an ice cream scoop.

"Will that be with one scoop or two?" a wicked voice asked.

THE END

Printed in Great Britain
by Amazon